Temporality

A Novel

DAVID STREETS

Copyright © 2023 David Streets
All rights reserved
First Edition

Fulton Books
Meadville, PA

Published by Fulton Books 2023

ISBN 979-8-88731-385-6 (paperback)
ISBN 979-8-88731-429-7 (hardcover)
ISBN 979-8-88731-386-3 (digital)

Printed in the United States of America

Chapter 1

Kankakee, Illinois
February 2019

When Tom Temporal's mother died, he had no choice but to empty the family home and put it on the market. He was the only child, and he had no desire to move back into it himself. It was extremely old and falling to pieces. It was also jammed with all kinds of bric-a-brac. So he and his girlfriend, Denise, rolled up their sleeves and set about the clearance. They divided the contents of the house into three categories: things of personal value that Tom wanted moved to his own apartment, things of broader but lesser family value that he couldn't get rid of honorably and wanted packed and stored for possible future use, and things he didn't want and never would want that could be auctioned off. Or donated. Or trashed. It was exhausting work, both physically and emotionally. They took a break after a couple of hours.

"Mom always said to me, 'Don't forget the attic!'" Tom said to Denise when many boxes had already been packed and stacked in the hallway. "'Don't forget the attic!' She was insistent." So he got up and went to the utility room and came back with a ladder. He placed it in the upstairs hallway and climbed up it. The trapdoor to the attic opened after a little pushing and wrenching. He clambered onto a joist and pulled Denise up after him despite her trepidation. After all that effort, there wasn't much there. Stacks of newspapers dating back to the thirties tied up with string. Hatboxes with no hats and shoeboxes with no shoes. An old armchair with springs protruding through the seat cushion. A tailor's dummy sporting a bowler hat.

They were surprised at how sterile the attic was. There were no spiderwebs draped across the low wooden beams, and not a single bug ran for cover when he pulled on the light string. No signs of the creatures they'd most feared: squirrels, bats, raccoons, pigeons. One thing there was plenty of was dust, all of it consisting of powdered wood. On one side of the attic were piles of very old books, and next to them stood an ancient trunk with leather straps. Tom went over and opened it. There were several items within. A box full of old postcards sent from assorted vacation spots. Two handwritten accounts books from the 1920s. A pile of frayed jackets topped with a dirty cap. A tartan bag containing an old chair leg. A box of baby clothes. And in one corner was a stack of stained documents and letters that had spilled out from between the threads of a decayed piece of pink ribbon. Tom stared into the trunk and then up at the rafters, disconcerted by this unexpected encounter with things past and long forgotten. History, it seemed, had ebbed and flowed all around his family home but left this island high and dry.

"Will you look at this stuff?!" Tom said. Denise peered over his shoulder. "It's ancient. I had no idea anything like this was up here. Mom never said a word about it. Why would anyone save a fucking chair leg?" He brandished the worm-eaten object in the air and then put it back in the tartan bag and returned it to the trunk. "And baby clothes! That's borderline sick!"

"Perhaps your mom didn't know what was up here," said Denise. "Perhaps it was your dad or your grandpa who stored it."

"Oh yeah. It probably was, now you mention it. My dad was a pack rat. Mom was just the opposite—use it or lose it. But this stuff goes back generations."

Tom gathered up the papers and carefully leafed through them. Most of them were bills or circulars or bank statements…commercial stuff. None of them looked the least bit personal. No reason to have saved them in the first place. At the bottom of the stack were two older items. The first one was a piece of card about three inches by four inches. It had clearly once been pristine white, but was now gray and blotched. Tom studied it. "It's an invitation," he said, "to attend a speech to be given by Senator Stephen A. Douglas at Kankakee County Courthouse on September 25, 1858. Formal attire required."

"*The* Senator Douglas?" asked Denise.

"Who?"

"He of the Lincoln-Douglas debates. Seminal in our history? When the eyes of the nation were on Illinois?" She waggled her eyes at him. "Civics class?"

"Oh, him," said Tom, only half-remembering the name.

"It must be him. That's a piece of history, Tom. Save that. Anything on the back?"

Tom flipped it over. "Just one word scribbled in pencil in the corner: *Father's*. Don't know who this father was."

"Nor the son or daughter who wrote it."

"No. They could at least have written their father's name."

Tom put the card back in the trunk. He squatted on the floor, hands on opposite sides of the trunk to keep his balance, and stared off into the distant, unrecognized past. Denise put her hand on his shoulder and patted it. The final item in the stack of papers was a thick document. It was folded in thirds and sealed with red wax. It looked old. Very old. Denise leaned forward, carefully lifted it out of the trunk, and examined it.

"No address on the front," she said. "It's not something that went through the mail. I'll take care of it for now." She slipped it into the pocket of her jacket with a businesslike flourish. "We can read it downstairs. You decide what to do with everything else. We don't have to deal with all of it this afternoon. You're not putting the house on the market tomorrow."

Tom's eyes came back into focus. "For sure. Let's leave this stuff in the trunk for now. We'll fill it up with anything else worth keeping and take it downstairs—if we can maneuver it down the ladder without killing ourselves. Everything else can stay up here for the movers to dispose of. Somehow, somewhere, sometime."

When they'd returned from their adventure in the attic and the old trunk was standing safe but aged and forlorn at the bottom of the stairs, Denise made coffee. They sat at the kitchen table and caught their breath. They were exhausted. Denise produced the ancient document from her pocket and placed it in the middle of the table between the two of them. They stared at it. The paper was waffle brown and very delicate, all the edges frayed. Tom tested the red seal. It was rock-hard and brittle.

"I'm going to open it," he said, looking over at Denise to see if she concurred.

"Do you think you should? You don't want to damage it."

"But I want to see what it is."

"Go on, then. But be careful."

"Here goes."

He toyed with the seal, and eventually it cracked. With the back of a kitchen knife, he was then able to pry enough of the cracked pieces off the surface of the paper so that the pages could be separated. He very carefully unfolded the document and straightened the seams as best he could. It ran to six pages, all handwritten. Tom gently blew dust off the first page and ran his eyes over the wording. The handwriting was childlike. Each individual letter, though crudely formed, had been carefully spaced apart, and the words were about as neat as an unsophisticated writer could contrive. It seemed that whoever had written it had wanted to make very sure that every word could be read and every sentence understood. It must have taken an inordinately long time to write. Neither the ink nor the thoughts had faded one jot. Tom took a deep breath and read it out loud from beginning to end.

Kankakee,
24 February 1870

My name is Thomas Temporal. I do not know where or when I was born. I do not remember the name of the hamlet we lived in when I was little, but it was close to the Village of Saxonborough in the County of Lincolnshire in the Country of England. When I was still a boy, my mother and my aunt brought me to America. I believe the year was 1810. We sailed from the City of Liverpool to the

City of Philadelphia on a cargo ship called, I think, the Gleamer *or some such name. The journey took about six weeks. All three of us were very seasick. My mother's name was Martha. She worked as a washerwoman in Philadelphia. My aunt's name was Jemmy. She worked as a waitress in the Pine-Apple Café owned by Miss Deloit, a relative of the farmer whose land we had lived on back in England. We all lived above the café on Juniper Street for ten years. I became an apprentice carpenter. I suffered badly from the night terrors.*

Aunt Jemmy took up with a sea captain. I don't recall his name. They were married a few years after we arrived and had two children. My mother died of the yellow fever in about 1820. She suffered terribly with it, but not for long, and her death shook me dreadfully. I felt the need to escape from Philadelphia and start afresh.

In 1816, the Treaty of St. Louis was signed that opened up the Midwest and made it safe from Indian attacks. So in 1822, with my mother newly in her grave, I came by stagecoach with my friend Batch Coleman from the City of Philadelphia to the City of Chicago in the State of Illinois and took up work as a carpenter with the help of a man named Mr. Alexander Wolcott. I don't know what happened to Aunt Jemmy back in Philadelphia. We were never in touch again.

I married late in life once the night terrors had faded. That was in 1840. My wife's maiden name was Fiona McCann. Her family was Scotch. She was a little younger than me. We had three children, George and Martha and Henry. My wife died in Chicago in 1850 during the third childbirth. She was really too old for birthing. She was forty-two. I have always blamed myself for her death, but Henry doesn't blame me. In 1854, I moved with my children to the new City of Kankakee, south of Chicago, to build the courthouse and homes for new settlers.

My eldest son, George, was clever and brave and handsome. I loved him dearly. He joined the Seventy-Sixth Illinois Volunteer Infantry and was killed five years ago in the charge on Fort Blakely in the City of Mobile in the State of Alabama. He was twenty-two years of age. They did not know that Lee had just signed the surrender of the confederate army a few hours before they charged. So my George died for nothing. It has made me bitter ever since, they say.

I am now in my late sixties, I believe. My daughter, Martha, looks after me. I am ill. I expect to die before the year is out. I needs must die so that my Martha can go and wed. She is already twenty-four. Henry can take over this house and work this plot of land. I write down these words today because I do not know who I am, and it haunts me. My children and grandchildren and all those who come after me deserve to know their forebears. It is their right given by God. I have told herein what little I know.

I say once again that I do not know who I am. After they set foot on American soil, neither my mother nor my aunt ever again said one word about our life in England. So all that I know about my childhood is stitched up in worn patches of memories of a young child. I have pictures in my head of things that I saw and words in my ears that were spoken to me or spoken in my presence. But they do not make sense. I do not remember my father. I believe he had the same name as me, but nobody would tell me anything about him. He might have been a bad man. They called me Tommy when I was little but Thomas thereafter. I recall that we lived in a cottage on the edge of a big field outside the village. My Aunt Jemmy walked me a mile to and from school every day for the two years before we emigrated. Even in the snow.

The first thing I can call to mind is the sound of weeping: a high-pitched yowling, a steady sobbing, and a gentle whimpering. Three different kinds. I don't know who these people were. I was little more than a baby then. And I remember that birds were an important part of my childhood. My school friends teased me in the playground and called me Tom Tit. And there was a strange, tall tree with a bird's nest in it where the blue tits lived. My aunt once showed it to me. It was by the roadside outside the village. I also remember a lot of wasps trapped in a jar of marmalade in the garden of our cottage. And I heard talk of a ghost that had something to do with my family. It haunted a bedroom at a tavern in Saxonborough called The Plough. In America we would say The Plow. Guests would not sleep in that room. But the ghost was never explained to me, and I was too frightened to ask about it. It often appeared in my night terrors.

Many people, I guess, wonder about their origins: where, when, and how they came into being. These things concern me too. But I have always been more interested in WHY I came into this world. Why is it that these two fingers in front of me work together at this very moment to hold this pen? Why does the pen not just rest on the desk with no fingers to hold it? For that matter, why are there a pen and a desk and fingers at all? I have always had a feeling that it was some sort of miracle that fashioned my existence, whether divine or not... That the heavens burst open one day and pushed me out into the world. My very breath is wondrous to me as it flows

> *out of my mouth and settles over this desk. I cannot explain it more clearly, but sometimes in my childhood my mother or my aunt would look at me in amazement that I should exist at all.*
>
> *This is my story. This is what little I know. My name is Thomas Temporal of the City of Kankakee in the State of Illinois in the United States of America. If it is within your ability to find out more about me...who I am...where I came from...please, please do so. Then tell all my family. Thereafter, I shall rest in peace. But not until then. Thomas*

Tom was stunned. He carefully laid the sixth and final page down on the table and held his head in his hands. Denise sat opposite him, uncomfortable, and said nothing. Tom looked up at the kitchen wall and then over to Denise, his face screwed up in anguish. "What the fuck?"

"It's just a letter," she replied. "You don't have to do anything with it if you don't want to. You could just put it back in the trunk. Let someone else worry about it. One of your sons perhaps. Or grandsons. It's already trickled down a long line of ancestors to get to you—the line could always stretch a little further."

But Tom didn't hear her. "My dad was born in 1950, right? He married late, just like this Thomas guy did. My dad was forty-two when I was born. So...so if we allow for, let's say, twenty-five years per generation...then this Thomas must be my"—he counted on his fingers—"great-great-great-great-grandfather. Four greats. I think they call that your four times' great-grandfather. Is that right? Did I do that right?"

"Yes," said Denise. "Something like that. I don't know."

"He says that his first son was killed in the Civil War, almost certainly without marrying. And his second child was a girl, who would've changed her family name when she married. So I must be descended from this third child, Henry. Probably. He was born in 1850, and his mother died giving birth to him. So Henry must be my three times' great-grandfather."

"I suppose. Tom, I'm not—"

"And birth dates after that would be my two times' great-grandfather in about 1875, my great-grandfather in about 1900, and my grandfather in about 1925. Yes, the math works."

"What do you know about your grandfather?"

"Not a lot. He had a farm outside Manteno. We didn't see much of him."

"And your great-grandfather?"

"Nothing really. I remember my dad saying he served in World War I. Something like that. I don't remember. We didn't talk much about our relatives. Just drove up to see Grandpa once in a while. Christmas. Thanksgiving. You know. That's about it."

"Right." Denise paused and then asked, "So what do you want to do about the letter?"

"I don't know. I feel like I should do *something*. This man asked me to find out who he was. He sounded pretty desperate, didn't he? He said he wouldn't be able to rest in peace until his origins were unearthed. Somewhere his soul is still squirming. He's a relative in my direct ancestral line. He had the exact same name as me for fuck's sake! I feel sort of obligated. Do you know what I mean?"

"I do," said Denise. "I do."

Tom looked from the kitchen to the living room. He saw his father sitting in an armchair in the business suit and tie he'd worn every weekday for as long as Tom could remember, sipping on the glass of cider that Tom's mother brought him after he arrived home from work every weekday for as long as Tom could remember, waiting for a quarter of an hour with his eyes half closed while he switched from salary man to family man. Behind the armchair, hands on the headrest, stood Grandpa with his close-cropped white hair, his tanned and lined face, his visage stolid from years of toil in Illinois fields. Behind Grandpa and slightly to one side, near the front door of the house, was a young man in a doughboy's uniform with a rifle by his side. Behind the soldier was a man in a three-piece suit, a high-necked white shirt and necktie, and a derby hat, looking hurried and late for work but staring into the kitchen at him. Continuing on up the staircase was man after man after man, each one fainter and less substantial than the one in front of him, lined up past the diagonal row of his mother's flying porcelain birds on the wall, back across the Atlantic Ocean, gradually fading to transparency, to Tudor doublets and hose, and then to mere sketched outlines at the top of the stairs, disappearing into Normandy, Denmark, Saxony. Stretching backward in space and time.

"Are you all right?" Denise asked him.

"I just never…I never thought of myself as being at the end of a chain of ancestors. Sorry, sorry."

"No, I understand."

"They're all dead. Each and every one of them. And I'm the next in line. I get to live for a little while and then die and join them. In the future, I'll be just like them, somewhere in the middle of the chain. Halfway up the stairs. With a distant descendant staring up at me from 2100…2200. Such things never crossed my mind before now."

"It's all right, Tom. It's just a letter in a trunk. Leave it till tomorrow."

"I should, yes."

"It's getting late. Why don't we go back to the apartment?"

"Sure. We'll take the letter with us and leave these boxes and the rest of the stuff for another day. The trunk too. You take the letter to the car. I'll lock up."

Chapter 2

Kankakee
February 2019

LATE THE FOLLOWING AFTERNOON, TOM and Denise had returned from work and were sitting on the couch in the living room of their apartment with the ancient letter brooding on the coffee table in front of them. They were a well-matched couple. Tom was twenty-seven; Denise was twenty-six. They'd met at Southern Illinois University when both of them were studying for degrees in economics. Tom now worked for a bank in Kankakee. He'd liked the work initially, learning the ins and outs of the banking business. For sure, he'd enjoyed his interactions with the other staff members and with customers. Then he'd gotten promoted into their investment branch, in which he was taught how to create investment portfolios and the like. He didn't enjoy that as much. He spent his days in front of the computer, and his personal interactions were limited to one or two wealthy, standoffish farmers. He was seriously contemplating a career change.

"So what should I do about it?" Tom asked, picking up the letter and weighing it.

"I suppose you could fulfill his request and find out more about him," Denise replied. "Trace his genealogy or something like that."

Denise worked in the financial department of a big chemical corporation on the outskirts of the city. She was second-in-command of their budget division. She prepared monthly financial reports of income and expenditure, staff time allocations, economic forecasts for different departments. Her boss was not as competent as she was, so a lot of people bypassed him and came straight to her for information. This had made her valuable to the company in a behind-the-scenes fashion. When she'd first joined the company, she'd been shy and unwilling to dive into conversation with the staff. She'd had a hard time distinguishing flirtation from legitimate requests for information. She declined to participate in office gossip. Some people turned against her because of this, but the more astute ones persisted in talking to her, and once they'd gained her confidence, they discovered how sweet she was.

"Is it possible to research family history on the computer?" Tom asked. "For a country overseas?"

"I think so. My dad dabbled in it for a while. But I remember he said you have to pay for a subscription to one of the family history sites. Otherwise, you can only find out if a record exists, but you can't actually see it. And these sites are not cheap. Look, Tom, it was a long time ago, and this Thomas guy provided only a little bit of muddled information. It won't be easy to find out more. Don't have high expectations."

"I won't. But it would be a place to start."

Tom and Denise had lived together for three years. They'd talked of marriage and children and owning a house, but so far they'd not committed words to deeds. Thomas was dark-haired, skinny, and wore wire-framed glasses. A bit geekish, some thought. Denise was blonde with delicate features. They were of equal height and weight. A well-matched couple, everyone agreed. And so it seemed as they sat side by side on their couch that cold February afternoon.

Thomas handed the letter to Denise, and she sized it up, flipped it over and back, and returned it to him. He clicked his tongue twice against the roof of his mouth, like he was urging a horse to move on; as he did so, a strange feeling passed over him, something like a low rumbling and tumbling of agencies of ancient significance, but he didn't know why.

"I'm also curious about this ghost thing," he said. "I wonder if there's anything on the internet about it. Pass me my laptop."

Denise did so, and he set it up and logged in.

"Let me search for *ghost…Lincolnshire…UK*."

"Add the name of the village as well."

"Good thinking."

He looked at the fifth page of the letter and added the word *Saxonborough* to his search. After a brief pause, he observed, "There's only one thing that comes up. It's an extract from a local newspaper. Er...from five years ago, 2014. Three kids rented a bedroom above a coffee shop one Halloween. They said they saw things. Heard a baby crying. They...er...seem to have caused a bit of a ruckus. Got kicked out by the manager. It wasn't a pub though, like Thomas said in his letter. It was a coffee shop. Perhaps this is a different place. I don't see anything else."

"Delete the name of the village and try again."

He did so and pored over the results.

"There's more stuff now. Hey, look at this! A scientific article. In the *Journal of Paranormal Phenomena*. From just last year. It's titled 'Ghostly Manifestations: Evidence of Quantized Temporal States.' See, it came up because the authors were investigating ghosts in a church in the county of Lincolnshire in the UK."

"Wow."

"It was authored by B. Kenning, H. Groh, F. Koslowski, and J. Kenning. Hmm."

Denise peered over at the screen, pointed to the bottom of the page, and said, "Look here! Do you see this footnote?" She became very excited. "The first and last authors—the guys with the same family name—are both affiliated with King's College in the University of London. They're probably brothers. But the two guys in the middle, Groh and Koslowski, are affiliated with CIU! Central Illinois University! That's just up the road in Joliet. What a coincidence!"

"Wait now." Tom tapped a fingernail against his front teeth. "I've heard those names before. Just recently. Let me think...Groh... Groh...How do I know that name? Wasn't it in the news not long ago?"

He rapidly typed *Groh* and *Joliet* into the search engine, and up popped a list of newspaper articles and police reports from the previous August about the death of a man by the name of Frank Koslowski. They also mentioned a CIU student named Karen Butler who'd gone missing. These events had happened at a place called Hoyland Church in Lincolnshire. Ghost hunting was mentioned in the articles. Paranormal occurrences. Groh was the leader of a research group at CIU studying sensory deprivation. Koslowski had worked for him.

"That's right," they said, almost in unison. Denise took over. "Remember? It was all over the news. That guy Koslowski was found dead over there. And there was an investigation in Joliet about it and about Groh's role in his death or something."

"There was, yes. I saw it on the local news. I don't remember any follow-up though. I don't think there was a trial or anything. Let me download this scientific article."

Tom continued to skim through the search results, then logged out and closed his laptop.

"How about that? I wonder if this Groh character heard anything about the Saxonborough ghost while he was over there. It's in the same county. Perhaps it's close to this Hoyland place that was mentioned. Perhaps the ghost wanders between the two places." He chuckled and made a fake ghostly moan. "I am the long-dead Master Temporal, your worst nightmare!"

"Quit it!" said Denise. "Look, Groh is a professor at CIU. Why don't you call him and find out what he knows?"

"It's less than an hour from here. We could drive over and see him. I've been there before. In my student days. We could."

"And why don't you sign up for one of those family history websites and see if you can find out anything about your great… whatever…grandfather?" said Denise. "After all, that's what he asked you to do."

"Okay."

"I'll go get something for dinner. I'll be back in half an hour."

Denise returned with Thai food and served it up in the kitchen. Tom joined her, and they talked while they ate. She asked Tom if he'd had any success while she was gone. He took a deep breath and tried to sound enthusiastic.

"A bit. Not much for a couple of hundred bucks. There are plenty of parish records out there for Lincolnshire but only a few with my family name. I think I might have found his birth though, which was one of the main things he seemed to be concerned about." Tom looked at his notes. "He seems to have been baptized at a tiny village called Marton, which is about five miles northwest of this Saxonborough place, according to the Google map. On the River Trent. The entry in the parish register for St. Margaret's Church at Marton shows that a Thomas Temporall—spelled with two *l*s by the way—was baptized there on April 12, 1801, the son of Thomas and Martha Temporall."

"The year sounds about right. He said he thought he was in his late sixties in 1870. That could well be him."

"Right. And remember that he said he believed he had the same name as his father. His mother's name is correct as well—he said she was called Martha. So it's spot on. And I also found what I think is the marriage of his parents in the same church. Thomas Temporall married Martha Ransome at Marton on March 5, 1800, about a year before the birth of their son. Just at the turn of the century. That entry was pretty clear and easy to decipher. There were also some entries twenty years or so before that, back in 1779 and 1780, that might be the baptisms of these two folks, but I can't be sure because the handwriting is pretty much illegible. I guess the registrar changed between then and 1800."

"Great. You cracked it."

"Yeah, but I didn't find everything. Obviously, there's going to be nothing more about Martha and her son because they'd emigrated to America in…about…when was it?"

"Thomas said they came in 1810. He said he was a young boy then. That would make him nine or so."

Tom paused for a moment. "Actually, when you think about it, that's a bit surprising. If he'd lived in England until he was nine years old, you'd think he would have had a better memory of his upbringing there. I'm pretty sure I knew all about my relatives when I was that age."

"You'd think so, yes. That's pretty old to know nothing at all about your roots."

"Anyway, I kept searching. I thought I might find the death of his father. Somewhere between 1801 and 1810. I thought that might have been the reason they left England—no husband, no father, no source of income…no future. Right? But I could find no burial record for him in Marton or Saxonborough or even in Lincolnshire as a whole. Nothing."

"Perhaps he simply deserted them and ran off to some other place. That would also be a reason for them to emigrate."

"It would. But I found no burial record for him anywhere in England."

"Huh." Denise was stumped. "Did you find anything else?"

"I did. Something very surprising. Something I didn't expect, the marriage of a Thomas Temporal to someone called Mary Kirkham at St. Swithin's Church in that Saxonborough place on October 26, 1803."

Denise's eyes widened. "1803? But he was already married! And his son was…what…two years old? Two and a half? Are you sure it's the same person?"

"No way to tell."

"Could he have divorced Martha?"

"No, I don't think divorce could come into it. I thought of that. I found a social studies article on the internet. Divorce was unheard of in those days among the working poor. It took an Act of Parliament, and only the rich could afford it. If the relationship cracked and seemed about to break, most couples simply glued themselves back together and carried on. Like a broken coffee cup that looked ugly as sin but still held your coffee. The couple would have been miserable, but they carried on. The only alternative was to simply walk away from your marriage and pretend like it never happened. Walk far enough away and marry someone else perhaps. It was unlikely that anyone would ever find out."

Denise thought about that for a minute. "So…bigamy?"

"It looks like it. Even though Marton and Saxonborough were only five miles apart. Perhaps that was a huge distance in those days. I guess nobody knew he was already married when he took up with this Mary Kirkham."

"That doesn't sound right to me, Tom. Not when he had a baby son. Who would do that? That entry must be for a different person with the same name—perhaps a cousin of your ancestor."

"Yes, it could be. But that still begs the question of what happened to Thomas's father—whether or not he was the man who married this Mary Kirkham. He certainly didn't come over to America with Martha and young Thomas in 1810. And he doesn't seem to have died and been buried in England either."

"Could he have emigrated by himself, then? Or with this Mary Kirkham?"

"I guess that's possible. To America or Australia or somewhere else."

"Canada. There might be immigration records."

They nodded and thought about the possibilities.

"Or I suppose it could just be a misspelling in the parish register," said Tom, "or a transcription error. His burial could be recorded somewhere over there in a handwritten entry in a dusty parish register. It just never got elevated to a findable entry in a computer database. Perhaps it's not even been digitized yet. I'd be surprised if they've been able to scan every single parish register in the whole country, spanning hundreds and hundreds of years."

Denise muttered her agreement and set down her chopsticks. "Nothing else?"

"Not on the website I was using."

Thomas finished eating too. "I did just a little bit of searching for other things. No mention on the internet of a pub called The Plough in Saxonborough. Maybe he got the name wrong."

Denise carried the dishes back to the sink and said over her shoulder, "You know what you need to do."

"What?"

"Get your DNA analyzed. That would tell you what your roots are, which might point the way toward Thomas's roots. I think you could just order a kit from the website."

"Do you have to give blood?"

"Just a saliva swab, I think. I've heard it's very easy."

"I'll look it up on the website. I'll do it."

"And put your family tree up on the website as well—at least the branches that you know so far: Thomas and his parents and his children. And the modern branches for your dad and grandpa. You could leave the in-between bits blank. You never know, some distant relative might have a DNA match and also recognize parts of your family tree or the places where your ancestors lived. They might contact you. That would pinpoint Thomas's origins even more accurately. It could happen."

"That would be awesome!"

Tom spent the rest of the evening cobbling together a crude family tree from the information that was laid out in his ancestor's letter and a few inferences that could reasonably be made from things he'd found online. When he'd finished, he showed it to Denise.

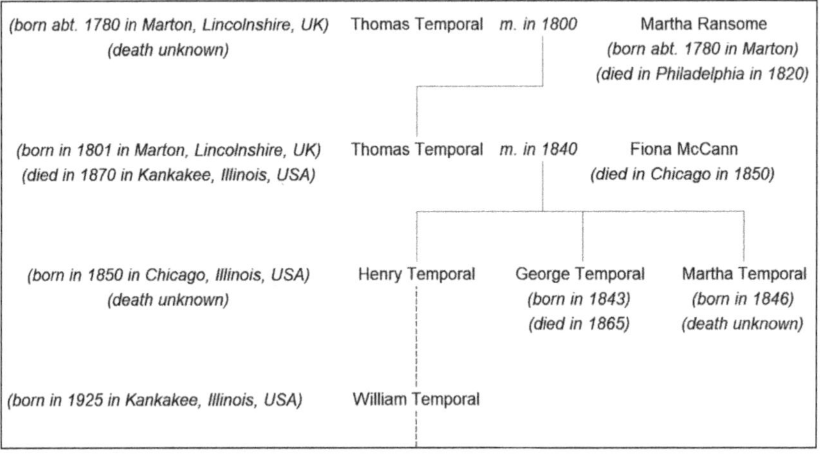

"What do you think? I tried to put in as much as I could about names and dates and places. Things that a reader could latch on to. At the bottom, I put a dashed line down to my grandfather, but I decided not to say anything about my parents or myself. If necessary, I can expand on that later. Keep it private for now. The middle period is still a mystery, but I guess that could be filled in by doing research at a later date on American genealogical records—connecting Henry Temporal to Grandpa Will, I mean by that. I thought it most important to get the older stuff in there first. I would have liked to say more about Thomas's Aunt Jemmy, but he didn't give enough information to place her in the tree. I don't know if she was a Ransome or a Temporal or something else. I didn't find anything about her when I did my search online. And sadly, I could find no place to mention Saxonborough either. But that's life. That's death."

"Yeah, it looks really good. Post it and see if you get any responses. And once your DNA is posted, you'll probably get additional responses from your matches. They may not know the people in your tree specifically, but the combination of family names and places might suggest a link. People do that all the time."

So Tom checked it over one more time and uploaded it to his family history website. As he did so, he said to Denise, "Can you imagine what life was like in rural England at that time? The French Revolution had only just ended, for Christ's sake! The internet says that the ruling powers in England were worried that the English peasants might rise up, too, and chop *their* heads off. A guillotine in Trafalgar Square! Wild! I wonder if the Temporals felt rebellion in their blood or had to endure repression from the powers that were. Perhaps they were too far away from London to feel anything. Lost in ancient fields, their working life dictated by the sun, their home life ruled by candlelight and firelight. How many of them could read and write? What did they eat for breakfast? What did they wear on their feet?"

Chapter 3

Marton, Lincolnshire
March 1801

TOM TEMPORAL WAS BORN ON the third of March in the year of our Lord eighteen hundred and one in the bed of his maternal grandparents at Marton, a tiny village just a few miles south of Gainsborough on the east bank of the River Trent. It had been decided months earlier that if the baby was a boy, he would be named after his father, in keeping with Temporal family tradition, but with the abbreviated form *Tom* to tell them apart. Winter had abated none that year. Great gusts of wind blew down from the Wolds under an iron-gray sky. As a result, the best attempts by the Ransome family to keep the lying-in room warm and dark had come to nothing. The drawn curtains were periodically blown inward and upward by drafts, and the keyhole plug was already on the floor. Warming pans were of little help. Candles fluttered every which way.

The birth itself was comparatively easy. Martha screamed and moaned a lot, but it was more by way of inducing guilt in her husband and parents for inflicting such suffering upon her. The baby was small and sickly looking. The midwife had to hold him up by the heels and slap his bottom four times before he choked up some mucous and began to howl. Martha's mother frowned and said the child might not survive long. Ten minutes after the birth, Martha was rolled out of bed, and her mother gathered up the sheets and underclothes and threw them in the washtub.

The father sat with the grandfather in the kitchen. They didn't know each other well and didn't know how to speak to each other.

Thomas and Martha had been married for two days shy of a year—the ceremony conducted just three months into the bright new century. For the first half of that year, they'd lived with Thomas's parents, and for the second half, they'd lived with Martha's. In order to make the transition, they'd had to walk a mere fifty yards, for the farms of the Temporal and Ransome families were literally a stone's throw apart. Thomas and Martha had known each other since they were toddlers. They'd walked to school together. They'd played marbles together…hoop and stick, diabolo…held tea parties with their teddy bears. They'd remained close throughout their teenage years, but it could never be said that they'd seriously courted. Nevertheless, to the surprise of all, they married as soon as Martha turned twenty-one, the legal marriage age. Martha's parents had no idea why their daughter thought to marry this man other than for his pretty face and his muscular body. And for convenience.

Since the marriage, Thomas had shown no inclination to seek out proper employment, which vexed Mr. and Mrs. Ransome no end. He just worked on and off on the farms of his in-laws and parents, did odd jobs in Marton, and otherwise moped around their cottage. And now a child was come to bind him tighter to their daughter. If the child had been born in October last or earlier, they could have presumed that Martha had been forced to marry him because she was pregnant. But that was not the case. Childbirth a year after marriage was usual and above board, so they were doing their best to accept their son-in-law. But they still couldn't fathom Martha's mind.

Mr. Ransome cleared his throat. "So," he said, "you're a father now, eh?"

Thomas nodded.

"You'll be wanting to get your own place and a decent wage-earning job, I suppose."

Thomas looked over at him but still said nothing.

"The same thing happened to me and Mrs. Ransome, you know. We drifted after marriage. Tried this and that. You know how it is. Dithered. But as soon as Martha came along, we pulled up our socks and set about making a home for her. You'll be wanting to do the same for Tom. After all, you're twenty-two now."

Thomas didn't seem inclined to undertake any such action.

"Are you kicking us out?" he asked.

"No, no, Thomas. I didn't mean that. But it's the way of the world, isn't it? The missus and I can't have the three of you underfoot all the time in this tiny cottage. Mrs. Ransome has the bad heads, as you know, and the babby's bawling won't bring her any comfort. And more'n likely there'll be more kiddies on the way soon enough, now that you've started the ball rolling."

"Martha and me, we haven't said we wanted any more kiddies."

Mr. Ransome ignored Thomas's response and pressed on with his own agenda. "It's no good for a man to settle for piecework, Thomas. Mending fences, delivering piglets, washing windows. Drinking ale in between times. No good at all. A man must have a steady job. A wage that comes in a packet every Friday, rain or shine. We all need it. Martha and young Tom need it."

"Where's the hurry? Martha's going to need her mother's help for weeks yet. Till she gets back on her feet and knows the ins and outs of caring for a babby. She knows nowt about it. It's going to take weeks and weeks."

"Thomas," said Mr. Ransome, more sternly now, "it takes weeks and weeks to find a decent job—to find an honest farmer who'll support you for as long as you needs it. Jobs like that don't fall from heaven. No one's going to show up at our doorstep and hand you a job on a plate. You needs to get up off your arse and go find one. We've all had to do it. I had to do it. Your father had to do it. Whether we liked it or not. Ain't that the truth?"

Thomas shrugged his shoulders and began to pick his teeth with a splintered matchstick.

"Listen to me. The statute fair is coming to Stow next month. You needs must go there and find yourself a job—one with a tied cottage."

"Statute fair?" A puzzled look came over Thomas's face.

"Statute fair!" exclaimed Mr. Ransome, incredulous that Thomas was not familiar with the term. "The mop fair! You know what I'm talking about. It's held in April every year, just up the road at Stow. All the farmers and landowners hereabouts will be there looking for workers. It was at the Stow Fair years ago that your father and I both got hired by Farmer Hubbard and ended up as neighbors here. It's good timing for you. It's next month."

"I'm not interested."

"You needs *must* be interested, Thomas. It's the only way for men like us to get settled in this world. How else will we? Land ownership in the county is all tied up and sealed with a magistrate's ribbon. Has been for centuries. We're never going to own our own land or our own home. We have to work for them as does. Stands to reason."

"What makes you think a respectable farmer would want to hire me? They only want men of good character. I have no references and nobody to speak for me. It'd be a waste o' time."

"Nonsense! References mean little. A farmer will often give a good reference just to shift a layabout off his land. Character don't lift bales of hay or wrestle carthorses. Never did, never will. Listen, Farmer Allsop of Gate Burton near here told me how he got a glowing reference for a young waggoner last year, but when he saw the lad, he found him to be knock-kneed, weak in the back, and weak in the head. No use at all. Let me tell you true, when a prospective hiring man sees your shoulders and thighs, he'll be well interested. Take my word on it. That's why the mop fairs are *held*, Thomas. Employers want to size up the prospects with their own eyes."

Thomas said nothing. He continued to slouch in the kitchen chair and pick his teeth. Mr. Ransome went and poured himself another cup of tea. Then the baby started screaming again, and Martha began sobbing. Mr. Ransome turned and said, "At least go and see your wife and child. Take an interest. You haven't been in the room yet. It'll bolster their spirits and yours." But Thomas just stood up and walked out of the kitchen into the back garden. Chickens clustered around him, thinking they might be fed, and then scattered when he kicked one of them. He saw for the first time that he'd been handed a life sentence, and he'd be expected to serve it with a smile on his face. There would never be enough strength in his shoulders and thighs to do a thing about it. *I should never have married her*, he said to himself.

A fine morning in the middle of April saw Thomas walking away from Marton down Tillbridge Lane toward Stow. The previous week, he had dutifully played his part at his son's christening in St. Margaret's Church on a rainy Saturday a little more than one month after the birth, as was the custom—though in young Tom's case, Martha's mother had wanted the ceremony brought forward in order to avert the terrible consequence of the death of an unbaptized child. The Temporals, the Ransomes, and one or two close friends comprised the gathering around the font, supervised by an empty-headed vicar. One verse of a hymn by the organist. A name assigned, "Tom, not Thomas, if you please." A wet cross drawn on the baby's forehead. Screams from the newly christened. Cake afterward at the vicarage. Only Thomas's sister, Jemima, did more than just play her part, doing her best to engage her downcast sister-in-law in uplifting conversation about the delightful future ahead of her, which Martha said she doubted. Thomas dawdled in a corner of the room and wolfed down slices of cake and waited for it to end.

Now, once again, he was doing his duty. One foot in front of the other. Tillbridge Lane was an old Roman road that led from a crossing over the Trent straight as an arrow up the nave of Lincoln Cathedral—or so it seemed to Thomas as the road stretched out in front of him toward the three tiny towers on the horizon. He walked and he walked with not the slightest of curves to break the monotony. After a mile, the entrance to a big estate appeared on his left. An ornate gate and beside it a small sentry box with a broken window, dense trees on either side of them. Beyond the gate, in a grassy expanse, a herd of deer grazed. He recalled that Martha had once told him her mother used to work at Stow Park, the ancient Bishops' Palace. This must be it.

He walked over and pressed his face against the ironwork of the gate. Looking beyond the deer, Thomas saw that the palace itself was in ruins. He laughed. *"Here endeth the lesson,"* he said to himself, one of the few phrases he could recall from those Sundays when he'd been forcibly dragged to morning service as a child. He had no time for the church. It might capture the minds of the weak and hold them in thrall, but he had no time for it. Let it spin its webs high above his head and tell lies about his fate after death all it wanted. It did not make his life on earth any easier. Thomas spat on the gate and walked on. Another mile and he came upon a village with a small pond at its center. Two ducks floated on the water, and two old women sat on a bench looking at them. There was no one else to be seen. Thomas walked up to them and tipped his cap.

"Where is everyone?" he asked.

"Everyone who?" one of the women replied.

"The men. The laboring men."

"All at the mop fair."

"And where is that?"

"At Stow."

"This is not Stow?"

"This is Sturton. Sturton *by* Stow. Not Stow, for goodness' sake." She giggled, and her partner on the bench giggled too.

"Where be Stow, then?"

"Stow's thataways." She pointed to the road leading northward.

Thomas cursed and plodded out of the village to the laughter of the old women behind him. Ignominy and ignorance, they forever dogged his footsteps, and he loathed them both. Yet another mile and he came to the massive Stow Minster and then quickly into a square full of people. The young men and women were distributed in clusters, each sporting the emblem of their occupation: dairymaids carried pails, coachmen carried whips, shepherds carried their crooks, and cowmen had whisps of straw in their hats. Naturally, housemaids carried mops, which was how the fairs had originally got their name. While these young people stood motionless in their anointed groups, the old farmers—their prospective employers—meandered among the groups, like a tidal wash among islands, occasionally lapping up against an interesting outcrop.

Thomas guessed there were a couple of hundred people at the fair, more bodies than he'd ever seen in one place before. And while the center of the ring was organized and hushed but for a whispered undertow of giggling and gossip, the perimeter was decorated with a colorful variety of stalls offering food, drink, games, music—anything to entice the newly hired to spend the token shilling they'd just been given by their new employer to seal the yearly contract: the *fasten-penny*, as it was called. But seeing as how it was still early in the day, the avaricious stalls were mostly quiet too.

Despite his response to Mr. Ransome when the topic had been brought to his attention at the kitchen table on the day his son was born, Thomas had heard of the ritual of the mop fair, but he'd never attended one. And because he had no particular calling, he did not know where he should go to try to find employment. Eventually, he spied a group of slovenly young men displaying no particular emblem and seemingly having no great interest in the proceedings. These he judged to be general agricultural laborers. The only ones among them who conversed were the ones who had arrived together and already knew one another; the rest merely shuffled from one foot to the other, hands in pockets, eyes downcast, silent as the grave. Thomas went over and stood at the edge of this group and thought it the most degrading activity in which he'd ever participated. At first he, too, put his hands in his pockets, but then he thought that that was perhaps not the right attitude for the occasion and took them out.

Periodically, farmers wandered over to him, sized him up, and asked him the name of his previous employer. When he said he didn't have one, they always sidled away. He began to realize that he was not going to get hired that way. So when the next farmer came up and asked him the same question, he invented an answer.

"Josiah Lofton from Gainsborough."

"Never heard of him."

"Big farmer. A hundred acres. Very big—"

"I'd've surely heard of him, then," the farmer said and walked away.

"—with an arse as fat as yours," Thomas muttered after him.

This wasn't going to work either. He felt ashamed and defeated. He glared at the ground and felt his cheeks burning like coals. He wanted to fart in each of their fat faces and head down to London. Then he recalled something that Mr. Ransome had told him, and the next time he was asked the question, he changed his answer yet again.

"Mr. Allsop from Gate Burton."

"A fine gentleman," the farmer replied, looking to one side with apparent indifference, yet smiling. "I know him well. How long did you work for him?"

"Three years, more or less. Had to leave because of a newborn."

Nodding and turning to glance over Thomas's physique.

"What kind of work did you do?"

"The usual. Ploughing, planting, weeding, harvesting. Looking after the horses and pigs. A bit of everything, you might say."

"Versatile, yes. Any physical disabilities?"

"None."

"Recurring illnesses? Infections?"

"No."

"Family?"

"Just the wife and son."

"Did Mr. Allsop give you a character?"

"No letter, no. He cannot write…very well…you know."

The farmer nodded again.

Thomas was asked to turn around, and the farmer clamped his hands on Thomas's shoulders and pressed down hard several times. He turned him back to the front. "You have the best body of any man I've seen here today. How soon would you be available?"

"I suppose I could start in a week or two. Just waiting on the wife to recover."

The farmer paused and thought for a moment and took a last look about him at the other candidates in the group. "And your name is?"

"Thomas Temporal. We live at present with my in-laws, the Ransomes, at Marton."

"I'm Deloit. From Fallow Fields. It's a couple o' miles south of here. What would you say to seven shillings a week, a decent cottage, and all the firewood you can burn and cereals you can scoff?"

"All right."

"You're hired, then."

The farmer took from his pocket a piece of paper with his name and address on it and scribbled a start date at the top. He handed it to Thomas. He then reached into his other pocket and took out a shilling coin and pressed it into Thomas's palm. They shook hands and the farmer wandered off in search of a housemaid. Thomas looked at the coin. King George the Third stared snootily off to one side, not unlike the look that Farmer Deloit had first given him. But a shilling was a shilling. Something better than nothing.

Thomas felt he ought to be excited by his success—Martha and his in-laws would certainly be over the moon when he told them about it—but he wasn't. He was humiliated. It felt more like a horse fair than a hiring fair and he the stallion. Feel the fetlocks, stare into the eyes, lift up the hooves and examine them. Slap the bottom and flip the tail. Why did it have to be that way? Why couldn't the young men and women circle a group of fat farmers and ask them about working conditions? Are the beds warm and comfortable? Is the food hot and tasty? No more than eight hours a day in the fields, yes? Poke *them* with sticks and see if *they* squealed. He would've enjoyed that kind of a hiring fair.

He thought he would walk home immediately, but when he arrived at the edge of the fair, he came upon two men leaning on a window sill, drinking ale and eyeing him up and down. They each had a red ribbon hanging from the side of their cap. They knew at once that he wasn't from around there. A stranger to be needled.

"Not hired, then?" asked one of the men. He was big and ugly.

"I *was* hired," Thomas replied.

"But you ain't got no ribbon."

"What's that mean?"

"You don't know?" The man guffawed. "Once you're hired, you're supposed to throw away your emblem and wear a ribbon." He waggled the one on the side of his own head. "Housemaids throw away their mops, coachmen hide their whips. Time to celebrate. Time to spend your shilling!"

"Nah, you didn't get hired," said his companion, laughing. He was of the opposite build, thin and wiry. He turned to look at his friend. "He ain't got no shilling."

Thomas pulled the piece of paper from his pocket. "Read this. This is my new employer."

"*You* read it," big and ugly replied. "If'n you can."

"What's the farmer's name? Where's his farm?" asked thin and wiry.

"He can't read. Go on, read it to us!" Both of them were now laughing.

Thomas folded it up and put it back in his pocket.

"He can't read, and he ain't got hired, and he ain't from Stow. What a mopey dick!"

"Aye. Mopey dick!"

Thomas took his time to respond. "Well, some of that might be true, lads, but one thing's for sure and certain. There's no problem with my cock. It's big enough and hard enough to bust apart either of your arses any day of the week...but I suppose you'd rather go home and fuck each other."

Their smiles faded. Big and ugly slowly placed his mug of ale on the window sill and stepped forward, blocking Thomas's path. "What did you say?"

"Hmm. Perhaps your ability to hear is worse than my ability to read. Fuckhead."

The man's hand coiled into a fist.

Thomas stood silent and still.

Thomas knew the secret to fist-fighting. He'd been in six fights in his short life. The first one, in the schoolyard, had consisted of one wild swing each, both off target, and degeneration into wrestling; it didn't count. The next five he'd won. The secret was to be able to take a hit. That first hit. In the countryside, the ruffians always took a wild swing at you. It was called a haymaker by real Lincolnshire makers of hay. You pulled your head back, and the fist either missed entirely or gently swiped your cheek or jaw. The secret was to remain composed and alert. After his swing, the assailant always found himself with his fist down in front of his crotch, his face and torso turned sideways, and his feet off balance—even more so if he'd been drinking. You then instantly punched straight and hard into his exposed cheek with your right fist—actually, not *into* his cheek but *through* it. Five times it had worked for him. And it worked this time too. He'd caught a sideswipe on the jaw, but big and ugly was lying spreadeagled on the road. Thomas took one step backward and raised both his fists, but thin and wiry thought better of it and decided to revive his friend rather than go after their adversary.

Thomas pondered his situation for a moment and then turned round and walked back into the center of the fair. He suddenly cared little about Farmer Deloit and the new job. He cared nothing about a weekly wage packet or a tied cottage. The fair had now transformed itself into a lively celebration, red and yellow ribbons flying everywhere, and he intended to make the most of it. Now there was dancing and fiddle playing. Laughter and singing. A penny whistle skipping up and down amidst the throng. Thomas found a pretty young dairymaid and drew her away from the crowd and bought her drinks with his shilling and by eight o'clock was on top of her in an orchard, and her head was banging against an apple tree; and when he woke up, it was dawn, and the grass was wet, and he walked back to Marton.

Chapter 4

Kankakee
February 2019

A WEEK AFTER THE SPIT-AND-SEND, TOM looked up from his computer one morning and exclaimed, "The results are here!"

"What results?" asked Denise.

"My DNA! It's posted!"

Denise came over and looked at the results with him.

"So what are you? Ten percent Martian?"

Tom laughed and checked the computer screen for the ethnicity estimate from his DNA.

"Okay. I'm sixty-two percent English."

"That's the Temporal mob and their cohorts."

"Sixteen percent Scottish."

"Not surprising. Remember that Thomas's wife was Scottish."

"Eleven percent Irish."

"Presumably they would be American Irish from relatively recent ancestors."

"And then five percent Sweden and Denmark. Who would they be?"

"Could also be immigrants. Didn't a lot of Scandinavian families settle in the Midwest? Or they could be Vikings who settled in Lincolnshire."

"Yes, I read something about the area where the Vikings settled. It was called the Danelaw. About a thousand years ago. Lincolnshire was a big part of that."

"I wonder how far back one's DNA stretches. What else?"

"Finally there's three percent Germanic Europe and three percent France."

"Okay. Probably Angles and Saxons and Normans from way back. Do you think?"

"I have no idea. But it does all seem reasonable. And look here, there's a list of people who are my close relatives. DNA matches, they call them. I guess they're other people who have taken the test and produced results similar to mine. It actually shows how much of my DNA I share with each of them."

Tom pointed his finger at the computer screen and scanned down the lengthy list of his DNA kin. He stopped after a few pages as the relationships became increasingly tenuous and distant.

"Not a Temporal among them!" he said with frustration.

"Well, think about it. There'll be very few lines down from Thomas to the present that still have the Temporal name. You could be the only one. Most of the other branches spanning six or seven generations will have different family names through marriage. They may still be close relatives even though they have unfamiliar names."

"Then what good is this list? It doesn't help me at all. I don't know any of these names. Not a single one."

"Yes, it is a bit disappointing, I agree. But perhaps one of these people will see *you* and recognize *you* and send *you* a message. Think about it. You've just popped up on all of *their* lists of DNA matches." She swept her arm above the computer. "*'Hey, here's a Tom Temporal,'* one of them will say. *'I know how I'm related to him. I'm going to contact him.'* See the message button at the top? You'll get pinged when someone messages you with a query."

"Okay. Still, it's rather disheartening. I was expecting a lot to come from this. Not one name in this long list do I recognize."

Denise put an arm round his shoulder and kissed him on the temple.

"Perhaps you'll have better luck with Professor Groh."

"If he's still at CIU. If he hasn't been kicked out or moved on to pastures new."

TOM AND DENISE DROVE FROM Kankakee to CIU one brisk sunny morning in early March. Tom knew the campus from previous visits to the dorm of an old high school friend and soon found the building that housed the Illinois Center for Psychological Studies. They sat in the car outside the main building for several minutes while Tom plucked up the courage to enter.

"Do you think you should have called ahead?" Denise asked him.

"I thought about that. But then I thought that would give him an easy option to blow me off. *'Sorry, I don't have time for that. Bye-bye.'* Then I'd be screwed. I thought I would have a better chance of success if I could just show up and talk to him in person. Explain everything. Show him the old letter. It'd be hard for him to blow me off when we're sitting face-to-face."

"That does make sense."

"Will you come in with me?"

Denise shook her head and said she would wait in the car. Tom got out and walked up to the front desk and took a deep breath.

"I'm looking for Professor Groh. Is he here?"

"Do you have an appointment?" asked the security guard.

"No. I'm an old friend," Tom lied.

"I'll call him."

The guard spoke softly into a phone on the counter, and a few moments later, Harry emerged from a side corridor and said, "You were asking for me?" Tom replied that he was and indicated the two armchairs in the lobby. They went over to them and sat down, Harry rather reluctantly and glancing at his watch.

"I'm sorry to come here unannounced, Professor," Tom began, "but I have something rather important to ask you…well, important to me, that is."

"Yes? Do I know you?"

"You don't, no. My name's Tom Temporal. I live over in Kankakee. The thing is, I was going through some old papers in the attic of our family home, and I came across a strange letter from my great-great-great…" He paused and took a deep breath. "My four times' great-grandfather. He was born in Lincolnshire in England in

1801 and emigrated here when he was nine. We think, anyway. The letter referred to a ghost that was connected to our family in some way. Totally bizarre, I know. Anyway, I did an internet search, and your name came up in connection with a ghost that you and some other scientists investigated over there. In England, that is. In a place very close to where my ancestor was born, as it turns out. So I was wondering if you might be willing to help me some. I'm sorry if this is all a bit off the wall."

"How do you know about our experiments?" Harry replied, slightly puzzled.

"I found your paper online, *'Ghostly Manifestations…'* blah, blah, blah. Sorry, I don't remember the rest of the title. In the *Journal of Paranormal Phenomena*. I was searching for any information about ghosts in the county of Lincolnshire. It just popped up. We thought it quite a coincidence that you worked so close to where we lived. Close enough to drive over."

"The stuff at Hoyland Church? Oh, okay. I was assuming you'd come about my discovery of the Sphere of the Planets. Not the ghosts."

"The what? I don't know anything about that."

"Well, after the investigations in Hoyland Church had finished, I was able to recover a fifteenth-century French artifact of great value. It's in the British Museum right now being cleaned and restored and having its history researched. It was known as the Sphere of the Planets. I thought you might have read about it in a newspaper."

"No. I only found the ghost stuff online. And reports of the… er…the tragic death of Dr. Koslowski. We remembered seeing that on the news."

"Yes," said Harry, leaning back in his chair and looking uncomfortable.

"Are you still doing those kinds of experiments?"

"No. No, I'm not. It caused no end of a ruckus here at CIU. Admin wanted to fire me for improper conduct, but after reading the British police reports and receiving a stern letter from my lawyer saying I hadn't done anything wrong, they had to keep me on. I'm tenured, see. No more experiments though, but that was mainly because DOD wouldn't renew my funding. I have a special kind of adjunct position here now. My lab was given to this Aussie guy, Professor Wilkinson, and my tank now has dolphins in it. My lab tech Connie Cammaretta went to work for him. I moved from Joliet to Plainfield and just come to the office a couple of days a week now. So that's my current situation. I sit at my desk and do pretty much whatever I want. I'm tolerated."

"What sorts of things? Are you still involved in ghost research?"

"We prefer to call it sensory deprivation research, chief. I still tinker around with it a bit. I collaborate with Professor Lieshman at Northwestern University on what we call zeta drugs, mind-altering drugs, if you will. I write the occasional journal article. I have one graduate student. And I'm helping out long-distance with the research at the British Museum. You can gather from all of this that my work's rather low-key nowadays. Admin wants me to keep my head down as much as possible—except when it comes to the Sphere of the Planets, of course, when they want me to raise my head up as high as possible. Positive exposure for CIU, you know. They *do* like that. It's all very ironic."

"Would you be willing to help me out a bit? Would you at least do me a favor and read my ancestor's letter and tell me what you think of it? I may be blowing it way out of proportion. Please?"

"I guess I could at least do that much."

Tom reached into his jacket pocket and pulled out a photocopy of the letter and handed it to Harry. As he did so, he took a gamble and said, "I'm thinking about going over there. I want to find out as much as I can about my ancestor and this ghost he mentioned. For his sake. It may be that other people in the village know about it. You'll see at the end of the letter that my ancestor asked for his descendants—people like me—to find out who he was and what'd happened to him in his childhood. He was pretty much completely ignorant about his roots. I feel under some kind of blood obligation, you know. Perhaps you'll be able to understand. Anyway, you'll read all about it in the letter." Harry nodded, and so Tom pressed his case a little further. "I don't suppose you'll be going over to England again?"

"As a matter of fact, I will. There's going to be an official unveiling of the Sphere of the Planets at the British Museum the second week of April. It'll be all bright and shiny and documented and installed in its own glass case. I'm invited as the guest of honor. The discoverer, yeah? I'm gonna go. CIU even said they'd pay for my trip. Surprise, surprise."

Tom pursed his lips and thought for moment. "Could I come with you? Could we spend a day or two in Lincolnshire after the ceremony is over? Nose around?"

"I don't know. I really don't know anything about you. What do you do?"

"I work at a bank. In Kankakee. In the investment department. I advise rich folks and manage their investments. Mostly big farmers from the county. I have a BA in economics from SIU. My girlfriend's outside in the car. She's got the same degree as me, not that that has anything to do with it."

"Do you have any science background?"

"Very little. Sorry. High school is all."

"I see." Harry stared out the window above Tom's head.

"Read the letter," Tom pleaded. "Please. I feel the need to follow up on it. You seem to know all about this paranormal stuff. Plus, you've been over there before and know the lay of the land—even locally in this Lincolnshire county. If I could just come with you, I would feel much more confident. If you want to know more about me, maybe I could come over to Plainfield one afternoon and better introduce myself."

"Give me a day or two to think it over. Let me read this letter. Write your phone number at the top here, and I'll give you a call. Would that be okay?"

"Yes. That'd be great. Thanks very much."

Tom and Denise drove back to Kankakee. Clouds had drifted over the low-set March sun, and sprinkles of snow already covered the fields and verges. It seemed colder to Tom. He knew that he ought to be in the warmth of his office at the bank, learning the depth and breadth of his trade, planning for a cozy future with Denise. Instead, he couldn't escape the feeling that he was crawling out on a frozen limb of his family tree that could snap at any moment and hurl him into oblivion.

Chapter 5

Fallow Fields, Lincolnshire
February 1803

Fallow Fields was not even worthy of its official designation of hamlet: three farms and five cottages straddling a nondescript intersection of two narrow country lanes in the middle of nowhere. There were a few hedges. There were one or two trees. But in February there was not a leaf on anything, just bare, angular branches pointing either upward to a perpetually overcast sky or downward to wheat and barley stubble that stretched as far as the eye could see in every direction. The only animals to be seen were a few chickens in the backyard of one of the cottages, for these were croplands only, with no cows or sheep raised anywhere and horses only in the stables of the well-to-do. Each cottage had one pig, but no snouts poked out of the shelter of their covered sties this chilly morning.

The Temporals lived in the middle cottage of the three owned by Farmer Deloit and occupied by his agricultural laborers. Farmer Deloit was several generations removed from France yet living in Lincolnshire only on the sufferance of his neighbors. Still and always a foreigner. The Temporals' tied cottage was tiny and in a state of disrepair—leakier even than the Ransomes' cottage at Marton. Winter wind had no trouble sidling under the doors and creeping around the window frames and even bellowing down the chimney if there was a storm and no fire burning in the grate, which there usually wasn't.

Thomas Temporal had nothing to do on this particular Thursday morning, just like he'd had nothing to do on the three previous mornings. If there'd been ale in the kitchen, he'd have been drinking it, as early in the day as it was, but all he had was Martha's weak tea, a feeble substitute. The baby was crying in the only other downstairs room in the cottage. Thomas was restless and unhappy and hadn't shaved for a week. There didn't seem to be any point.

"I work six days a week for seven shillings," he spat. "Half of that goes on bread and bacon. I can't remember the last time I ate beef. What kind of a wage is seven shillings a week?"

"It's wintertime," said Martha, sitting across the kitchen table from him. "There'll be more work on the farm come spring, what with planting 'n' all. We can survive on seven shillings till then. Don't fret so."

Martha always did her best to reassure Thomas and keep him calm. In all honesty, she feared what might happen if she failed to do so, as quick-tempered as he was. Martha was not a pretty woman. She was the kind of woman most men would want to have as a sister, capable and never one to shirk responsibility or hard work. She had a round face and a square jaw, very pale. White almost. Her eyes were blue, her hair mousy and thin. She smiled a lot—not because she was happy but because she knew that that was what people expected to see on a plain round face like hers; flirtatiousness and petulance were out of the question. Just keep on smiling. But she hadn't done much smiling in recent months, as Thomas grew increasingly morose and the baby cried all the time and never seemed to progress from the sickly state it'd been in when it dropped out of her at Marton nigh on two years before.

Martha increasingly felt that their marriage was a mistake. Thomas had married her for three reasons: he'd known her his whole life, she got on well with his parents and his sister, and she let him do anything he wanted in bed. She'd known no other man and had no frame of reference for the art of passion. But her acquiescence under the sheets, she now realized, was no longer sufficient to keep Thomas content. There was no way it could last a lifetime. And thinking back on occasion, she could no longer recall why she had ever wanted to marry Thomas.

"Wintertime. Oh, aye," replied Thomas, nodding his head. "Survive, aye. Right easy for you to say. You don't have to take orders from old Frenchy. All he has me doing these days is hedging and binding faggots. That's no kind of life for a laboring man. I've had my fill of him. This is no kind of a life."

"But he owns the land we live on," Martha stressed. "He owns this cottage, the roof over our heads. If we upset the man, he'll turf us out, and then you'll have neither work nor home. We mayn't survive that." She glanced up to see if she'd upset him, but he was deep into his grousing soliloquy and paid her no mind.

"And now there's young Tom to feed 'n' all. Soon he'll be stuffing his gob with meat and fish. Twice as costly. And new clothes. Ever bigger, ever dearer. You can just sit here and knit, but I'm the one as has to provide. Nay, we cannot survive as we are, I tell you."

"Think about it. We pay no rent, and we get free firewood. And wheat and barley scratchings. There's summat to be said for that."

"I'd rather earn a good living and pay rent. Honorable like. I'm in shackles here."

"What, then, Thomas? What do you want to do?"

Thomas gritted his teeth and stared down into his mug of tea.

"I've talked to me mates, and they say that work's just started up on the Fossdyke bank below Saxonborough. They're widening the canal at the moment, and then they're going to set stone slabs up against the sides of it. Word is there'll be loads more barge traffic soon through Lincoln to the Trent. I'm going to sign on with them Monday."

Martha was instantly frightened by Thomas's words and leaned toward him, reaching out a hand to touch his sleeve. "But that's more'n two miles from here. You can't walk it twice a day and break your back betwixt."

"I don't intend to. I'm going to stay with Jeb and Danny. They've got a room at a doss house in Saxonborough. Only two shillings a week. I'm set on it."

"But what about me? What about young Tom? We can't live alone out here in the middle of nowhere. You can't just up and leave us. This is a tied cottage—Farmer Deloit will kick us out."

"Canal banking pays fifteen shillings a week, Jeb says. They's in a hurry to finish the work afore next winter. That's more'n twice what

Frenchy'll pay me even when there *is* work to do on the farm. Which there ain't nohow. Nay, lass, I'm off to Saxonborough on Monday. My mind's made up." He slammed his mug down on the kitchen table, and tea slopped over the sides. "Anything's better than what I have now."

Martha's face began to crinkle and fold in on itself. "Thomas, please! You can't! Tom is not two years old and poorly. It takes me all my time to look after him. I can't keep up the cottage and cook and clean all by myself. And what about the shopping? I can't carry Tom to market twice a week. He's not strong enough." She burst into tears.

"None of that, woman," Thomas said out of the corner of his mouth. "I'll come back every Sunday and bring you something. Ten shillings. That's more'n I give you now. So shut up with your bawling—you're worse than the babby."

"It's not just the money. Not the money at all. I can't live weeks and weeks by myself with Tom crying all through the night and me getting no sleep. I'll lose my mind. I know it for sure and certain. I'll lose my mind." She clutched tightly at his shirt sleeve and jerked on it several times, trying to make his eyes turn and look into hers. "Please, love!"

Exasperated, Thomas pulled his arm away, jumped up, and walked over to the window, running his hands through his hair as he went. He looked out at their neighbor's dilapidated cottage and the dismal view of the flat winter landscape beyond. He gripped the grubby drapery. It took all his strength of will not to rip it off the curtain rod and tear it to shreds. He hated to have to make choices of this kind, of any kind.

"All right!" he snapped. "I'll ask our Jemmy to come and stay with you. She ain't got nothing better to do these days. She can keep you company and help look after the young un. We'll feed her, and she can sleep up in the loft. Or in your bed if that'll make you any happier."

"But it's *you* I want, Thomas. *You.* Not Jemmy. We've only been wed nigh on three years. I still loves you, Thomas, and needs you beside me in the night. That's the only thing that keeps me going through the day. Don't you need to be with me?"

Thomas snorted. "In that way? Not so much anymore. You knew nothing about what I needed afore we wed, and whatever you learned in those first few months, you forgot the day young Tom was born. And you ain't recalled none of it since. Well, I don't feel inclined to teach you again. That's the truth on it. I'd as soon drink ale with Jeb and Danny as lie in a cold bed."

Martha renewed her sobbing with greater vigor.

"All right, all right!" Thomas shouted. "I'll go to my father's on Saturday and fetch Jemmy."

"I don't want Jemmy! I want *you*!" She picked up the cup on the table in front of her and threw it at him. It missed by a mile, bounced off the wall, and landed in a chair by the hob. It didn't even break, her throw was so pathetic. Thomas paid no attention.

"I'd be better off joining the army, truth be told. Word in The Plough is that we'll be at war with France come the spring. Did you know that? They say that King George is set on it. At war!"

"I didn't know."

"You know nothing. Humphrey Norris says that Boney's fixing to invade our shores. How would it be if we had Frenchies running the taverns and the market and the stables as well as this farm? Did you ever think about that? Deloit would love it—he'd probably get to run the county. No, I'd rather fight and be killed and be done with it."

"No, Thomas! You mayn't say things like that!"

"I can say whatever the fuck I like in my own house!" He turned and ripped the curtain off its rod as he did so, the wooden rings clattering together like sudden hail. "Deloit may own it, but I'm the master of it! You're no better than him! You think you can tell me what to do any time of the day. Change the babby. Mend the fence. Feed the pig. Just like Frenchy. I'm a strong man, Martha Temporal, strong in mind and body. Don't you forget that! I can't abide being pushed hither and yon by weaklings like you and him—weaklings I could knock through this here window with a single punch any time I wanted to. I'm deserving of better." He pounded on his chest with his fist. "Don't you *never* forget that!"

"I'm sorry, Thomas, love. Don't take on so. I don't mean to push you around. Honestly, I don't. I know things need to change. You're right. But what will Farmer Deloit think if you're not here when he needs you?"

"I don't give a fuck anymore. You and Jemmy can work for Boney's pal on weekdays, and I'll come back for planting and harvesting and weekends. If I feels like it. I don't give a fuck. Get that through your head. I deserves better."

"You *do* deserve better, Thomas, I know it. But *I* deserve better too."

"Well, then, it's our Jemmy you'll get, and I'll go build dykes."

Despite their fight, Thomas was as good as his word, and on the Saturday he walked to his parents' farm at Marton, gathered up his sister, and returned to Fallow Fields. When they came through the front door of the cottage, Martha ran up to Jemmy and tried to hug her, keeping her tears in check, but Jemmy held her at arm's length and spoke firmly to her, "All right, Martha, love, save the sentiment. You listen to me. We're going to make the best of this. If our Thomas has to run off to Saxonborough, let him. You and I'll manage this place together. He'll soon get tired of the navvying and come back. Nothing surer. It's brutal work. So let's fill a warm bath for my nephew and leave Thomas to brood on his future. Mother gave us this pheasant for dinner." She handed a parcel to Martha, who accepted it gratefully.

"You don't mind staying here with me?" Martha asked.

"Given a choice, I'd rather bed down with my sweetheart, Billy Allsop, at Gate Burton farm. But I don't mind it here. Thomas is my brother, Lord love him. And it's only for a short while."

"Do you think so?"

"He's a strong man, that much is true, but canal banking is infernal, I tell you. He'll only be able to take so much of it."

"Where will you sleep?"

"Somewhere. Anywhere."

Martha stared into Jemmy's eyes and tenderly extended her fingers to brush Jemmy's hair back behind her ears. "Thank you," she said. "You're an angel come down from heaven."

And this time Jemmy didn't prevent Martha from stepping up and hugging her tight against her bosom. Jemmy smiled and patted her on the back. "There, there," she said. "There, there. We'll manage."

The two of them bustled about the cottage for the rest of the weekend, sparing only an hour for Sunday morning service over at St. Swithin's Church in Saxonborough. By Sunday night the cottage was in the best shape it had been in since the day Thomas and Martha moved in. Young Tom was clean and dry and happy. Good food was on the table, meaning meat. Jemmy slept on the couch for a second night and was woken the next morning by the sound of Thomas stomping around the cottage in his boots. He was chewing on a piece of bread and gathering his belongings.

"You're determined, then," Jemmy said. "You're going to do this."

"I am," Thomas replied. "I'm rejoining the world of men."

"Doing the things that only men do, I suppose."

"It's past time. For me anyways. Women and babbies live in a different world."

And he walked out the door, slamming it shut behind him.

Scarcely an hour later, just a few miles north on the edge of the village of Marton, Mrs. Temporal hurried across the small field separating their two farmhouses to have a natter with Mrs. Ransome. Hot milky tea and biscuits were the perfect accompaniment to the exchange of information about *goings-on*, such consultations being ever necessary in the precarious lives of tenant farmers and their families in the remote countryside. Usually, each one tried to outdo the other in the lurid portrayal of their news, but this time it was personal. This time it was serious.

"There's something particular I needs to tell you," Mrs. Temporal said, leaning forward across the kitchen table as if there were gossipmongers behind the curtains.

"Do tell," Mrs. Ransome replied, leaning forward to meet her by the teapot.

"Thomas came home on Saturday. Out of nowhere. Surprised Harold and me no end. Thomas was all of a tiz-woz. Said he was going to work at Saxonborough for a while. Canal banking. Leaving the farm, can you believe?"

"Well, I never."

"And he took our Jemmy back with him when he left. To help Martha out while he was away. We were shocked, but he wouldn't heed a word we said. Not even a scolding from Harold."

"Did he say anything about our Martha?"

"No."

"She must be really upset about it."

"He said nothing about her. But she's probably all right. And she'll be better with Jemmy there. They get along well together."

"And what about our grandson? He's yours and mine both."

"Thomas said he wasn't doing too well. Not sick but not thriving neither. Much the same as the day he was born."

"I should go and see them," Mrs. Ransome resolved there and then. "It's young Tom's second birthday on the third of March, so I'll take him a present. See how he's faring. It'll give me an excuse to check on our Martha."

"And on Jemmy if you would be so kind."

"On Jemmy too, yes. I'll come over and let you know the lay of the land when I return."

Young Tom had been small and sickly looking when he was born. Eyebrows had been raised by his grandmother and the midwife once he'd been cleaned up. For the first two years of his life, he'd been fairly well nourished, mostly on mother's milk and barley gruel and mashed apples—with the addition of a little ground-up bacon or fish whenever Martha could afford it on Thomas's seven shillings a week. But the baby was always hungry and crying for food whenever he was awake. He ate anything within reach of his mouth. But he never gained weight, never developed fat or muscle, and showed no interest in living.

When Mrs. Ransome did visit Fallow Fields on Tom's second birthday, her jaw dropped when she saw him, and she repeated the words she'd uttered by the birthing bed, "He might not survive long." It had gradually dawned on everyone during those first two years that the baby was not altogether well, that he likely had some malady that held him back and pinned him down in his crib. Martha did her best but always felt like she was fighting a losing battle.

When she returned home that night, Mrs. Ransome told her husband about the condition of their grandson, and he went and talked to their landlord, who, graciously and after more than a little coaxing, paid for the doctor at Marton to travel down to Fallow Fields and examine the child. Doctors rarely, if ever, visited Fallow Fields—it might have been in the Sahara or at the North Pole for all they knew of it. The doctor asked many questions of Martha and prodded and poked young Tom till he screamed. The doctor tapped his chin, pondered for a few seconds, and then said a single word, *marasmus*, and left, leaving them none the wiser.

Martha and Jemmy didn't know it, but Thomas was well aware that Tuesday—the day after he arrived in Saxonborough and moved in with his workmates and got a job carving out the Fossdyke—was Valentine's Day. He'd known it and had factored it into his plans. Jeb had told him that there was to be a party that evening at The Plough, and Thomas intended to enjoy himself. It would be the first time in months that he'd be out of earshot of the sobbing and chattering of women and the whimpering of babies, the first evening that he would not have to worry about Farmer Deloit knocking on their front door the next morning with orders to undertake some new, menial task. For once he would be unfettered.

The Valentine's Day celebration, however, turned out to be not quite the kind of party that the landlord, Humphrey Norris, had foreseen when he'd hung red hearts from the ceiling of the great room. There were no young couples sipping cider in the firelight and staring dreamily into each other's eyes, no elderly couples holding hands and reminiscing over good times long gone. There were just one or two married folk blathering on about their naughty children, and they had left early in the evening when they saw what the party was descending into: a drinking contest among a horde of crude, muddy, laboring men. As the night wore on, Humphrey became increasingly concerned for the durability of his furniture and his waitresses both. He prayed that the constables would be close at hand come closing time.

Thomas's mates were boisterous. At times they would glare in fury at one another across the table and then burst into uproarious laughter and clash mugs of ale together. But they were entirely focused on the chatter at their own table, the grins on the faces of their mates, and the tales of experiences they'd all shared and really didn't need reminding of. They had no interest at all in their surroundings. All save Thomas, that is. Thomas could hold his liquor better than any of them. He'd been known to drink ten pints at a sitting and walk a furrow home as straight as a prize plough horse. He always had his wits about him. Always. He made a point of it. While his friends caroused and spilled ale and slowly descended into stupor, Thomas was glancing around him. Several times during the evening his eyes settled on a young waitress he did not know who was serving drinks to tables on the far side of the room.

When Nancy Barnes next brought a round of drinks to their table, he beckoned her over. "Who's that pretty thing yonder?" he asked, directing Nancy's attention with his finger. Nancy turned to look.

"That's one of the occasional workers here," she replied. "She only comes in on holidays and party nights to help us out."

"What's her name?' Tom asked, continuing to stare over at her.

"Mary. Mary Kirkham."

Chapter 6

Plainfield, Illinois
March 2019

Harry Groh called Tom Temporal a few days after their brief meeting at CIU and invited him to come to his place the following weekend so they could get to know each other better, chat about the past experiments, and discuss the possibility of doing things together in the future. Harry lived in a small farmhouse way out on Wheeler Road, west of Plainfield, surrounded by cornfields. He'd bought the property early the previous fall soon after he'd returned to the States and mostly recovered from his traumatic experience in England in July. The farmhouse had been abandoned by the previous owner and was largely derelict, so he'd spent the fall and winter rehabilitating it by himself. Nobody knew why Harry had bought the place. He wasn't even sure himself except that it was a terrific financial deal—once he had sold off its two fields to a neighboring farmer—and there was more than enough work to do on it to take his mind off his troubles at work and the deaths of two of his colleagues.

Tom accepted Harry's offer and didn't have difficulty finding the farmhouse. Their meeting on the doorstep was awkward for both of them. Harry was a giant of a man with a full beard and a professorship; Tom was a slender young bank employee. Big differences at the outset: fifteen years in age…a foot in height…eighty pounds at least in weight. It seemed that the one might look to kill and devour the other, but they shook hands instead.

The farmhouse was crammed with books, and Harry hadn't yet had time to install bookshelves. Tom squeezed himself onto the couch between piles of books and Harry's two dogs. Harry had accepted Karen Butler's small library after she'd disappeared and when the owners of her complex wanted to take back her apartment. Everything save Karen's books had been put in storage. Thus, Tom found himself torn between examining the front cover of J. W. Dunne's *An Experiment with Time* on the top of the pile to his left and studying the butt of a golden retriever to his right. Harry brought coffee and sat down on a kitchen chair opposite him. Neither was certain how to begin, but Tom eventually realized that the onus was on him as the one who had initiated contact.

"So did you get a chance to read the letter from my four times' great-grandfather, Professor? What did you think of it?"

"You can call me Harry. Yes, it was fascinating. And so old. 1870! I wish I had that kind of connection to my own ancestors. I got nothing. I'm presuming we Grohs came from Germany eons ago. But…no details." Harry walked over to his desk and retrieved the photocopied letter and began to leaf through the pages as he spoke.

Tom then continued his introduction, "What did you make of him saying that he thought his birth was something very special? Don't we all think that at some time in our lives?"

"I wouldn't read too much into that. He might have been… er…adopted or illegitimate or simply had a difficult birth, and his parents laid some kind of miraculous trip on him."

"I guess so. Anyway, I've started to do some genealogical research to see if I can find out more about his origins. I think I've already found his birth and the marriage of his parents in English parish records. I think. No indication of what happened to his father though. I've still got work to do from that angle. Denise thinks the record of the burial of his father might still exist in its original paper form somewhere over there. But it might not have made its way into digitized, searchable databases yet."

Harry did not respond, so Tom forged ahead.

"What did you think about the reference to a ghost? That's really why I contacted you. When we examined our internet search results, it just seemed too much of a coincidence to Denise and me that you knew all about ghosts over there in that same English county and that you also lived so close to us. We thought we must be destined to get in touch."

"Yeah. I searched the internet too. I found the same newspaper reference you did. What I think that means is that there's a local legend in the village that a certain place is haunted, and some teenagers decided to horse around in the room on Halloween and see if they could encounter the ghost. Impress the local girls, if nothing else. God knows what they would've done if they'd seen it. But the manager of the place rightly kicked them out. Of course, this doesn't mean that the place is *not* haunted in some way."

"No. Right. Do you think there's a chance it could be connected with your experience?"

"How could it be? No, not possible. I looked on a map, and Saxonborough and Hoyland are fifteen miles apart. No direct connection."

"Nevertheless, we're still left with my ancestor's story. Whether or not a ghost does exist, he said there was a connection to our family. Perhaps this supposed ghost was a member of our family."

"I understand. Perhaps your family was the beginning of the legend of the Saxonborough ghost. In which case, the locals might know something about it."

They took up their coffee mugs and sipped on the implications of Harry's notion. One of the dogs roused himself and knocked two books on the floor. Harry took no notice.

"So...Harry," said Tom, "perhaps we could begin by you giving me a brief explanation of what happened to you over there. I read that journal article of yours but couldn't really get to grips with the theory. I need a layman's summary. And there was very little by way of a description of what actually occurred while you were in the church. I'm wondering if there are any aspects of your experience that we could transfer to Saxonborough."

"Sure. Well, it all started for us when I got a phone call at CIU from a buddy of mine in England. A physics professor at London University. He's the one who was the lead author of the paper and wrote most of it himself, Brian Kenning. A nice guy. We got on well together. I got to know him when he did a postdoc over here at

Northwestern. We bumped into each other in Chicago and became friends. Some mild razzing—baseball versus cricket, football versus rugby, lifts or elevators...that sort of thing. All in good fun. Anyway, he called me one day about eighteen months ago, out of the blue, and said that his girlfriend back in Lincolnshire claimed to have seen a ghost in a church. What did I think about that? I brushed it off at first, as you do, but then I began thinking about the research we were doing at CIU. Sensory deprivation stuff. Our best student, Karen Butler, had just started having the most peculiar visions in the tank. We both wondered if there could be a connection."

"And was there?"

"Surprisingly, there was. We all went over there, and Karen was able to *conjure up*—I don't know how else to put it—a ghost in the same church as Brian's girlfriend had. We found one or two other people who could do it as well. Brian developed a theory that they generated some kind of a cerebral field when they went into their *trances*—again, for want of a better word. Frank Koslowski, who worked with me, named it the zeta field. In our research world, there were already cerebral brain wave types named alpha, beta, dot, dot, dot, and he wanted to give this one a Greek letter at the end of the alphabet so no one could ever surpass us. He didn't realize that zeta was *not* the last letter in the Greek alphabet."

"Alpha and omega."

"Right. Frank was a bit of a dipshit, God rest his soul. But we kept calling it zeta, and it stuck in the end. So it was this zeta field that caused the ghosts to come into existence. Brian had an inspiration and hypothesized that many people used to be able to do this—probably many that can do it today. People from all walks of life all over the world but especially in the past when we didn't know much about the physical world, and the spiritual world was so much more important. Shamans, druids, witch doctors, sorcerers, clairvoyants... all of them capable of generating the zeta field—or at least playing around its edges. It's like we dismissed them all individually, on a case-by-case basis, never realizing that they were all part of the same phenomenon. A brilliant insight by Brian, I thought. None of it proven yet though."

"I kind of got that from your paper. It was the time stuff I didn't understand."

"And that's the hardest part to grapple with. We owe all of that to Brian. I'm not sure I fully understand it myself—even now. And I need pencil and paper to explain it clearly." He walked over to his desk and got them and drew a diagram, which he brought over and showed to Tom. "This diagram shows the temporal theory in its essence…Hey! Temporal! That's your name!" Tom gave a wan smile and waited for Harry to explain the figure.

Harry was not quite ready to dive into it, however. It had been months since he'd thought about those days back in the squalid apartment in south London, those long days when he and Frank had helped Brian and Karen to hammer out the full meaning of the temporal disturbances. Brian and Karen entranced on the couch in the center of the room. Curtains drawn tight. Vials and syringes of anoxyseriphin and other liquids on the only table in the room. He and Frank poring over the electronics and examining data from their measuring devices. Then the dramatic interruption by Brian's brother John and Brian's erstwhile girlfriend Sarah Harcourt. Insults thrown, accusations made. Things he had sworn to forget.

Harry stared out the window at the cornfields and wondered if the real reason he'd bought this remote farmhouse was to transport himself as far as possible from that tiny room in that claustrophobic city in that foreign land where he and the others had been trapped for so many days. Where they'd been so excited to develop the theory of the time quantum. Where they'd broken hard new ground that soon turned into quicksand and swallowed them whole and alive.

"Here goes, then," said Harry at last, turning his attention away from the distance and the space outside his farmhouse window to recollections of past confinement in a tiny flat come laboratory and the here-and-now reality of the anticipatory look on Tom's face under which he thrust the diagram he'd just drawn. "Layman's terms. Sure. So what we observe in our everyday life is that all the molecules

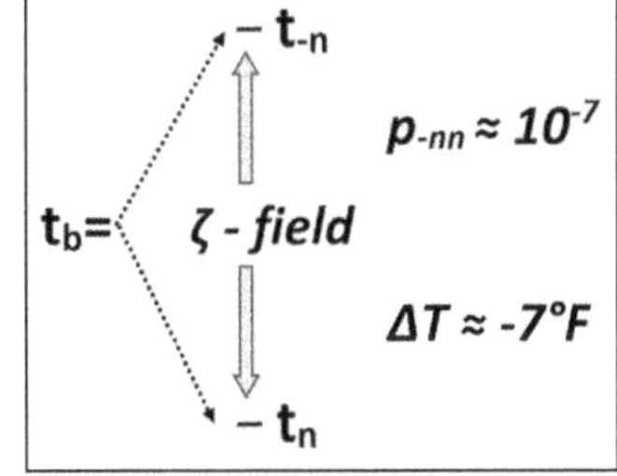

that comprise the objects in our world exist in one temporal state, which Brian christened the *now* state, indicated by the parameter *t⟨sub n⟩*, shown as this bar at the bottom of the diagram under the arrow." He pointed to the bottom of the page. "Brian's theory was that a molecule has the *potential* to exist at *any* moment in time, that time is, in fact, quantized. All things being normal, a molecule has one hundred percent probability of being in the *now* temporal state and zero percent probability of being in any other state. But in actuality, there are alternative time frames or quantum states that the molecule *could* exist in. Perhaps infinitely many. Always and forever. Past and future. But they are unpopulated. Right?"

"Under normal conditions."

"Exactly. The conditions we experience every day. But Brian's idea was that this may not necessarily always be the case. He postulated that imposition of the zeta field—see it here in between the arrows with its Greek letter, the *ζ-field*—could cause some molecules to populate an alternative temporal state. Karen Butler and Sarah Harcourt, just like the shamans and the clairvoyants, *et al.*, are particularly adept at generating this zeta field. Having no accurate way of measuring just how many molecules make this transition at any given time, Brian thought the probability might be as high as 10^{-7}. That value was just his guesstimate. See this *p⟨sub -nn⟩* value here on the right. That is to say, at any instant, one in ten million molecules are in the alternate temporal state. Brian thought that would be sufficient to make the object visible. Vague and insubstantial, of course—but visible. This alternate temporal state is shown in the diagram as *t⟨sub -n⟩* at the top of the page, above the arrow. It's a mirror version of *now*. The subscripts Brian used are, like, *n* for *now* and *minus n* for *minus now*, so to speak.

"So what we have is a ghost object, an exact, dilute replica of the object in the *now* time frame. Molecules are continually transitioning to the alternate temporal state when they're in the zeta field and then relaxing very quickly back to the *now* state. So when we see a ghost, we are seeing a faint representation in our time frame, *t⟨sub n⟩*, of an object that really exists in another time frame, *t⟨sub -n⟩*. And the transitions can go either way. Molecules can move up or down in this diagram. We can see objects that are in the past, and others can see objects that are in the future. Brian hypothesized that it was a reciprocal phenomenon, and we did actually observe that. It's all pretty straightforward when you think about it."

"And what does this $\Delta T \approx -7^{\circ}F$ mean?" Tom asked, pointing to the lower right side of the drawing. "Is it something to do with a temperature change?"

"The zeta field *creates* the alternate temporal states and *enables* them to be populated, but a source of energy is still required to push the molecules into those states. We are pretty sure that the energy is drawn from the surroundings. In our experiments we observed a temperature drop of as much as seven degrees at the center of the phenomenon. It gets cold when you see ghosts. Isn't that what people say? You shiver and rub your arms? Huh?"

Tom nodded. And then nodded some more. "I get it now," he said. "And what about this parameter *t⟨sub b⟩* on the left?"

"That was another stroke of brilliance on Brian's part and on the part of his brother John, too, as I understand it. We'd been observing the ghost of an old monk in this Hoyland Church that you've heard about. Well, in addition, I recorded some very faint sounds on a special tape recorder I built. They turned out to be a monastic chant. Super ancient. And somehow it was discovered that the sounds were recorded backward. A linguistics professor at Brian's college figured that out, as I recall. This meant that we were seeing the ghost monk from the early time period *t⟨sub -n⟩* in reverse. This prompted Brian to postulate that the mirror states were generated by something that had happened at the precise midpoint in time, this *t⟨sub b⟩* state, and the ancient and modern states were symmetrical around it, one running forward in time and one running backward. Get it? When you see ghosts, you're actually seeing them in reverse time. And it's only that single quantized state *t⟨sub -n⟩* that's accessible from *now*. No others. Theory absolutely demands it."

"Really?"

"Yep. And that's the essence of our work. The time quantum. Time is quantized just like energy at the molecular level. Are you listening, Mr. Einstein?"

"So what happened during your experiments?"

"Well, everything was going swimmingly for a while. We were able to explain what was happening in the church. We knew which time periods we were observing and the base state that was causing it all to happen. We in the present, *t<sub n>* = 2017, observed the ghost of an Anglo-Saxon monk, *t<sub -n>* = 1057, courtesy of the religious ecstasy of an Augustinian abbot at the exact midpoint in time, *t<sub b>* = 1537. Levitation, electrical sparks, flashes of light…the whole ecstasy shebang. We published the paper. Great. A tremendous discovery. We should have stopped there and waited for the Nobel Prizes to be awarded."

"But?"

"But that wasn't enough for Brian and Karen, who, by the way, had become an item by this time. They wanted more. They wanted to observe a transition from *t<sub n>* to *t<sub b>* in order to explore the event that had caused it all to happen in 1537. Understandable, I guess. Brian called it a resonance transition, from its physics analogy. He believed it must be possible to accomplish such a transition under the right conditions. We got a guy at Northwestern, Professor Lieshman, to prepare a drug to facilitate greater contact—anoxyseriphin, he called it. Karen taught Brian how to achieve the zeta effect, and they both experimented with anoxyseriphin. Frank and I helped them do the background work in Brian's apartment in London. It all worked. All too well."

"And?"

"And so we moved our base of operations back to Hoyland Church." Harry got up and walked around the room. He seemed suddenly anxious and unsure of himself, chewing on his fingernails. "I was there with them, but I have to confess that I still don't know what exactly happened when they achieved that resonance transition. It was all chaos and confusion. There was a fire, you see. This was the time of the dissolution of the monasteries, and King Henry's force had set fire to the church. There was smoke everywhere. Monks being chased hither and yon. Soldiers brandishing swords. But nothing could be seen clearly. And I was super stressed out by that time. I'd pretty much lost it completely, to be honest.

"And then this figure…this figure suddenly appeared in front of me out of nowhere. It looked like a man out of history. By his clothing. Do you know what I mean? But I'm not sure anymore. It happened so quickly. He had a big sword in his hand. He chased me and Frank out of the church. I was out of my gourd. I ran to the car and drove off as fast as I could. This dude must have caught Frank and killed him just outside the church door. I found that out later. I think Brian and Karen ran off too. Perhaps through the vestry. I'm not sure." He turned and walked back across the room. "I remember that I was speeding. The car ran off the road. I was lying in a field. I was spouting nonsense to the ears of wheat around me. And then a newspaper reporter who'd been hounding us about what we were up to in the church found me and helped me. Called an ambulance. Due credit to him. I ended up in a hospital somewhere. It took me weeks to recuperate. Then I flew home. To this day I'm not entirely sure what the fuck happened in the church."

"So that's what caused all the trouble you ran into at the university?"

"Yep. Nothing's been the same since then. Frank's death changed everything. I was held responsible at first, but then common sense prevailed, and I was seen as just another victim."

That appeared to be the end of Harry's account, so Tom waited a few moments and then pushed his luck. "That's a remarkable story. You seem to have discovered such a lot—and endured such a lot as well. Is it too much to ask if you would be willing to help me follow up on my ghost?"

"I don't know. I guess I might. I wouldn't make a special trip, but if I'm going to be over there anyway, I guess I could spare a day or two to go back up to Lincolnshire."

"And what about this Brian Kenning? Could we get him to come with us? He seems to have been the brains behind the discovery."

"Not possible, chief. He hasn't been seen since that day. Not hide nor hair. Karen neither. I already told you that the two of them were having an affair during the time we were doing the background research in London. Nobody knows where they went after the debacle in Hoyland Church. Myself, I think they'd had enough of the supernatural. Run off together to Tahiti."

"Oh. I didn't realize that. Sorry. What about the other author? This *John* Kenning. You said he was Brian's brother?"

"Exited stage left, also. He wasn't with us in the church, but we never saw any more of him after he stormed out of the apartment in Clapham. I guess he'd also had his fill of the supernatural. He always said he wanted to go and live in the South of France. Don't know if he did or not. I liked Brian and John both. Real smart, the pair of them. I wish we could have kept in touch. But it wasn't meant to be."

"And this Sphere of the Planets thing? What's that all about?"

"Yeah, well, during our experiment in the church I saw one of the monks brandish the object above his head to try to ward off the marauding soldiers. Like some kind of a precious talisman. But it didn't work. So he ran through into the Lady Chapel, where he fell down and was killed. At that very same time, the burning roof caved in and enveloped everything. But I was watching and saw exactly where the relic fell. Later I contacted the county archeological authority and asked if they would dig under the floor of the church in that precise location to see if the relic was still buried there. It was. And it turned out to be very rare and very valuable. Late fifteenth century. French. Hence all the palaver at the British Museum. Official unveiling coming up next month. Fame for Harry Groh instead of notoriety. For once."

"That's amazing. That you should have seen where it fell."

Harry nodded. "I had my wits about me that one time."

"Well, all I want is for us to go up to this place called Saxonborough. Find the inn that my ancestor mentioned. Dig around for information—metaphorically in my case. Find out what the locals know. See if the Temporal name means anything to anybody. I may stay on and search the local archives in Lincoln, but you can come back after we're finished with the ghost part."

"I'd be willing to do that much. I'm scheduled to leave on April 7 by the way. The ceremony at the British Museum is on the Wednesday, April 10. You can find details about it on the internet."

"Great. Thanks so much. I really appreciate it. I'll check with Denise, but I'm sure she'd love to come with me. We've been talking about a summer vacation in Europe. I'll confirm everything with her and let you know our travel plans."

"Okay. If you want to look through that pile of books next to you on the couch, feel free. You might find something of interest. That one on the top is particularly interesting, *An Experiment with Time*. It's fantastic. They were Karen Butler's. She was much deeper into the spiritual world than any of us. She was a special kind of lady. I wish I knew where she was. I wish I could see her again. I don't even know if she's alive or dead." He looked at the floor and closed his eyes. "We messed up so bad."

Chapter 7

Hoyland Abbey
1537

LEAVING THE FOOTPRINTS OF HIS sandals imprinted in the ash that now covered the floor of the chancel at Hoyland Abbey, Abbot Gervase rose, inch by inch, up into the smoky air. His cowl had been ripped away to reveal his bald head, now glazed a solemn, dull purple. On his neck the veins pulsed, and the sinews stood out tight and rigid, stiff as whipcord. His eyes bulged. His gaze was fixed on the arms of Jesus reaching out to him, welcoming him. The taste of electricity was suddenly in the air, and the ring of hair surrounding the monk's tonsure spiked out in all directions. Brian's notepapers flew off the bench. The abbot continued to rise above the floor: six inches…a foot. His voluminous brown habit began to undulate from ankle to neck. Blood dripped from his nose and ears. A maelstrom of dust and ash and paper began to swirl under his feet, blue sparks crackling back and forth across it. Tiny stars twinkled in the column of air that stretched above him into the blackness of the abbey roof.

Richard Crossly was unconvinced by this extraordinary display. He very much doubted its religious significance; to his mind, wizardry was a more likely cause. He took one step forward and swung his sword in a full circle against the abbot's neck, decapitating him. The abbot's torso collapsed onto the stone slabs, jerking violently. Blood was everywhere. The severed head rolled to a halt against a bench. A swatch of cloth remained stuck to Crossly's sword, and with a single motion he used it to wipe the blade clean. He then gave a single shout of defiance, drew the sword back with one hand,

and hurled it up at Brian with all his might. The sword cartwheeled through the air, sliced through Brian's left hand, and embedded itself in the rood screen behind him. Brian emitted a harsh cry of pain and clutched his arm in horror. Crossly walked over to retrieve his sword and finish off Brian, who had sunk to his knees. Simultaneously, Karen leapt up off the bench on which she had been sitting. Harry Groh and Frank Koslowski stood statuesque and silent in the back row of the choir stalls, unable to comprehend or react to the fantasy unfolding in front of them, their science of no value now. Harry kept his eyes on the flames billowing in the Lady Chapel, wondering if they would be able to escape with their lives.

And that was when it happened. The figures of both Brian and Crossly began to fade into a delicate, shimmering blue haze. Without hesitation, Karen ran and jumped in between the two men, grabbing hold of Brian to protect him. The two of them fell in a heap on the flagstones, Karen's arms wrapped tightly around Brian, her eyes squeezed shut in anticipation of the fatal blow to come. But it did not come. It did not come. After a moment, Karen turned and looked up, still clutching Brian to her. She saw that all the monks were on their knees by the altar, praying. Many of King Henry's soldiers were praying also—though one or two of them, disbelievers no doubt, remained standing, swords down at their sides. These soldiers were unable to make sense of what they'd just seen with their own eyes, but they, too, doubted its religious significance. Richard Crossly was nowhere to be seen.

"Help him!" Karen screamed. "Help him!"

Brian lay motionless on the floor, in shock, blood pulsing from the stump of his wrist.

"Help him!"

A young soldier walked over to them. He took off his neckerchief and wrapped it tightly around Brian's wrist. He then bent Brian's arm at the elbow and indicated to Karen that she should hold it tightly in that position. Soldiers who'd been on the battlefield knew these things. He was surprisingly casual about the whole thing even as Karen panicked.

He turned and shouted to the monks, "Who among you is from the infirmary?"

A stout monk stepped forward and jogged over to them.

"I am Friar Anselm," he said. "I can take care of him." He turned toward the altar. "Brother Bonaventure, come, please!" Another monk stood up. "Quickly now!" The monk ran over to join his colleague.

"But what of Abbot Gervase?" said Brother Bonaventure as he approached.

"There's nothing to be done for him," the soldier replied, indicating the body on the floor. "He is with the Almighty. Take care of the one who can yet be saved."

Friar Anselm looked up and pleaded with the soldier, "Have mercy on us, sir! Save our brethren, I beg you! Do not burn any more of our buildings. We will take this man to the infirmary and treat him."

"Very well," said the soldier. "Enough is enough." He turned and bellowed to the soldiers around him, "No more this day! Take these monks outside. All soldiers and monks to assemble in the courtyard. Tell Master Clinton! Tell all of our men!" They hesitated. "Go, I say!" The soldiers dispersed and escorted the monks outside, some roughly, some compassionately. Friar Anselm and Brother Bonaventure picked up Brian and carried him outside also. By this time the entire Lady Chapel was ablaze. The roof had fallen in, and patches of gray sky could be seen through the burning rafters.

The soldier wiped Brian's blood off his tunic and escorted Karen out of the abbey, out of danger.

"This is inexplicable," he said to her, once the flames were behind them. "How do you and the wounded man come to be here? Can you explain this occurrence? And where is our leader, Master Crossly?"

Karen could answer none of these questions. Even if her mind had not been befuddled and jittery, she could not have answered, for she did not know. So she took the easy way out. "All these questions will be answered very soon," she replied. "But first I must attend to the wounded man and make sure he is properly cared for. It is my bounden duty."

"Very well. But rest assured that he is in the best of hands. He is fortunate to have been injured at the site of one of the best infirmaries in the county. The monastery here at Hoyland is renowned for the skill of its monks. Only the hospital in Lincoln and the Benedictine monastery at Croyland on the Norfolk border are its equal. Have a monk take you to see the condition of your colleague and the treatment that he is presently receiving. We shall convene in the refectory in one hour for explanations."

"Very good, sir, you are most understanding," said Karen. "And you should be aware, first and foremost, that a fantastic miracle has been worked here by Abbot Gervase this day. Do not think lightly of it. I suggest the next hour be spent in prayer by all here present, monks and soldiers alike." The soldier nodded. "And might I ask your name, sir?"

"I am William Cecil, the son of Sir Richard Cecil, Master of Burghley. I am young, but I am of high birth and considerable experience. I and Edward Fiennes de Clinton of Lincoln are the officers appointed as second-in-command jointly of King Henry's force here present under Richard Crossly's leadership. Clinton is presently in charge of the force outside the abbey, keeping the villagers at bay. Now have one of these upstart monks escort you to the infirmary."

Karen and the monk walked across the grassy courtyard that separated the abbey from the monks' quarters and the communal buildings. She was desperately worried about Brian and whether he would survive the attack on him, but also, swirling around in another corner of her mind were ideas as to how she was going to explain their sudden appearance in the abbey. She was also deeply frightened of their predicament. But she knew she had to keep a calm and calculated demeanor if they were to survive.

They came to a long, low stone building, and the monk ushered Karen inside. There were no more than a dozen beds, laid out in two rows facing inward. Two of the beds by the door were occupied, and the eyes of those two patients were glued to a bed at the far end of the room, which was surrounded by half a dozen monks. The escorting monk indicated that Karen should go over to that bed. As she approached, the monks saw her and made way so that she could come to the bedside. There she saw the unconscious figure of Brian wrapped in sheets that were white and lying on a bed that was mostly red.

Friar Anselm came to her side. He spoke in low tones but with assurance.

"He is not yet conscious, madam, but he is as well as can be expected."

"What have you done to treat him?"

"We have used the best and most advanced of treatments. In another place and at another time, he would have had his wrist seared with a red-hot iron to cauterize the wound. He may have died of shock at once. Many soldiers do. But in this monastery, we know better. We are fortunate to have among us Brother Bonaventure from France. He has learned new and more humane surgical practices from the great Ambroise Paré. Brother Bonaventure?"

One of the assembled monks stepped forward and bowed deeply in front of Karen. "Madam, I am Brother Bonaventure," he said with a strong French accent. "Your friend is indeed in good hands. I have come to this monastery earlier in the year. Before that, I accompanied the army of King Francis on its advance from Marseille into Northern Italy. It was there that I renewed my friendship with Ambroise Paré. We had previously been trained together at the hospital Hôtel-Dieu in Paris. He is a brilliant surgeon, madam. As we marched onward into Piedmont, our army fought battle after battle, and many soldiers were brought to our tent suffering from wounds caused by the arquebus and other firearms as well as sword thrusts and slashes—wounds such as the one this man has suffered. At the siege of Turin, Dr. Paré saved many lives with his innovations for the treatment of the gravely wounded."

"That is very gratifying to hear," said Karen.

"Ambroise is fearless, madam. He is never afraid to try new techniques to save the lives of soldiers. He prefers slow and gentle methods over quick and brutal ones. He has made particular strides in developing methods to treat amputations, following the advices of that most accomplished physician of antiquity, Claudius Galenus—who some call Galen of Pergamon. As Friar Anselm said, cauterization causes indescribable agony to the patient and often results in a quick death. So Ambroise developed a less savage method. I observed his work in the battlefield tents. I have since copied his methods, and that is how we have just treated this young man."

"What exactly have you done?"

"Well, first, we tied off the arteries with ligatures—using what Ambroise christened *le bec de corbeau*."

"The what?" Karen asked.

"Ah—*je suis désolé*—pardon me, madam, er…*the beak of the crow*. That is what we call the instrument. It is a special device to seal off the arterial flow. It is a curved clamp, like in appearance unto a crow's beak."

"Oh, I see."

"Then we treated the exposed surfaces with an ointment made of egg yolk, rose oil, and turpentine. It is both soothing and effective against infection. All is then tightly bound in clean cloth that has been soaked in boiling water for one hour. See here." He pointed to Brian's arm.

Friar Anselm then interjected, "The flow of blood appears to be stemmed now, madam. Thanks be to God. Brother Bonaventure will continue the treatment according to Dr. Paré's techniques. Periodically we will unwrap the wound and reapply the ointment. The danger is not yet passed, but with the grace of God he will survive."

"It is most fortunate that you were here at the abbey at this time when we needed you most desperately," Karen said to Brother Bonaventure with tears in her eyes. "If you had not been here, my friend would surely be dead by now. We cannot thank you enough."

"Thanks are not necessary," he replied, bowing once more and looking away from Karen's watery eyes. "I am a servant of the Lord. I have dedicated my life to treating the sick and injured among his flock. If this man is otherwise healthy, I believe he will not die. I have seen such amputations by sword at Turin. Some of them with the entire arm or leg lost. Perhaps ten of them in sum. I would guess that eight of them survived under Dr. Paré's treatment."

"Thank you. Thank you so much," said Karen again. "It is a great mercy that you found your way to this remote English abbey. How long have you been a monk?"

"After what I saw in Piedmont—the terror in the eyes of the injured and dying soldiers, the desperate methods of the ill-trained barber surgeons—I decided to leave the army and join the

Augustinian Order. And to avoid retribution, I decided to come to England. I thought it better to serve God and mankind as one, rather than to obey a single king and despise all of his enemies. And I hoped that I might also, in a small way, heal the wounds that have existed for so long between our two countries. So this is now my life's work. I take my guidance from Dr. Paré. Whenever he treated a patient who survived, he would always say, *'Je le pansai, mais Dieu le guérit.'*"

Karen raised her eyebrows for a translation.

"*'I bandaged him, but God healed him.'* These are the words I live by."

Karen returned the gesture that the monk had twice bestowed on her and bowed deeply before him. She would have hugged him if she'd thought it appropriate. Their work completed for the time being, the monks left Karen sitting by Brian's bed, holding his one remaining hand tightly in hers. He did indeed look peaceful and likely to survive Crossly's attack. As she sat, finally in a tranquil setting, the desperate nature of the situation in which they found themselves stepped out from the corner of her brain in which it had been gestating and came forcefully into the front of her mind. Through some unknown temporal phenomenon, they had been transported back in time, into Tudor England, about which she knew nothing. Brian could perhaps explain what had happened and where they were, but she could not.

Nevertheless, some kind of a story needed to be concocted. And concocted quickly. They were in a violent age, among a violent people. Their lives could be at stake. *But don't use the word* stake, she said to herself. *They might believe me to be a witch and think to burn me at one.* In addition, as near as she could tell, the leader of the soldiers had vanished…also transported to a different time perhaps? Could they have switched places? There was no way for her to know. But if the authorities were to decide that she and Brian were responsible for his disappearance…for his death perhaps…then their fate might be sealed. Indeed, a compelling story was needed, one that the people of this time and place would accept. Something that would save her own life and Brian's. Something believable. And she was the one who had to come up with it.

When the prescribed hour was up, a soldier entered the infirmary and escorted Karen to the refectory. There she sat down at a table with William Cecil, Edward Clinton, and Friar Anselm. Two soldiers guarded the door.

"Where is Richard Crossly?" Edward Clinton shouted at once before even they had made themselves comfortable, banging his fist on the table. "What have you done with him?"

"You were not there, Edward," said William Cecil, indicating the need for calm by placing his palms toward him. "You did not witness it."

"He is not here at the head of this table, is he? As he rightly ought to be. So where is he? What has the witch done with him?"

"Let me begin the proceedings, Edward, if you will. I know more of what occurred than you do." William Cecil turned from Clinton to Karen. "Who are you, madam?" he asked her. "There were no women on the church grounds until you appeared. Will you tell us your name?"

"Let us begin elsewhere," Karen replied. "I will tell you my name later."

"See! She is a witch!" Clinton spat. "I can sense it. Flown in from that Burstoft coven."

"Edward, please!" said William. "Restrain yourself! If you cannot tell us your name, madam, then what can you tell us?"

Karen mustered her thoughts and slowly began to relate the story she'd dreamed up during the previous hour. "You saw what transpired, sir. You saw the maelstrom on the chancel floor…the levitation of the abbot's body…the stars…the sparks…all the work of Abbot Gervase. He achieved a high state of religious ecstasy." Clinton scoffed, but Karen pressed on. "The abbot performed a miracle, I say. He summoned all his power against the man who would destroy his church and his monastery: Master Crossly. A man who would desecrate all the works of the Almighty at this abbey and far beyond.

"And God answered his call. It is as simple as that. God effectuated a transfiguration." She hoped she'd correctly remembered the meaning of that word. "Abbot Gervase desperately wanted to change Master Crossly's view of himself and of the abbey and of the monks under him—in order to halt the destruction of all he had worked for his entire life. And so he summoned God to perform the transfiguration of Crossly from an evil vilifier into a benevolent man. And God heard his plea. God acted upon it."

"What are you saying?"

"I am saying that the man on the floor, the man whose hand was severed and who is now lying in the infirmary, is, indeed, Richard Crossly, the *new* Richard Crossly."

"How can such a miracle be worked? I have never heard of such a thing."

"When great faith meets heavenly intercession, many things are possible."

"I cannot believe it."

"You cannot?" Karen decided to be more forceful. "Can you explain the disappearance of the *old* Richard Crossly, the Richard Crossly that *you* knew? Can you explain the appearance of an unknown man on the floor of the abbey? What other explanation can you offer?"

William Cecil looked down at the table. "In truth, I can offer nothing."

"Offer witchcraft, William!" said Edward Clinton. "Offer sorcery! There are many alternatives to celestial intercession."

Friar Anselm, who'd observed these exchanges in silence, now spoke up, "I do not believe that sorcery can be the explanation, gentlemen. Abbot Gervase was the holiest of men. He could never initiate it or permit it to be practiced in his presence. That is impossible. There is an impenetrable wall around a high-status abbey such as this one—a wall that no devil can breach. This much is beyond dispute.

"I prefer to think that Abbot Gervase was the originator of a miraculous event, just as this young woman has described. Such things have been seen before. Indeed, here at Hoyland we still relate the story of Bricstan of Ely, who prayed to St. Benedict to release him from the chains in his prison cell. St. Benedict descended to earth and shattered Bricstan's fetters. The prison guards saw it with their own eyes and swooned in amazement. That much is true. And Brother Bonaventure has related similar miraculous interventions in

France by Our Lady of Rocamadour. The precedents are numerous, gentlemen."

"So, madam," William Cecil continued, acknowledging the friar's endorsement. "Are you telling us that the man in the infirmary is, in fact, Richard Crossly, even though he bears no physical resemblance to him?"

"It is he. Indeed, it is."

"And how do you know this? What part do you play in it all?"

Karen took a deep breath and began the second part of her story.

"My name is Ka-Ren. I am…I *was* a lowly member of the celestial body. When Abbot Gervase summoned the help of the heavenly host, the Almighty answered his plea and transfigured Master Crossly. He also sent me down to earth to protect him, for as long as it took for him to be accepted into the world of man. For God knew that mankind would not readily believe what had happened." Emboldened, she pointed across the table at Edward Clinton. She felt she had nothing to lose at this point. Audacity had a better chance of success than hesitance. "As has just now been demonstrated by this arrogant man!"

"Are you telling us that you…you…that you are an *angel*?" Edward Clinton said with utter contempt. "Preposterous!"

"I was an angel before I descended to earth. I was Ka-Ren."

Friar Anselm jumped to his feet at this point. "It is true! That much is true! The wounded man was part-conscious as we carried him across the courtyard, and he said several times, *'Help me, Ka-Ren! Help me!'* He spoke that name several times. *Ka-Ren!* So I can vouch that that much is true." He dropped to his knees and prayed before her.

Both William Cecil and Edward Clinton were unnerved by this outburst from the friar. It served to support the notion of heavenly intervention. This was a development that cast a whole new light on the matter. Neither of them had any desire to offend the deity.

"I said that I was an angel before I descended to earth," Karen continued, "but I am no longer one. The heavenly host does not permit angels to live among men. There must ever and always be a boundary between the two realms. I am become an earthly woman. I am to be called Ka-Ren no more. I have been given the name Catherine, a name with which you are all familiar. I am here to watch over and protect the wounded man, the new Richard Crossly."

"And you will remain on earth?"

"That I do not know. For the time being at least. Perhaps I will be taken up when the new Richard Crossly is safe and renewed and accepted. I do not know. I was not told. I only serve God's plan."

"I suppose this also explains your strange way of speaking. It is an ancient way?"

"It is. My accent is typical of the voices of the celestial host. It is the way people spoke in biblical times. It has been preserved in heaven throughout the ages."

"Enochian," said William Cecil, nodding, but none other present knew what that meant.

"How can we be sure that all this is true?" asked Edward Clinton, still deeply suspicious. "Master Cecil has confirmed that you appeared in the abbey from nowhere. Arose out of the dust and the ashes at the bidding of Gervase. But that, in and of itself, does not mean that you are of celestial origin. Can you prove it? Can you perform some miraculous illusion that will convince us? Madam?"

"I am not St. Benedict," Karen replied sternly. "I have not been dispatched here on some theatrical errand. I am here to protect the wounded man now and on into the future. As I just said, in such circumstances, we are made human. I am the same as you. I cannot perform miracles. I can only observe and guard. Though, if it should become necessary, I do have the power to report human transgressions back to Almighty God. So be aware of that."

"And what of the hand of the new Richard Crossly?" William Cecil asked her. "What has happened to it? It was not to be found on the floor of the chancel when the smoke cleared. My men have looked everywhere. Can you explain that?"

"It is my understanding that it was taken as penalty, so that he, Richard Crossly, although transfigured, would ever be reminded of his previous life and his misdeeds. And that the men around him would ever be reminded of it also. The hand has been taken up. It is possible that it will be returned to the abbey in the distant future as a relic...as a remembrance perhaps...of all that has taken place here today. If the future be sufferable."

Cecil and Clinton looked at each other, each one waiting for the other to utter some conclusory statement. Friar Anselm glanced from one to the other and back again. Finally, young William Cecil took matters into his own hands.

"Well, I, for one, am not willing to countersay this woman at this time. I am a God-fearing man and would not want to be the one who upsets the course of heaven and the stars. Unless Master Clinton has an objection, I will take this woman at her word—for now. I rule that the wounded man be treated here in the monastic infirmary under the care of Friar Anselm." The monk nodded. "There will be no further action to dissolve this monastery at this time. King Henry can shoot his arrows at other targets in the meanwhile. I will return to Tattershall Castle and confer with my father and the Duke of Suffolk. No monks shall be evicted today."

He turned pointedly to Friar Anselm. "But you should not construe this cessation to imply that we will not return at a later date to enforce King Henry's will. This Catholic blasphemy must indeed be expunged from our nation." The monk made no gesture in response; this time it was Clinton who nodded. "You, Friar Anselm, may report on the death of Abbot Gervase and the damage done to the abbey to whomsoever rules you on these matters in these isles. I suggest that your order rethinks its position and reorganizes itself. Perhaps the course of events here today will divert your path to one that is tolerable to the king."

"You, madam," he said, turning to Karen, "shall remain here to watch over the man you call the new Richard Crossly. I suppose you may be afforded the right to sleep next to him in one of the infirmary's beds for mutual comfort and protection—if there is no danger of contagion from the other patients, that is, you being altogether human as you assert."

"There is no risk," responded Friar Anselm. "There are but two other patients at this time. One suffers from a broken leg incurred at the harvest. The other is just slightly delusional. I will have Brother

Bonaventure explain to them the situation at the other end of the infirmary. Brother Bonaventure will watch over the security of… of—"

"Of Catherine," said Karen. "From this point onward, I am to be called Catherine Crossly. Do not forget this."

William Cecil wound up the meeting with these words to the group, "I myself will ride to Ketteringham Lodge this day. I will lay rushes in the path ahead. I will explain to Sir Adam Crossly what has happened here. He is an old man, feeble in the head, so perhaps he can accept the change in appearance of his son and the sudden arrival of Catherine. Or perhaps it will kill him. I cannot say. But I will try my best. The servants will oblige without question. Friar Anselm, I suppose it will take two weeks or more before the man is healed and can leave the infirmary?"

"At least two," Friar Anselm responded. "Possibly three. Brother Bonaventure will have the final say on when our work here is done."

"Very good. At that point in time, then, you two may journey to Ketteringham Lodge and make your home there. I will leave soldiers on guard here at the monastery and the abbey, and one or two of them can accompany you when you are ready to depart. Is this acceptable to all?"

"It is," said Catherine Crossly.

"It is," said Edward Clinton.

"It is," said Friar Anselm.

"In that case, I will terminate this consultation and withdraw our men from the abbey this twenty-second day of August in the year of our Lord fifteen hundred and thirty-seven. I will prepare a brief report on events and all matters arising for the further edification of His Majesty and all concerned. God save the king!"

"God save the king!" replied Clinton.

They stood up and walked out of the refectory. Friar Anselm escorted Karen back to the infirmary, and as she walked beside him across the grass, her hands were trembling, and she muttered under her breath, "1537. Oh my god. Oh my god. 1537. Oh my god."

Chapter 8

Ketteringham Lodge
November 1572

A BRIGHT NEW STAR APPEARED IN the sky over Ketteringham Lodge in November of the year 1572. Richard Crossly first noticed it through the window in front of his desk. He went outside to look at it. The evening air was clear and chill, and the star sparkled brilliantly against the pale-blue sky. Catherine came out to join him, and they linked arms.

"What is it?" she asked him.

"There's a new star in the sky. I've not seen it before. It's bright—brighter, I think, than Venus on a clear morning."

"It's only just recently appeared?"

"Yes. In the constellation of Cassiopeia. See?" He pointed up at it.

"Ah yes, the big *W*! I remember my father showing it to me once."

"It's easy to remember. But that bright star off the right tip of the *W* is something new."

Catherine huddled against him for warmth.

"What do you think it is?" she asked, turning to look at him.

"It must be a supernova. I can think of no alternative."

"Come inside and put on your coat."

As they stood there staring up into the sky, their cook Joan and her daughter Alice, their maidservant, came to join them and took up positions alongside Catherine.

"What are you looking at?" Joan asked.

"A new star."

Richard pointed to it again, and Joan and Alice followed the angle of elevation of his arm.

"Where did it come from?" asked Joan.

"Probably a small star just recently exploded."

Alice, who was only thirteen years old and uneducated, looked at Richard and then into her mother's eyes. "I'm frightened, Mother," she said.

"No, no, no," said Catherine, putting her arm around the girl's shoulders. "There's no need to be afeared."

"But what if the flames should reach our house? We will be burned."

"It is very far away, Alice. Very, *very* far away. Only the starlight that you see here tonight can ever reach us."

Alice relaxed her shoulders under the protection of Catherine's arm and stared at the star in awe. At that moment their young groom, Nicholas, walked over and took his place at the end of the line next to the cook. He was sixteen years old.

"It's a new star," he said.

"Yes," Richard replied. "I just saw it from my desk a moment ago."

"I already knew of it," Nicholas remarked proudly, his years among the hooves of horses needing all the confidence building he could get. "They've been talking about it in the Red Lion for a week now. They're calling it the *Wise Men's Star*." Joan and Alice turned and stared at him. "They say it means that Jesus will return at Christmas. Or that a new holy child will be born on Christmas Day. They cannot decide which."

"Either one would be wonderful," said Joan.

"Wonderful," echoed young Alice.

All five members of the household stood in a line looking up at the new star. The denuded cornfields and scattered, leafless trees seemed to be curiously illuminated by the light of the visitor. It was a haunting, magical sight. Catherine finally interrupted their several and utterly different reveries, by urging them, "Come inside. It's cold out here. Hot spiced milk for us all, please, Joan."

TWO MONTHS LATER, IN THE middle of a cold but quiescent January, William Cecil convened a brain trust at Burghley House to discuss the new star. William had been elevated to Baron Burghley by Queen Elizabeth in 1571, and in July of 1572, he had been appointed to the most prestigious position of Lord High Treasurer. As a result, his days were spoken for, and he had to prevail upon his eldest son, Thomas Cecil, then aged thirty, to host the get-together. John Dee had been the one to request the meeting because his adopted son and acolyte, Thomas Digges, had developed some new ideas about the star's origins and its significance for the structure of the universe. Also invited was Thomas Allen, one of the nation's prominent mathematicians and astrologers, who had already been summoned by the queen to give advice on the new star.

Richard and Catherine were invited as well. Why? Because over the thirty-five-year span since they'd been washed up on this unfamiliar shore, they had developed a reputation as two of the preeminent thinkers and savants in Britain; and despite their seclusion at Ketteringham Lodge for much of this time, they had already cultivated a friendship with John Dee and made several trips to his home at Mortlake for discussions. Their friendship with William Cecil, naturally, stretched back to the day of their initial shipwreck. At this particular time, Thomas Digges was especially excited to run his new cosmological ideas by Richard.

And so Nicholas smartened up the Crossly carriage, brushed down the horses, and conveyed Richard and Catherine the few miles over to Stamford and the majestic Burghley House, the pride of Lincolnshire, built on the foundations of the lucrative wool trade enjoyed by the Cecil family. Construction of the mansion had begun seventeen years ago, but it was still not completed, and one wing was out of commission. Nevertheless, Richard and Catherine were overawed by its grandeur as they rode up the driveway.

"Remember," Richard said to Catherine, "what we agreed when we first found ourselves marooned here. To reveal nothing about the future. We must not direct the course of events. Our motto is EAST: encourage, applaud, support, teach. Nothing more. The unfolding of the scientific truth about the world—and in the case of today's meeting the structure of the universe—we must leave for Hubble, Einstein, and Dirac to uncover."

"And Hawking," said Catherine. "Agreed."

"Actually, I do not recall the name of Thomas Digges as a leading light in this area, but that's not totally surprising. I was more of a molecular physicist, not an astronomer. I never heard of a supernova in 1572 either. We'll see what the experts say."

They were escorted up the main staircase to the library of Burghley House. It was called the library, but there were precious few books to be seen; one didn't rise up through the political strata of Tudor England by hiding in corners and reading. There, a fine buffet lunch awaited them on the highly polished sideboard: twice-cooked ham stuffed with apricots, spit-roasted mallard, and pheasant with orange sauce, all accompanied by fresh white bread and pickled quail eggs. On a side table were three kinds of dessert: marzipan treats, gingerbread, and a jam tart conceit with fondant cream. Though there was also one plate of potatoes and one of pumpkin, there was no green vegetable to be seen, much to Catherine's disappointment—though something to which she'd become accustomed over the years. She managed to locate an apple, however, and added that to her plate. Every guest praised the delicious food.

After lunch, the discussion began. Six people sat around the library table: Thomas Cecil, the host; John Dee and Thomas Allen, both renowned natural philosophers; Thomas Digges, the up-and-coming young scientist; and Richard and Catherine Crossly. The first part of the discussion concerned the facts of the appearance of the new star.

Digges described his own observations, all of which were confirmed by Allen. "I hung a six-foot ruler from a tree," Digges said, "to see whether the new star moved in relation to the other stars nearby. It did not. I concluded, therefore, that it was not a planet. In addition, common wisdom of the day—which I will come to in a moment—is that the new star must lie between the spheres of Earth and the moon, for that is the only place in the heavens where change can occur. But I found no daily parallax against the background of fixed stars, and therefore the new star had to be much farther away than the moon. These two conclusions I am certain of. I am presently developing trigonometric equations to determine the parallax of the star. I hope to publish my findings next year in a book, which I tentatively entitle *Alae seu Scalae Mathematicae* or *Mathematical Wings or Scales*. I am deeply engaged in the writing of it these days."

Allen then said, "I might add that our ambassador in Italy has received word that Clavius and Maurolico have both made similar observations of the new star. The ambassador reported back to Her Majesty, who tasked me with enlightening her on the matter. This I am doing from time to time. I hope today's meeting will enable further edification of Her Majesty."

"On the basis of my observations," Digges continued, "I am confident that the sudden appearance of this wondrous new star will provide the ideal circumstance to permit alternative views of the universe to be entertained."

"Take care, Master Digges," Cecil interjected. "I believe that any assertions of alternative cosmologies will be viewed as heretical by the Catholic church."

"Be that as it may, Thomas, I have already asked your father for funds to support additional astronomical and theoretical works, for I believe that we are on the verge of a great new understanding. But we need additional observations in the first part. We need careful observations of this new star and of all wandering stars in the firmament. We need to note changes in their appearance: their brightness, color, and texture. Only then can we say whether the divine Nicolaus Copernicus has fully and accurately described the realities of the fantastical organization of celestial globes."

"My father showed me the letter you wrote him," said Cecil. "I was greatly impressed by it and urged my father to support you. I most particularly liked the words you chose in framing, from the viewpoint of the astronomer, the nature of your observations *in the various regions of this dark and obscure terrestrial star, where, wandering as strangers, we lead in a short space of time, a life harassed by various fortunes*. Such beautiful words. It brought home to me most forcefully the vicissitudes of the natural philosopher in plying his trade amidst the convulsive forces of politics, the monarchy, and the church. Such a torturous path it must be."

"Please explain to us how Copernicus transformed our prior understanding of the structure of the universe," said Catherine. "I for one need some background."

"Well, of course," said Digges. "Copernicus upset the long-standing applecart of Ptolemy that Earth is the center of our solar system. *'No, it is the sun,'* said Nicolaus. A most inspired declaration. His revolutionary treatise on the subject, *De Revolutionibus Orbium Coelestium*, or *On the Revolutions of the Celestial Spheres*, was published in 1543, a mere three years before I was born. Part of my present work is an informed translation of this document.

"Copernicus espoused that all heavenly bodies move within celestial spheres. All the spheres surround the sun as if it were in the middle of them, and therefore the center of the universe is near to the sun. The distance of Earth from the sun is imperceptible in comparison with the height of the firmament, the outermost celestial sphere that contains the stars. All apparent motions of the stars arise purely from motions of the Earth—none of them can move of their own volition. This is the essence of the work of Nicolaus. I myself have encapsulated his system in this paltry but informative diagram." He drew from his files a piece of parchment and laid it on the table before them. "You see, here we have the spheres that contain the positions of the planets surrounding the sun. There are six of them, of course, but here I only show the outer three: Mars, Jupiter, and Saturn."

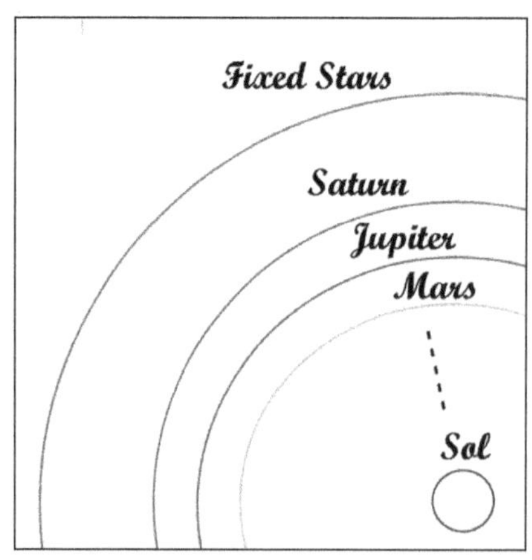

"If I may interrupt you for just one moment," said Richard Crossly, "you may be interested to know that my father, Sir Adam Crossly, once owned a jeweled representation of this view of the heavens. It was known as the Sphere of the Planets and was given to him by the King of France for his skillful framing of the Treaty of Étaples. It was presented to him in 1492, suggesting that a heliocentric view of the heavens existed prior to Copernicus. Ten or twenty years prior no less."

"That much is true," John Dee said. "I can affirm it. The Vienna School and others had already proposed it informally. Before Copernicus brought forth his powerful treatise. May we see your father's treasure, Richard?"

"Sadly, it is no more. My father gave it to the church…to Hoyland Abbey…many years ago, and it was lost during the dissolution. We have asked William Cecil if it was carried off to the Royal Treasury, but he said not. It simply vanished."

"Most regrettable," said Dee. "Please continue, Thomas."

"With pleasure, John. Well, beyond the six planetary spheres, Nicolaus proposed a seventh sphere that contained the stars…*all* the stars in his view. He described this seventh sphere as *stellarum fixarum sphæra immobilis* or *the immovable sphere of the fixed stars*. You can observe it here on my diagram. Nicolaus maintained that this orb of stars that were fixed extremely high up in the sky extends itself in altitude spherically and is immovable. He said little about what lies beyond the sphere of fixed stars.

"However, from what I have observed and conjectured, the existence of this farthest fixed sphere is not correct. The stars are not contained within a fixed sphere. I believe they are scattered through endless space." Digges drew out of his file a second diagram and laid this one on the table next to his first offering. "Like this," he said with no elaboration.

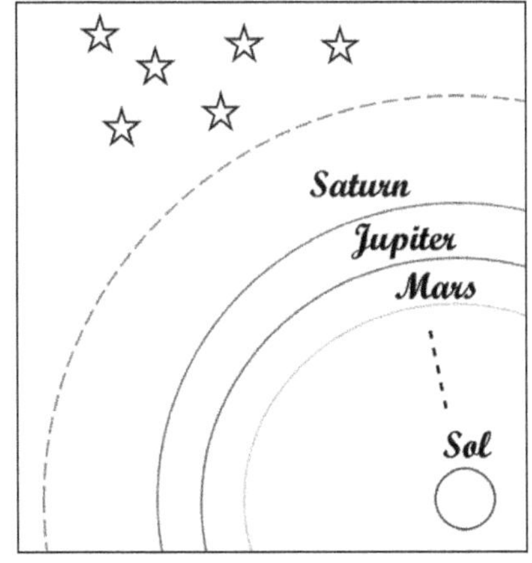

Richard Crossly smiled and said, "I think you may be the first person in this world to propose such a theory."

Digges shrugged his shoulders and replied, "I have done but little. I have merely embraced the system thought up by the mind of Nicolaus and grafted onto it… nothingness…an endless space. And then I have cracked the seventh sphere and scattered the stars throughout this endless space. It is but a small extension of the profound revelation made by our divine Copernicus."

"It is very far from being a small thing, Thomas."

"Do you think it is correct, Richard? You have an unmatched comprehension of the physical world. Do you think it might be correct?"

All eyes turned to Richard Crossly.

"Indeed, I do. I encourage you to finish your investigations and publish the results as quickly as possible. You will not regret it, and the world will be forever in your debt. It seems to me that your observations and conjectures imply that the universe is what Aristotle termed *infinite*. I think you are the first human being to come to this conclusion."

"I would not make so bold."

"I think so. But let me ask you this. Do you think that time may be boundless also? That there was no creation? That this boundless space has existed forever and will exist forever?"

Digges chuckled and said, "If there are no cardinals hiding behind the paneling, then I would have to say it is a possibility."

Everyone in the room broke into laughter.

"But it will take the Tom Digges of 2072 to prove it."

They laughed louder, and Thomas Cecil shouted, "Huzzah!"

This seemed like a perfect ending to the discussion, so Thomas Cecil brought the meeting to a close. While they were still seated, however, Richard Crossly leaned across the table and said to John Dee, "I have an idea to undertake some experiments of my own in a different area. I wish to investigate communications with the spirit world. Perhaps with the celestial host or with the shadows of past and future worlds. Would you be willing to assist me?"

"That is a subject in which I have a keen interest," Dee replied, "but I have no experience in it and no time available to participate. Nevertheless, I would be most interested in your findings, should you succeed in such an endeavor."

"The problem is that I am unable to achieve such connections by myself. Catherine has some ability in this area, but she is unwilling to help me."

"Why so?" Dee asked, turning to Catherine.

"It is quite simple, John," she replied. "I do not believe it is possible. Richard has desired to make such connections for many years now and has made some initial, fruitless attempts. But I believe it to be impossible. Furthermore, the continued failures have dampened his energies and weakened his spirit. I think it is better that he and I focus our attentions on the *real* world and what is possible therein. I myself am engaged with Sir Humphrey Gilbert on plans for requesting a charter from Her Majesty to explore and colonize North America. You may recall that Verrazzano explored the southerly coastline of North America some fifty years ago, but King Henry did not pursue it—I know not why—and there the matter languished. There is much promise in acquiring new lands for the crown."

Dee nodded but had no words to offer on this topic either.

"I respect my wife's views," said Richard, "but I would still like to find a scryer or a fortune teller to assist me. If you hear of one, please connect me."

"Well, as a matter of fact," said Dee, "I might know of such a person already. I have been contacted several times recently by a man calling himself Edward Talbot or Edward Kelley—he has used both names on occasion. He claims to be an alchemist...a scryer... an occultist. Many things. He speaks very highly of himself. He says he wishes to work alongside me."

"That same person has approached me also!" exclaimed Thomas Allen. "He claims to have attended Oxford University, though I have been unable to confirm that. He says he knows Latin and Greek. He dresses himself as an esteemed intellect."

"So far I have ignored the advances of this man," said Dee. "I do not fully trust him. But if he should capture my attention in the future, and I can vouch for him and his art, I will put him in touch with you."

"Many thanks," said Richard just as Catherine turned her face away.

Meeting adjourned.

The afternoon light was fading into a dewy dusk as the Crosslys drove away from Burghley House and set out for Ketteringham Lodge. By the time they arrived home, it was almost dark. Catherine stepped down from the carriage and stood off to one side, shivering in the cold air, awaiting her husband. Richard alighted and approached Nicholas, looking up at the darkening sky as he reached his side.

"The new star is still ablaze," he said. Nicholas nodded, looking upward at it.

"Tell me, Nicholas, what do you think of the starry heaven? Do you think it is like a painting on a ceiling? An engraving on an upturned bowl?"

Nicholas did not respond.

"You see, the stars never move, do they? The planets move. The sun and the moon move. Comets come and go. But the stars do not move. Why do you think that is?"

"I have never thought much about it, sir," he replied. "I suppose it could be such as you describe. A painted bowl."

"This is what we have been discussing at Burghley, Nicholas. Thomas Digges has a new hypothesis that there is no starry sphere. He believes that the stars are scattered throughout an immense void—some of them nearer to us, some farther away…some so far away as to be invisible. Do you think such a thing is possible?"

Nicholas gazed from horizon to horizon.

"Yes. I could believe that were possible."

Nicholas thought about it for a moment and then pressed the tip of his index finger against his lips and gently tapped them. "But if that were so, then would not every place that we look in the night sky encounter a star? Would not there be a star of some kind in every direction? And then would not the entire sky shine a silvery light down upon us? There would never be darkness, sir. There could be no night."

He turned to stare at Richard, who smiled back at him and said, "For a stable boy and groom and to be but sixteen years of age, you have the mind of a philosopher, Nicholas."

Nicholas said nothing, and the blank expression on his face did not alter.

"See to the horses," Crossly said, "and then come eat supper with us. You've earned it."

Richard walked away and put his arm around Catherine's shoulders and led her to the door.

"Olbers' paradox," he whispered as they entered the house.

Chapter 9

London
April 2019

In the minicab from Heathrow Airport into central London on Monday morning, April 8, Harry Groh laid out the timeline and geography for their stay. "My travel agent added you two to my itinerary, and thanks for paying for your tickets up front, Tom. We're going to be staying at the Russell Hotel—at least, that's what everyone called it when I was here before. It's now the Kimpton Fitzroy apparently. It's old, with a lot of ornate carvings and statues and stuff. You'll love it. We're registered there for the week. It's close to the British Museum and also to King's Cross Station if we have to take a train up to Lincolnshire.

"I'm going to be doing my thing at the museum on Wednesday afternoon, which you're welcome to attend by the way. I have no idea what it will be like, but they want me there tomorrow to discuss procedure. A kind of rehearsal. You can do some sightseeing this afternoon and tomorrow. We'll regroup Wednesday night after the ceremony and decide then what to do for the rest of the stay. We can go up to Saxonborough for a few days or whatever. You can decide that. The flight home is a week from today, Monday the fifteenth. Sound good?"

"Yes, yes, Harry," Tom replied. "Terrific. We'll definitely come to the British Museum on Wednesday to see your treasure on display and watch you get your due recognition. I may spend tomorrow at the National Archives to see if I can find out more about my illustrious ancestor. Denise can come with me or do some sightseeing by herself."

"Or…do some shopping," Denise responded. "My credit card is itchy. I've heard that Oxford Street is the place to go scratch."

Tom did go to the National Archives at Kew on Tuesday but was rapidly disheartened by the incredible volume of material stored there and the complexity of the organization of records. It seemed like you needed to know precisely what kind of information you were looking for and which set of records it could be found in. Wanting to know more about your ancestor was not an option. He soon became disoriented and disheartened and was reluctant to show his ignorance by requesting help from the harried employees. Head bowed, he left within the hour. Perhaps the county archives in Lincoln would be more his speed. Or perhaps online shopping for records was all he was cut out for. He met up with Denise in Trafalgar Square, and they spent the afternoon gawking at all things ancient and modern.

Wednesday afternoon found the three of them peering into a glass case set against the back wall of Room 46 (Europe 1400–1800) of the British Museum at Bloomsbury, while an archivist pointed out to them the beauty of the cleaned and restored Sphere of the Planets.

"You can see the brilliance of the workmanship at once," he began with great enthusiasm. "The background is white enamel set in a gold outer frame. In the center is the sun, made of gold, about two centimeters in diameter. Around the sun and connected to it by fine gold filigree work are representations of six planets and the moon. No planet beyond Saturn had been discovered at the time it was made." The three of them nodded to hide their ignorance of the fact.

"Generally speaking, the planets are represented by their appropriate gemstones, according to the astrological wisdom of the day. Mercury is an emerald, Venus is a diamond, Jupiter is a sapphire, and Saturn is an amethyst. Mars is a ruby, but it really ought to be red coral. Perhaps the craftsman was out of red coral at the time. You can see that the moon, off to the side here, is a circular silver ingot, also about two centimeters in diameter. However, our tests suggest that it's a later addition, and perhaps originally there was a pearl in that position. A pearl would have been more appropriate. There's no sign of planet Earth though!" He looked at them and laughed. "You might describe the piece as an iconographic portrayal of what a person sees when looking up from the surface of Earth into a clear nighttime sky. It's so evocative. So…exquisite frankly.

"The workmanship is very similar to that of the Holy Thorn Reliquary that's here in this museum as part of the Waddesdon Bequest in Room 2a. You should go take a look at it later. It was made in France in around 1400. We know that the Sphere of the Planets was given to Sir Adam Crossly in 1492, so perhaps it was a treasure of King Charles VIII that had already been in the French royal family for some years—though we can find no record of it in extant inventories of crown jewels of the period. We have a student over in Paris hunting through French archives even as we speak. It's possible we could find out more about it in the coming months."

"It's beautiful," said Denise, truly spellbound. "Absolutely beautiful."

"And though it has tremendous appeal and significance for art historians," the archivist continued, "it's also of huge importance to *science* historians. Do you know why?" He didn't wait for an answer. "It's because of its heliocentric representation of the solar system. Yes? Our art historians have been collaborating with a professor of science history at University College to establish its place in astronomical epistemology. It clearly predates the work of Copernicus by a decade or two, but a general transition from the ancient geocentric theory of Ptolemy to a heliocentric construct was already taking place in the latter half of the fifteenth century. Based loosely on the work of Aristarchus, Western European philosophers were already shifting toward heliocentrism at the time the Sphere of the Planets was made. The Vienna school of astronomy, led by two scientists called Peuerbach and Regiomontanus, had already proposed a heliocentric theory of the solar system by the 1470s based on observations of the motion of the heavenly bodies. So our guess is that dissemination of this revolutionary new theory among the intellectual elite of Western Europe had…had *stimulated* the creation of the Sphere of the Planets, as it were—perhaps in 1480 or thereabouts—as a kind of symbolic affirmation of the true architecture of the solar system. For the edification of the masses. It must have been truly groundbreaking in its time.

"Another fascinating thing we came across is the role of an Englishman in making the Copernican heliocentric model, as outlined in his book *De Revolutionibus*, available to the English-speaking world. Not only did Copernicus write in Latin, but his book also bore the wording *'Let no one untrained in geometry enter here'* on the title page! Can you believe that? So it was pretty much inaccessible and unreadable. But this Englishman, Thomas Digges, translated it in 1576 with the addition of his own groundbreaking elaborations under the title, *A Perfit Description of the Cælestiall Orbes*. What an appropriate tribute to the Sphere of the Planets! Digges was a Londoner and deserving of far greater recognition than he presently receives."

The three of them were speechless, words failing to express their appreciation of either the artistic merits or scientific attributes of the treasure; their brains simply had no foundation on which to assemble a sensible comment on the archivist's esoteric words.

"We all—the museum, the nation, the world—are forever in your debt, Professor Groh, for salvaging this treasure." The archivist beamed. Harry nodded and smiled. "We've got a couple of French experts coming over from the Louvre next week. Everyone's very excited. And you can rest assured that the artifact will remain safe and secure and permanently on display for as long as the museum exists. And we will always assist students and scholars who come to examine it as part of their research."

A small ceremony followed in the Ruddock Gallery, attended by museum dignitaries and donors, a few professors and students, two newspaper reporters, and one cameraman. Perhaps twenty-five people in all. Visitors took turns to stare at them through the window of the closed door into the hallway. The departmental director gave a short speech, describing the new exhibit and its historical importance. He introduced Harry as the discoverer, but no mention was made of how it came to pass that Harry miraculously and inexplicably knew where to find it under the floor of the Lady Chapel at Hoyland Church. Harry stood up and said a simple thank-you to the room. There was a smattering of applause, and it was over. Ten minutes total. Harry shook the hands of the most important attendees as they left the room and graciously accepted their flattery. When the last of them had departed, he emitted a huge sigh of relief. Frankly, he was glad it was over. This was not his kind of thing. The director and the archivist were the last ones to thank him and depart. Left to their own devices, the three of them decided to head to Room 2a to check out the Holy Thorn Reliquary that the archivist had mentioned.

They had barely exited the gallery when a woman approached them. She seemed to be in her sixties or early seventies. She was slim, with short black hair delicately wisped in gray. She was dressed neatly but casually. She captured their attention and ushered them over to the side of the hallway. They assumed she was an eccentric devotee of medieval art who wanted to chat about their artifact. But far from it—so very far. She spoke softly and furtively. All three of them leaned in toward her voice.

"I have something of the utmost importance to tell you," she said, addressing Harry.

"Really?" Harry replied with a deep frown.

"Please just listen," the woman replied, "and listen very carefully."

"Okay. I guess."

"I know where you're planning to go. I know what you're planning to do. Please don't ask me how I know. Just follow my instructions exactly. To the letter. Lives depend on it. You must leave for Saxonborough tomorrow—"

"Saxonborough?" exclaimed Harry. "How the hell did you know we plan to go there?"

"Just listen!" the woman replied fiercely. "Go up there tomorrow morning. Not today. Not the day after tomorrow. Tomorrow. In the morning. Go to the coffee shop in the village. It's called Speed the Plough."

"No," Tom interjected. "That's not right. We need to go to the local pub."

"That pub is now a coffee shop. It used to be an old tavern called The Plough, but it was converted and renamed years ago. It has two guest rooms upstairs for vacationers and casual travelers. Both those rooms are reserved for you for three nights. Thursday through Saturday. Got it? They're reserved under the name Groh. For three nights. Remember that."

"What the…we didn't…," Harry stammered and stumbled as he tried to make sense of this confrontation. "How did you know my name was Groh? Who in God's name *are* you?"

"Here's what you must do. And you must do it precisely as I say. Tomorrow night, Thursday, you must go into the main bedroom that overlooks the street. You must sit quietly in that room for the whole night. Wide awake. Sometime during the night, ghostly apparitions will appear. Do nothing. Just sit and watch. Then on the next night, Friday, you must do the same thing. Sit in the main bedroom all night. But this time, Friday night, you, Professor, must periodically repeat your name and where you come from—especially when the spirits are present. They will need to confirm your identity. Repeat it several times in a loud, clear voice. Your name and where you come from. Nothing else. Remember that. Otherwise, just watch and listen and remember what happens. All will be explained to you on Saturday. Do you understand me?"

Harry turned to look at Tom, who was staring back at him.

"Do you understand me?" the woman repeated with emphasis.

Harry asked Tom, "Did you get all that?"

Tom nodded. Denise nodded also.

"Is this all so very important?" Harry asked the woman.

She stared fixedly into his face. "It is absolutely vital. Like I said before, lives depend on it. You must do precisely as I've said."

"But *why*?"

"Now is not the time. Saturday will be the time."

"Okay, then. If it's that important, we'll do it. But you won't even tell us your name?"

The woman shook her head.

"Well, can I at least ask about your accent? It's so strange. Where do you come from? Some remote part of Britain? Scotland? It's very peculiar."

The woman shook her head again.

Harry stared deep into her face.

"Are you sure—"

But before that question could be asked, the woman had turned and hurried away. They started after her, but she soon melted into the crowd milling about in the entrance hall of the museum.

Chapter 10

Ketteringham Lodge
December 1587

Edward Kelley closed the door of Catherine Crossly's apartment and turned to face the large and forbidding entrance hall of Ketteringham Lodge. He was lost. He was fifty-eight years old, and he was lost. His proposal of marriage had just been rebuffed by Catherine, and the future looked altogether bleak. He was painfully aware that the elbows of his doublet were patched, that the knees of his hose were threadbare, and that he had precious few coins jangling in his pocket. His alchemical experiments were getting nowhere. He looked around, and the dark oak paneling of the entrance hall pressed him on all sides. From above the staircase, a large painting of Richard Crossly glared down on his melancholy and bewilderment. Kelley was much disoriented. Which way to go, this moment and forever? Which way even to turn? A door to his left opened, and the housemaid emerged hurriedly, wiping her hands on her apron and seeming to think herself somehow at fault.

"Sir?" asked Alice.

"Where is Robert, my coachman?"

"In the kitchen with me, sir. He was hungry. I fed him pickled samphire, bread and butter, and small beer. I thought it would be all right."

"Well, thank you for that, Alice."

"But he wouldn't eat the samphire, sir. He said it made him feel like he was at the beach on his hands and knees chewing seaweed."

Edward couldn't help but chuckle, and Alice bowed her head and smiled. "In these parts they say it is powerful against the winter scurvy," she noted.

"Better to burn it and use the ash to make glass. That's what the French do."

"Yes, sir."

"Ask Robert to come here, if you would."

"Yes, sir."

Seconds later, Robert Rimes hurried through the kitchen doorway, wiping the back of his hand across his mouth and then buttoning his collar.

"We must away to York, Robert. John Dee awaits us this evening."

"I'm afraid we cannot reach York today, sir. The distance is too far."

"Only fifty miles, is it not? With a change of horse we can make it by nightfall."

"Nay, sir, we cannot."

"Not with the wind at our backs and Jesus Christ in our hearts?"

"Not e'en with the devil nipping at our heelbones. York is more like seventy miles from here, sir, and by the time we reach Winteringham, there will be no more ferries across the Humber for the day."

"What if we head for Newark instead and then up through Doncaster?"

"It is even further that way, and we would still have to cross the Trent. Nay, sir, it cannot be accomplished today. It is best we follow the Ermine Street and cross the Humber. It was good enough for the Romans."

Edward turned aside and muttered, "*Abus Fluvius*. Damned Agricola."

"I suggest we head for Lincoln," Robert continued. "We can arrive there this afternoon. I suggest we stay overnight at the Spread Eagle. You recall it, sir. We mounted our horses there after Richard Crossly's funeral in September before riding out to Hoyland. The rooms are clean and the stables well provisioned. You can eat your dinner and sleep soundly the night. Then we can take to the road early the morrow and be in York soon enough. If needs must, we can change horses at Brough or Market Weighton."

"Very well. You know your business, Robert. But Dee will be sorely vexed. I have tarried here too long, I know. I lost track of time. It's my fault. Bring the horses and carriage round and we'll set off for Lincoln promptly."

Robert returned to the kitchen and went out the back door. Alice led Edward Kelley over to the front door, pulled it open, and stepped aside. Edward tightened his doublet around his neck in anticipation of mist and chill and turned to the maidservant. "Thank you, Alice," he said. "I'm sure I shall return ere long. Please to take good care of your mistress in the meantime."

Alice bobbed her head and gave an awkward curtsey.

Edward stepped out onto the front porch, glancing up and about him at the pinched and graying December sky—Christmas would soon be upon them. Was there drizzle in the air? Travel was distasteful to him at the best of times, and soon there would be much more of it across all of Europe: France, Poland, Bohemia. All foreign and fierce. He studied the carefully groomed flower beds around him and the raked stone driveway in front of him. He admired the lovely groves of alder trees in the near distance for which Ketteringham Lodge was famous. Yes, he would like to see out his days here. It would suit him well. The wide, flat marshlands with sturdy trails through them. The open sea beyond. All very pleasant. *If only Catherine could somehow be persuaded*, he thought, *then we could enjoy these peaceful surroundings together*. And once again the feeling of missed opportunity swept over him.

It took his coachman a few moments to roust the horses, harness them, and hitch them to the carriage. Then they emerged as one from around the side of the house and came up to join him. Edward tossed his bag into the carriage and climbed in beside it. He took one last look at the house and grounds and shook his head sadly. Robert chivvied up the horses, and they set off across the marshland for Lincoln. In due course, the spires of Lincoln Cathedral peeked over the horizon, and before long the men were installed in the Spread Eagle Inn on the High Street. Robert bedded down the horses and washed the carriage wheels, while Edward sat in his room trying once more to make sense of Dee's *Monas Hieroglyphica*. Then it was beef, sleep, dawn, and oat porridge; and soon the spires of the cathedral dwindled back to nothing behind them, and they were set due north on the Ermine Street.

When the door of her apartment closed upon the departing figure of Edward Kelley, Catherine Crossly returned to her writing desk. Her thoughts turned first to her beloved husband, perhaps as salve against Edward's approaches. She reminisced about their life together. She relived the six days and six nights they'd spent in bed together in that hotel in London long, long ago. She could still see the color and texture of the wallpaper, the feeble desk lamp, the worn carpeting. She recalled the shape of the green pears they'd practically lived on during those days. The varied sounds from the street below…night following day, day following night. She had fallen so deeply in love with him then, though it had taken her time to fully realize it. And she still loved him just as much even though he'd now departed this world. She'd never felt lonely these four months since his passing. His arms were still around her, keeping her warm. His words were still in her ear to reassure her. His ideas, implanted in her brain, guided her each and every day.

But then she began to wonder if she'd spoken too harshly to Edward. Too bluntly. She'd left no avenue open for him. It was not his fault that her love lay elsewhere. And he'd always behaved in a most courteous and gentlemanly fashion toward her. She could have said, *Who knows what the future will bring*, or *Not under the present circumstances*—words that would have built a hidden door in the corner of a garden that he might one day discover and open. Or indeed, a door that she might one day want to open herself. Would it have been a betrayal of her husband not to expunge all hope?

Alice tapped on the door and entered with a glass of claret. She set it carefully down on the desk.

"Thank you, Alice," said Catherine and then as she was leaving, added, "Alice, I'm sorry that we keep burdening you with Mr. Kelley's coachman."

"Robert? Oh no, madam. It's quite all right. We get along well."

"Oh…good! That's good to know."

"He's a nice young man. I am happy to sit and chat with him."

"You like him?"

"Yes, madam. He's charming." Her eyes dipped to the floor. "Do you know what I like the most about him? He doesn't boast. He's not like the young men in the village—always telling you how many foxes they've killed, how many pints of ale they drank last night. Robert has been in many of the great houses of England. He's traveled on the Continent. But he never brags about those things. He just tells interesting little stories of things that have happened to him. Often I needs must ask, *'Was that at Chatsworth?'* or *'Did the Earl of Lincoln say that?'* He never uses high-flown words or drops names just to impress. And he's considerate enough to request similar little stories from me—though mine cannot hold a candle to his. I like that in him."

"Well, good. I'm glad. However, I'm not sure when you will see him again. Mr. Kelley and I may not converse as much in the future. After what happened just now. We'll see."

"Very good, madam," said Alice and left the room.

Then finally, Catherine's thoughts wandered away from both the men in her life and sailed over the sea to America. She took up quill and paper and wrote a letter to Richard Hakluyt, just returned from five years in Paris in support of the English ambassador to the French court. He was a leading advocate of the colonization of the Americas, and Catherine had met him several times at the subscribers' meetings in London. He had befriended her at those meetings, especially at the early ones, when she'd felt isolated and inferior. He was a great writer, a mapmaker, and geographer, and she respected him. In her letter, Catherine urged Hakluyt to continue his support of the Roanoke colony and to prepare and distribute maps of the coastline and the settlement in order to encourage further interest and more donations. If possible, and if it was known in some way, she said these maps should highlight the inland areas of coal and minerals and timber. "The more people know about its potential, the greater its chances of success," she wrote. "America holds unlimited possibilities." She thought about making mention of the expedition of Jolliet and Marquette—the former having a particular connection to her—but she could not remember if the two explorers had already ventured into the Upper Midwest or if their journey was yet to come, so she decided not to mention it.

She then wrote a letter to Sir Richard Grenville, urging him to do all he could to outfit and provision ships to transport John White back across the Atlantic. She promised him fifty guineas of her own money toward the venture. She acknowledged that in these perilous times he had greater responsibility to assemble a mighty English fleet to oppose the Spaniards, but she reasoned that there must be one or two ships available that were too small to fight galleons but large enough to battle the sea. In her own mind, she was sure they would not make it to Roanoke, but she knew the attempt was worthy and necessary.

Finally, she wrote to John White. She commiserated with him on having had to leave his daughter and granddaughter in his wake and then to suffer seven weeks of indescribable hardship on the open ocean. She encouraged him to be brave. To endure. And to return to Virginia at the earliest opportunity. The colony, she was sure, would survive. One way or another. She offered her help if ever he should need it.

She folded each of the three letters, sealed them with red wax, and then impressed her initials in the wax using the signet ring on her little finger. She set them aside. Soon Alice tapped on her door and entered with lunch. On the plate was a small piece of broiled fish and some vegetables. Alice set the plate down on the table by the fireside. Catherine picked up the letters and handed them to Alice for delivery. Then she sat down and began to eat. The fish was nice and fresh, and the vegetables were from her own garden: carrot, turnip, parsnip. Chopped small, doused in olive oil, and sautéed. Delicious. But as she ate, Catherine could not help but think, *What I wouldn't give for an ear of corn with this fish.* She half-closed her eyes. *Fresh-picked, lightly boiled, and dabbed with butter. Alice is a good cook, but…oh! Mom's Iowa corn!*

Chapter 11

York
December 1587

Edward Kelley and Robert Rimes arrived at the Humber pier in good time; and before noon they were crossing the river on a barge together with several families, three cows, and a queen's messenger. The children were heaving over the side within minutes even though the water was smooth. The ferry arrived at Brough within an hour and a half, and Robert drove the carriage to Market Weighton, where they changed horses. By midafternoon, York Minster had assumed the place of Lincoln Cathedral on the horizon and in the gathering gloom of dusk.

"Where do we stay in York?" Robert turned and shouted down to Edward in the carriage, as fenced land and rows of cottages signaled the outskirts of the city.

"Dee has made arrangements for us to stay at the Old Treasurer's House. It will be very comfortable. Sir George Young is to be our host. His father was the Archbishop of York many years ago. Dee stays there also. You will find it most agreeable."

Robert nodded and turned his attention back to the road.

"Head straight for the Minster," Kelley instructed him. "The mansion is close by."

Robert nodded once more.

As grand as it was, the house was not easy to find. Four times Robert had to stop and ask directions from locals, all of whom seemed to have more important things on their minds than where the rich people lived. Eventually they arrived in front of the broad facade of the Old Treasurer's House with its nine windows and protruding wings at each end. Edward Kelley climbed out of the carriage and walked up the stone steps to the front door, tired and dirty and splattered with mud and a little vomit from his long journey. He dusted himself off and pulled on the bell cord. A maid quickly opened the door wide and held out an arm in welcome.

"I am Edward Kelley, here from London by way of Ketteringham and Lincoln. Here to see Dr. Dee and Sir George."

"I know who you are, sir. We were expecting you yesterday. You are right welcome. My, my, you look exhausted. Please to come in and rest yourself."

Edward dragged himself through the doorway and immediately flopped down on a bench in the vast entrance hall of the house. It always astonished him how exhausting it was to be jostled for hours in a carriage with rough wooden seats and thin cushions on a road made of nothing but dirt inscribed with wheel ruts. Soon John Dee approached him, stooped from his sixty years, beard almost down to his navel, wearing a long robe and plain black skullcap. Edward rose, and they collided in front of the bench grasping forearms tightly. Edward began to speak at once.

"John, I must apologize for stealing a day from you like this. We—"

"No, no, Edward. It is nothing. Nothing at all. I filled yesterday afternoon with the Minster and this morning with Sir George. No time was stolen."

"I'm afraid I dallied too long with Catherine at Ketteringham. We left insufficient time to spur the horses on to York."

"Again, it is of no consequence." Dee smiled. "I know you admire Catherine greatly. We all know it. Even Laski remarked on the solicitous attention you paid to her that afternoon after we had laid poor Richard to rest and were hurrying from Hoyland churchyard. But Burghley thwarted you then, I think." He smiled again, mischievously this time.

Edward Kelley cast his eyes downward and to the side and began to look uncomfortable as he replied, "I know. I'd hoped I could be the one to provide solace to her that day, but it was not to be. Nobility won out, as it always does in England. And…on that same subject…perhaps I should tell you at once that I made an overture to Catherine yesterday. I…I asked for her hand. I took destiny by the scruff of the neck and asked for her hand."

Dee stepped back aghast, his eyes wide, then thrust his head in Kelley's face and spluttered, "But you are married, sirrah! What about Jane and the children? Did you forget about them?"

Edward shook his head vigorously from side to side. "I know, I know. But the marriage is not what it was. You know that, John. You've seen it for yourself. And the children are not mine. I have loved them and educated them—but they are the seed of another man. He is dead, it is true, but somehow that means little to me now. It has all gone sour. And Catherine is something very special indeed. I would give up everything to be with her."

"Did she accept your offer?"

"She did not. She said that Richard was the only man for her. E'en in death. She could love no other. It pained me like a javelin through the heart."

Dee thought for a moment and then led Edward back to the bench, and the two men sat down together. Kelley clasped his hands tightly between his knees and waited for Dee's advice.

"I think it is too soon, Edward. Richard has been dead but four months. And despite her advancing years, Catherine still sees options and opportunities for the future that lies in front of her. In a year or two, Richard's memory will have faded, and time will have begun to close in on her. Her options will have dwindled. Then you may try again. If you will."

"There is not much of time remaining for either one of us."

"I understand that. But most importantly, it would give you time to resolve your relationship with Jane. You could propose next time as a free man. That would be better in God's eyes—if you feel you must do it at all."

Edward nodded in reluctant agreement, but his mind was made up. "I must, John. Catherine is not like other women. In fact…" Edward looked up and stared straight into John Dee's eyes. "In fact, I think she may be a scryer."

"A scryer? How so?"

"The things she says. The things she knows. Just yesterday she told me things about the Roanoke colony in the Americas that simply astonished me. About John White's voyage. The birth of Virginia Dare…and the *fate* of Virginia Dare no less. How could she know that? And she said that John White will not return there next year as planned. Can you believe that? She even foretold that the Spanish fleet will sail on our shores. Soon! This coming year!"

"Mere supposition, Edward. Perhaps she has heard that Drake singed the king's beard at Cadiz last April. Everyone knows that King Philip will not be Philip the Prudent much longer. An invasion is not out of the question."

"But the other things. Her knowledge of events to come in the Americas. How can she know such things unless a scryer?"

"Surely it cannot be thus. She is merely surmising. She has not practiced the art."

"Not to our knowledge, John, but recall some of the things that Richard said about his wife. He told us that the experiments at Hoyland Church would be more likely to succeed if she would participate. Do you remember? Several times he regretted that she were not present…that she would not agree to help us. Once he told me in confidence that she had what he called a special gift. He called it something like the *zeta power*. Like the sixth letter of the Greek alphabet. I forget his exact words, and I do not know what it means, but she has the gift of second sight, I feel sure."

"Edward…these presumptions…they are so hard to believe. Do not dwell on them. They will deflect you away from resolving your familial relationships in an honorable way."

"All things considered, Catherine Crossly is a very special lady, John, and I am afeared that I love her greatly."

They sat in silence on the oak bench in the drafty hallway of the unfamiliar mansion at York, both far from home and both despondent in different ways. Dee sought to raise the mood.

"Well, anyway," he said, "Sir George has promised us a fine dinner tonight at eight of the clock. Then tomorrow we will set off on foot for the shop of Evergreen Jones, the apothecary I told you about—he who says he has found vulgar gold in a vial of molten silver and quicksilver."

"With sulfur as seed?"

"I do not know. We will find out tomorrow. Off to your room now and rest until dinner. Ask the servants to fill a hot bath for you—you have half the Ermine Street in your hair. Oh, and Thomas Digges will join us soon. He is somewhere on the road from London at the present."

"Our good friend Thomas!" Kelley said. "I shall look forward to seeing him again."

"The maid will show you to your room. Rest now. Restore your spirit."

"I will. And please ask that care be given to Robert Rimes, my coachman. He has done more good work than I have these past few days."

The following morning, John Dee and Edward Kelley took a brisk walk around the Minster and located the tiny apothecary's shop on Stonegate. They peeked through the smeared and dusty glass in the door but could see no light nor proprietor within. The door was unlocked, however, so they entered. The walls were stacked from floor to ceiling with bowed shelves on which stood every size and shape of blue bottle, each bearing a large label stamped with Roman numerals and mysterious abbreviations. There was a stuffed cat on a table. Dee walked over and rapped on the counter with his knuckles. A door creaked open in the wall behind the counter, and in walked a small elderly man with snow-white hair. He was bent nearly double. He shuffled over to the counter and blew his nose on his sleeve.

"Mr. Evergreen Jones?" Dee inquired, bending down to the height of the old man's face and peering inquiringly into it.

"Indeed. Indeed, I am, gentlemen. Please to excuse the delay. My ears have fallen into decrepitude over the years. And pardon the snot also—my manners have declined along with my hearing. You must be Sir Dr. Dee, your eminence." He dipped his head slightly.

"You may call me John or Dr. Dee, as you wish. I have had no knighthood bestowed on me. And this is Mr. Edward Kelley."

"Mr. Kelley. Yes, sirs. Please to enter my…my humble…my shop."

"It is most agreeable," said Edward but thinking otherwise.

"There are just four rooms," the apothecary continued. "In this one I dispense. In the back room, I mix the potions. In the room above this one I sleep, and in the back bedroom lives my lodger. Without him I would be in the poorhouse. There is a small yard behind and a shed where sits my largest oven—it would be all too easy to burn down the desiccated wood that is Stonegate. It may or may not be missed." He chuckled. "This is my world, gentlemen. Small but sturdy."

They followed him into the back room to find it littered with bottles, vials, spoons, scales, and all manner of apothecarial tools. On a table by the window was a chemical apparatus consisting of an alembic with the distilling retort removed and a sturdy cucurbit resting part ways inside a small oven, shielded on all sides by sheets of metal. The wooden surface of the bench was blackened in many places, records of fiery failures.

"This," proclaimed Evergreen Jones proudly, "is my latest experiment. This is the one I told Dr. Dee about. I have tried several alternative arrangements of apparatus before this, but I find that this one produces the ideal temperate conditions for maturation of the metal—so that the spirit of the metal may be quickened and the tangible parts opened, you understand. The Dutchman overfired his work, you know. The making of gold is a subterranean work in nature where little heat comes to its aid. That must be mimicked. And the device of the lamp was folly, I have found."

"Indeed. And what are the main ingredients of your present concoction, the one that achieves the transmutation?" Edward Kelley asked with growing eagerness.

"I have read the works of Paracelsus and others, and I conclude that the use of lead is too ponderous and that quicksilver alone cannot endure the prolonged heat of the fire. Copper, I think, might be a plausible metal, but I do not possess sufficient quantities of it. I have begun with silver, which, as you know, in nature is the closest in symbolization with gold. I place the silver in a small furnace at a temperate heat that will hold the metal perpetually molten."

"And what as accompaniment?"

"To the silver I add a tenth portion of quicksilver and a twentieth portion of niter. I find that these two additives quicken and expose the body of the metal."

"No sulfur as seed?"

"I have tried both ways. With sulfur and without. I find it makes no difference."

"Recall the *tria prima* described by Paracelsus: salt is the body, mercury the spirit, and sulfur the soul—the emotions and desires. Sulfur may be necessary."

The apothecary shook his head. "That was for directing the curing of ailments, sir. I find that sulfur is *not* necessary for transmutation." He seemed insistent.

"Very good, Mr. Jones. We take your word on it. And then?"

"Well, sirs, I am aware of the importance of astrological symbols and their vital influences on the formation of gold. I have done my best to read Dr. Dee's instructions on the matter. Regrettably, I am unfamiliar with how the zodiacal alignments and those of the planets conform to our daily calendar. So I could not arrange my experiments around them. Not meticulously anyway. Not in every detail. But one thing I made sure to do was to mix the earthy substances and place them in my furnace on the evening of the summer solstice last June. I set them out in the sun for the whole day. Then I let the mixture simmer for four months. This gives nature an undisturbed space to work in. That is most necessary. Celerity is the scourge of transmutation—as it is of most things in this modern world."

Kelley turned to Dee and said, "We should have Mr. Jones speak with Thomas Digges, John. Thomas has the clearest and best organized view of the heavens of anyone in this land. With his knowledge of the motion of celestial bodies, he could steer the timing of these experiments with some precision." Dee agreed.

"Once each month," the apothecary continued, "I added a teaspoon of the tincture of oil that they use to recover gold. This helps the parts to lay closer and smoother and reduces the churlishness of the materials that liken to separate them. You can appreciate the need to limit any vexatious separations, gentlemen. And one most vital aspect of the prolonged simmering is that no part of the spirit be emitted. For if there are any releases, the body of the metal will be hard and churlish. This must be achieved partly by the temper of the fire and partly by the closeness of the vessel. After the four months of heating and two days of cooling, there was revealed a yellow powder that was soft to the touch and smooth and pliant. It has been immune to rust these two months. The quantity of the preternatural powder was in the proportion of one one-hundredth of the weight of the silver."

"And how do you know it to be gold?"

"It has all the properties according to the axioms. Let any man dispute whether it be gold or not!" The apothecary was once again firm in this assertion, almost indignant.

"Have you tried to heat it and melt it into a sliver of the metal?"

"I have not. I did not dare. I wished for you gentlemen to regard it first."

"So now let us see it."

Evergreen Jones shuffled to another bench nearby and held up in front of them a small flask with a yellow powder at the bottom of it. Dee and Kelley leaned forward until their noses were an inch or two away from the flask. All three peered into it, silently, for several seconds. Then Dee and Kelley turned to look at each other, and Dee spoke, "Indeed, it has the color of gold."

They turned to look at it again. "And the texture of powdered gold," Kelley replied. "I have seen the product from the making of potable gold from urine, and it appears quite similar to this." They stared at it once more, and then Dee and Kelley returned to their normal upright bearing, while the apothecary turned away, still hunched over, and replaced the flask on the bench.

"We are most grateful to you, Mr. Jones, for explaining your experiments to us," said John Dee, "and I hope that you will continue them and report the results to us at some future time. Mr. Kelley will try to replicate your arrangement in his own laboratory." He reached into his purse and took out a gold sovereign. "This, sir, is your reward for hosting us this morning." Evergreen Jones held both palms outward in front of his chest to refuse it. "It is not my own money, sir,"

Dee explained. "It is England's money. I have permission from Lord Burghley, the Lord High Treasurer, to give one sovereign to every subject who assists me in pursuing the truth behind my alchemical and astrological pursuits. It is for the further edification of Her Majesty, you understand. Verily, it is yours by right."

Evergreen Jones fussed and simpered and then accepted the sovereign.

"And *that*, my friend, is true gold," said Kelley, pointing to the coin and laughing. "Let no man dispute *that*!"

Chapter 12

York
December 1587

When Dee and Kelley returned from the apothecary's shop, they found Thomas Digges waiting for them in the hallway of the Old Treasurer's House. Following the untimely death of his father, Thomas had been brought up under John Dee's guardianship and was a cross between an acolyte and an adopted son. He had grown into a renowned astronomer and mathematician under Dee's tutelage. Though he paid respect to the work of Dee and Kelley on mystical topics, he personally did not believe in such things. He was forty-one years old and at the peak of his accomplishments. All smiles and fine greetings, the three friends embraced heartily.

"So, gentlemen," Digges asked them after the formalities, "have you found a new pathway to gold?"

"We think it doubtful," Dee sighed.

"One more disappointment, I'll wager," Kelley added. "The tincture cultivated by Mr. Jones had the appearance of gold and the color, but I doubt that it was gold."

Dee continued, "We think it most likely that an impurity in the niter had reacted to form some yellow compounded substance. Perhaps married with a trace of the silver or the quicksilver. The mixture matured in the cucurbit for four whole months, and closeness of the vessel cannot be assured for such a long time. When you think of the smoky haze that descends upon York in the winter months, then Mr. Jones's laboratory surely held seeds from the soot and ash suspended outside his shop that would on occasion penetrate the alembic as a whole. And Mr. Jones unsealed the alembic once each month to add a soothing oil. That, too, could taint the admixture."

"Those seeds would then assault the fiery silver or quicksilver and leave a taint of yellow," said Kelley. "Over time, the impediments would multiply into a stain of odium across the entire surface of the formerly uncorrupted silver. I agree with Dr. Dee. I, too, doubt that it was gold." Edward Kelley seemed disappointed and frustrated. "Despite our misgivings, however, we encouraged the alchemist to continue his work and report back to us."

"Well," said Digges, "there are many roads to paradise. Some say that nature intended to make *all* metals gold, and if only the crudities and impurities and leprosities of metals were cured, they would eventually all *become* gold. It is only necessary to write the correct prescriptions. If Emperor Rudolf will build you laboratories and grant you educated apprentices, then you can write prescriptions by the hour."

"Let us hope so," said Kelley. "Let us hope so, indeed."

"Come the spring, Edward and I will attend on the emperor and find out," said Dee.

Later that evening, four men sat around the fireplace in the smoking lounge of the Old Treasurer's House: John Dee, Edward Kelley, Thomas Digges, and Sir George Young. The weather had turned blustery during the day, but their surroundings were warm and sumptuous, and the three visitors were in no hurry to leave. On each side of the fireplace hung exquisite Belgian tapestries. Sir George noticed that Dee and Digges were admiring them and remarked, "My father acquired those in the 1560s in Brussels. They are replicas of pieces hanging at Hampton Court. Smaller, I grant, but equally fine. Betimes, Her Majesty has a similar view as you now do. They are from de Pannemaker's series on *The Story of Abraham*. We are extremely proud of them."

"Such splendid needlework," said Dee, squinting into the dim shadows alongside the firelight. "Gold and silver thread, to be sure." The four of them settled into their armchairs and sipped their wine. Slowly conversation began. Much of it cycled around the three old comrades, and Sir George mostly just listened and interjected occasional observations on religious matters when appropriate and when he knew what on earth they were talking about.

Edward laid his glass carefully on a side table and began with a polite question, "How was your journey here, Thomas?"

"Good," Digges replied. "Tolerable anyway. I traveled part of the way with my friend Thomas de Whitmore. Do you know him?" Dee and Kelley shook their heads. "We are of the same age and attended school together. I have known him my whole life. He mostly lives in Hertfordshire these days—at the home of his wife's family—but he grew up in Nottinghamshire and is the Baron of Tuxford Hall. We rode together up the Great North Road."

"Tuxford? I have not heard of it," said John Dee.

"You would not have. It is but a tiny market town. And the land thereabouts is poor and heavy with clay. *Tuxford in the Clay*, some call it. Or *Tuxford le Clay*. Riding through it is laborious in the extreme. The clay weighed down our horses' hooves, and periodically we had to halt the carriages while our grooms picked at the hooves. Awful conditions for traveling. But I stayed overnight at Tuxford Hall with de Whitmore before continuing on to York. That was exceeding pleasant."

"Well, we are most glad that you're here," said Dee, and Edward nodded. John Dee then leaned forward in his chair and spoke the words that had been on his mind since first they sat down, "So what's to be done about the calendar, Thomas?"

"Little, I fear," Digges replied despondently. "Every day it seems further removed from adoption. Though Pope Gregory has been dead of the fever for two years now, Sixtus is woven from the same cloth. All the Catholic countries are firmly committed to the new calendar."

"And rightly so."

"Yes, of course. The astronomical calculations are beyond dispute. We are without doubt ten days too long by the Julian calendar. The fixing of Easter is a mess across all of Christendom. The *Playne Discourse* that you delivered to Lord Burghley four years ago made it crystal clear. And the subsequent report that I and Savile and Chambers delivered merely served to confirm your words. I don't find a man in London with any claim to scientific knowledge who disputes it."

"We simply cannot persist with a calendar that clashes with most of the countries of Europe. What about trade and commerce? Diplomatic meetings? Many highborn men will show up unexpectedly, while others will leave an empty seat. Are we only to trade with Germany and the Low Countries in future?"

"I have done my best to explain this wherever I go and whomsoever I converse with."

"What about Lord Burghley? Can he not help? He is a great friend to us all. Recall that as a young man he saved the lives of Richard and Catherine during the dissolution of Hoyland Abbey. He has been cordial ever since—to you in particular, Thomas."

"Burghley supports our view. He has said as much. But even *his* influence at court is limited. And Walsingham will not commit, calling it *a mixed civil and ecclesiastical matter*."

"But it is *not*. You know that better than I, Thomas. It is a matter of the physical realities of the earth and the moon...of the sun and the stars. Their positions in the heavens and their movements across the sky are not influenced by religious tendencies. Pope Sixtus cannot pull the sun one way, while Archbishop Whitgift drags it another."

"Even the nation's judges can find no fault with our argument," Kelley added.

"I think Walsingham believes it in his heart too, but he recognizes the power of the church and feels he must incorporate it into his advice to Her Majesty. He has said forcefully to me that the views of the church cannot be ignored."

"And the bishops remain unmoved?"

"They do. Though your *Playne Discourse* may have killed Archbishop Grindal—pardon my sacrilege—nothing has changed."

"Grindal, I knew," said Sir George. "He succeeded my father as Archbishop of York. He was a Puritan sympathizer and held in scant regard by the city."

"Many in Parliament disliked him also," Digges continued. "And his support for the Puritans' position on prophesyings was much to the distaste of Elizabeth. But e'en though he has been dead these four years or more, his successors hold their stubborn chins up high as if supported by Grindal's palm. Bishop Aylmer remains unmoved. He and Bishop John Piers of Salisbury have reiterated to the court and the Privy Council that the Pope is the Antichrist, and therefore we may not concur with him or confer with him or harmonize our views with the Vatican on any matter. If Rome says black, England must say white. End of the matter."

"But to say that we must oppose papal doctrine on clear matters of science is nonsense!" said Edward angrily.

"It is. It is pigheadedness," said Digges. Then he turned to John Dee with a bashful look on his face. "But if I might add a slight criticism, sir—in these amicable surroundings—your proposal to recalculate our calendar to the time of Christ's birth rather than to the time of the Council of Nicaea in 325 has further inflamed the church."

All eyes turned to observe Dee's response.

"Is the birth of Jesus Christ not the radix of time itself for all true Christians?" Dee replied, somewhat indignant. "I cannot be faulted for saying such. If the calendar must be changed at all, then there is no better way to do it than to begin from the true beginning. And it means an adjustment of just one more day. Eleven instead of ten. A small price to pay."

"But yet another line of charge to the account." Digges raised his brow and tilted his head.

"I know, I know. Perhaps it *was* a step too far. I would be willing to discard it if the rest of the proposal would find approval."

"The religious viewpoint has political overtones too though," Digges continued. "If we were to agree that the Pope was correct in this matter and we were to follow his teachings on it, then it would signal to the nation that we fear the Pope, that he still exerts dominion over us. That would encourage our own papists and unnerve the weak among us. We cannot afford to embolden any more Babingtons and Ballards to try to kill Her Majesty and seat a Catholic queen on the English throne—e'en though it can now no longer be Mary. This is another reason Walsingham tiptoes down the center of the road."

After a brief silence and the shaking of heads, Dee turned to their host and asked, "Did not your father work diligently to conform religious views in the North of England, Sir George? I saw his monument in the Minster. At the east end of the choir. Very impressive. As Archbishop of York, he must have adjudicated many religious disputes in this part of the world."

"He did indeed. My father saw his role as being to pacify the north and forestall Catholic revolt. And Elizabeth gave him charge of Charles Stuart no less—the son of the Countess of Lennox—with the aim of repressing the Catholic tendencies of that family."

"He did much good work, your father," said Dee. "We will need more like him. The struggle is not yet behind us."

"But back to the calendar," Kelley persisted. "What about the parliamentary act giving Her Majesty the power to alter the calendar herself?"

"It was defeated in the House of Lords, Edward," said Digges. "Leicester attacked the bishops on the matter, but to no avail. Then other business pushed it to one side. And with all the warlike talk now spewing from the mouth of King Philip, I fear it is lost for many a year."

Dee then nodded toward Kelley to indicate that he was about to raise a topic of interest to him and asked, "Thomas, do you remember Catherine Crossly, Richard's wife? You met her at Burghley House when we discussed the new star in Cassiopeia."

"I have a recollection," Digges responded.

"Well, Edward says she has foreseen the invasion of England's shores by a great Spanish fleet."

"I have reason to believe that Catherine is a true and fearsome scryer," Edward added, his eyes wide and piercing, but nobody wanted to delve into that topic.

Thomas Digges nodded. "An invasion would not surprise me. I have heard rumblings of such things in the halls of Parliament. Walsingham's spies have reported several galleons sailing into the Port of Lisbon and there being outfitted for battle. If that should happen, we can forget the new calendar entirely."

"Catherine thinks they will set sail for our shores quite soon. Early this coming year."

After these words, the company drank in silence for some considerable time, pondering the most unwelcome prospect of England becoming a sovereign state under the rule of Spain.

"I will have no time to work on the calendar next year in any case," Thomas said at last, staring into his wine glass. "As you know, I have been appointed muster-master general for our forces that fight the Spanish Netherlands. There is much work to be done at the Port of Dover, and Raleigh is insistent that it be completed quickly." He clenched his jaw. "All I want to do is to map the stars, but next year I will only be able to map sluices and channels."

"Good wishes for that, Thomas," said Kelley. "The time will pass quickly enough. And John and I might meet up with you in Dover when the time comes for us to pass through the port. We expect to travel to Poland before long if the conflict permits. And then on to Bohemia. As John has already mentioned, Emperor Rudolf has promised us great wealth if our alchemical experiments yield gold—such wealth as will support the two of us and our children for life."

"The opportunity cannot be turned down, e'en though age acts against our best interests and desires," Dee observed. "If Her Majesty would reward us half as much, such wearisome travel could be avoided. I for one would be happy with that."

"I for another," said Kelley.

Further silence and further drinking.

Thomas Digges suddenly jerked upright in his chair. "Gentlemen, I forget to tell you something that will interest you greatly—you in particular, Edward. Something quite remarkable transpired while I was at Tuxford Hall. On the evening of the day we arrived, several notables from the parish joined de Whitmore and me for dinner. One of them was the local curate. You will scarcely credit the story he recounted over the dinner table. I will relate it.

"The curate described an incident that had happened lately at a tavern in a village that sits midway between Tuxford and Lincoln. I believe the name of the village is Saxonborough. The vicar there told him that he had communed with angelic voices in a bedroom of the inn. Truly! It is an old travelers' inn called The Plough. Several visitors who had stayed in that room reported hearing spirit voices during the night. They had hurried away swiftly the next morning—several of them cursing the landlord and refusing to settle their bills. The landlord feared his business would suffer, so he made contact with the clergy to beg for succor. By way of response, the vicar offered to sit up in the room one night with the landlord to confirm or belie the rumors. A young servant girl sat with them. This girl was well-known in the village. She was reputed to have encountered otherworldly spirits before and was believed to possess the power of second sight. So all three of them took up positions to see what angels—or perhaps demons—the mysterious bedroom would reveal to them.

"The vicar said that, indeed, for a spell of fifteen minutes or more, faint voices could be heard all around them. High-pitched and ethereal. The light seemed to modulate during this time, but no spiritual forms could be discerned. Neither could every word be distinguished. But the vicar said that certain phrases were repeated by the visitors, and he believed he might be able to decipher them. Given time and paper and a sharpened quill."

"In truth?" said Edward. "Did the curate at Tuxford appear credible?"

"He did. Most certainly. But here is the fascinating part. He said that the vicar thought the words were spoken in the Enochian tongue that you and John have heard and recorded. He professed to have read your treatise *Liber Loagaeth*, Edward. He claimed to have noted similarities to the forty-nine magic squares. Thus...so the vicar believed...the visitors must be...angels."

"I doubt that it could be so—or that he could decipher the wording thus, if it be Enochian," Kelley scoffed. "Translation is a most laborious and convoluted process. And I rarely hear the language spoken. Usually the words are directed to me through the crystal or the black obsidian mirror—that which John calls the *shew stone*. The angels write their guidance for mankind on holy strips of paper that I read and transcribe. They do not chatter in tavern bedrooms."

"Nevertheless, the curate sounded most sincere. He said that the landlord of The Plough confirmed it all, though he knew nothing of celestial speech."

"What is this Enochian language?" asked their bewildered host. "Is it something spoken in Bohemia?"

"Oh no, Sir George!" said Dee, smiling. "Far from it. It was the first language spoken on earth. The words in it are the words that Adam used to describe the things he saw around him."

"Why called Enochian?"

"From the lost book of Enoch in the Bible. Enoch was the father of Methuselah and the great-grandfather of Noah. It is said that he lived for 365 years. A magic number. Read Genesis 5:21, sir. Enoch was the last man on earth to know this primal language. It is said in the Bible that he was taken up by God. He did not die. Taken up. That was his reward for his great faith."

"His likeness may be in one of these tapestries," said Kelley, and all four men looked over at them and stared into the array of bearded faces.

"Doubtful, Edward," said Dee. "Abraham came eleven generations or so after Noah. His story cannot stretch back to Enoch. But we digress. Sir George, the Bible says that only Enoch and Elijah were so righteous as to be taken up to heaven alive. They have the highest standing under the Almighty in the realm of the heavenly host. This primal language was quickly debased on earth, however, and lost to the Hebrews. But it is the language of God and of the angelic host e'en to this day. Enoch was its champion. Edward communes with the angels in the Enochian language. The heavenly host has told us they are trying to reseed the language of God among men. They have anointed me with the task with Edward's help. Edward is the ears and eyes of mankind, and I am the mind that infers the meaning of the words."

"Extraordinary!" exclaimed Sir George. "I knew nothing of this. It almost sounds to be blasphemous. You only speak with angels, sir? What about the envoys of Satan? Do they not try to shout down the celestial voices?"

"We are most meticulous in our purification ritual, Sir George," said Dee. "Before contacting the celestial host, we fast, and we light holy candles, and we pray at length. It is only angels who hear the call."

"Whom you summon is one thing. Who responds to your call is another."

Kelley smiled nervously and looked to Dee for reassurance.

"Uriel…Anael…Madini," said Dee. "Angels all."

Sir George nodded acknowledgment but stretched back in his chair, desirous of playing no further part in what, to him, was a disturbing conversation. Dee and Kelley exchanged glances and then looked to Thomas Digges to change the subject. "How remarkable your story is, Thomas," said Dee. "The vicar must be a true scholar." Thomas merely shrugged and finished his wine.

"This village is off the Great North Road, you say?" Kelley asked with some eagerness.

"Saxonborough," Digges confirmed. "No more than five miles to the east of Tuxford."

"What say we stop there on our return to London, John? See if there be truth to it."

John Dee did not reply but also shrugged and stared deep into the firelight.

Chapter 13

Saxonborough
December 1587

It was two days before Christmas when Edward Kelley and his coachman finally arrived on the outskirts of the village of Saxonborough. They had ridden hard from York throughout the morning and reluctantly parted ways with John Dee at Tuxford. Dee averred that he would rather continue on to London to spend Christmas with his family than to chase wild geese across Lincolnshire fields. "Take stock of the situation," he had told Kelley. "If anything seems of value, we can return at a later date better prepared. I grow weary of strange beds and unfamiliar food. I wish to return to the things I am accustomed to."

Saxonborough was surprisingly lively when they arrived there just as dusk was painting the western sky with streaks of vulgar gold. Several smartly dressed couples meandered arm in arm down the muddy street that comprised the only thoroughfare in the village. Mothers carrying baskets and children trundling hoops hurried to and fro. Robert Rimes maneuvered the carriage around a dozen turkeys walking to Retford for Christmas dinners.

"No working in the fields today," Robert said to Edward, presuming him unfamiliar with country ways. "Only grooms and herdsmen are unspared for the season. Women and girls may not spin neither. Those are the rules. Everyone else may choose to rest or beat the drum."

Their carriage pulled up in front of The Plough, and both men went inside. There was one great room on the other side of the door, filled with activity. Three girls were hanging boughs of holly and mistletoe around the pelmets and from the ceiling beams. Unseen bells jingled. Tables were being washed and floors swept. A yule log lay in the hearth, and a large wooden bowl of mulled wine decorated with slices of orange stood by the entrance. A brawny man with his sleeves rolled up came over to them.

"May I assist you gentlemen?"

"Are you the landlord of this tavern?"

"Yes, I am. Indeed. Samuel Stringfellow at your service."

"My name is Edward Kelley, and this is my coachman, Robert Rimes." Kelley looked around the room and swept his arm in a half-circle. "What is happening here?"

"It is the night of the Feast of Fools, sir. Have you come to enjoy it with us?"

"What? Nay, nay. I am here as the representative of Dr. John Dee, advisor to Her Majesty Queen Elizabeth." The landlord was momentarily stunned and took a step backward. He could find no words, but he bowed deeply and then looked up and swallowed hard. "Be not alarmed, sir," said Kelley. "I am not here on official business. I am here consequent upon a tale told to us by the curate of Tuxford, who had heard it from the vicar of Saxonborough. He said that this tavern was wont to be visited by spirits."

The landlord promptly took Kelley's arm and walked him out of earshot of the servant girls. He glanced from side to side and then spoke in a whisper, "Please to moderate your voice, sir. Visited? Yes, perhaps it is. Spirits? That I do not know. Some people believe so. But it is bad for business. Very bad. And it is only a single bedroom that is accursed. The rest of the tavern is as it should be. But what can an illustrious gentleman such as yourself possibly want with us?"

"Dr. John Dee and I are studying such phenomena. With your permission, I would like to stay the night in this accursed room, as you call it, and see if anything untoward should happen to me. Just sit in the room and observe. And gaze into my obsidian mirror. Nothing more."

"Sit, merely?"

"Mr. Stringfellow, do not be alarmed, I say again. It might well be that it is the celestial host that wishes to commune. There can be no danger involved in that. We have had much experience in such matters. Dr. Dee and I have published scholarly articles on the subject."

"Well, you may do as you wish, sir, of course. Let it never be said that Samuel Stringfellow forbade the queen's envoy from residing here. That would be the final blow to my business." He laughed nervously and scratched his chin. "Will your coachman be staying in the room also?"

Robert shook his head vigorously.

"No," said Kelley. "He does not wish to. Do you have a room for him to sleep the night?"

"Certainly we do, sir. There are very few travelers at Christmastide."

"We will pay to hire both rooms for tonight, then. The haunted room and a sleeping room."

"No payment will be necessary, sir. We are happy to host the queen's men without charge."

"Might I request that the sleeping room be as far removed as possible from the haunted room?" Robert Rimes asked. "If you please."

"Certainly, certainly. But, sirs, I must point out that the night you have chosen for the purpose you describe may be a bad one. The Feast of Fools will begin soon. Half the village will be in this very room. There will be revelry and gaiety. Perhaps the spirits will think better of it than to visit this night."

"When will the festivities end?"

"Each year we ask that everyone leave at eleven of the clock. The servant girls must away to their homes, you understand. Their mothers demand it. But I cannot guarantee that there will be instant quiet the minute the clock strikes eleven. Some of the heavy drinkers...you know."

Edward Kelley pursed his lips and thought for a moment. "We will proceed anyway, Mr. Stringfellow. We are here now, and we will see what can be done. We will examine the room and prepare ourselves during the early evening. And then we will seek out the spirits after midnight. If all should be silent this night, Dr. Dee and I may return anon for further experimentation."

"Very good, sir. I will have a girl prepare the sleeping room for your coachman. There is no bed in the haunted room at present. We have deemed it wise to shut it up until such time as the ghostly visitors and the disruptive rumors may both be quashed. There are just three chairs, which should prove adequate, I hope. One of them is a good-quality armchair that you yourself could rest in, sir."

"It all sounds most satisfactory."

"And…and…if perchance you could *banish* the spirits from that room, I would be eternally grateful. If it is within your power, that is." He bowed deeply to Kelley, then turned and summoned a girl over from a corner of the great room and gave her instructions. She hurried quickly to a back room in search of bedsheets.

"One more question," Kelley said. "The curate of Tuxford told us there was a servant girl who might perhaps be…shall we say…attuned to the celestial world. That often the angels would come to visit when she was present. Might she be persuaded to sit with me? Perhaps to increase our chances of a successful encounter?"

"That would be Jane. Jane Oughtred. Her family are small farmers on the Torksey Road. They and half the village believe she possesses the second sight. Indeed, she did sit in the bedroom with me and the vicar, as you say. She is over there." The landlord pointed to a slim, fair-haired girl hanging a wreath of bay leaves on the far side of the room. He called her over.

"Jane," said the landlord, touching her shoulder, "Jane, these two men have come from London. From Her Majesty the Queen, no less. Mr. Kelley wishes to sit in the haunted bedroom with you this night to see…to see…if…" He faltered.

"Jane," said Kelley, "if you are willing, I would like you to sit this night with me to see if we can summon the angels. Just like you did with Mr. Stringfellow and the vicar once before."

"Yes, I have heard the voices several times, sir. You think they are angels?"

"That is what Dr. Dee and I believe. We have communed with the celestial host many times already. The voices in The Plough we are yet to comprehend. And I should add that we are not here on the queen's business, Jane. Nothing will be reported back to Parliament or to Her Majesty. It is just a personal interest in unusual phenomena of the natural world that drives us."

"Well, as you say, sir." She glanced over at the landlord, who nodded back at her. "I will help you with pleasure. If Andrew the scullery boy can carry word to my mother that I stay here the night?" She glanced again at the landlord, and he nodded again. "Very well, then," said Jane. "I will be most honored to assist you." She gave a small curtsey.

Kelley added, "And there will be a shilling for you in the morning, Jane."

For a third time she looked at the landlord, and for a third time, he nodded, but this time, he added the words, "But it will be my shilling, sir."

"You are exceeding generous, Mr. Stringfellow," said Kelley. "We will prepare ourselves at once. And perhaps Jane would be kind enough to come up to join me at eleven after this…"

"Feast of Fools," said Samuel.

"After this Feast of Fools is ended."

Jane Oughtred curtsied again and returned to help the other servant girls decorate the room.

The landlord led the two men up the narrow, decrepit wooden staircase to their two rooms. At the top of the stairs, he said to them, "There will be souse served fresh and hot at six of the clock, sirs. Be welcome to come down and dine with us."

"I'm sure Robert will oblige, but I will not. I do not eat souse. Like all swine, I hold that feet are for walking and ears for hearing. My thanks for the offer though."

The landlord turned and walked back downstairs. Edward and Robert entered the haunted bedroom. The room was small and bare. There was one leaded window overlooking the street, flanked by two tiny oak tables each with a lit candle on it. No curtains. There was no bed, just a rectangle of floorboards lighter in color than its neighbors, marking where a bed had once stood. The walls were bare and badly stained, with no pictures thereon. There was one armchair and two kitchen chairs. The maid had thoughtfully brought in a small table with a third candle on it and placed it in front of the armchair. Little light found its way in through the dirty window, and a wintry dusk had already descended on the street below. Robert and Edward did a quick inspection of the walls and floor, finding nothing out of the ordinary. No secret points of ingress at least.

"You may go now, Robert," said Edward. "Enjoy the festivities below if you wish. Eat some souse. I shall not need you the rest of this night. We will breakfast together in the morning and then be off to London. With luck you will be able to spend Christmas Day at Islington with your parents. I am sorry that this trip has taken longer than planned."

Robert smiled his gratitude and left the room.

Edward Kelley sat down and placed his obsidian mirror on the table. He polished it with his neckerchief and stared into it. Nothing but black rock and twinkling candlelight. He sat back in the armchair and rested for a few moments. Then he pulled out of his bag a notebook, quill, and inkpot, and finally a copy of Dee's *De Heptarchia Mystica*. He spent the next hour charting the current positions of the planets and the phase of the moon and similar items of astrological import in case Uriel should deign to visit him that night and wish to discuss them. "Two days past the winter solstice," he muttered. "Perhaps that will prove a lure." He wrote it all in his notebook.

At six o'clock, faint sounds began to drift into the room from the street below the window. Not angels, no. He heard bells and then a falsetto voice:

The boar's head in hand bear I
Bedecked with bay and rosemary.
And I pray you, my masters, merry be
Quot estis in convivio.

"The wassail," Edward groaned. "Truly it is the worst night of the year for quiet and contemplation." He did a quick translation of the last line of the carol, rather proud of his Latin skill: *"As many as are at the feast."* The singing grew louder and louder until it stopped outside the tavern and was followed by a loud rap on the door. The door was opened. Drinks were offered to and by the landlord, and then the revelers entered, and the Feast of Fools began.

Darkness was now total. The noise from beneath his feet was unrelenting. A fiddle played, throats warbled, and feet thumped. The candles burned low. Edward laid down his quill and closed his notebook. It was a little too early to begin the purification ritual that he and Dee had perfected for the angelic calls. He read Dee's tome again. Then, unbidden, his thoughts drifted back to the words Sir George Young had spoken at York the previous day: *"Whom you summon is one thing. Who responds to your call is another."* Such thoughts had occasionally drifted through his mind before—but it had only been angels who had responded to their calls. Would it always be thus? Must it *necessarily* be thus? Was their purification ritual absolute protection against evil?

The boar's head, as I understand,
Is the rarest dish in all this land,
Which thus bedecked with a gay garland
Let us servire cantico.

Another verse of the carol pushed its way up through the floorboards. *"What about the envoys of Satan?"* Sir George had asked. What about them? Could they also hear the summons? Could they respond if they so wished? If they did, how would he recognize them? Did not Satan take on disguises to outwit the careless? Uriel was clearly one of the celestial host...but what about the lesser angels who'd communed with them? Madini had said some peculiar things on occasion. What of him? In the darkness of an unfamiliar room in the middle of an unfamiliar village far from home, it was easy to doubt that angels were the only listeners.

Time passed slowly, and the candles burned down to stubs. Edward began to wish he'd insisted that Robert sit with him. At nine o'clock, he went down to the kitchen and asked for some bread and bacon and a half pint of small ale, which he took back to his room and consumed slowly. He read some more and polished his shew stone again and then began his prayers. Eventually, the hour of eleven o'clock neared, and the revelry below lessened and moved out into the street.

"Get yourself cleaned and readied to go up to the gentleman," Samuel Stringfellow instructed Jane Oughtred in the great room below.

"Yes, Mr. Stringfellow," she responded.

"And you'd better be on your guard. It is never certain what will happen when an older gentleman finds himself alone with a pretty young servant girl. There is a kissing bough at the top of the stairs, and I saw Mr. Kelley glance up at it as he went by. Do not let him kiss you."

"I will not, sir," Jane replied. "Be assured of that."

"You say that now. You say it in earnest. But you would not be the first servant girl of The Plough to find herself with child after such a dalliance. Cry out if you foresee an unwelcome advance. I will be up the stairs in an instant."

"But he is a gentleman. Come from Her Majesty."

The landlord snorted. "Nowhere near a guarantee of gentlemanly conduct. Envoy of Her Majesty or not, I will punch his nose and turf him out onto the street if he tries anything."

Jane Oughtred nodded and lit herself a candle and mounted the stairs. She knocked on the door of the haunted bedroom and came in at Edward's urging.

"Jane, come in, please," said Edward. "Put that candle on my table and sit you down over there. My sincere gratitude for your assistance this night."

"With pleasure, sir."

"Tell me, Jane, what is your experience with the spirit world?"

"I have had the gift since I was a child, sir. I saw several spirits at my grandmother's house when I was a child."

"And here? At The Plough?"

"Perhaps three or four times. The last time was with Mr. Stringfellow and the vicar that you know about."

"And how do these visions come upon you?"

"I really cannot say, sir. It is something I learned in childhood. I used to like to float in my grandfather's pond, and the sensation is something like that. It seems that I relax my whole body and feel to sink down into the pond. It seems like a watery substance envelops me, and I lose all sense of my surroundings. Then the lights come to my eyes and the sounds into my ears."

"The spirits seem to be actually in the room with you?"

"Yes, sir, sometimes they do. But whether they appear or do not appear on any occasion is beyond my control and most unpredictable. Whether there will be any visitors this night I cannot say. If there are not, I do heartily apologize."

"Not necessary, Jane. But your method does sound much like what Richard Crossly used to call the zeta state. That which his wife, Catherine, possessed. Possesses."

"The what?"

"Never mind, Jane. And do not be concerned if the night turns out to be uneventful." Jane nodded. "At times you will see me looking into this black stone here. Do not be concerned about that either. It is only a way to tell if the spirits are with us." Jane nodded again. "Are you afraid?"

"Afraid? Oh no, sir. I have grown up with them. They do not harm you."

This time it was Kelley who nodded.

Nothing had happened by midnight. Jane Oughtred remained sitting bolt upright and alert in her kitchen chair. However, the long evening and the small beer began to make Edward drowsy. Sitting back in the armchair, his eyelids drooped several times. When the clock downstairs chimed midnight, Edward roused himself and declared that he needed to empty his bladder.

"There's a privy next the stairs," said Jane.

Edward got up, opened the bedroom door, and stepped into the small hallway. He relieved himself in the privy, pinching his nose against the terrible stench rising up from the cesspit far below, and turned back into the hallway. He halted. Something was different. The lighting. The angle of the shadows. He looked to the end of the hallway and was shocked by what he saw.

There was a figure standing at the far end of the hallway. Facing the wall. Edward squinted to try to get a better view of it, but it was almost entirely hidden in shadow. Only a few thin shafts of light coming up from downstairs through the ill-fitting floorboards cast a faint light on the man. Or woman. Or beast. Edward said nothing. He just stood and stared. Then the figure turned toward him, and Edward at once made out the two horns protruding from the top of its head, the two tusks hanging down from its mouth, and the large ears drooping down almost to its neck. This was neither man nor woman. This was beast only. It emitted a low growl from the back of its throat, followed by a single sharp bark. Edward jumped. He began to tremble. Could Sir George be right? Had he inadvertently conjured up an envoy of Satan as a result of his misplaced contemplation in the early evening? Then another possibility occurred to him, and he quickly turned away and pushed open the door of the haunted bedroom and stepped inside.

"Jane?" he asked in agitation. "Have you already begun to—"

The servant girl was still sitting upright on her kitchen chair. She turned to him, her face at first impassive, then slightly puzzled.

"No, you haven't," said Edward. He stepped back into the hallway. It was empty. He took two steps forward, then thought better of it and returned to the bedroom. He closed the door gently behind him. For a moment he stood in silence, his back pressed tightly against the wooden door. Then slowly and carefully, he walked over to his armchair and sat down. For the next ten minutes, he sat quietly, his mind racing backward and forward across what had just transpired and what its meaning might be. Jane was the first to break the silence.

"Are you unwell, sir?"

"No…no. Did I sleep just now?"

"I believe you might have, sir."

"Did I go to the privy though?"

"You did, sir. It was before that that I think you might have slept."

"So I did not dream it. It really happened."

"What did?"

"I saw something in the hallway."

"A man?"

"I don't think so."

"A woman, then?"

"No."

Jane stared at him. "Do you want me to see if the spirits will visit us now?"

"In a moment. Let me gather myself first."

Edward Kelley did his best to divert his mind away from the beast in the hallway. He focused on the angel Uriel, who had led all previous celestial contacts. Uriel would not permit any satanic intrusions. Surely. He removed his neckerchief and polished the shew stone again, more in hopes that the rhythm would calm his mind. The room was colder now that the log fire in the great room below was no longer being stoked. He thought of the approaching daylight and how he could soon depart from this place, no matter what might happen during the next few hours. He was under no obligation here. The December air in the street below the window was now perfectly quiet and peaceful. The inn had shed its feast and the fools that had enjoyed it and extinguished its lanterns. Only Edward and Jane remained alert in their candle-lit box.

"Very well, Jane," said Edward. "Put match to your second sight."

She closed her eyes but did not change her position. For two hours, they sat there. Only once did anything untoward happen. Vague and distant sounds could be heard. Sometimes with a hint of laughter. Edward would have dismissed them as distant revelers, but occasionally the sounds seemed to come not from the street below but from inside the walls of the bedroom or from some corner of the tavern beneath their feet. He could make out no words, however, English or foreign or Enochian. The blackness of the shew stone was never disturbed. Edward was confident that the sounds were unearthly, but he could conclude nothing more. When the clock on the tower of St. Swithin's Church struck two, Edward whispered, "That is enough, Jane. You have done enough. Go find yourself a place to sleep. I will stretch out in this armchair till morning."

"Very good, sir," Jane replied and left the room.

Edward pulled his coat tight around his legs and drifted off to sleep.

Come morning, the landlord approached Edward and Robert as they sat at the kitchen table with a breakfast of brown bread and egg and warm cider, the best he could offer. He pulled up a chair and sat down with them, drawing himself a glass of cider.

"Food satisfactory?" Samuel said.

"Yes. Thank you."

"Any success last night?"

"A little," Edward replied. "I believe I did hear some distant voices of heavenly communication—but not loud enough to decipher. I think the rumors of spirits here are perhaps true. But something stranger than that happened in the hallway outside the room. I saw a figure. A very strange figure."

"Yes? Well, after the festivities concluded, we did have two unanticipated guests for the night. One of them a hungover reveler. Had to carry him up the stairs."

"I don't think it was one of them. The figure I saw had…seemed to have…the head of a beast. A large, misshapen beast head. And in all other wise dressed in black."

The landlord chuckled nervously. "Well, I hope you banished him and all like him from our tavern, sir."

"That is not one of my skills, Mr. Stringfellow, I'm afraid. Perhaps your vicar could perform that task."

The landlord shook his head. "The vicar will not come here again. He said if called upon by the bishop, he would seek a new parish."

"Well, perhaps Dr. Dee and I will return after the winter is ended. Study your haunted room more thoroughly."

"You would be welcome at any time."

Breakfast finished, Edward and Robert gathered up their belongings and prepared to leave and return to London. As they opened the front door, the landlord ran up to them excitedly.

"A beast, you said? Like a wild animal?"

Edward nodded.

"Why, that was the Lord of Misrule!"

"Who?"

"The Lord of Misrule! It is he who convenes and oversees the Feast of Fools. Do you not know the tradition? It is like an overturning of the normal way of the world. The village chooses a poor mischievous idiot from its ranks and dubs him the Lord of Misrule. He governs the entire village for just the one day and night. Even squires and clergy are required to obey him. Within reason, of course."

Edward shook his head this time, but Robert nodded. He knew of such things.

"In Lincolnshire it is the tradition that the Lord of Misrule wears a boar's head during the festivities. The women of our village made it years ago out of cloth and paper and wool. Did you not hear the *Boars' Head Carol* sung by the wassail choir earlier in the evening? All our festivities before Christmas revolve around the boar. It is a very ancient tradition. Harkening back to the days when real boars roamed the forests hereabouts. Very ancient indeed."

"I did hear the singing," Edward confessed. "A boar *was* mentioned in the lyrics."

"Yes, yes! And that was the beast you saw in the nighttime," said Samuel Stringfellow, much relieved. "The Lord of Misrule wearing a boar's head!"

"Very well. A relief, as you say. I thought for a moment that Jane Oughtred might have accidentally conjured up the devil in animal form."

A smile broke out on Kelley's face even as the smile on the landlord's face evaporated.

"Jane?" said the landlord. "She was there? What time did this happen?"

"Shortly after midnight."

"Surely not. You must be mistaken. The Lord of Misrule drank too much last night and was carried home by his wife and son before ten of the clock."

Chapter 14

Saxonborough
May 1803

MARY KIRKHAM GATHERED UP HER picnic basket and walked out the front door of The Plough. She crossed the muddy main street of Saxonborough and made her way down an alley between the butcher's shop and the local brewery onto a path that sloped down toward the Fossdyke. She had lately turned twenty years of age and was considered by the village to be both pretty and sweet-natured. Her mouth was small and delicate, her eyes large and bright. Her hair was jet-black, and she wore it tied up on the top of her head, revealing a narrow, shapely neck. Most of her social life was enjoyed within the confines of a bevy of village girls in order to hold the boys at bay, but lately she'd been lured away from her girlfriends by a handsome but slightly older man with an irresistible physique. On this particular morning, she wore a pretty dress, snow-white and embroidered with bluebells and forget-me-nots, cinched tight at the waist. As she walked, she swung her basket from side to side in an unknowingly seductive fashion.

It was late spring, and the day held the tepid beginnings of summer's warmth. The sky was painted a creamy blue that matched the color of the flowers on Mary's dress. She noticed that there were a few banked cumulus clouds with gray underbellies scattered across the western horizon. It might rain later, but the day promised sunshine well into the afternoon. On the eastern horizon, the towers of Lincoln Cathedral stuck up like three tiny fingers of a baby. Mary was happy but nervous. In her picnic basket was luncheon for two.

She walked down the slope toward a group of seven or eight men standing knee-deep in the water of the canal and hacking at its banks with pickaxes. All were bare-chested, tanned, and muscular. Several of them had colorful kerchiefs wrapped around their heads. One was chanting some kind of monotonous work song in what she thought was an Irish brogue. High up on the bank stood a foreman staring off into the distance. He wore a three-piece suit with a conspicuous watch chain dangling from his waistcoat pocket; periodically, and with a flourish, he would pull out the watch and examine the hour, then put it back. He also flaunted a top hat and a handlebar moustache. Mary held her distance from the group.

"Thomas," she called out, then louder, "Thomas!"

One of the men turned toward her.

"Mary? What in blazes are you doing here?"

"I've brought lunch for us," Mary replied. Thomas glanced over at the foreman, who nodded to him. Thomas laid down his pickax and walked barefoot and dripping up the slope to her side. "Ham sandwiches," she added. "And an iced cake. And lemonade."

"I'm with me mates," Thomas said with undisguised irritation in his voice. "We always drink in the *Goat and Compasses* at midday. No soppy girlish food. No…picnics."

"But I needs must talk with you this day," Mary said. "I must. Come sit under yonder tree with me. Please, Thomas."

Thomas clenched his jaw and looked around. "It's not twelve yet. Go sit under the tree you've chosen particular. If you must. I'll join you when the church clock strikes."

"Yes, Thomas," said Mary and obediently walked over to the tree and sat under it.

Thomas returned to his colleagues and renewed his attack on the canal bank with a fury born of chagrin. Clods of earth flew off the bank and splashed into the water. A couple of his workmates glanced over at him but said nothing. They knew better than to mess with him when he was in this kind of mood. As soon as the bell on the tower of St. Swithin's Church struck its twelfth note, Thomas threw his pickax onto the shore and climbed out of the dyke. He snatched up a threadbare shirt off the slope, draped it around his shoulders, and marched over to join Mary.

"What must be so important as to make you trespass on my laboring? To make me look a schoolgirl in front of me mates?"

"Take a sandwich," Mary said, apprehensive at her lover's rising anger. "It's from the best cut of the sow's thigh. With mustard. I made it myself."

"I don't want nor need no sandwich. I need ale. I'm parched to distraction."

Mary pulled the jar of lemonade from her basket and held it out to him. He bent over and knocked it out of her hand. He did not sit down beside her.

"What do you want? Tell me now, and then I'll go join the lads at the inn."

Mary bit her lip and looked away from his threatening eyes.

"All right, then."

"Come on! Out wi' it!"

"I'm with child," she confessed at last. "I don't know no other way to tell you."

"What?" Thomas was astonished. "With child?"

"I'm sorry, Thomas."

"Did you not take care to prevent it?"

"I'm sorry. I did not know about such things. My mother…she never…"

"How far gone are you?"

"Two months. Perhaps three. I know I've missed several of the bleeding times. I only realized it last week. I'm so sorry."

Thomas shook his head and looked away.

"We needs must marry," Mary added.

"Marry? *Marry*? Does it look like I'm the marrying kind? Did I not tell you many times that we had only the day and not the morrow?"

"You did, yes." Mary's eyes moistened. She looked up at him, but no words would come.

"No, it's out of the question. You must find an old woman to prevent it."

"I cannot, Thomas, I cannot. My mother says it's too late for that now. I must carry the baby to term. We needs must marry."

"I will not."

After standing there a minute, his legs and feet sodden, Thomas finally sat down beside her. They spoke not a word for a long time, Mary sobbing quietly, Thomas pulling clumps of grass and throwing them up into the wind. Eventually Mary said the second thing in her mind, "I spoke to my father this morning. He says he's willing to carve out a tract of land for us from his farm. Up the Torksey road. He says he'll pay for a cottage to be built on it that all three of us can live in together."

"Three of us?"

"You, me, and the baby."

"Oh, right."

"Failing that, he says he would be willing to give us money so that we can go and live elsewhere. Especially if we are afeared of village scandal."

"Money?" Thomas paused. "How much money?"

"He did not say. But a goodly amount. Perhaps then you could give up the laboring work, and we could buy a small farm of our own. Somewhere. Work the land together. You and me."

"Five hundred pounds?"

Mary's face was blank.

"A hundred?"

"Perhaps not so much. But what about a cottage on his farm, then?"

"So that I can chew the gristle of gratitude at your family's table my whole life? With a smile on my face, even as I chew? No, ma'am."

"All can be negotiated. Please come with me and talk to my father. We can reach some agreement that will suit you. Suit us both. Come now, please, Thomas." She looked up at him and held out her hand. "Could you not love a child that we have made together?"

Thomas ignored her plea. "I needs must work this afternoon. If I leave now, I'll lose half this day's pay and a sixpence penalty besides. I've said my piece." And he got up and walked down to the canal without a backward glance. When he realized that his mates were not there, he turned and went halfway up the bank, dried off his feet and trousers, and put on his boots. He thrust his arms violently into the sleeves of his shirt, tearing the cuff of one of them. Then he strode to the top of the hill and headed for the *Goat and Compasses*.

Mary wiped her eyes and blew her nose. For a long time, she sat under the tree, staring off into the distance. Her mind was empty. She was not angry at Thomas nor sad at her predicament. She did fear her father, but there was little she could do about that. Fate held her in its fist and would toss her from one palm to the other over the year to come. She must accept that.

A ragged boy walked by. She called him over. "Hungry?" she asked. He did not reply. "Here," she said and handed him the sandwiches and the cake and the bottle of lemonade.

His eyes opened wide. "Ta, miss!" he said, accepting them eagerly. He bit into the sandwich and ran off. After a few more minutes, Mary stood up, walked a step or two down the grassy slope, and hurled the empty picnic basket into the center of the canal.

Chapter 15

Mortlake, London
February 1588

THE WINTER OF 1588 WAS hard. The Little Ice Age was firming its grip on Europe. The River Thames froze over in several places but not as thoroughly as it would two decades later when the first frost fair was held on it. But the winter of 1588 was sufficiently hard to freeze Kelley in his laboratory and Dee in his library. Kelley tried to replicate the experimental setup he had seen in Evergreen Jones's shop at York but without success. No yellow carapace formed on his silver ingot. Either he had not held the mixture at the right temperature and for long enough, or—as Dee had suspected—it was all the result of accidental adulteration. Dee spent these same winter months copying an important manuscript called the *Steganographia*, prepared by Trithemius, a German abbot, which Dee believed might contain cryptographic codes that would circumvent the need for astrological mediation with the angels.

Kelley and Dee did not meet again until early February when the air had warmed somewhat, and Kelley felt sufficiently energized to take a carriage to Dee's home at Mortlake on the south bank of the newly thawed Thames. Kelley and Dee did not dwell on their recent alchemical experiences but rather on their plans for another trip to the Continent in search of wealthy patronage; both of them were finding that their incomes were no longer adequate to support their lavish lifestyles. Over lunch, Kelley described his recent European overtures.

"I sent a missive to Olbracht Laski at the turn of the year. I asked him to contact the court of King Stefan at Krakow with a view to us both earning a station at court, underpinned by considerable finances, so that we could further our experiments and hire apprentices for the laboratory and ultimately provide him with gold in profusion. I sent a similar missive to Lord William of Rosenberg requesting an audience with Emperor Rudolf. I suggested that we might spend April in Krakow and May in Prague, depending on the extent of favors granted us."

"Any responses?"

"Not yet, John. The winter has been as bad on the Continent this past month as it has been here. But I expect to receive their letters of reply any day now. I feel sure Emperor Rudolf will agree, but I am uncertain about the Poles. Laski is certainly supportive, but I am less persuaded about the eagerness of their monarchy."

"It seems like a good plan, Edward. Is there any other news from across the Channel?"

"Well, in truth, I am a little concerned about possible interference and intervention by the Catholic church. Lord William said in his last letter that the papal nuncio in Prague had learned of the court's interest in alchemy and feared it to be aligned with necromancy. Germanico Malaspina, the Bishop of San Severo, requested a consultation on the matter, but thus far it has been rebuffed. I don't know if that possibility will sharpen after we arrive there."

"Let's hope not. Surely we can shelter under the emperor's wing?"

"One would think so. Does he not hold greater sway in Bohemia than the Pope?"

"He must. Let me know as soon as the responses are received."

"Yes, of course."

The two men finished their meal and settled down in armchairs by the fire.

"Since we cannot return to the continent before April at the earliest," Kelley continued, "I should like to return to Lincolnshire as soon as the weather makes travel convenient—while the ground is still frozen and before the mud and clay lose their solidity. That tavern at Saxonborough holds strange secrets, I am sure of it."

"You talked of voices…and a demonic figure?"

"Yes. My experience was most unusual. It was unlike our typical angelic discourses. But I feel I only scratched the surface. I still do not understand what happened that night. I feel that the walls of that singular bedroom hold some dark secrets that perhaps only Uriel and the servant girl, Jane Oughtred, know of. If we were to return there under more propitious circumstances, I believe we could open doors that have thus far remained locked."

"All right. I will accompany you. Shall we wait a week or two for the weather to better shade our journey?"

"I think so," said Kelley. "Perhaps the last week of February or early March would suit."

"Very well, then. Make arrangements, my good man." They smiled at each other.

And so it was that on a clear and cloudless evening in late February, Edward Kelley and Jane Oughtred once again sat side by side in the haunted bedroom of The Plough at Saxonborough, this time with John Dee enthroned beside them on a third kitchen chair. Dee had persuaded the landlord with five shillings to keep the fire stoked in the great room throughout the night, so they were less chilled than Edward and Jane had been in December.

This was to be a show of sound more than light. True, several times as the night progressed, the candlelight was modulated somewhat, and the shadows shifted a little, fading, then brightening. And several times Kelley thought he saw two figures on the opposite side of the room, but he could never be certain. One figure might have been large and bearded; one seemed of smaller build, clean-shaven, with huge round eyes like an owl. Kelley strained his eyes mightily, peering into the depths of the shadows, sorting and reassembling the varying shades of gray. But he saw nothing of angels or devils—nor of horned beasts, thank the Lord. But at those times when he was most convinced there were beings of some kind in the room, there were definite sounds. These sounds gave the impression of being trapped in the high corners of the bedroom, whimpering to be released from confinement. Their pitch was high, their tone reverberant. They tinkled: a cowbell in a far-off field, a waterfall in a distant stream. At times, the sounds seemed to scurry across the ceiling as if searching for a means of egress. At other times, they would settle on their haunches in one place, disheartened, and grumble to themselves. Kelley followed the sounds with intense concentration, his goose quill in his hand and his notebook on the table in front of him. He desperately wanted to wring words out of the ethereal sounds. Anything meaningful that could be transcribed and processed and passed on to John Dee for interpretation.

At the outset he hoped for names. In past calls the angels had always imparted their names by way of introduction. He thought he heard the name of their primary and most distinguished contact—Uriel—mentioned once, but it was not with the same intonation that he recalled from previous contacts. It was more like *Eriah*. Or something similar. Or different. He could discern no name for the second angel, except perhaps *Sammod.* The spoken words were visceral, pervasive. Neither could he say if the sounds came out of the mouths of the figures opposite to him. He doubted it, as the angels had never before shown their physical nature, but it was not impossible.

Gradually, the sounds became louder and distinctly clearer. Edward nodded to Dee, cocked his ear to one side, and, without looking down, dipped his quill in the inkpot and began to write in his notebook. Eventually getting a grip on the intonation, he began to notice similarities in certain noise strings. They were repeated. They were emphasized. They must be messages. There was a pause of ten minutes or so and then resumption. The same strings. Kelley corrected what he had written before. He wrote down alternative possibilities. He tried to attach meaning to the transcribed words but without success. His own brain could add nothing to improve the transcription. Light fumbled in from the street to reveal Jane Oughtred slumped in her chair, chin on chest, eyes closed. Perhaps she had fallen asleep; there was no way to be certain. It seemed that the sounds breathed a sigh of relief at this point and found a cleft in the ceiling beams through which to escape. Time passed in silence until Dee at last rose up and replaced the candles that had expired. Kelley slapped both knees with his palms.

They roused Jane and with much gratitude bade her leave for another room and sleep away the remainder of the night. They lit two more candles and placed them on the table. Kelley opened up his notebook, and they both peered at his scratchings.

"Let us decipher the message, Edward," said Dee excitedly.

"There was much talk, but most of it either too faint or indecipherable. There were two phrases, however, that were repeated. Did you observe that?"

"I did. I could discern them. The angels appeared to stress them on our behalf. Their enunciation was most earnest. They must be of the highest import."

"I don't know if this was Uriel and Madini or another angel. I thought I heard the names *Eriah* and *Sammod* spoken."

"New angels descending?"

"Perhaps. But to my ear, there were no formal introductions from on high, as in the past."

"The voices, too, did not sound like any of the ones we have heard before."

"They did not. Perhaps I was mistaken in that particular. Nothing was clear. And it was all different this time, was it not? I heard the words, and I somehow could see them in the shew stone. However, it is possible that they were merely in my mind, and my mind imprinted them onto the shew stone. I do not know which. But my ears held the sounds fast, and I transcribed each word in Enochian as best I could. But perhaps they were not spoken in the Enochian language. Did you think of that? Perhaps it was some foreign tongue. You know foreign speech better than I do, John. Did you recognize any part of it? Was it perhaps German? It sounded somewhat Germanic. All was *very* different this time."

"I did not recognize any part of it. It was all mere sound to me. It is best we assume at first that it *was* Enochian and see if any meaning can be extracted on that basis."

Edward Kelley picked up his notebook and showed Dee the entries. "This was the first part of the repeated speech." They stared at the characters.

"It is mysterious in the extreme," said Dee, pointing at Kelley's handwritten notes. That first word seems to be *van-med-don-ged,* does it not? That is not a word in the English language. *W-O-R-G.* That is not a word. The other characters do not appear to be words either. Might some of them need be run together?"

"I heard them distinctly and saw them clearly as separated. Four words. The angel was trying hard to make a clear statement to us."

"That fourth word might be *tal-un-gon*. That is an English word, *May*. The month of the year."

"Or perhaps the present tense of the auxiliary verb, as in *'It may rain.'*"

"Yes. That is also possible. Do you think it could be linked to the second part of the celestial message? How does it continue, Edward?"

"If you remember, there was a pause and then a second, longer utterance. I have it written thus." And he again pointed to his notes in the appropriate place.

"Also mysterious, Edward. I cannot see any sense in it."

"It is strange, indeed. But I am not sure if it is to be read from left to right or right to left. We know that the Enochian language is *meant* to be read from right to left; but on occasion, as you know, we have found that the messages are transmitted to us in reverse. We do not know which way to read this message, as its mode of transmission was so different from previous ones."

Kelley pursed his lips and stared intently at the second of the phrases. Dee leaned over his shoulder and did the same. Neither spoke for a minute or more. Then Kelley tapped vigorously on his paper.

"Look at the first," said Kelley.

"Or the last," Dee pointed out.

"Of the words in this phrase. Do you see it here?"

"This one?" Dee asked. "The one with seven characters?"

"Yes. Examine it closely, John." He did so.

"It begins and ends with the same character, *un*," said Kelley. "Our letter *a*."

Dee struggled to translate the word into English. "Taking a literal view of the characters, Edward, it suggests to me that the word is *A-C-I-R-E-M-A*," he said, spelling out each letter and then linking them together.

"Or," said Kelley, turning and looking up into Dee's eyes, "*A-M-E-R-I-C-A*."

Chapter 16

Ketteringham Lodge
February 1588

ALICE WAS PREPARING A QUICHE for Catherine's lunch when the pounding on the front door began. She hurriedly wiped her hands and scurried out of the kitchen and across the hallway. The pounding continued unabated until she threw open the door to reveal Edward Kelley in a disheveled and rather distressed state. His fist was raised toward the door, preparing another blow upon it.

"Mr. Kelley?" she said, startled. "What in heaven's name are you doing here?"

"I must speak to your mistress immediately," he replied. "Is she at home?"

"She is, of course. You'd better come in."

"May Robert tend to the horses and then spend time with you in the kitchen? While I consult with your mistress?"

"Of course, he may."

Kelley turned and nodded to Robert, who flicked his whip at the horses and steered them round to the back of the house. Edward stepped across the threshold and looked meaningfully toward the door of the apartment—the same room in which he had been rebuffed by Catherine some two months previously. Alice saw great anxiety in his face.

"May I tell my mistress what this is regarding?"

"Just announce my arrival, if you would be so kind. Quickly."

Alice turned, walked over to the door of the private apartment, knocked on it, and went inside. A few seconds later, Catherine

Crossly emerged and walked over to Edward. He nervously looked into her face to see if there were any signs of affection or pleasure around her eyes. There were none. There was only passivity with a hint of concern.

"Edward? Is everything all right?"

"I have something of importance to convey to you, Catherine. You will, I think, be glad I called this morning when you hear of it. But do not be alarmed in the slightest. There is nothing of risk or danger involved. May we go inside?"

He gestured toward the room, and Catherine led him into it and closed the door behind them. She was dressed informally, and her hair was not prepared for visitors, but she seemed unconcerned about such things. "Tell me why you would come unannounced," she said.

"It is a long and convoluted story," Edward Kelley began, "but I will try to simplify it and summarize the background." He described what had happened at The Plough during the previous night: the vague figures, the sounds, the message…John Dee's impression that it was a most important contact with the celestial host.

"This message," said Catherine. "That is the reason you have come? What did it say?"

"Much of the message is yet to be understood. But there was one word that was crisply enunciated and readily transcribed by me. It was the final word of the message that we heard repeated many times. It was this word." And he showed a piece of paper to her.

"What does it mean?"

"Notice that the first and last characters are the same. This is the Enochian character *un*. It is like our letter *a*."

"And the rest?"

"I will not go into detail. It spells the word *America*."

Catherine looked up at him. "Are you sure?"

"John and I have been interpreting celestial speech for six years or more. We know the language well. This word jumped off the page at us. It is incontrovertible. The only uncertainty concerned in which direction it was intended to be read. We heard it spoken backward, and I found that I had written it backward. But that is not without precedent. Over the years we have found that about one-third of the celestial messages are received that way. We do not know why."

"So what do you think it means?"

"I will get to the rest of the wording in a moment. But we must first ask ourselves. Why would our Lord and the celestial host concern themselves with America? And why would they wish to impart those concerns to us? Is it because they wish to ensure the firm foundation of Christianity in the New World?"

"Do you think that is the reason?"

"Last night, Dee and I were convinced that it was. But this morning, upon further examination of the entire transcript and further reflection, I have a different opinion. I think it may have something to do specifically with the needs of the new colony. John Dee has posited an English claim to the New World for many years. You know that, Catherine. He asserted eight years ago that Queen Elizabeth, as heir to those intrepid sailors who discovered the land in ancient times, had a prior claim over Spain. So our second thought was that the angels were giving guidance for the further disposition of America."

"I do not think that God—" Catherine said with a smile.

"I know you are inclined to doubt the existence of celestial calls, Catherine, but what we can decipher of the rest of the message further supports our view that we were being provided with a message concerning the Roanoke colony—coming from their angelic guardians or possibly even from the settlers themselves. Perhaps it was a desperate plea from the colonists relayed through the celestial medium."

"And you thought that I—"

"You know more about the colony than any person in England, with the exception perhaps of John White," said Kelley. "You have the knowledge and a sense of comradeship with them. I thought to come to you at once."

"What of the rest of the message?"

"Well, it is not as easy to interpret as this one word. The sounds were insubstantial. Perhaps there are aural errors in my apprehension or cerebral mistakes in my transcription. Perhaps both. But our final interpretation is that the message concerns agricultural practices. We know that the colonists are struggling to grow their own food in a soil and a climate that are unfamiliar to them. If they do not succeed, they may starve. Mayhap they are starving already. Mayhap they are reaching out to the heavens for guidance. It may be a supplication. They may be at death's door!"

"So what more have you been able to decipher? What brings you to this conclusion?"

"Well, the first word appears to be *yam, gon-un-tal.* Initially, we thought it was the word *may*, but when *America* was shown to be reversed, we settled on *yam*. I did not know that such a word existed, but John had heard it before."

"I know the word well," said Catherine. "Yam is another word for the sweet potato."

"That is correct!" said Edward in surprise. "How did you know that?"

Catherine knew she had to be careful. "The sweet potato is new in England, to be sure, but I have seen it in London on occasion."

"They are grown in the New World and have come to our shores through Spain," Edward continued. "They say that Catherine of Aragon was entranced by their exotic taste and ordered King Henry to have them brought from Spain on a regular basis. John Dee had heard of this at court, but I had not. I have never seen a sweet potato."

"I believe they do not grow in the English climate. Perhaps the Roanoke colonists have learned of their existence and their hardiness under the conditions in which they find themselves. I would surmise that they are trying to discover the best way to grow them in Virginia as a staple."

"Yes! That is what I think! And there were other phrases that we read into the Enochian transcript. We saw the phrases 'how we grow' and 'from a plain field.' They are struggling to grow unfamiliar food in a new place."

"It would seem so, Edward," Catherine agreed, "though the mechanism by which the request was transmitted to you and Dr. Dee is far beyond my comprehension."

"I thought that you would want to know this, Catherine," said Edward earnestly, leaning toward her and touching her sleeve. "I thought you might have some ideas as to what action we should take. Can instructions be carried to the colonists on the next sailing ship? You are one of the most important subscribers to the present endeavor. What do you think?"

"As I told you in December, Edward, John White does indeed intend to return to Roanoke this year with supplies. He could perhaps carry a Spanish gardener with him, one who would have experience of growing yams and similar produce that are unfamiliar to our own people. But that voyage will be much delayed. I know it. As I told you before, the Spanish fleet will be all around our shores in just a few months from now. No English ships will be able to sail for the Americas."

"Yes, you told me that. You can see deep into the crystal, Catherine. Your skill is far greater than that of Jane Oughtred or me. And Thomas Digges affirmed to us that there is already nervousness in the Privy Council about the possibility of aggression by King Philip. Warships gathering in Lisbon. Thousands of troops mustered in the Netherlands. That sort of thing."

Catherine did not respond. Neither of them knew what to say next or where to steer the conversation. Romance was one of Edward's options, but not Catherine's.

"Would you be willing to come back to Saxonborough with me?" Kelley said at last. "I feel that you could help to solidify the angelic communication on this topic. And perhaps to elicit some speech that would be more forthcoming. I feel that Uriel and the rest of the host would empathize greatly with you and provide clarification."

"Edward, you know that my husband earnestly wished similar things of me years ago. He, too, felt that my powers would enhance the chances of his experiments succeeding. But I declined then, as I must decline now. The blow that descended on Richard and me in 1537 during the destruction of Hoyland Abbey was powerful enough to make me renounce all further involvement in mystical transactions of any kind. I would not have been able to survive thereafter otherwise."

"I know this. You explained it to me last Christmastide. But this is about *America*, the land you love. It could be the key to establishing our colony there."

"This is what I suggest," said Catherine. "Leave your Enochian script and your English translation with me here for one hour. And provision me with some kind of alphabetic equivalence. Then take a brisk walk around our gardens. Look for signs of an early spring. Relax. Drink cider with Alice and Mr. Rimes. Let these matters slip away from you for just one hour. Then return here to me. After I have studied your scripts, I will give you my considered opinion as to their meaning and their import and what I recommend as a next step. Does that sound reasonable?"

Kelley agreed that it did. Her words seemed to soothe him the moment they slipped from her lips, like a sweet balm on his forehead. He handed his papers to her and left the room. Catherine took them over to her desk and began to study them. Edward walked around the gardens and beneath the alder trees, enjoying the tidiness and tranquility of them; and for the moment, he set aside his desire to abandon his alchemical and astrological studies and enjoy a quiet old age in Catherine's company. Sweet nature was more than sufficient for the present. At length, becoming chilled, he took up Catherine's other suggestion and went into the kitchen to drink cider with Alice and Robert. When the hour was up, he took his leave of them and returned to Catherine's apartment. As soon as he walked through the door, Catherine stood up and pulled a shawl around her shoulders.

"Tell Robert to prepare the horses. We leave at once for Saxonborough."

"What? Why?"

"Your transcription is not accurate, Edward. It is not your fault. The true meaning could not have been known to you. Only I know what was said."

"And what was it that was said?"

"It is not 'Yam…how we grow…from a plain field…in America.' It is something entirely different—'I am Harry Groh from Plainfield in America.'"

Chapter 17

Saxonborough
February 1588

Catherine and Edward arrived at The Plough in midafternoon. Samuel Stringfellow welcomed them in his usual way, but they couldn't help noticing a smear of irritation in his voice. It seemed to suppress the thought of, *How many more times will you come here without banishing the spirits that vex me so?* Edward showed Catherine the bare room that was to be the seat of their investigations, and then they went back downstairs. As the afternoon was dry and not at all cold, they strolled around the village for an hour and then went back for a supper of stewed venison, turnips, and black bread.

"I'm afraid Jane isn't here today," said Samuel while they ate. "Her mother is unwell, and she must perforce remain on the farm. Can you manage without her?"

"I believe so," Edward replied. "Mrs. Crossly here as similar gifts to Jane."

"Yes, sir," Catherine added. "This time we will not require the services of Jane. Though I have to say that I would very much like to meet her on another occasion and confer with her about her spiritual experiences. Compare notes, one might say. The day may come when I *will* need her assistance."

"Yes, madam, I'm sure we can arrange that for another time."

Catherine and Edward then returned to the haunted bedroom and moved the chairs around so that they would be seated side by side against the end wall by the door. Before getting down to business, they walked over to the window together and stared down on the simple, bare main street of Saxonborough. They exchanged thoughts on what was to come.

"Do you expect the spirits to appear this night?" asked Edward.

"Indeed, I am certain of it."

"Why is that?"

"It is because of the message you received yesterday. There must necessarily be a second rendezvous today."

"But why must it be so?"

Catherine looked away and rubbed her forehead. "Listen, Edward," she said, "I cannot explain to you all that is happening. You would almost certainly not be able to understand it, and, if perchance you could, I'm afraid it would trouble your mind immensely. It is best that you leave things in my hands for the time being. Perhaps there will be an opportunity in the future for us to sit down together and discuss it. For now, I will tell you just three things. First, the message that you received yesterday does *not* have a celestial origin. No angel spoke to you and John. And the message was *not* transmitted in the Enochian language. It was entirely of earthly origin."

"Does the explanation have anything to do with beasts? Satanic beasts with the heads of animals? Perhaps a wild boar?"

"Of course not, Edward. You told me in the carriage about your experience at Christmas. There is no connection. The second point I feel able to convey to you is that it was to be expected that the message would be presented in reverse. But it was not by choice. The reason has to do with the fundamental causality of such occurrences, the explanation of which was discovered by my husband years ago. A quirk of time, let us call it. That is all I can say on that matter."

"Very well. I shall sit back and leave it all in your capable hands. I am assuming that Jane Oughtred was not needed because you yourself are an experienced scryer and can bring about spiritual contacts yourself, yes?"

Catherine turned to Edward and nodded.

"And third," she said, "you must take no part whatsoever in what should occur this evening, except to observe events closely and report back to me after I emerge from my trance. When I am deeply immersed in what my husband and the other scientists call the zeta state, I am mostly unaware of my surroundings. Occasionally, I do see things, but I will not be totally aware of all that has happened around me. So you must tell me when I awake. I expect that you will see people—perhaps one or two. You will not know them. Their dress will be unfamiliar to you. I do not expect them to try to communicate with us, though they may exhibit shock or surprise on their faces when they first appear in the room. I do not know in which part of this room they may manifest, and their appearance will be faint and translucent. For this reason, you must keep your eyes peeled. They are not celestial beings—nor their counterparts from Hades. They are people of this world but from a time and place that is not Saxonborough in the year 1588. Is it clear?"

"It is, Catherine. I shall do exactly as you bid."

And that was the end of their initial conversation. They went and sat in their chairs, and the evening turned into black night. Catherine eventually drifted away from the empty room and Saxonborough and from the physical world entirely. But her sojourn in the spiritual world was short-lived. After a period of little more than ten minutes, she dragged herself out of her stupor and asked Kelley what he had seen. He described the contact carefully.

"You had only been gone from me for a few minutes when the room and the whole environment began to alter its appearance. Subtly, but surely. For one, the window became brighter, and shortly thereafter the light in the room became brighter also. Not by much, but it was significant. These dirty brown walls suddenly appeared clean and white. The stains were gone, and there were square shapes on the walls that might have been paintings of some kind. The floor seemed softer and to have colored patterns upon it, which I took to be carpeting. And there was definitely the faint outline of a bed. A large bed. Up against the wall there." He pointed at the wall opposite the window. Then he lifted his hands in front of him and spread them around as he recalled the changed appearance of the walls, floor, and ceiling.

"And people? Did you see the shapes of people?"

"To the best of my poor sight, there were three spirits in the room—one more than yesterday. They were ranged across the room from us against that far wall. They appeared to be seated, but I could discern no chairs. I formed the impression that there were two men and one woman. I am certain that the two men were the same ones I observed yesterday. I could see them with far greater clarity this time. The third figure had hands clasped against the face until the very last moment of your trance. Then the hands were removed to reveal, I believe, a womanly appearance. At that very same time, looks of amazement transformed the faces of both men. They leaned forward. One of the men pointed toward us. The other man seemed to nod in agreement. Then they both stopped moving and simply stared ahead. Nothing more. Their images soon faded away. I do not understand what happened."

"Very good. Anything more?"

"Their clothes! Like nothing I have seen before. Stretched tightly against their bodies. No ruffs. No collars."

"Yes, yes. Excellent, Edward. You are a fine observer."

"But why did the connection fail so soon after it began? All the images faded to nothing within just a few moments of their appearance."

"I am not sure about that," Catherine replied. "I felt myself dragged out of the zeta state by a force unfamiliar to me. In my own mind, it seemed that the purpose of tonight's experiment had been fulfilled and nothing more was needed. Something of that nature. But I truly don't know why it ended so abruptly."

"Absolutely remarkable, Catherine," said Kelley, staring into her eyes. "Your talent is unheard of in this world. Your powers far exceed those of Jane Oughtred. This contact was much stronger and clearer than was achieved by Jane."

"It is because I know what is happening. And because I have practiced the art many times. My husband and I trained ourselves when we were still young to achieve such contacts with the spirit world. Jane will not know how she does it or why she does it. She will just believe that she has been blessed with second sight from some distant god. She does not know it is an internal power she possesses, and thus she does not know that it can be cultivated."

"So then, are you able to tell me who these three spirits were?"

Catherine Crossly looked away and bit her lower lip. "I suppose it could not hurt to tell you that the large bearded man was the one who gave you the message yesterday. His name is Harry Groh. You will recall my translation of the wording. He was the man who identified himself to you and John Dee. I know him. The other, younger man I do not know at present. Nor the woman you speak of. Perhaps I will learn their identities at a later time."

"And this bearded man. Could he have been the monstrous figure I observed here at Christmastide? He was of similar stature and of animalistic appearance. Only the boar's head was lacking."

"No, that is not possible. He was only here just now because I am here."

"Because of you?" A shiver ran down Edward Kelley's spine. Catherine had never before been in Saxonborough, let alone in this tavern. How could the spirits have known that she would accompany him this night? Were they omniscient? But if they were, why did they need to meet up with her here? They could have communicated with her at Ketteringham Lodge any time in the past fifty years. What was so special about The Plough? Why must The Plough be the confluence of the earthly and unearthly worlds? For such it seemed to be.

"Was it important that *I* was here?" Edward asked.

"No, Edward," Catherine replied with a smile. "They did not know that you would be here. They do not know you at all. And, therefore, you need not be concerned about future contacts by them if that is what you fear. The spirits are only interested in me. But you have played an important role. You are the reason I am here tonight. You brought word to me at Ketteringham Lodge, and I acted on that word. If you had simply shaken your head when you received the Enochian message and returned to London with Dr. Dee, then I would not be here. And this Harry Groh would not have been here. You will never know how important that has been for me."

"So what do you wish to do now? Where do the events of tonight take you the morrow?" asked Edward, both happy and unhappy to hear the mixed message, not knowing whether his chances of obtaining Catherine's hand had increased or decreased since the moment he'd pushed the tavern door aside to let her enter.

"I need to think," she replied. "This business is most convoluted. A false step now could doom me. But it might be that an opportunity has presented itself to me that I never dreamed was possible. Let us go to our separate bedrooms. You may sleep. I need to think on it and decide my course of action. Does that sit well with you, Edward?"

Edward Kelley agreed that it did. He might have wished for some more intimate end to the evening—or that the evening would not end at all—but it was clear there was no other path forward, so he agreed. Before they parted, Edward drew from his pocket a gold necklace. "This is a gift," he said. "A token of my esteem and great affection. As you know, Catherine, it is my wish that we live the rest of our lives together, but I sense now that it may not come to pass. So perhaps this is a parting gift, though I hope not." He pressed it into Catherine's hand.

"Edward, no—" she began.

"Say naught, my dear. Accept it and wear it on occasion and think of me."

She did so, and they stood facing each other for several awkward seconds. The very last thing he wanted was for them to turn and walk off in opposite directions down the hallway, but that was what happened.

Early the next morning, Catherine met up with Edward in the kitchen of The Plough. She had a determined look on her face. And among other things, the look suggested she had slept very little in what remained of the night after their ghostly experience.

"I must ask a very great favor of you, Edward. I have much to do and only a short time in which to do it. I need to borrow Robert and your carriage for two days, three at the most. I no longer have my own carriage and horses. I had to let Nicholas go after Richard died. I did not expect much future travel, if any, after I was left alone at my age. Would it be possible?"

"But…"

"I thought we could convey you to Tuxford, to the mansion of this Thomas de Whitmore, who is the great friend of Thomas Digges. You told me about him, remember?"

"But I do not recall ever meeting the Baron of Tuxford Hall. He does not know me. It would be most impolite."

"But you are both close friends of Thomas Digges. You will have much in common."

"But to arrive unannounced and ask to stay for two days—"

"Possibly three."

"Possibly three. It is unseemly."

"Please, Edward. Do it for my sake. For my life. I shall be eternally grateful."

Backed into a not wholly undesirable corner, Edward agreed. He was acquiring future credits at a prodigious rate.

"And I shall reward Robert handsomely," said Catherine.

Within one hour, Catherine and Edward were on the road, driving westward the short distance from Saxonborough to Tuxford. Edward entered the impressive double doors of Tuxford Hall and returned fifteen minutes later to tell Catherine that de Whitmore had been pleased to offer him the required hospitality. He then took Robert Rimes aside and explained that he should go wherever Catherine directed him and care for and protect her as he would his own mother. When Catherine no longer needed his services, he should return to Tuxford Hall to collect him, and they would return to London. Robert agreed.

"First back to Ketteringham Lodge, Robert," were Catherine's blunt instructions, and after they'd arrived, she said, "You go and hobnob with Alice while I ponder my next steps in the drawing room." Catherine sat in her armchair for half an hour without moving. Then she took a deep breath, rose quickly, and hastened to her dressing table. She grabbed quill and paper and wrote with a steady determination in a clear hand for another hour. She sealed her words in three separate letters, just as she had with the correspondence for the Roanoke luminaries. However, these three letters she did not give to Alice to deliver. These letters she placed in her dresser drawer. She then proceeded to her bedroom and pulled all the jewelry and coins and other small valuables out of their respective hideaways and placed them in a purse, which she hid inside her dress. Finally, she opened the doors of her wardrobe and scrabbled about in the bottom of it for an old bag of clothes, which she stuffed into a handbag. She stepped back, surveyed the room one last time, and hurried down to the kitchen. There she found Alice and Robert huddled together in what seemed like an intimate conversation.

"Robert, please ready the horses and carriage. We will leave shortly."

When he'd left the room, she turned to Alice. She did not know how to begin to speak the words that were necessary. Her eyes were watering well before her mouth could open.

"Alice," she said at last, "Alice, I needs must tell you something of great import—not just for me but for you also."

"Madam?" said Alice, her voice quivering.

"Where I am about to go and what I am about to do places me in some danger. There is a possibility that something may happen to me. Indeed, I may not return. If I am not back here in three days, you must go into my dressing room and open the drawer in the dressing table. There you will find three sealed letters. One is addressed to you, and you may open that one first. There are instructions for you within the letter that will guarantee your comfort for many years to come. The second is for my company of lawyers, Messrs. Crouch and Williamson. Please to deliver it to them promptly. The third letter is for Edward Kelley. Try your best to put it into his hands. He may come here anyway soon enough." She hesitated. "And please to take care of my beagles."

By this time, Alice had a hand pressed against her mouth and was sobbing. She could not speak. Catherine walked over to her and hugged her.

"Thank you for everything, Alice. No servant in this land has been as good as you have over as many years. And you have taken better care of me since Richard died than I could have hoped for. You and your poor late mother, Joan, were loaned to Ketteringham Lodge by the deity, I am certain of it. Rest assured that if I do not return, you are taken care of. The letter says as much." Catherine pushed Alice away to arm's length and smiled at her. "But it all may be for nothing, my dear. Perchance Robert and I will be back here the day after tomorrow. Who can know the will of the Fates."

Still Alice could not respond and could only reach out and wrap her arms tight around Catherine's waist. Catherine kissed the top of Alice's head and carefully disentangled her arms just as Robert returned to the kitchen. Catherine went back upstairs to comb her hair and calm herself and ready herself. When she heard Robert's halloo from the front of the house, she went downstairs, gathered up her bag of old clothes from beside the doorway, and went over to join him by the carriage.

"Saxonborough again, madam?"

"No. Not this time, Robert. Take me to Hoyland Church, if you please. You know it—you drove Edward there many times over the years."

"I do know it, madam. And I know the lanes that lead to it. It will take us perhaps thirty minutes. Forty-five at the most."

"Very good."

Robert hesitated, then plucked up enough courage to ask, "Madam, if I might be so bold, can I ask you about Alice? She seemed very distressed in the kitchen just now. She could not say why, but I am worried. She seemed very afraid of something. Is she to be sacked?"

"No, Robert," answered Catherine. "Actually, I think she is more worried about me than herself. I will always take care of Alice. Do not doubt that. She is precious to me."

Robert reddened and looked down at the ground. "To me also," he said.

Chapter 18

Hoyland Church
February 1588

ROBERT'S CARRIAGE CAME TO A halt outside Hoyland Church just before lunchtime. Catherine walked up the path through the churchyard and around to the vestry, suppressing bitter memories of the last time she'd been there. She found the vicar at his desk reading the Bible and scribbling notes for a sermon on a piece of vellum. He put the Bible down when he saw her through the window, stood up, and walked over to greet her by the door. They knew each other, but not well. It had been five months since he'd officiated at the funeral of her husband. Catherine had not been to church since then and had only gone infrequently before that.

"Mrs. Crossly," he said as she entered. "I am honored to see you again. You are most welcome at our church. You and your husband always were welcome. I grieve for his passing. But this is a surprise. What brings you here on this cold day?"

"Reverend Massey. A pleasure to see you this morning. I needs must speak with you on a matter that is of importance to me—and would have been to my husband. If your time permits."

"Of course it does. Please to come in and rest yourself."

"I'm afraid I have little time to dally here today, so I will come straight to the point. I wish to make a very unusual request of you. One might almost call it a...a proposed accord...a pact."

"A pact? All right. Please proceed."

"You know, of course, that my husband Richard spent a good deal of money to have a sarcophagus built and carved so that he and

I might be buried side by side in your church. We both wished it. And it was a fine piece of work done by the Hoyland stonemason."

"It was. And Richard was interred in it last September. The sarcophagus rests in that niche in the east wall of the church. It looks magnificent. Yes."

"It is completely finished except for the inscription that circumscribes the top of it. It has Richard's name and his date of death, and it has my name. A space has been left for my date of death to be added in due course."

"Yes. That is customary practice for those of distinction who die in the parish."

"Well, therein lies the problem. I plan to leave Lincolnshire soon. And I do not think I shall return. I shall likely die in a distant place…"

"Madam, I am sorry to hear this. Is there some mischief afoot that could be averted?"

"Nay, sir, nothing of that kind. It is my own undertaking. But I would not wish to leave the sarcophagus with no one by Richard's side and carved such as it is. It would appear that I forsook Richard upon his death. He would not like it, and the parishioners would not approve. And, therefore, I would not like it either. In addition, I do not like the idea of Richard spending eternity all alone inside that stony prison. A difficulty all round, one might say."

"What do you suggest? To build another tomb for Richard alone?"

"No, that would not do. Future generations must know that we were a happily married couple, devoted to each other in life and in death. For that we surely were and will be. Insisting on resting in peace together. The sarcophagus must remain as it is."

"And so?"

"Let me ask you a question, vicar. What happens to suicides in this parish?"

"Suicides, madam? Well, we very rarely have them. I can recall only two in the decade I have been here. It is a blasphemy to take one's own life, as you perhaps know. Suicides may not be buried in consecrated ground. Our community has the same custom as all in this county. If the coroner records a verdict of *felo de se*, then the parishioners carry the body to a crossroads about a mile from here. Our sexton digs a hole there, and the body is placed in it. A stake is driven through the heart to peg the corpse in place."

"Truthfully? I did not know that. Why thus?"

"You do not know? Everyone in the village knows that the ghost of a suicide will return to haunt their home. It is common knowledge. The body must be buried at a crossroads to misdirect the spirit, and the stake may prevent the spirit from rising at all."

"That is a shocking custom."

The vicar held his palms out in front of him and shrugged his shoulders. "Perhaps it is. But suicide is a shocking crime against God, he who most generously vouchsafed life to us all."

"And what about people who are not Christian? What happens when they die?"

"Not Christian? I do not think we have ever had such a person die in Hoyland. We may squabble among the Catholics and those of the various Protestant persuasions, but they are all Christian."

"But if such a one *should* die here?"

"I do not know. The bishop would decide. But there could be no burial in this churchyard."

"I see. So that brings me to the first part of my offer. Failing the possibility of the most desperate unfortunates among us being interred within these walls, I would wish that a poor old woman who has recently passed away be interred alongside my husband and *her* date of death carved into the inscription. I am thinking of someone who lived alone, had no relatives to bury her, and was supported by the parish. A respectable woman but someone destined for a pauper's grave. I wish that her interment be elevated to a safe and secure position within these church walls. This is what I wish. And my husband would wish it too. What say you?"

"I have never heard of such a thing. I do not think I could permit it. It sounds to be sacrilegious, though I cannot see exactly how at this moment."

"In return for this consideration, I will donate one half of my estate to this church."

"Truly, madam?" The vicar was taken aback. "But Ketteringham Lodge is a valuable property. The proceeds from its sale would dwarf the income of our tiny, impoverished church."

"I have committed one half of my estate to the support of John White's planned return to the Roanoke colony. And I have also granted some allocation for the support of my servant Alice. The remainder will come to Hoyland Church. And it will come quite soon, I expect—if you will grant me the favor I ask. I have so informed my lawyers, Crouch and Williamson."

The vicar stood up and walked to the far wall of the vestry, rubbing his brow.

"The interment of this old woman in my place will and must remain a secret," Catherine emphasized. "Only you and I will know of it. And probably your sexton, I suppose."

The vicar nodded and turned to face her.

"Very well, Mrs. Crossly. Your offer is too generous to be declined. When the time is appropriate on your side, the funds may be transferred to support my parish in perpetuity. And as soon as the funds are received, I will begin to search for an appropriate woman, recently deceased, to take your intended place alongside Richard. I will only inter a woman of impeccable moral virtue and kindly disposition who has found herself unfortunate and in solitary old age at the time of her death. And I pledge that it will be our secret alone. God may hold it a sin, but he should understand that I cannot think how it is one."

"Many thanks. It is a burden lifted from my shoulders. And we can both pray that the Lord will look kindly on our small and well-intentioned deception. And from the celestial realm, Richard thanks you also."

They shook hands on the deal, and Catherine Crossly left the vestry and returned to Robert and the waiting carriage. Before she climbed inside, she instructed Robert to head for Lincoln. "Take us to the Spread Eagle. You know it well, and you are acquainted with the staff thereof. We will partake of a late lunch there. Then I want you to discover from the landlord the name of the finest apothecary in Lincoln. Depending on where his shop is located in the city, we will walk or drive there this afternoon in order that I may purchase some special herbs and tinctures."

"Very good, madam."

In the late afternoon, Catherine entered the apothecary's shop on Silver Street that had been prescribed by the landlord of the Spread Eagle. A bald, middle-aged man in a long apron stood at the counter. He was grinding pestle against mortar but set them aside and wiped his hands on his apron as Catherine approached. "Madam?" he asked.

"Sir, I am in search of certain herbal potions or similar tinctures."

"Yes. We have a wide variety," he said, sweeping his arm around the room. "What is the ailment?"

"Hmm. It is not an ailment as such. I am searching for a potion that can be used to enhance the so-called second sight."

"You mean something that mystics and their kind might imbibe before a séance or some visionary practice? The reading of a crystal perhaps?"

"Precisely. Has such a request ever been made to you before?"

"It has. There are two ladies living in Bailgate, up by the cathedral, who come here regular before conducting their séances. There seems to be a demand for communing with spirits among the elderly and prosperous ladies who live uphill. Perhaps they desire to learn how they can transport their wealth up to heaven upon their death." He chuckled but then quickly stopped.

"And what do these ladies purchase?"

"We have several herbs that are believed to hold the properties you require. I have heard that the burning of gum mastic in the room enhances clairvoyance and, shall we say, the manifestation of spiritual entities. He turned and pulled a blue bottle off a shelf and showed it to her. It had the words *Pistacia lentiscus* emblazoned on it.

"Burning something might not be appropriate for my purpose," said Catherine thoughtfully. "Anything else?"

"Well, the two ladies I mentioned always purchase meadowsweet from me. It is known as bridewort by the countryfolk. They say its scent has the power to grant second sight and induce the ability to converse with fairies. Mugwort also. We call that *Artemisia vulgaris.*

Mugwort is said to be remarkable for divination. It is said to open the third eye. It may be drunk as a simple infusion."

"Excellent. And do you perchance have anoxyseriphin?" A blank look came over the apothecary's face, and Catherine laughed. "My little joke, sir. There's no such thing. Please give me small quantities of meadowsweet and mugwort, if you would be so kind."

"Very well. I shall grind them in preparation for use. One moment."

The apothecary carried two bottles into a back room and returned with two well-sealed paper sachets, which he handed to Catherine over the counter.

"Do not overuse them. I am told they are powerful."

"I shall be careful. How much do I owe you?"

"Shall we say, a florin each?"

"Somewhat costly, but I will take them."

Catherine reached into her purse for coins and paid the man. Before leaving the shop, she said to the apothecary, "Do you know, is there a reputable jeweler's shop nearby?"

"There is, as a matter of fact. Three doors down on the left. Morrisons. Just about the best in the city, they tell me."

"Many thanks." Catherine stored the information away and rejoined Robert on the street. "Time marches on, Robert, and I am beginning to tire. What say we return to the Spread Eagle for the night and then head to Saxonborough the morrow?"

"As you wish."

Catherine and Robert continued their ride through Lincolnshire apace, arriving on the outskirts of Saxonborough by midmorning of the following day.

"The Plough again?" asked Robert.

"Not yet, Robert. First, I wish to visit the home of Jane Oughtred. Ask a villager for directions."

That was quickly accomplished, and soon Catherine was knocking on the door of a small farmhouse, and two women were answering it.

"Is one of you good ladies Jane Oughtred?" asked Catherine.

The younger of the two women raised her hand and said, "I am Jane. This is my mother."

"My name is Catherine Crossly. I am from Ketteringham Lodge to the south of Lincoln. I am a close friend of Mr. Edward Kelley. You know him, Jane. You helped him conjure up the spirits at The Plough with Dr. Dee just a day or two ago and before that at Christmastime."

Jane nodded and relaxed somewhat.

"I wish to do the same thing as you did with Mr. Kelley, Jane, and I need your help. Actually, I also have the power of second sight. Just as you do. We are two peas in a pod in that regard. But there must be two masters of the scrying art for what I intend to do. So I am asking if you would be willing and able to come join me this evening."

Jane seemed doubtful and looked at her mother, who spoke up sternly.

"Jane's father and I are not at all persuaded that paddling in spiritual pools is appropriate for a young woman like our Jane. Not only for her own health and safety, you understand. We are also concerned that rumors of such…immersions…will lessen her chances of a match. No man will tie himself to a witch."

"No. That I can understand. But it is nothing of that nature, truly. Summoning spirits is an honorable activity. Mr. Kelley is certain that the spirits are, in fact, angels. It is akin to praying to our Lord. As I understand it, Jane has no such qualms."

"She may not. That is all by the by. Cherub or imp, the villagers know not which."

"Mother!" said Jane, offended.

Catherine pressed her case from a new angle. "Is Jane's father at home at present?"

"He is not," Jane's mother replied. "He is at Gainsborough. He is at an auction of farming equipment. He will not return until the morrow."

"That is unfortunate. I was going to offer him three gold sovereigns in return for allowing Jane to accompany me this evening."

"Three pounds?" Jane's mother was astonished. "You are a wealthy woman?"

"I own Ketteringham Lodge, as I said. It is a sizeable estate. The funds are merely an act of generosity on my part, you understand. I do not imply that I am purchasing Jane's services."

The offer of money changed the direction of the conversation abruptly, and all was quickly agreed. Jane Oughtred went inside to dress appropriately, while Catherine counted out three sovereigns into her mother's hand. Soon Jane joined Catherine in the carriage for the short ride to The Plough. Along the way Catherine laid out specific instructions for Jane. To do so, she cast her mind back fifty years to the events at Hoyland Church.

"Tonight you must do just as I now prescribe. If you follow my wording, you will come to no harm. All I ask is that you sit in the corner of the room and do exactly as you have done before for Mr. Kelley and before that for Mr. Stringfellow. But you must do it even better than those other times. Concentration is the key. There will first be an infusion to drink. I do not know how it will taste, but the portion will be small enough to down in one swallow. It will help with the coming of the second sight. I do not think our collaboration will last very long. Certainly not for the hours that you had to sit with Mr. Kelley. I know how to accomplish the raising of the spirits without great delay. Our previous session lasted but a quarter of an hour.

"The most important thing is that you remain seated no matter what you should see or hear in the room. It is possible that strange scenes will be summoned up. Of their nature I know not. But I have seen it happen before. If you see such strangeness, do not act upon it. Do not rush out of your seat to try to save anyone who is apparently in distress, whether it be me or some other person. It is pure imagery. But they that dash into the fire will be burned. Do you understand?"

Jane nodded but asked, "This fire will not spread into the corner of the room where I shall be seated?"

"It will not. Its extent will be but a yard or two."

Jane nodded again.

"You will be safe if you remain in your chair. And I will stay safe in the opposite corner. However, eventually, I may approach the fire. Or I may not. I am not sure how things will proceed. I may even jump into the flames. If I do so, again, do not be afeared. The fire will burn itself out in no time." She paused to make sure that Jane truly understood her analogy. "It is not *real* fire of which I speak, you understand, just a violent conflagration of spiritual energy. You will be safe if you stay in your chair, Jane. Remember that. When the fire dies out, all will be over and done. You will know when. Then you will be free to go."

"It seems that you are not certain what will happen to you."

"I am not, my dear. My goal is clear, but the path to reach it is not."

Chapter 19

Saxonborough
February 1588

SILENCE.

Silence. Rising up from the marshland like honey, thick and sweet and sickly. Dripping out of the clouds and oozing across a thousand cornfields. Pinning flocks of geese down on the water and hushing them. Muffling moorhens. Pinching the noses of exhausted laborers snoring in their beds. Assembling and mixing all its varied tones of emptiness. Settling over a prone, splayed village...a recumbent tavern. Enfolding, at its center, a small square wooden room. Flowing there down the midnight ganglia. Converging on the two cities of jewels: Manipura, Manipura.

Darkness.

Darkness. Slinking from behind the moon indecently. Seeping through the branches of apple trees, sliding gently down the Ketteringham alder trees. Suffocating the reflected moonlight on ponds. Greeting the upwelling silence like a long-lost sister, embracing her. Damping the candles in cottage windows, the lanterns above tavern doors. Smothering the starlight on silverware in quiet kitchens. Creeping under the church door and seeking out, slithering into, the cold stone tombs of Richard Crossly and Abbot Gervase. Permeating wood, flesh, water, air. Stretched tight over and under and throughout everything. Violating the prone, splayed village.

Time.

And time. Not absent, but its presence concealed behind the silence and beneath the darkness. Presumed to be crawling on hands and knees down the village street. Assumed to be skulking behind all those old, stained, plaster walls. Tiptoeing across the roofs of pigsties. Sneaking ever onward in the bedrooms of worn-out skivvies. Remorselessly aging the helpless village, stealing youth and childhood unnoticed. And yet within the small square wooden room, frozen. Imprisoned in a pulsating latticework, stretched tight around it on all sides. Puzzled. Going nowhere.

The scent of meadowsweet.

The taste of mugwort.

Consciousness reverberating on the edge of helplessness. Juddering back and forth. Searching across the years. Sifting pasts and futures. Ferreting through the crumbled dust and the yet unassembled crumbs of other physical worlds. Clawing for a foothold in the mental constructs of others. Did eyes have corners? Could they see around flattened palms? Was anything different beyond the palms? No, not yet. Nothing but silence, darkness, frozen time.

Stasis.

Stasis. Slowly polishing away the sensation of touch. Insinuating itself between inanimate surface and nerve ending. Contact rolled thinly to nothing across the bedroom floor. Disassembled. Dissembled. Was it touch or not touch? Being touched or not being touched? And slowly, then, water. Squeezed from the clouds and the mist. Raised up out of the marshlands. Regurgitating memories of a familiar pond. A familiar tank. Filling inward through ceiling, wall, floor. Rendering muscle to flesh, flesh to fluid. Lifting feet and legs as floating debris. Returning each jewel to her origins. Manipura, Manipura. A grandfather's pond. A professor's tank. Floating. Horizontal. No longer touching the physical world. Every sensation polished away. From the skin, from the hair, from the nails. From the mind.

Then…a barely perceptible change. A beginning. Delicate candlelight streaming up the walls. Dripping upward and out across the roof beams. Filtering into wormy crevices. Celestial light responding. Peering in at the windows. Pressing down on the roof. Tinkling and flickering like molecular ornaments on a blank, black tree. Slowly, some delicate shades of stained plaster demarcating the boundaries of the small square wooden room. A three-dimensional backwash of careless artistry. Existence not entirely muted, not quite invisible, slowly aware of time.

Out of those corners of those eyes, then, a faint tableaux. A woman floating above a bed. Arms outstretched. Leonardo's Vitruvian Woman. Face creased in agony. Lights and sparks and fluttering stars as frame. Creeping along every surface. Around the woman's arms and shoulders. The smell of electricity. The taste of charred wood. A man standing in front of her. The tableaux fading into nothingness.

Closing those eyes. Falling forward onto the bed of nightmare. Praying to her husband. Clenching her teeth. Sinking back into the tank. Pressing ever onward with all her strength. Remembering her lover's guidance. Clutching his love and pressing onward. Not moving a muscle. Thinking only *2019…2019…2019*. Ever onward. Back into…

Silence.

Darkness.

Timelessness.

A different bed, then. Bright, shining walls. Light no longer pinpricks but smooth folds of whiteness all around her. A deep breath. Turning. Eyes fluttering. Turning.

Jane Oughtred doubled over in a chair with her head tilted backward and her arms limply by her side. Time slowly beginning to rise up and stretch and drag its feet once more across the cobblestones outside the window. Silence sighing and soughing and moving on. Darkness sensing the low orange sun and bidding farewell. Jane roused by sounds she knew well. The clattering of irons against the fireplace of the great room beneath her feet. A raking of ashes. A brush sweeping soot off the walls of the chimney. Rising out of the chair and looking around. Finding her way to the door and tiptoeing downstairs. Both hands on the rails. Bewildered. A maid on her hands and knees in front of the grate, turning, surprised to see a woman at the foot of the stairs.

"What time is it?" Jane Oughtred asked.

"I don't know," the maid replied. "Dawn at the threshold."

"Is Mr. Stringfellow up?"

"He's in the kitchen brewing tea. Have you been here all night?"

"Yes."

Jane walked into the kitchen.

"Good morning, Jane," said Samuel Stringfellow cheerily. "You're up with the lark today. How is Mrs. Crossly?"

"I don't know. Is she down here?"

"What? No. Why should she be? Wasn't she upstairs with you?"

"No. I fell asleep. When I woke up just now, she was gone. Did she leave?"

"I shouldn't think so. Not this early. I haven't seen Robert Rimes yet either. She couldn't leave without him."

"Oh, that's right. He's going to drive her home first thing this morning and then run over to Tuxford and collect Mr. Kelley. I remember now. Let me go and see if he's in his room."

"I'm sure he is. The carriage is still in the back. And I just now went to check on the horses. They're still there. Go roust Mr. Rimes." Samuel Stringfellow set the kettle back down on the hob, concern beginning to replace cheeriness.

Jane lit a candle, went upstairs, and knocked on Robert's bedroom door. She had to do it three times before Robert's sleepy frame appeared in the doorway, clad in a rumpled nightgown, hair scattered to the four winds.

"Jane?" he asked.

"Have you seen Mrs. Crossly this morning?"

"No. You just woke me up. Why?"

"We're not sure where she is. We were in the front bedroom all night. I fell asleep at some unknown hour. And when I awoke, she was gone. Neither Mr. Stringfellow nor the maid in the great room have seen her."

"Well, nor have I. Let me get dressed and come down."

This time Jane hurried downstairs, trying hard to swallow her sobbing. She confronted Mr. Stringfellow. "No, sir," she said anxiously. "Robert just woke up. He hasn't seen her."

"Well, she can't have gone out walking before the dawn. Only a local would do that. Or a fool. Are you sure and certain she's not in the room? Or in one of the other rooms? You've no idea where she could have gone?"

"As Lord Jesus is my witness, I don't," she said, her voice now punctuated with heavy sobs. "But I just now remembered something from last night. At the time I thought it was a dream, but now I'm not so sure. There was blood on the floor. I had my head down on my knees, and I saw it spreading across the floor toward my feet. Blood. You'd better go up there, sir. Go right away. I can't do it. I can't go in that room again."

"Oh, good God, Jane. You should have mentioned this when first you came down."

"I'm sorry, sir. I didn't recall it until this moment. And when you go up there, sir, you'd better take a pail of water and a mop. I'm sorely afraid there's blood on the floorboards. And perhaps Mrs. Crossly's dead body in a corner of the room for all I know." Jane burst into tears. "I can't stay here any longer, Mr. Stringfellow! I must away home. And I can't work here never no more! I fear the curse of that room has taken a hold of me. Please forgive me!"

She rushed out the door into the first light of day and ran down the road.

Samuel Stringfellow went into the kitchen, filled a pail with water, grabbed mop and rags, and with much trepidation climbed the stairs. At the top, he bumped into Robert Rimes coming out of his bedroom.

"What in heaven's name is going on?" asked Robert. "All this commotion so early in the day. Have the skies opened?"

"I don't know. We can't seem to locate Mrs. Crossly. She appears to have vanished."

"But I'm supposed to take her back to Ketteringham Lodge this morning. And then go on to Tuxford. What do you mean she's vanished?"

"Jane is afraid that something frightful happened in the haunted bedroom last night. She has already run on home. I have to see what is in there. Please to come in with me, Robert, for I am most trepidatious."

"All right. You go first. I'll be right behind you."

The landlord carefully opened the door and stepped inside. Robert followed and halted beside him. They stared around the room, softly lit now by the dawn light seeping through the window. The floor was clean. The room was empty.

Chapter 20

Saxonborough
April 2019

A different bed, then. Bright, shining walls. Light no longer pinpricks but smooth folds of whiteness all around her. A deep breath. Turning. Eyes fluttering. Turning. Eyes flashing open.

It took her a couple of minutes to fully wake up and realize that she was lying on the bed of the guestroom above the inn. To her great relief, there was no one alongside her in the bed nor anyone seated in the chair in the corner of the room. The clock radio on the bedside table informed her that it was 5:00 a.m., but she had no idea what the day was or the month or the year. She did know, however, that she had no time to waste. She had just half a day to locate her boss and contrive to bring him to this same bedroom, otherwise… She dreaded to think what that otherwise might be. She jumped out of bed.

She grabbed the bag she'd brought with her and rummaged through it. She undressed and put on her old moth-eaten blue jeans and jacket. She stuffed the clothes she'd arrived in into the same bag and hid it under the bed. She picked up the purse containing the jewelry and coins and slipped it into the pocket of her jacket. She checked herself in the mirror. Good enough. Everything was dark and quiet as she crept downstairs. And to her great surprise, downstairs was a coffee shop, not a pub.

As if placed there by the Almighty, two courtesy computers stood on a table in the corridor leading from the stairs to the front desk. She switched one on and discovered that it was Wednesday, April 10,

2019. She fist-pumped the air. She googled her boss's name. He was definitely somewhere in the country, but where? She found him and learned of the ceremony that was to take place in London that very afternoon. At that point she knew how to locate him and what she must do beforehand. There seemed to be just enough time to accomplish everything, though she regretted that she'd not waited one more day before making the trip up to Saxonborough. Nevertheless, in her heart she already felt she was halfway home. She switched on a light and waited for someone to arrive. One by one, the staff turned up for work, stared over at her, and disappeared into the back room. The manager then came out of the back room and took his place behind the front desk. She walked over to him.

"I wonder if you could help me," she asked him. "My name is Karen Butler. I need to get to Lincoln this morning. As quickly as possible. It's important. How can I do that?"

"Well, there's a bus, madam. Every hour on the hour, starting at seven o'clock. It takes about forty minutes. A couple of stops along the way unfortunately."

Karen grimaced.

"But if it's very important, I might be able arrange a ride for you with my daughter. She'll be leaving the village in about half an hour and going straight there. She works in the Guildhall."

"Oh, that would be awesome," Karen responded with obvious signs of relief. "I would much appreciate it."

"Umm…you're not a guest here, are you." It was a statement, not a question.

"No, not yet. I'm scouting the village out for a friend of mine. We plan to stay here later in the week. Which brings me to my second favor. Could you reserve both of your upstairs rooms for us for, let's say, three nights, Thursday through Saturday?"

"Certainly. We don't have many guests here, to be truthful. Nobody at all, actually, at the moment. We're a little bit out of the way unfortunately. We mostly make our money from locals in the coffee shop. What name should I put it under?" He opened the register and grabbed a pen. When Karen didn't immediately respond, he looked up at her.

"Yes…please make the reservation for a Mr. Harry Groh and friend," said Karen. "That's G-R-O-H. Both rooms. But the problem is, I don't have a credit card to give you."

"No credit card?"

"I'm afraid not. Mr. Groh has mine. And he's in London at the moment. There was a mix-up when we parted earlier in the week." She pretended to look embarrassed, while the manager looked disconcerted. But with a little soft soap, she managed to persuade him to accept an unsecured reservation. It was not like there was competition for the rooms.

"Thank you so much," said Karen. "Mr. Groh will be here tomorrow. I'll be back on Saturday and make everything good. Shall I sit over here and wait for your daughter?"

The manager nodded, and by the time the shops were opening up in Lincoln, Karen was waiting under the Stonebow. She walked over to Silver Street and to her surprise found that the jeweler's shop she'd seen before was still there. It was a totally new building, of course, with a totally new name, *Gems Tones*, but it was exactly what she was looking for. She went inside and showed the owner the gold Tudor bracelet she wanted to sell. He was just a tiny bit suspicious, mainly because of her worn-out clothing, but he thought, on balance, she seemed honest. She asked for one thousand pounds cash. He could tell at once that the bracelet was worth upward of three thousand, so he could not refuse. He went and got the money from a safe in the back room. Karen pocketed the money and walked quickly into a nearby department store and bought some new clothes. She changed in a public restroom. Then she hurried to the railway station and caught the first train to London. By lunchtime, she'd arrived at King's Cross Station and eaten a sandwich. From there she took the short walk to the British Museum.

Chapter 21

The English Channel
May 1588

THE OMENS WERE NOT GOOD. It had been reported in early April that a battalion of fleas had mustered on a window of one of the queen's residences, and thirty porpoises had swum up the Thames to wait upon Her Majesty's pleasure. A sense of foreboding had quickly spread through the royal household. The shadow of King Philip lurked in every corner. The threat of invasion had escalated on April 25 when Pope Sixtus blessed the banner of the Armada in Lisbon Cathedral upon its presentation by the commander of the Spanish forces, the Duke of Medina Sidonia. The banner proclaimed, *"Exurge Domine et vindica causam Tuam!"* Arise, O Lord, and vindicate thy cause!

It was all getting very serious. Walsingham's spies in Portugal had lost count of the number of galleons, galleys, galleasses, carracks, and hulks anchored in the Port of Lisbon. The Privy Council, acting on the concerns of Queen Elizabeth, had already issued a general stay on shipping in the waters around Britain. How were John Dee and Edward Kelley to make their way to the Continent? Was it even safe to do so? Kelley had received a response to his missive to Olbracht Laski. He and Dee would be most welcome at the court of King Stefan. No extravagant promises were made except that they could live at court and work with Polish alchemists to contrive a method to manufacture gold. Their living expenses would be paid. If all went well, riches beyond their wildest dreams would be showered upon their heads. April in Krakow was suggested. Emperor Rudolf offered them similar terms in Prague for a later date.

But as with many things in those troubled times, delay compounded delay. April came and went. In the end, Thomas Digges interceded on their behalf. Unbeknownst to the general population, Walsingham's men had been negotiating a peace treaty with Spain. Talks were ongoing with the Duke of Parma in the Spanish Netherlands, where thirty thousand troops were massing with the intention of being collected by the Armada and deposited on English soil. Valentine Dale, jurist and diplomat, had been selected to lead the English side of the treaty negotiations, and he had been in London in early May to report back on the latest Spanish demands and to receive instructions from the English court. He was soon to return to finalize negotiations.

When Thomas Digges heard of this, he approached Lord Burghley and suggested that Dee and Kelley might be permitted to accompany Dale across the Channel under the protection of the royal ensign. Burghley talked to Walsingham, and in light of Dee's favored standing with Her Majesty, approval was granted. Thus, on May 22, Dee and Kelley boarded a three-masted royal pinnace for the short trip across the Channel. The wind was favorable but strong, and there was a chop in the water. Halfway there, Dee and Kelley found themselves seated at the long table in the captain's quarters, while the captain and Dale pored over nautical charts by the stern window.

"Tell me again what happened to Catherine Crossly," Dee asked of Kelley.

"It is a complete mystery, John. The first news of it fell from the mouth of my coachman, Robert Rimes. He arrived at Tuxford Hall posthaste after Catherine and Jane Oughtred had held their séance in the middle of the night. He would not stop chattering. It seems that Jane fell asleep, and when she awoke, Catherine was gone. Vanished. *Disparoo*, as the French would say."

"Surely she was hiding in the tavern. Resting in another room. Perhaps Jane snored."

"Robert said not. He and Mr. Stringfellow looked everywhere. Nary a trace of her."

"She cannot have walked off into the night."

"No. They don't believe so. That would have been sheer folly. They thought it most likely that Catherine had prearranged to be picked up by a different carriage in the early hours. And had departed without a word to anyone. Though why she would decline to tell anyone about her plans, we cannot imagine. Poor Robert was beside himself, as he'd promised me that he would take good care of Catherine and ensure that she came to no harm. He felt an abject failure."

"But what would make her leave like that?"

"I cannot imagine. I am so worried for her, John. Robert said that Jane Oughtred thought she'd seen blood on the bedroom floor. Perhaps Catherine had been injured. But when Stringfellow entered the room a short while later, there was no blood anywhere. Not spot nor smear."

"A dream, then? Jane had dreamed it?"

"I pray it was only that."

"And afterward? You said something about letters?"

"Yes. There were three letters. Written by Catherine before she left Ketteringham Lodge. One for her maidservant Alice, one for me, one for her lawyers. In the event she did not return."

"You have seen the letter she wrote to you?"

"Robert mentioned the existence of these letters when first he arrived at Tuxford. And when nothing had been heard from Catherine for several weeks, I dispatched Robert to Ketteringham Lodge to collect the letter that was addressed to me. He found the grounds much deteriorated—a fallen tree across the driveway, ivy grown wild above the doorway, a dead fox—and he said that Alice was in a dreadful state. She was looking after the place as well as she could, but the lawyers had already put it up for sale, and she expected to be asked to leave any day. I wish I could buy the lovely place myself, but upon reflection I realized that without Catherine by my side, it would quickly lose its luster.

"At that point, Robert confessed to me that he and Alice were sweet on each other and wished to marry. Where he'd failed with Catherine, he was committed to taking care of Alice. He could not bear to see her suffer the way she was—all alone in that great mansion.

With all of the responsibility. So I'm trying to arrange employment for the two of them elsewhere. Perhaps with Sir Francis Willoughby at Wollaton Hall. We'll see."

A steward entered the room and placed two cups on the table between them. They stared into the oily black liquid and sniffed it. "What on earth is this?" Dee asked.

"Mocha," the waiter replied. They stared up at him. "Some call it *coffee*."

"Captain?" said Dee, looking over at the ship's captain. "Are we supposed to drink it or rub it in our hair to become young again?"

The captain looked up from the charts, laughing. "Why, drink it, sirs! It is tasty and of high medicinal ranking for ailments of the stomach. So they say. It comes from a bush called the *bunnu*. We discovered it in the Port of Trieste last summer. They import it from the Horn of Africa. We traded a sack of our best Darjeeling tea for a parcel of it. Try it!" They each took a sip, and each screwed up their face. They set their cups back down on the table in unison.

"S'truth!" Dee exclaimed. "Medicine indeed! It should be taken by the spoonful while pinching the nose with thumb and forefinger. It will never take hold as a beverage."

The captain and Valentine Dale both chuckled. "Well, they seem to like it in Italy. Bring them ale," the captain instructed the steward.

Dee resumed his interrogation of Kelley. "So tell me what Catherine said in her letter to you—not the intimate parts, if there were any."

"There were none," Kelley replied. "It was all very matter-of-fact. She said things like, 'I do not belong in this time and place' and 'You must erase me from your thoughts.' She instructed me to *'repair the broken threads in my family.'* I was overcome with sadness to read it. To be cast aside in such a severe, impersonal way. For seven days I could do nothing, John. Speak to no one, read no book, do no work. I barely slept. I walked the streets of London. I sat and cried in taverns. I was especially heartbroken by her parting words, 'I shall never return.'"

"Poor Edward. That must have been very hard to take. Was there no clue at all as to where she might have gone?"

"None. Except for one thing. She said something that I already knew from our earlier conversations. Near to the end of the letter were the words, 'My heart beats in the New World.'"

"What do you think she meant by that?"

"I cannot say. She always had such a great interest in John White's colony. You know that. She supported their voyage with generosity. And when I reported on our discovery of the word *America* in the Enochian call at Saxonborough, it immediately energized her and made her desperate to come to The Plough with me. She wanted to converse about it with the angels. In some way, therefore, I believe I am responsible for her disappearance. If she had never gone to Saxonborough, she would never have disappeared therefrom."

Valentine Dale looked up from the charts this time. "Did I hear you mention John White?"

"Yes," Kelley responded. "He that founded the Roanoke colony."

"I am aware. Did you know that he has returned to America?"

Kelley sat bolt upright, shocked.

"Returned?" he exclaimed.

"Raleigh told me at court last week. He recounted that John White had left Bideford Bar about a month ago. In a bark called the *Brave* and a pinnace called the *Roe*, laden with provisions for the colony. Victuals, grain, garments, and the like. And ten seedsmen. Initially, Sir Richard Grenville had assembled a fleet of eight vessels for him. They were all laden with supplies and waiting at anchor at Bideford in late March for a fair wind. But then the Privy Council recalled six of the vessels as being required to join the fleet gathering to face the Spanish Armada. The *Brave* and the *Roe* were considered too small to be of any value in war, and so Sir Francis Drake released them to go relieve the settlers that had wintered at Roanoke. Thus, John White is on his way. He has probably left the Bristol Channel by now."

"He will fail," the captain said bluntly, joining the conversation. "A bark and a pinnace cannot cross the Atlantic, believe me. They cannot withstand the ocean swell…those late winter storms. White will either be blown back home or float face down on the water with seaweed in his hair." He then pointed a finger at Dee and Kelley as another possible fate occurred to him. "Or…or French pirates will capture them. Those villains cruise our western and southern shores freely now that their Spanish allies harass our navy. Nay, there is little chance that the *Brave* and the *Roe* can reach the Americas."

"Piracy, you say?"

"Oh, indeed, sir. It is rampant now. Instead of maintaining order and prosperity on the high seas, the English and Spanish navies both have their blinkers on and their noses pressed onto sword-sharpening grindstones. They have no time for knockabouts. But do not worry, sirs, our little ship is protected by the queen's ensign, so its passage to Calais is safeguarded. Probably."

Kelley stood up instantly, pushing his chair to the floor behind him in the process.

"Do you not see it?" he asked Dee. "Catherine has gone with John White! She made prior arrangements for a carriage to collect her from Saxonborough and deliver her to Devon. She is on one of his boats at this very moment! Even as we speak! It makes perfect sense. That is why she told me in her letter that her heart beats in the New World. She has sailed to it. Oh, God speed, my love! God speed!"

Chapter 22

Saxonborough
April 2019

HARRY, TOM, AND DENISE WALKED through the elegant streets of Bloomsbury from the British Museum to the Kimpton Fitzroy, chatting excitedly about the mysterious woman they'd just encountered and the bizarre instructions she'd given them. How could she have known about them and where to find them? How could she have known of their intentions? When they reached the hotel, Harry marched directly to the front desk and asked them to order a rental car for early the following morning. They slept off the rest of their jet lag on Wednesday night, and by the middle of Thursday, they were in Saxonborough.

They quickly located the coffee shop called Speed the Plough and learned that, indeed, the two upstairs bedrooms had been reserved in Harry's name. The manager was unable to tell them the name of the person who'd made the reservation, but he did describe a woman who sounded very much like the one who'd accosted them in the museum the previous day. They took an hour to settle in and rest up. Though their nights were spoken for, they were perplexed as to how to spend their days in such a tiny village. They wandered the main street, window-shopping, without the courage to ask anybody about ancestors, let alone ghosts. Tom and Denise were fascinated by almost everything they came across: the wording of signs, the cuts of meat in the butcher's shop window, the red postbox, the unknown birds chittering above their heads…all new and delightful. Nevertheless, their walk took no more than thirty minutes. Back at the coffee shop, bored, Harry sat down at the desk in the larger of the two bedrooms and pounded away at a new journal article on his laptop. Tom went downstairs to talk to the manager.

They smiled at each other across the counter. "Good afternoon," Tom began casually, cautiously. "We're here on a family history expedition. I had an ancestor who used to live here. Or somewhere around here." He smiled again. "Believe it or not."

"Really? You're American, aren't you?" the manager replied. "All three of you?"

"That's right. We come from Illinois. It's a state in the Midwest." Tom paused and tried again. "My ancestor mentioned the village of Saxonborough in an old letter of his that I found."

"Seriously?"

"Yeah. It was upstairs in a trunk in our family's attic. He mentioned this particular place, believe it or not, and said it was a tavern in his day. Early 1800s." Tom looked up and around the ceiling as if searching for Georgian or Victorian wooden beams.

"Yes, it could well have been. It was called The Plough back then. That's the origin of our shop's name today."

"When was it converted?"

"Oh, it must have been about ten years ago, I think. A couple of years before we took it over. All the upstairs rooms were guest rooms once upon a time. Nowadays we just keep the front two for guest rentals, and me and my wife live in the back."

"Hmm."

"It's nice country around here. You should go for a drive. And go to Lincoln. The cathedral there is fantastic. And the castle—the castle is awesome. It's still got dungeons and stuff. Nothing like it in America." He smiled and flashed his teeth. "And go to a football match—soccer, I suppose I should say. Lincoln City is our local team. They're not bad. The Imps."

"Hmm."

"So...your ancestor...what was his name?"

"Oh, it was the same as mine, Thomas Temporal. He lived somewhere around here in the early part of the nineteenth century.

Then he emigrated to America. We think he was born in about 1801. In a place...is it called Marton?"

"Could have been, yes. Marton's just up the road from here. By the Trent."

"But he said he went to school here in Saxonborough before his family emigrated."

"Fascinating. Yes, the school here serves all the rural areas round about."

"So that's why we've come here. To see what it's like and to see if we can learn anything more about him."

"*Temporal*, you say," said the manager, wrinkling his brow and nodding. "*Temporal*. It does ring a tiny bell. But I'm pretty sure there are no families by that name here today. It's a rather unusual name, isn't it? I think I would have remembered it."

"Yep. But that doesn't surprise me. He was only nine years old when he emigrated. There might not have been anyone left behind to continue the family name. You know what I mean? There might still be relatives of his in Marton but probably not here. Anyway, we just wanted to see where he came from."

"I understand. We get quite a few Americans and Australians doing the same kind of thing. We've hosted one or two of them here. Upstairs."

"I'm searching for my roots, you might say," said Tom, a little embarrassed.

"Well, I hope you enjoy your stay. I have to get on now—"

"Before you go," said Tom, "there is one more thing. A small thing. When I was looking up this place on the internet, I found a newspaper article. Just a clipping from a local paper. It said there was a bedroom here that was haunted. Do you know anything about that? Do you think it could be true?"

"Haunted? Hmm. No, I don't think so. You shouldn't believe everything you read in the papers. There have been rumors about it in the village, that much is true. In fact, I had to evict some teenagers from the room a few years ago. One Halloween. They were messing about in there all night and causing a bit of a rumpus. Another guest had complained. Silly stuff mostly, apparitions...a baby crying.

That's what they said. But no. No ghost to my knowledge, and we've lived here day and night for eight years. Not a spooky squeak in our ears. It's just village gossip. You know how it spreads."

"Like wildfire. Sure. The rumpus you just mentioned is what the newspaper article talked about. So tell me, which room was it?"

"The one overlooking the street. One of the two you've rented."

"Okay. Silly stuff, as you say. Who believes any of that stuff nowadays?"

"Only cable TV and the sensational newspapers. Now I really must—"

"Sure. Thanks for your time. We'll just poke around in the village some more. Perhaps check out the church. See if there are any family gravestones, you know." Once again, Tom felt uncomfortable for no good reason. His voice faded away. "That sort of thing."

"Well, enjoy your stay, sir. If you need anything—towels, soap—just come and knock on this door behind the counter." The manager smiled and left Tom to make his way back upstairs and rejoin Denise, who was immersed in online shopping. When Tom was halfway up the stairs, he heard the manager's voice again. "You said *Temporal*, right?"

Tom turned.

"Something makes me think that name *was* important around here in the past. In the dim and distant. Didn't a man by that name once kill someone?"

Chapter 23

Saxonborough
October 1803

Thomas Temporal was in a bad mood. He'd quarreled with the foreman earlier in the day and then broken his pickax on an unseen rock lurking in the bank of the Fossdyke. He would have to buy a new one. Unable to work, he threw the ax into the bushes and marched up to The Plough to drown his anger in brown ale. Nothing seemed to go right for him these days. He pushed the door open and entered the great room. To his surprise, there were five well-dressed men seated around a table, each one of them staring at him. Ethel Hodgson, the housekeeper, was washing glasses in a sink behind them and did not look up. Mary Kirkham, eight months pregnant, was sitting in a chair by the fire, looking down on her huge belly, her hands clasped beneath it. Thomas did not acknowledge any of them. He merely switched into fighting mode, composed and alert.

The five men got up as one and arrayed themselves between Thomas and the table.

"Please go into the kitchen, Mrs. Hodgson," said the landlord, and so she did.

Thomas was not the least bit afraid. He was quite willing to fight all five of them at once if it came to that—even the one on the end in the uniform.

"So?" he asked, placing his hands on his hips.

A tall man stepped forward and spoke first.

"I am James Kirkham, Mary's father." He pointed to the other four and counted them off. "Constable Perkin. Godfrey Fry, overseer of the poor for the parish. Arthur Goodwright, deputy overseer. And I think you know Mr. Norris, the landlord here, all too well."

Thomas didn't move a muscle. He stared into their eyes, one by one.

James Kirkham thrust a piece of paper at him, which he did not take or look at. "Thomas Temporal, this is a marriage license. You will wed my daughter. Like it or not."

At these words, Thomas turned toward Mary, who looked over at him in anguish and pleaded, "I did not know of this, Thomas, I swear it. I thought we were just coming here to consider our future. With my father alone, I thought." She turned her head. "Father? Is that not what you told me at home? Father?"

James Kirkham shook his head in the direction of his daughter. "There is nothing more to be discussed, Mary. You are eight months gone and may deliver any day. This is the only path forward now. The parish will not support an unmarried mother and her baby. And no more will I. There is no alternative."

"Mr. Temporal, you must marry the woman you have impregnated and be responsible for the support of her and the baby," Fry the overseer said to Thomas. "If you do not do so, there will perforce be a bastardy examination before the magistrate when the baby is born. You will be named as the father, and the parish will seek a weekly maintenance from you. This obligation you cannot escape under any circumstance—save for pondering it in a prison cell. It is best that you marry the woman."

"I will *not*." Thomas spat on the floor in front of Fry. "Such would be a knobstick wedding and naught less. I will have nowt to do wi' it."

"Indeed, you will, sir," said Kirkham. "It is the way of the world around here. Where were you brought up not to know such things? And *how* were you brought up not to cherish my Mary?"

Constable Perkin walked over to Thomas and circled behind him. He took Thomas's hands off his hips and handcuffed his wrists behind his back. Thomas did not resist but continued to glare at each of the men in front of him.

"When must I marry?" he said.

"Now."

Constable Perkin grabbed Thomas's left arm. Arthur Goodwright took hold of the right, and the two of them escorted Thomas out of the tavern and frog-marched him down the street. Mr. Fry walked behind them, while Mary and her father took up the rear. Mary wept and remonstrated with her father, who maintained a stiff expression and an upright bearing and answered her supplications only with terse yeas and nays. Thomas could have struggled against this coercion, but he simply complied with it, a look of disdain on his face. The unfamiliar group walking through the village caught the eyes of several villagers, but the handcuffs were hidden, and there was nothing to suggest that this was anything other than a group of men intent on farming business. The pregnant woman *was* a bit of a puzzle though, they had to admit.

Thomas was marched up to St. Swithin's Church and through the small, decrepit wooden gate into the churchyard. The procession made its way between the rows of gravestones and entered the church. The curate was waiting for them, seated on the back row of the pews reading a hymnal. He jumped to his feet as soon as they entered.

"Let's get this over with," snapped Mary's father.

"Certainly, certainly," the curate replied as he scurried to the altar and set up the lectern in its correct place. Constable Perkin removed Thomas's handcuffs.

The ceremony was short and far from sweet. Mary swore her marriage oath through tears. When prompted to do the same, Thomas mumbled a single word that the curate took to be a response of agreement, whether it was or not. He closed his prayer book and led the group into the vestry. The entry for the marriage in the parish register had already been completed in its main parts, and all that was required was for Mary and Thomas—both being illiterate—to scrawl crosses next to their names in lieu of signatures. Mary dutifully made her mark, but Thomas refused. Mr. Kirkham grabbed the pen, thrust it between Thomas's fingers, and enfolded his own two hands tightly around Thomas's hand. "Feckless jackanapes!" he exclaimed as he forced Thomas to make a misshapen cross on the paper. The pen was then passed to the two overseers of the poor who signed as witnesses.

"Is the bride twenty-one?" the curate asked.

"Twenty," Mr. Kirkham replied.

The curate nodded and entered the words *"With the consent of the parents"* on the form. He then signed the form himself at the bottom and checked that all was legal and binding, superficially at least. He closed the register.

"Can I go now?" said Thomas. "Or do you intend to heap more shame on me?"

"No," said Mr. Kirkham, "you may not go. There is one more thing that you needs must do. Your relationship is now legitimized by the act of marriage, but it must also be ratified in the eyes of the village. Only then will my daughter's child be born innocent, and there will never be a stain of bastardy upon it. A room has been booked for you at The Plough for this night. You and Mary will remain in that room for at least one hour under the guardianship of these three officials and in the eyes of the landlord and the servants and any villagers who may have an interest, prurient or otherwise. And interested villagers there will be, believe me.

"After that hour you may remain or leave, I care not which. But you will be forever married and true parents. You may take up my offer to live with Mary on my land and in a cottage that I will build for you. Or you may accept my dowry and live with her in some other place. Or you may desert her, I suppose—though your legal and financial responsibility for your wife and child will dog you to the ends of the earth. But, Thomas Temporal, this one hour is what you owe our family for your debasement of my daughter. Let us proceed. Constable?"

The policeman reapplied the handcuffs, and the group retraced their steps to The Plough. The landlord escorted them up to a bedroom overlooking the main street of the village. There was nothing in the room save for a bed and two chairs. The constable brought Thomas in and removed the handcuffs. James Kirkham pushed his daughter into the room. The couple was left alone, and the door was closed behind them. Constable Perkin and the two parish officers settled into the three chairs that had been placed for them outside in the hallway.

"You may go home now, sir," said the constable to Mr. Kirkham. "We three will see that they remain in there for the hour, as you have prescribed. You may rely on us. Then they will be left to Providence and their own devices."

James Kirkham stood stock-still for a moment, reenacting the afternoon in his head and reviewing the current situation, then he nodded and turned away. He went downstairs and conferred with Humphrey Norris. Mrs. Hodgson brought them each a tumbler of whiskey.

"I knew naught else to do," James Kirkham said to the landlord, clearly unhappy with the course of action he'd been forced to take. "Mary is greatly aggrieved and much disappointed in me. But I could think of naught else to do. I had to decide if she would be the more despondent as an unhappy wife or as the debased mother of a bastard child."

"A choice no father should have to make."

"I knew she would resent my actions no matter which path I chose."

"With luck it will last but a short time, Mr. Kirkham. Mary is such a sweet girl. We have all enjoyed having her work here betimes. I feel sure she will make the best of whichever future circumstance befalls her."

James Kirkham first nodded, then shook his head. He took a long draught of whiskey and slammed the tumbler down on the counter.

"It may matter little very soon," said Humphrey Norris.

"How so?"

"They say the war with France is aflame."

"Why?" Kirkham asked. "What did the French do now?"

"One of our guests up from London said it had nothing to do with an aggressive act by the French. It was all to do with some business over an island in the Mediterranean Sea. I know not its name. France said we had agreed at that Treaty of Amiens to remove our citizens from the island, but the prime minister was no longer willing to do so. Addington wanted to be the one to make the first move. Reopen hostilities on our own terms."

"What nonsense," said Kirkham.

"I know."

"Who cares about a faraway island? Let them have it. Foreign soil for foreigners, I say. Now if they'd landed on the Dover beach, I would already have my musket in my hand. That would be a different matter. But to fight over a distant island is an act born of lunacy."

"I'm afraid that it will upset trade soon enough," said Norris, but Kirkham seemed to think that trade was of no great concern either. "But think about it in another way, sir. This war might have a beneficial effect on the marriage of your daughter. It might knock some sense into young Temporal's noggin."

"I doubt even a French trebuchet could do that."

Norris leaned in closer to James Kirkham and whispered, "I heard tell that Addington and the king plan to beef up the army very soon. It's possible that *we* might invade France before *they* can invade *us*. That would soil Boney's breeches, eh?"

"It would indeed," said Kirkham with the merest of chuckles.

"And that would mean a general enlistment of all able-bodied young men who have no protected type of employment. Agricultural laborers, for instance. Eh? Navvies. Eh?"

"Perhaps he'll enlist!" The idea suddenly flashed into Kirkham's mind. "Perhaps Temporal will enlist!"

Norris nodded. "Or be called up."

"Mary once said that he'd talked about joining the army."

Norris nodded again. "There you are, then."

"That would open up a third possibility for my Mary, the hapless widow with the fatherless child."

"That eventuality is better than the other two, for sure and certain."

"Yes. Most definitely."

"God save the king!"

They raised their glasses and toasted His Majesty. James Kirkham finished his drink and set his tumbler down on the counter—carefully this time. He shook hands with the landlord and bade him, "*Adieu*!"

"No French to be spoken in here no more," said the landlord sternly.

James Kirkham agreed and apologized and walked out the tavern to begin the trek back to his farm. The Plough was quiet again. The dull October afternoon was slowly turning to a misty silver dusk, and the landlord lit lanterns in the great room. He yawned and stretched and then went out back to feed the pig.

No sound escaped from the marital bedroom. The three sentries chatted and dozed. Arthur Goodwright took out a pack of playing cards, and the two overseers played noddy on their laps. When the constable deemed it time, he stood up, rapped twice on the bedroom door, and shouted, "The hour is up, Mr. Temporal. Your freedom is vouchsafed back to you. We three will leave now." There was no response from within, so leave they did.

Fifteen minutes later, the sounds of two bangs from above were heard in the kitchen below. Mrs. Hodgson looked up at the ceiling. She thought to go and see what was amiss but then decided that someone must have bumped into a chair and knocked it over. She went back to scrubbing the tiles around the sink and thought nothing more of it.

Chapter 24

Saxonborough
April 2019

THEIR TWO NIGHTLY SOJOURNS IN the main bedroom of Speed the Plough went exactly according to the instructions of the woman from the museum. Shortly after midnight on the Thursday, two figures appeared on the opposite side of the room, a man and a woman, even as that side of the room descended into semidarkness and the walls became brown and stained. Denise had come with Tom and Harry, mostly out of a sense of camaraderie, but as soon as the figures appeared, she clapped her hands over her eyes and bent over with her elbows on her knees. She didn't move again until it was all over. Though transparent and vague, the two figures outlined against the wall on the opposite side of the room were revealed much more strongly than Harry had expected based on his experiences in Hoyland Church. In fact, the figures were revealed so strongly that both he and Tom instantly recognized one of them.

"That's the old woman from the museum!" Harry exclaimed, pointing. Her face was clearly that of the woman, though everything else about her—her hair, her clothes, her makeup—were decidedly different.

"How is that possible?" Tom whispered. Both ghostly figures sat impassively, staring back at them until it was over. No more than five minutes.

Denise, shaken by these events, declined to accompany Harry and Tom the following night and went to bed early in the smaller room that had been rented for them, a sheet pulled over her head.

Harry and Tom assumed the same positions in the main bedroom that they'd occupied on the previous night. And sure enough, just as foretold, figures appeared at about the same time as the previous occurrence, though this time they were decidedly indistinct. And this time there were three figures: two male and one female, as near as they could tell. The woman was younger this time and quite clearly *not* the old woman from the museum. They had absolutely no idea who any of them were. Dutifully, Harry recited the words he'd been instructed to deliver. He repeated them on a number of occasions over the next ten minutes until the apparitions faded away.

Early the next morning, Harry, Tom, and Denise sat in the coffee shop munching on bagels and speculating on how a woman could approach them in London one day, in the flesh, and then appear as a ghostly image in their Lincolnshire bedroom twenty-four hours later. Was it possible that the woman in the British Museum had been a ghost? No, definitely not. That was not possible. Could the woman have staged her own appearance in the bedroom above the coffee shop? Was it some kind of electronic wizardry—perhaps an image from a projector in the opposite wall? That didn't seem possible either; they would have seen the trail of the image, light reflected from dust particles in the air. A hologram perhaps? What then? A facial double? No, both Tom and Harry were clear that it was the exact same woman. Alive or dead? Nope, they couldn't even decide that much. And with what motive? There was none.

Most mysterious of all was the fact that the woman had known what would happen on the two nights they were in the bedroom. She correctly told them that ghostly figures would appear. How did she know that? Assuming she could not predict the future, it had to be that she engineered the whole thing herself somehow. Or was it possible that the apparitions were *always* there? As some kind of latent potentiality that merely required their presence for them to be drawn out? That explanation had a certain appeal, but the visitors were different each night, so that rather ruled against the possibility of it being just a matter of hitting replay. However much they pondered over it, they could not figure it out.

"The museum lady said we'd get an explanation today," Harry said.

"I guess we'll just have to wait," said Denise.

"Yeah? Well, one thing's for certain," said Tom in a tone of disappointment and exasperation. "It's got fuck all to do with my ancestor. And that's why we came all this way."

Harry had just gotten up to get a coffee refill when the outer door to the shop opened, and in walked a small, delicate woman. The same woman. The woman who had confronted them in the flesh at the British Museum on Wednesday afternoon and in the spirit on Thursday night in the room above the one they were presently in. She and Harry stared at each other across the room, while Tom and Denise, seated and puzzled, stared at both of them.

"It's you," said Harry, in the most startled and amazed voice he'd ever used. "You."

"Yes," the woman replied. "It's me."

"I guess it must be the time for explanations."

"It is."

"Can you first tell us who you are?"

She walked over to him. When she was just a few feet away, she raised her eyebrows, shrugged her shoulders, and replied in a calm and matter-of-fact way, "I'm Karen."

"Karen? Karen who?"

"Karen. Your student. Karen Butler."

Harry continued to stare into her face. "Karen Butler? How can you be? You're an old lady."

"Nevertheless."

Harry shook his head and then leaned forward and examined her face closely, his eyes slowly widening in astonishment. He stepped back and surveyed her up and down.

"Karen… It *is* you. But how can it be?"

"Well, let's just say I've been on a long journey. A journey nobody ever went on before. And I put on ten pounds and fifty years. Let's go over to the table, and I'll explain everything. Come on."

Harry continued to stare at her in silence and then began to tremble slightly. "I thought I would never see you again. I didn't know what'd happened to you, but I knew I was the cause of it. All this time I hoped for the best but feared the worst."

"Easy does it, Harry," she said. "Come and sit down."

Harry opened his mouth as if to speak again and then closed it. Suddenly, his eyes watered, and he stepped forward and grabbed her and hugged her so tightly she couldn't breathe. Eventually, he relaxed his grip, pushed her out to arm's length, and continued to stare into her face as if searching for better clues to confirm the impossible.

"The table," Karen said again, gently taking Harry's arm. "Let's go over there, and I'll explain." She smiled at him.

They walked over to the table, and Harry introduced Tom and Denise. They shook hands. "I've seen you before," said Tom. "Twice."

"Same here," said Karen.

The four of them drew up chairs around the table. Eyes flashed around the group, everyone waiting for someone else to begin. It was still early in the morning, and the coffee shop had not yet seen its influx of elderly men and women participating in the ritual of morning coffee—or as it was generally known in the area, *elevenses*. There was just one couple who'd come in out of the bright but brisk morning air and taken a table near to them. These two both possessed that well-known village art: to be able to hold a sensible conversation while simultaneously listening to every other conversation within earshot. Such was the necessity of being able to both generate and apprehend gossip in villages such as this one.

"Where the fuck do we start?" Harry asked.

Two pairs of ears instantly pricked up at the utterance of that forbidden word.

"Let's start at the point you and I parted ways," Karen began. "That day last July. In Hoyland Church. How much do you remember about that day?"

"Well, like I told Tom a few weeks ago, it's all a bit of a blur. There was so much smoke for one thing. I couldn't make out who any of the people were or what the hell was happening around me. In the end, Frank and I just bolted. We were both terrified. Someone was chasing us, I remember that much, but I didn't know who. I drove off, but Frank was caught and killed."

"Frank was killed? Oh no! I had no idea. I'm so sorry."

"Hmm. I was a complete mess. I crashed the car into a field and ended up in hospital. It took me weeks to recover. And I still couldn't remember exactly what'd happened. I didn't see any signs of you or Brian after the smoke descended on us. I never did know what happened to the two of you. The cops didn't find your bodies in the church after it was over, so I kind of assumed you'd escaped as well. Run out of the church, like Frank and I did. And that you'd decided to end the experiments there and then. I formed the notion that you'd run off together in search of a quiet life. But I really didn't know. It seemed like a reasonable explanation."

"Or a comfortable one at least."

"Yes. One that I could live with. My mind's circled the matter many times since."

"Did you never think that something terrible might have happened to us?"

Harry hesitated before replying, then looked down at the table and confessed, "It did cross my mind. But I guess I shied away from it. I had my own problems to deal with. And I really liked you and Brian. I couldn't bear to think that something bad might have happened to you. Imagining you on a beach in Tahiti was more acceptable."

"So what happened to the man who chased you and Frank?"

"He was found dead in the crypt of the church about a month later. And I'm sorry to have to tell you that Dan Patzner was with him. Dead too. I'm really sorry."

"Dan? Dead as well? How in God's name did Dan get involved?"

"I have no idea. I didn't have anything to do with that."

"And what about Brian's brother, John?"

"I don't know about him either. He disappeared as well."

Karen looked aside for a moment, clearly pondering what could have happened. Her brow wrinkled, and she stared at the counter. Then she looked up in an instant and clicked her fingers.

"It was John!" she exclaimed. "John must have brought Dan to the church!"

"What? *John*?"

"How else could Dan have gotten involved? You didn't bring him over to England, and Brian and I certainly didn't. But John also knew of Dan's existence. John is the only common thread here. He must have brought Dan over from Illinois to try some new experiment. That's the only possible explanation."

Harry thought for a moment and nodded. This was new to him.

"Yes…yes. That would make sense. It was *John* who brought Dan over. Yes."

"He must have. John must have been planning an experiment of his own, and Dan was the only person he knew who could help him achieve his goal—whatever that was."

Harry picked up his coffee cup with both hands. "So…the man who chased me and Frank…you know who it was, I guess?"

"Richard Crossly," said Karen. "The real Richard Crossly. The *old* Richard Crossly."

"Hmm. Yes. I'd hoped that it wasn't. That it was just a man in a costume. That it was the vicar playing a trick on us. I lied to myself. But then when they found the body—"

"It *was* Richard Crossly. Most definitely."

"And he died with Dan somehow. The authorities have been unable to identify his body. No surprise there. He and Dan were found kind of wrapped up together in the crypt of the church."

Karen shook her head sadly. She'd had no idea that people had died at this end of the time loop, while she and Brian had been coping with their own calamity. Harry was quietly recalling the same events from his own viewpoint.

"So," said Harry, finally looking up at Karen, "it's time for you to tell me what happened on that day. From your perspective."

"All right. Ready or not. So you know that Brian wanted to find out more about the base time frame in our experiments, *t⟨sub b⟩*. I guess you remember the terminology he used?"

"Yep. And Tom knows it too. I explained it to him last month."

"The base year was 1537—the year Hoyland Abbey was dissolved. Brian wanted to do what he called a resonant interaction between the present and 1537. He wanted to understand exactly what'd happened to Abbot Gervase and how he'd managed to create the time warp. That was still a big mystery to us. Brian and I had it all planned. You remember the tests we did at Clapham? Professor Lieshman's drug, anoxyseriphin? We had it all worked out, but—"

"But it worked a little too well, I guess."

"It did. The connection was strong. We could see everything very clearly. Brian was up on a bench with his hands outstretched, trying to calm the soldiers who were harassing the monks."

"Yes, I did see some of that."

"And that was when Abbot Gervase went into his religious ecstasy. He thought that Brian was Jesus Christ come to save him."

"All hell broke loose."

"Afterward, Brian called it a psychic tsunami."

"I saw the sparks and flashes of light...the abbot's levitation. But smoke filled the air so quickly. I lost sight of what was going on with you all."

"Before we knew what was happening, Brian and I found ourselves on the floor of the chancel. Crossly was gone, Gervase was dead. The monks and the soldiers were going nuts."

"Pandemonium. I sensed it."

"Brian's hand had been cut off by Crossly, but there were a couple of monks there who had medical training. Their names were Friar Anselm and Brother Bonaventure. I need to look them up in Wikipedia, by the way, when I get a chance. The three of us managed to apply a tourniquet to Brian's arm, and he survived."

"That's good news. Just so you know, the hand landed on this side of the time barrier. The cops found it in the chancel. Sarah Harcourt recognized it as Brian's hand when she was brought up from London with John. Something to do with a ring he'd been wearing. So what did you and Brian think had happened?"

"Brian said it was a case of population inversion. Like the action of a laser. The molecules in the vicinity of the abbot spilled over into their alternate temporal states—*t⟨sub n⟩* and *t⟨sub b⟩* switched places, if you like. As Brian would say. But only in that small volume of space near to the abbot. As a result, you and Frank had to do battle with Crossly, and Brian and I were stuck in 1537."

"Yes. Yes, I see it now. I hadn't worked all that out. And you survived!"

"We did. Somehow. I don't know how we did it, but we did. I managed to convince the soldiers that there'd been a miracle. A miracle caused by the abbot's religious ecstasy. The evil Richard Crossly had been transformed into a new man. A good man. A kind man. Transfigured by the Almighty. At first, they were inclined to doubt it. But Crossly was gone, and Brian was there. Can't argue with that. The soldiers were very ignorant and superstitious, and most of them quickly bought into the idea. Many of them actually prayed to Brian. The monks did too. It was all so fantastical. But the ruse worked. Deep down, King Henry's men had disliked Crossly, and so now they loved his replacement, Brian. Brian sent by God."

"And what about you?"

"I came up with a story that I was an angel sent down in human form to protect Brian. They stared long and hard at me, but they treated me with respect. I guess they loved me too."

"Or were fearful of the consequences of not loving a true angel. And after that?"

"Crossly's second-in-command that day, young William Cecil, who later became Lord Burghley, the Lord High Treasurer and chief advisor to Queen Elizabeth, took charge. He accepted Brian's explanation and rode directly over to Ketteringham Lodge, the home of the Crossly family. Fortunately for us, Richard Crossly had few relatives. Only his father, Sir Adam Crossly, was living at Ketteringham Lodge at that time, and he was in poor health, both physical and mental, so William Cecil was able to persuade him of the miracle that had just occurred. Sir Adam accepted us when we showed up a couple of weeks later after Brian's arm had healed. The servants did what they were told. So we slotted into the household. Sir Adam died soon afterward, and Brian slash Richard inherited the house and grounds. And we lived there for the next fifty years."

"That's totally amazing," said Harry, pulling back from the table. "I can't imagine how you managed to survive in that strange place and time. I couldn't possibly have done it."

"Actually, it wasn't so bad after the first couple of years. I was with Brian, and I loved him immensely. We had a nice property. We had a sizable financial inheritance, and we made some money from farming. The countryside around us was absolutely gorgeous. Brian took charge of our interactions with the local community and the Lincolnshire gentry. This gave me time to focus on what I found fascinating about that time period: what was going on in the Americas. This was the time of Roanoke and John White and Walter Raleigh… Ananias Dare, Virginia's father. I knew them all. I joined the subscribers' group and donated money, so I got to meet all the explorers and settlers of the day in London. That part of it was truly, truly amazing. You might say that I'm partly responsible for the settling of America! In my own small way. I actually acquired a bit of a reputation as a fortune teller as well, because I knew so much about the country and the settlements in Virginia and future events in general. All thanks to my civics teacher in high school!"

"And now I realize why you have that funny accent," Harry said out of nowhere, pointing at her with a smile. "I couldn't place it before."

"Yep. Part Tudor England, part rural Iowa. A unique combination. I'm trying to suppress the former now. Age aside, I'm slowly adjusting back to the way I was last July."

All the while, Tom and Denise said nothing. They were enthralled dumb. Tom had heard the essence of the theory of the time quantum from Harry, but that was all. The rest was new to him and barely believable. It was at this point that he asked Karen the million-dollar question: "How did you get back?"

"Yes. Well, for some years Brian had been trying to find a way to reverse the transition that had landed us in the past. He made friends with some of the leading scientists of the day and brought them in to help him. You may have heard of them…John Dee?"

All three of them shook their heads.

"Edward Kelley? Olbracht Laski?"

Nothing.

"They were notables of the day, each one some kind of a cross between scientist and mystic. Well, anyway, they couldn't get it to work. They didn't have anoxyseriphin, and none of them knew how to attain the zeta state. Brian couldn't do it by himself."

"And you?" asked Tom. "You didn't participate?"

"For a long time, I thought it was a mistake to try. I didn't think it could be done, and I thought it dangerous to keep trying. Failure was making Brian miserable. He blamed himself for landing me in such a horrendous predicament. I told him not to be so hard on himself. I tried to persuade him that under the circumstances, the best thing we could do was to accept our fate and live out our lives there as best we could. Try to be content with our lot. But Brian wouldn't accept it…couldn't accept it. Even as the years rolled by. He and Dee and Kelley and the others kept going back to Hoyland Church to try to achieve a resonant connection with the present."

"While you stayed home."

"Rightly or wrongly. It was just how I felt at the time. It was hard…and harder still when Brian thought it best that we not have children in case he might succeed in his experiments and the two of us would be able to return. Children would have smoothed the rough path we trod."

"But something must have happened to make you change your mind."

"Brian died last year. In September. He was seventy-three. My attitude began to change after that. Because of being alone so much, I guess. I began to think more and more of what I'd missed. My parents back in Iowa. My apartment in Joliet. My homeland. Even just the modern way of life—electric lights, television, central heating, cars. Memories of them came flooding back to me. Brian had been a distraction from all of that, but now he was gone.

"On top of that, one of these mystics, Edward Kelley, started to pay a great deal of attention to me. A few months after Brian died, he actually proposed to me. But I turned him down. He was a nice gentleman, but I had no interest in marrying him. Then one day—about six days ago, if you ignore the centuries in between—he burst into our home at Ketteringham Lodge and told me this amazing story about how he and John Dee and a local girl had seen ghosts at a tavern in the village of Saxonborough, which was not far away, close to Lincoln. Most important of all, he said that he'd received a message from the spirit world. He and Dee claimed to do a lot of that kind of stuff. But they couldn't understand most of the message, and what they thought they'd understood was wrong. I was able to figure it out. The message that had been conveyed to them was very simple: *'I am Harry Groh from Plainfield in America.'* Sound familiar?"

"Yes, that was me!" said Harry excitedly. "That was what I said! But…but…wait…you *told* me to say those words! How in hell could you have told me to say them in the present and then have your colleague hear them in the past?"

"In a minute. In a minute. So this guy, Edward Kelley, had figured out that the word *America* was in the message. That was the only word he got right! And because I was so knowledgeable about America—and also because he fancied me, I guess—he came racing down to Ketteringham Lodge to tell me about it and ask if I could help him and Dee understand what the celestial host was trying to impart. Kelley told me he'd made contact with this spirit, i.e., you, in this place called Saxonborough. We went up there together the next day and repeated the experiment. I knew how to achieve the zeta state, so it was all rather simple and quick for me. No need for the local scryer girl this time."

"Scryer?"

"A Tudor word, sorry. Spiritualist…diviner…gazer into crystal balls."

"Never heard the word before."

"Very common in those days. So anyway, during our little séance, I saw that, indeed, you *were* one of the spirits. You know, the beard and everything. It had to be you. Your introduction to Dee and Kelley the previous night had been real."

"Sure. I did exactly what you told me to do."

"So I thought about it overnight. All night, in fact. It dawned on me—literally—that the tavern at Saxonborough must be a similar focus of temporal turmoil to the church at Hoyland. It was another, but different, *t(sub b)*. Different place, different time. Something must have happened there that was similar to the religious ecstasy of Abbot Gervase. That was why we were able to make contact with you. I thought about it and thought about it and decided to use that knowledge to try to return to the present. The Plough at Saxonborough was another gateway, do you see? In just a few hours, I lost my contentment with Ketteringham Lodge and was overcome with a desperate desire to be back in the twenty-first century. It was funny how my mind switched so quickly and completely."

"Wait a minute," said Tom. "You're telling us that the tavern at Saxonborough went through some kind of explosive psychic event?"

"It must have done. That's how we get to connect with other time periods. It's an exact analogy to what had happened at Hoyland Church. Though at the time I hadn't the slightest idea what that event could have been. It wasn't necessary that I knew."

"Let me get this straight. There was a significant event. If I recall the diagram that Harry drew for me back in March, there has to be symmetry around the base year, *t⟨sub b⟩*, as you call it. Correct? That significant event must have occurred midway between your time period, Karen, and ours. Am I right?"

Both Karen and Harry nodded.

"So…1537, you say?"

"No," Karen replied. "That was the date of our transportation back there at the time of the dissolution of Hoyland Abbey. This recent connection occurred fifty years later. In February 1588, local Tudor time."

Tom grabbed his cell phone and began punching numbers into the calculator.

"1588…2019…3607…divide by 2…1803.5! The event at Saxonborough must have taken place in 1803. Or let's say somewhere in the period of 1802 to 1804. Give or take. My ancestor Thomas Temporal was born in 1801, according to parish records. This must have something to do with him—or with his mysterious father! Remember what he wrote about a ghost in the tavern and his mysterious origins, Harry? It has to be connected with what Karen is talking about. Too much of a coincidence otherwise. Let's face it, that's the reason we're here in Saxonborough in the first place. There must have been another psychic tsunami here, *circa* 1803, that has something to do with my family. Don't you think?"

Chapter 25

Lincoln Castle
March 1804

THOMAS TEMPORAL SPENT FIVE MONTHS in the dungeon of Cobb Hall in the northeast corner of Lincoln Castle. For six hundred years, Cobb Hall had held the most dangerous of prisoners, and its walls bore the final testimony of many of them, scratched into the stone. Thomas added his own inscription—using a shard of rock, the occasional utensil, and often his fingernails—in an empty space underneath the barred, arrow-slit window: *T. Temporal 1804*. Then one morning in March, two prison warders led him out of his cell and up the wooden ladder and out the doorway and across the green sward to the county courthouse. Through the door and into a large room with vast arrays of polished oak everywhere. Pushed into the dock in front of many seated people, some wearing robes and wigs. One or two of the people he recognized, most not. He paid little attention to any of it. When Thomas and the warders were settled in their places, the man in the red robes sitting on high and facing the assembled vacant faces uttered one simple sentence to set the proceedings in motion, "You may begin, Mr. Knollys."

A short man in wig and spectacles stood up and spoke from in front of the bench, continuously rotating so that all in the courtroom might feel the gravity of his words, "Herewith commences the Lent assizes of the year eighteen hundred and four in the city of Lincoln for the Midland Circuit before Sir John Monson of Burton-by-Lincoln presiding. May it please your lordship, gentlemen of the jury, it is my painful duty to solicit your attention to the facts that will be laid before you in evidence in order to direct your minds to a verdict of guilt or innocence of the unfortunate prisoner now standing before you at the bar. The crime imputed to him is as high a crime as any that is known to the laws of the land or, if I may make so bold, to any laws human or divine. The person is charged upon this inquisition with the murder of a young woman who was carrying his child."

Mr. Knollys nodded toward the dock, indicating the impassive prisoner standing there.

"Gentlemen, Thomas Temporal is here indicted for that he, on the twenty-sixth day of October last, not having the fear of God before his eyes but rather being moved and seduced at the instigation of the devil, with force and arms, feloniously, willfully, and of his malice aforethought did beat about the head one Mary Kirkham of the village of Saxonborough in the county of Lincolnshire, of which blows the said Mary Kirkham did expire at once.

"Gentlemen, I beg not to be understood in this my opening address to be attempting to divert your minds away from the fair judgment that you should form in your own minds from the facts that will be laid before you today. All in this courtroom, prisoner and judge and members of the public alike, will be satisfied with the determination that you make. Of this I am sure.

"Gentlemen, it is my duty to inform you that by the law of this country, wheresoever and whensoever a death, either accidental or by violence, occurs, an inquisition is directed to be taken at once before the sitting coroner. Such an inquisition in this case took place in the said village of Saxonborough in November of last year. The coroner's jury thought fit that the charge be willful murder committed by the prisoner at the bar. Therefore, because of its extreme severity, the case has been brought before the present assizes for resolution.

"Gentlemen, the prosecutors of this indictment are the officers of that parish where the death occurred, one of whom, Mr. Godfrey Fry, overseer of the poor for the Parish of Saxonborough, is sitting here before you as one intimately familiar with the case and who was, in fact, in the company of the prisoner and the victim on the day the murder took place. He will present evidence later this day. I think you will agree that the officers of the parish have done no more than their duty in submitting this case for your consideration. They are to be commended.

"Gentlemen, I will now lay the broad facts of the case before you..."

The words that Mr. Knollys proceeded to deliver faded from Thomas's mind the minute they entered his ears. He could think only of the rage that had come upon him on that autumn evening. Of the petty village officials and the dishonest curate who'd forced him into a false union. And above all, of Mary's wicked father who was at the root of it all, the instigator of all that had transpired, and who by rights should be standing in his stead this day. Only rarely did Thomas's mind stray back to the long winter nights of twelve months' past when he'd lain in sweet contentment in Mary's arms. There was no profit to be gained by recalling that.

He was only pulled out of his reverie by the sudden appearance in the box on the other side of the courtroom of the housekeeper at The Plough, whom he knew well. Another man in wig and spectacles rose and turned to address her.

"Mrs. Hodgson, welcome. Please state your full name and describe your present situation."

"Yes, sir. I am Ethel Hodgson, housekeeper of The Plough inn at Saxonborough, sir. I have been employed in that capacity by Mr. Humphrey Norris the landlord for eight years. I oversee the maidservants and generally make sure the premises are shipshape and Bristol fashion."

"What can you tell us about the day of the murder in October of last year?"

"Well, it was a most uncommon afternoon, sir. Several gentlemen arrived at the inn about midday and conferred with Mr. Norris. One of them was a police constable. I didn't know any of the others. Mary Kirkham came with them. Her I knew because she'd worked for us on occasion in the past. For parties and suchlike. She was very great with child."

"Did you know the purpose of this gathering?"

"No, sir."

"Mr. Norris had not explained to you why the visitors were assembling there?"

"No, sir, he had not. And I was ordered out of the room when Mr. Temporal came in."

"Did you know Mr. Temporal?"

"Oh yes, sir. He was a regular customer of ours."

"Was he alone?"

"Yes, sir."

"And just to be clear, you did not know why they were meeting that day?"

"No, sir, I did not."

"Please continue."

"Well, sir, there was some heated discussion straight away. I could hear the raised voices through the kitchen door but none of the words. And then they all left. Mary as well. They were gone for more than an hour, and then they returned. All I know after that is that Mr. Norris asked for the bed to be made up in the best bedroom—the one at the front of the inn—and that three chairs be placed outside the room in the hallway. So I asked our maidservant Nancy—Nancy Barnes, as is—to fetch the sheets and make the bed and carry up three kitchen chairs. I heard the lot of them stomp up the stairs a short while later. I'm not sure what happened after that. I was busy running hither and yon doing my chores.

"At some point, Mary's father came back downstairs, and I served tumblers of whiskey to him and Mr. Norris. The two of them talked about politics and war and suchlike. I didn't listen to any of it because I don't know nothing about such things. Mary's father finished his drink and departed. All was quiet for some time after that. Nary a peep. Eventually, just as night was falling, the police constable and the two other gentlemen came downstairs and left. I was not aware that they'd been upstairs all that time. Or else I'd forgotten. Then it was peaceful once again. It seemed to me that all the commotion was finally ended for the day, and I was glad of it. I sat down at the kitchen table and began to peel potatoes for Mr. Norris's supper. He always eats something before the evening customers arrive. Then I took to cleaning the kitchen tiles. They were so filthy, you wouldn't believe."

"Had you any comprehension of what was taking place upstairs? Please be candid, Mrs. Hodgson."

"I don't like to say, sir."

"Come now, Mrs. Hodgson, this is not a children's tea party. This is a court of law. Your words are necessary for the jury to hear in order that they may make a just decision on the fate of the prisoner. Your words will be protected under the law. Nothing you say will go beyond these four walls. Please tell us what the rumor was in The Plough that afternoon and evening."

"Very good, sir. Yes, sir. Well, our Nancy—the one that had made up the beds, like I said—she was a good friend of Mary Kirkham's. They often used to go out walking together of an evening. With the other village lasses, you know. Well, Nancy said that Thomas and Mary had been put in that bedroom together…to…to consume their marriage."

"I think perhaps you mean to use the word *consummate*."

"Yes, sir. Sorry, sir."

"Did you know that, in fact, they had been married just that very afternoon?"

"At the time, I did not, sir, no."

"But Mary was already great with child, was she not?"

"She was. Very much so. Our Nancy was of the opinion that Mr. Temporal was probably the father, but he might not be, and that the consumption…*consummation*…was necessary to bind the marriage in the eyes of the village. That was what Nancy thought, anyways, but none of us really knew. How could we?"

"Indeed, you could not."

"I told Nancy that Mary was a virtuous girl and not the kind to have more than one lover. Thomas had to be the father of her child."

"Yes, Mrs. Hodgson. However, the identity of the father of this unborn child is of secondary importance to this case."

"Is it? I would have thought it very important."

"Come, come, Mrs. Hodgson. Let us move on. Now did you know that Thomas Temporal was already married to another woman named Martha Temporal, born Ransome?"

"Indeed, I did not. *What, sir*?" The housekeeper was greatly surprised to hear this.

"And that he lived in a cottage at Fallow Fields to the west of Saxonborough?"

"What? No, I don't think that's right, sir. He lived in Ma Livingstone's doss house across the street from the inn with Jeb Sparks and Danny Murphy. The three of them came in The Plough regular of an evening. They all worked down at the canal. Laboring sorts, the three of them. I'm sure of it."

"Please just answer the question, Mrs. Hodgson. Did you know that Thomas Temporal lived at Fallow Fields?"

"Sorry, sir. No, sir, I did not."

"And that he had a young son, baptized Tom Temporal in Marton?"

"*Indeed*, I did not. Is all this true, sir, what you just said? A wife and a son across the fields? I had no idea. Nobody at the inn knew of it. And I would bet a pound to a penny that Mary Kirkham didn't know it neither."

"It is all true, Mrs. Hodgson. But let us continue. How soon after all the gentlemen had left the tavern and Thomas and Mary were alone in the bedroom did you hear noises?"

"After perhaps a quarter of an hour I heard two loud crashing sounds from upstairs."

"What did you suppose those sounds were?"

"I truly did not know, sir. I thought perhaps someone had fallen over the furniture."

"Did you take any action?"

"No, sir, I regret that I did not." She bowed her head.

"And what then?"

"Just a few minutes later, I heard a sort of a bustle and the sound of blows. Then I heard Mary scream twice. That caught my attention straight away, and I was so startled that I dropped my scrubbing brush on the floor. I thought at first to run and fetch Mr. Norris, but instead I hurried out of the kitchen and made for the stairs. All the while Mary was crying out and…moaning like."

"Where was Mr. Norris at this time?"

"He was in the back garden feeding the pig. He likely heard nothing."

"Please continue."

"When I got to the top of the stairs, Mr. Temporal ran out of the room and pushed himself past me and hurried below, taking the steps two at a time. I entered the bedroom and came upon the most piteous scene, God have mercy on me. It was a spectacle the like of which I'd never seen before and hope never to see again, God willing. I still have nightmares about it."

"The court understands and sympathizes, but please describe it as best you can, Mrs. Hodgson. We do apprehend your reluctance."

"The candles were still lit, so I could see quite well. Mary was lying back on the bed. Her nose was knocked quite sideways across her cheek, Lord love her. There was blood everywhere—perhaps half a pailful. One side of her head seemed stove in. Her nightdress was torn away from the left side of her body, and I could see blood rushing out below her breast. I saw also that one of the chairs had been broken, and a bloody chair leg was lying at the foot of the bed. I cannot speak more of poor Mary's body, if you please, sir—it is too much for me. And her such a pretty thing." She bowed her head again and placed her right hand over her eyes.

"That is adequate, Mrs. Hodgson. Please take a moment to compose yourself."

The proceedings were halted. A glass of water was brought to the witness, which she sipped. Several women in the well of the court could be heard sobbing. Counsel cleared his throat and looked over at the witness. When he thought the time was right, he straightened his wig and resumed his questioning.

"Now, Mrs. Hodgson, if you would be so kind, when you appeared before the coroner's inquest at Saxonborough, you described some most unusual circumstance about the condition of the bedroom when you entered. Please tell His Honor and the gentlemen of the jury what that circumstance was."

"Yes, sir. Well, sir, it was all most peculiar. It was as if lightning had struck the chimney breast or something. I'd never seen nothing like it my whole life. There were little sparks rippling along the sides of the iron bedstead and across the curtain rail." She stretched out her arm in front of her and made a fluttering motion from side to side with her hand and fingers. "Anywhere there was metal, it seemed. And tiny flashes of light in the air. The smell of scorched wood. And there was a buzzing sound, like as if there was a beehive somewhere close by. All unfamiliar to me. That's the best I can say to describe it, sir, and I'm sorry if my poor words make it hard to imagine. I'd never seen the like before in my entire life."

"So what did you do next?"

"Well, like anyone would, I ran directly to the window, threw it open, and shouted down into the street as loud as I could manage. *Murder! Murder most foul! Call the patrol! Stop that man!* Words like that."

"And as you now know, the patrol was fortuitously close by, heard your cries, and apprehended the prisoner after a brief pursuit and struggle."

"I saw none of that, sir."

"No, Mrs. Hodgson, but you must be aware that you alone are responsible for the prisoner being captured and arraigned. For this the county holds you in high esteem."

"Thank you, sir, but I care naught for that. I am only sorrowful every day for poor Mary."

"You may be seated, Mrs. Hodgson. Thank you for sharing your painful testimony."

Other witnesses were called. Thomas recognized several of the men who had confronted him in The Plough that day—Godfrey Fry, Arthur Goodwright, Constable Perkin, Humphrey Norris—but their words were unnecessary, so he blanked them out and withdrew further into himself. It was all just more and more of the same. Poor Nancy Barnes was called to the stand but could not bring herself to utter a single word and was excused. Only James Kirkham was not called as a witness. He remained silent, but Thomas could see his tall figure standing at the rear of the courtroom, ominous, brooding, his eyes fixed on Thomas's eyes the whole of the morning. Making sure and certain that he would be convicted. The sun dragged itself slowly up into the sky over Lincoln and dispelled the clouds that in the early morning had hidden from view the tops of the cathedral towers framed in the window directly opposite him.

Mr. Knollys read a statement attributed to Thomas himself but prepared by a legal clerk because Thomas could neither read nor write nor fashion any kind of fancy sentences in his mind. The statement declared that he, Thomas Temporal, had been unable to work that day due to an accident down at the dyke; he would lose several days' pay that he could ill afford. That had annoyed him. Then he'd been forced to marry Mary in the afternoon, against his will; that had angered him. It had also placed him in an intolerable bigamous situation not of his own making. He had then been forced to bed Mary, though the two of them had merely sat apart for an hour. They had been brought together by others; so that, too, was not of his making or his desire. He had not sought her out or chased her down. The events of the day, all combined together, had made him lose his mind. When Mary had tried to get him to agree to their living together in wedlock, he had lost his temper and struck her. He had not meant to hurt her. He regretted that she had died as a result of his actions. He pleaded not guilty to murder by reason of temporary insanity.

There was then a delay of several hours, during which time Thomas was permitted to sit. Eventually the judge ordered him to stand up, and a common man of the city in a rough brown suit stepped forward and said some few words in a soft, nervous voice that he did not hear. He slowly became aware that the proceedings were drawing to a close. Through the window he saw shadows beginning to creep up the cathedral towers. The warder standing beside him shook his elbow so that he might pay attention to the closing speech by Sir John Monson.

"Prisoner at the bar, after a most deliberate and humane consideration of your case by a jury of honorable men, you have been convicted of the most horrid crime of murder, a crime so malignant that it is difficult to find words to express its atrocity. All civilizations are agreed in punishing this enormous offense with death, and by the law of the land, the murderer is justly condemned to die. It is a law that has the sanction and authority of the sacred scriptures. Even in the atrocious crime of murder, however, there are different shades of malignity, and your crime is of the deepest hue. You have, in savage brutality, spilled the blood of an unarmed, innocent, and helpless young woman, who, by all accounts, loved you and was carrying your child.

"This act, prisoner, was one which nothing can justify. Your statement that you were forced into a marriage earlier that same day against your will does in no way mitigate the callousness you later showed to this poor young woman, of whom you had brazenly had carnal knowledge for several months prior. *She* did not enforce the marriage. *She* did not deserve any malice done to her whatsoever. What, then, could excuse such an offense? Nothing short of the deprivation of reason, some might say. However, this jury, in the discharge of their duty, has found that the deed was done in sound mind and in most wicked heinousness. The plea of not guilty by virtue of *non compos mentis* is without merit.

"Inasmuch as your offense is of the greatest enormity in the sight of God and man, so ought your contrition be the most sincere and unfeigned. I earnestly implore you, therefore, to make the best use of the short space of time that you will be permitted to remain among us to make your peace with Almighty God. Pray that the execution you are about to suffer in a most public manner may be an example to deter others who might be disposed to commit such similar outrages. All this in accordance with the Murder Act of 1751 of the Parliament of Great Britain."

The judge paused to let his words sink in.

He then reached under the desktop in front of him. He drew out a small black cloth and placed it atop his white wig. He cleared his throat.

"Nothing remains for me but that I pass upon you the dreadful sentence of the law, this seventh day of March in the year of our Lord eighteen hundred and four. That you, Thomas Temporal, be taken from hence to the place from whence you came and from thence to a place of execution, there to be hanged by the neck until you are dead, this execution to take place within two days from now, also pursuant to the aforementioned statute. In light of the extreme atrocity of your offense, I find no other course but to impose the most extreme penalty. That some further terror and peculiar mark of infamy be added to your punishment for better preventing the horrid crime of murder, also pursuant to the aforementioned statute.

"I mandate, therefore, that your cadaver be hung in chains in the close vicinity of the villages of Saxonborough and Fallow Fields in the county of Lincolnshire as a signal beacon to the community *in perpetuum*. The location for the gibbet shall be alongside a well-traveled road to be selected by the village council of Saxonborough and agreed to by the landowner. Prisoner, may the Lord have mercy upon your soul."

Chapter 26

Saxonborough
April 2019

When Tom pointed out a connection to the year 1803, Harry let out a long "Fuuuck," and the couple at the nearby table tut-tutted, tossed Harry a haughty glare, and walked out. "That does seem plausible," he continued, "when you put it that way. Your earlier observation that this has fuck all to do with your ancestor now seems to be off base, Tom. But we can come back to that. Finish your story, Karen. Just how *did* you get back here?"

"Well, so I decided I would go to The Plough at Saxonborough and try to do a transition back to the present. That meant a transition from *t⟨sub -n⟩* to *t⟨sub n⟩*. A double jump, you might say. Something we hadn't ever tried before. But I figured, what did I have to lose at this point? Without Brian, my life had lost all meaning. If I blew myself into a million molecules scattered across the lifetime of the universe, I didn't much care. I spent a day and a half putting my Tudor affairs in order, and then I went to the tavern and stayed overnight.

"I enlisted Jane Oughtred to help me because I knew I would need a strong zeta field. And it worked! I distinctly remember passing through the *t⟨sub b⟩* state. I momentarily glimpsed some really freaky stuff that was going on there: a man with a stick in his hand, a young woman levitating just like Abbot Gervase. I had no idea what was happening, but I couldn't afford to stay and find out. I didn't want to get stuck in 1803! So I sank back into the zeta state and pressed on.

And eventually I woke up in the bedroom above here on Wednesday morning. I could hardly believe I'd succeeded."

"But that still doesn't explain the sequence of events. I don't understand the logic of it."

"Well, that's the part I'm still not totally clear about myself. Listen to this reasoning and see if it makes sense to you. I made the double jump two days after seeing you and Tom and someone else—"

"That was Denise," said Tom.

"In the bedroom at The Plough. But remember that our two time periods are moving in opposite directions. They have to do so in order to preserve symmetry around *t⟨sub b⟩*. This meant that I actually arrived in Saxonborough the day of your presentation ceremony in London, Harry. Wednesday. I had to rush down to London to catch you at the British Museum. I've been hanging out in London since then."

"What?"

"Yes. I arrived *before* you'd even conducted the séances in the bedroom above the coffee shop! I quickly realized that I needed to find you in London and talk to you and tell you what to go and do at Saxonborough. You had to tell my colleague Edward Kelley who you were—mentioning America—so that he would come and tell me so that I would rush to Saxonborough, confirm that it was you, and then make the transition.

"Here is what I was concerned about. Imagine if I'd simply introduced myself in the British Museum and told you who I was and that I'd just returned from the past. You might well have been very happy…so happy that you didn't think anything more needed to be done. Karen has returned! That was what I was desperately afraid of—that you would no longer see the necessity…the imperative…of going to the coffee shop and talking to the spirit of Edward Kelley. But then Edward wouldn't have received your message and come to get me, and I wouldn't have rushed up to Saxonborough, and I wouldn't be here now. So it all needed to be carefully coordinated. Thank heavens you did what I told you to do! If you hadn't, I guess I would've simply vanished from 2019 a day or two ago and continued my life back in 1588. Or been consigned to the infinite everlasting. Who the fuck knows." She paused. "Well, Brian would have known." She clenched her jaw and pursed her lips to avoid breaking into tears.

"We didn't know why we were doing it," said Harry, "but we did what you asked of us."

"I still can't quite get my head around it though…how it was that the connections were set up. Sometimes I think it was an inevitable coordination of interactions across the two time frames, but I still can't quite figure out who *initiated* it. Was it me or Edward Kelley or you, Harry, or you, Tom? We all had essential parts to play in creating the…the symphony of it all. If any one of us had broken the circle, I would not have returned." She paused and reflected on her last sentence. "I said broken the *circle*, but I don't think that wording is quite right. For a while I viewed it is a circular connection between the two time periods, but later on I decided it was more like a kind of *spiral* of related connections. Anyone got a pen?"

Denise reached into her purse and pulled out two pens, one black and one blue. Karen grabbed a napkin and drew a diagram on it. "It's actually not a circular connection, see, because the two time periods are both continually in motion. No sooner have you resolved a state in one period than the other one has moved on, either backward or forward. You shift your attention to that second time frame, and then the first one has moved. And so on. In fact, of course, they are both continually in motion and have been ever since that single instant when they were united as *t(sub b)*. So I've found it easier to visualize the two time frames spiraling away from each other and from the base year that created them. Like this. Yeah?"

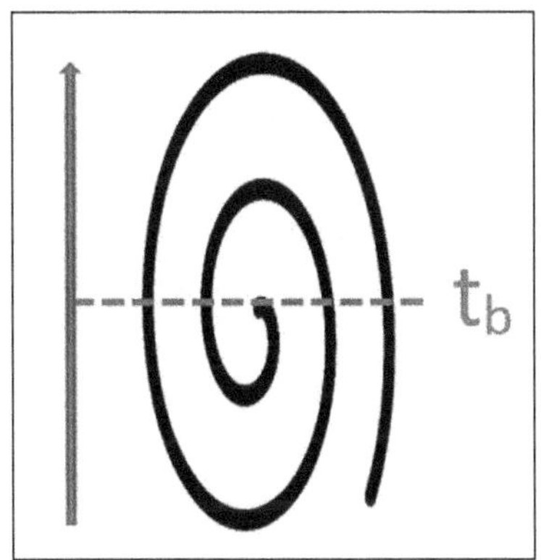

"That's astonishing," said Harry.

"And if you think about it a little bit more, you realize that when you're in the past, the forward movement of time brings you ever closer to the future. Whereas when you're in the future, you're always moving further and further away from your mirror state in the past. It all follows from Brian's theory of the symmetrical connectedness of the quantized states. I should write a paper on it, *The Spirality of Mirrored Temporal States*. My first publication!"

"I would read that," said Tom. "Jeez."

"I don't claim to fully understand what's going on. I've wracked my brains, but I still don't completely get it. Perhaps it will come to me one day. A lightning bolt in a cloudless sky. Brian would have been all over it in no time. For now, I'm just happy that it worked and I got home."

"Me too," said Harry. He beamed and reached across the table to hold Karen's hand. "Welcome home! Don't worry about your stuff either. Nothing has been lost." He released her hand and said, "So what do you want to do now? We have the two rooms here reserved for the night. We planned to drive back to London tomorrow and then fly home on Monday."

"I haven't had time to think it through. But it did occur to me this morning that I have no paperwork. I don't know what happened to my passport. It might have been left at the cottage of Brian's uncle. Or if it was in the Clapham apartment, it's likely gone for good. I can't remember. Perhaps the police have it. And anyway, it's for a nineteen-year-old, not an old woman like me. I'm going to have documentation problems when I attempt to travel."

"Ah, that's right! You're not young Karen Butler anymore. Even if we find your passport, Immigration will never buy your photo and your birth date. What are you going to do?"

"I have no idea. I'm just happy to be in the right time and the wrong place."

"I'm sure we can find a solution," Harry reassured her. "You're still an American citizen after all, so there must be some way to get you back across the Atlantic."

"I suppose I could bluster my way into a Central American country and then sneak across the border."

"No, no, no. We'll find a legal way to get you home."

"You're also going to have problems when you *get* home," Denise added. "Social security…medical insurance…even getting a new driver's license. The difference between your birth record and your apparent age is going to raise red flags everywhere."

"I know. But I'm thinking that if I can just get back home, the rest doesn't matter that much. I might be able to mostly avoid interactions with government in the future. I'm no spring chicken. I just want to sit on a porch somewhere in Iowa and watch sunsets till my time comes. Dream away my last few years in peace and solitude."

"Lots of people would like to do that."

"Let me relax for the rest of today and review my predicament. I'm utterly exhausted."

Tom chimed in, "Denise and I thought we'd like to check out the local church this afternoon and see if we can find any gravestones of Temporal family members, seeing as we're here, if that's okay with you all."

"Sure," said Harry. "You go do that. I'm going to keep working on my paper. It's settled, then. And tonight Karen can bunk down with Denise, while Tom and I will make the best of the big bedroom. And tomorrow we'll have a full English breakfast and head back to London."

AFTER LUNCH, TOM AND DENISE left the coffee shop. Before heading for the church, they crossed over the street to enjoy the view to the south. They stood at the head of the footpath that led down a slope to the stripe of calm, limpid water below. They surveyed the broad quilt spread out beyond the river, made up of hundreds of rectangles in various shades of gray, black, and brown, picked out here and there with green edging, and all stretched out under the sun to a horizon lost in mist. An elderly man approached and stood beside them.

"American, eh?" he said, grinning.

"Yes," Tom replied. "How could you tell?"

"Me and the wife saw you in the coffee shop this morning."

"Ah yes. That was you."

"Your friend certainly knows how to swear." His grin widened.

"Yes, I'm sorry about that. Harry forgets himself sometimes."

"Oh, it didn't bother me," the man said. "I was in the army. But it got the wife's goat."

Puzzled, Denise turned and stared at him. "Your wife has a goat?"

"What? Er…no. We had a pig once."

"Oh."

"I was in the Falklands."

Denise was even more puzzled by that. With the communication gap widening by the minute, Tom quickly said to the man, "We were just remarking how clear and calm the river is."

"That's because it isn't one."

"What?"

"A river. It isn't one. It's manmade. That there's the Fossdyke. The Romans built it."

"Really?"

"Really. See, it connects the River Witham at Lincoln to the River Trent just west of here. The Witham goes east to the North Sea, and the Trent goes every which way. So it's ideal for transportation inland from the coast. The Vikings certainly found it useful. Invasion-wise. And it was busy as could be years ago, carrying coal and grain and stuff like that up and down. Salt, too, probably. Once upon a time. Backward and forward. Very busy it was."

The three of them stared down at it.

"The Romans built it, you say?" said Tom. "But it looks so neat…so modern."

"That's because it's been rebuilt. Navvies came in and deepened it and widened it and fortified the banks."

"When did that happen?"

"Oh, years ago."

"Really."

"Yes." The man paused. "It's not so busy these days."

They'd run out of things to say to each other, so Tom and Denise made their excuses and stepped backward onto the hundred yards of narrow asphalt that comprised the main street of Saxonborough. They headed west and then made a right turn up an incline to St. Swithin's Church. They entered the churchyard through the lych-gate and surveyed the large collection of gravestones distributed on three sides of the church. There was one large array of relatively modern gravestones immediately to the right, a group of slightly less modern ones under some yew trees over to the left, and a small, compact group of really old ones huddling around the skirt of the church like frightened children. Behind the church was a single line of tall, densely packed trees stretching beyond the boundary wall of the churchyard on either side and entirely obliterating the view to the north.

"Right, honey," said Tom. "We're mainly looking for the name *Temporal* obviously. Perhaps spelled with two letter *l*s—or perhaps with other variations. *Temple* maybe. Also, keep an eye out for the name *Ransome,* our Tom's mother's maiden name, and *Kirkham,* the name of this other woman Tom's father might possibly have married. I can't think of any others."

"And what dates again?"

"Hmm, starting in about 1800, I would say, and then going forward to maybe 1850."

They divided the churchyard into two halves and began examining headstones. After twenty minutes they reconvened by the church door.

"Nothing," said Denise.

"Nothing," Tom replied. "I haven't seen anything that old. Most of the early ones are, like, 1870…1880. One or two are earlier…1850-ish, but those ones are heavily eroded. Perhaps no *really* early ones have survived. We're on top of a hill here, so two hundred years of wind and rain have taken their toll."

"Let's work our way around the church walls," said Denise. "Most of the very old ones are close to it. But like you say, many of them are pretty much worn away. You can hardly read the person's name let alone any of the other details."

They did as Denise had suggested, their progression much slower than before. Often they had to squint and lean in close to the gravestone to even hazard a guess at the name of the deceased. The worst ones also had a layer of green moss obliterating much of the wording.

"I should have brought a toothbrush," Tom said to himself.

Eventually, on the west side of the church, just a few feet from the vestry, they found one. "*Kirkham*!" said Denise. "A *Kirkham*! Come look!" Tom trotted over to join her, and they stared at the inscription, most of which was surprisingly readable, perhaps because it was sheltered by the vestry wall on its northern side and a gorse bush to the west. Tom brushed dirt and grime off the upper part of it. They tried their best to read it.

"Who is it?" asked Denise, turning to stare at Tom, hoping she'd made a useful discovery.

"It says *James Kirkham*, I think," Tom replied, "*of Saxonborough*. That much is clear. He died in 1836 at the age of seventy-six. Perhaps he's the father of that woman, Mary Kirkham, who married a Thomas Temporal in 1803. Remember that mysterious marriage entry I found online? We still don't know if he's part of my ancestral line—or even if he's our Thomas's father. You said at the time that you thought it could be a cousin or some other relative. But if this Mary Kirkham was, let's say, twenty-one or twenty-two at the time she married in 1803, then her father would have been…er…something like forty-five then, which would make him in his mid to late seventies in 1836. Just like this man here, seventy-six. So the age is about right. This might well be Mary Kirkham's father if I'm remembering everything clearly, and my math hasn't let me down."

> ***IN AFFECTIONATE***
>
> ***REMEMBRANCE OF***
>
> JAMES KIRKHAM,
>
> OF *SAXONBOROUGH,*
>
> WHO DIED AUGUST 6th, 1836
>
> AGED 76 YEARS
>
> "*BLESSED ARE THE DEAD WHO*
> *DIE IN THE LORD*"

"There's no mention of James Kirkham's wife on the gravestone though," Denise responded. "I've noticed that a lot of these older gravestones start with the death of a man and then add underneath it words like, *Also of his wife*…blah,

blah, blah. I guess it was the practice of the day to bury husband and wife together. The first one to die was buried alone, and then after the death of the second one, they buried him or her in the same grave as the first one and carved a new gravestone with both of their names on it. And of course, the husband's name was always first. No *Also of her husband* wording. Excuse my gender bias."

"You're excused. See if you can find a Mrs. Kirkham or any other Kirkhams around here. Families tended to be buried in groups if they could arrange it. The Victorians seemed to like things neat and organized."

They didn't have to look far. Right next to the gravestone of James Kirkham was another one, smaller and lopsided. In addition, it was cracked across the center and partly hidden under the gorse bush. It proved to be very difficult to read, but after they'd deciphered the word *Kirkham*, Tom got down on his hands and knees and set to work to clean it up. He first pulled a handkerchief out of his pocket, spat on it, and scrubbed the stone with vigor. He had to hold on to the top of it with his left hand to prevent it splitting in two. They then pulled out the long grass that was obscuring the bottom part. When Tom was finished, about half of it had become legible. He stood up and surveyed his handiwork, wiping his fingers on the filthy handkerchief.

IN MEMORY OF
MARY KIRKHAM

WHO ———BER 26th 1803
"IN BLOOM OF LIFE
SHE'S SNATCHED AWAY
SHE ————————
—— *MAKE DEFENCE*
—— *HERE* ————
IN ———— *CLAY*
UNTIL THE RESURRECTION DAY"

"Okay," he said. "Let's see what we've got here. This must be James's wife, Mary. She had the same first name as her daughter. I can't read the month when she died, but it's a long word that seems to end in…*ber*. It could be any of the months from September through December, I guess. The day of the month looks like the *twenty-sixth*, and the year looks like

1803. As near as I can tell. No other information provided about her. No mention of where she lived. And then just this poem, 'In Bloom of Life'…blah, blah, blah…'Until the Resurrection Day.' I can only decipher one or two of the words in between. She must have died young. Thirty-three years before James. Probably in childbirth. If she was the same age as him, she'd have been…what…forty-three when she died? Right?"

"Right. Seventy-six minus thirty-three. Right," Denise responded. "A dangerous age for giving birth. Just like your Thomas's mother, Fiona." She mused on the poem that someone had thought appropriate to put on the foot of the gravestone. "So when does life begin to bloom, do you think?"

Tom chuckled. "Bloom? Early twenties? I don't know. Have you begun to bloom yet?"

"I don't think so," said Denise with a smile, "but I'm working on it."

"It doesn't begin at forty-three, though, that's for sure. But then again, she could have been quite a bit younger than James. If she'd been ten years younger, then she would have been only thirty-four when she died. Twenty years younger and she was twenty-four. That's more in the *blooming* range, don't you think?"

"I guess so. If it is, then I might have bloomed and missed it."

"I'll take a few photos of these two gravestones, and then we'll move on."

They completed their circumnavigation of the church, even delving into the roots of the huge trees massed behind it, and then returned to the two Kirkhams.

"No Temporals anywhere," Tom said, clearly disappointed.

"And no Ransomes either."

"I didn't really expect any Ransomes to be honest. Thomas and Martha were married in that other place, Marton. To the northwest of here. Probably the Ransome family came from Marton, and all the Ransome gravestones are in Marton cemetery. It would be unlikely that any of Martha's relatives would have followed her to Saxonborough."

"That's true. And the Temporal family probably came from Marton too."

"Good point. I hadn't thought of that. So there's no reason to think there would be a whole lot of Temporal gravestones here either. But I thought we might at least find the grave of the elder Thomas, our man's father. I still think that Thomas and his mother and aunt most likely emigrated after the elder Thomas died and left them destitute. I just can't imagine them up and leaving the head of the household and emigrating for any other reason. Emigration would have been a huge deal for two women and a kid. Huge."

"True," said Denise. "Even if he was a bad husband and father, he provided some degree of security for Martha and their son. I imagine that would be Martha's primary concern in those days. Probably every woman's concern. Nobody wanted to be left penniless. Nobody wanted the workhouse."

"I was really hoping we would find his gravestone."

"I know you were, Tom," Denise said with sympathy. "And there's no sign of a Mary Temporal, née Kirkham, here either." She paused and thought for a moment and then started up again, "And this aunt, Jemmy, why would she get involved? Only because Martha needed help surely? Think about it...because Martha had suddenly been left alone with a baby to look after. I can't imagine why else she would be inserted into the household."

"I wonder if Jemmy was Martha's sister or Thomas's sister," said Denise.

"I'd kind of assumed she was Martha's sister. A Ransome. Being close family, Jemmy might have felt an obligation to go and help out her sister. But we can't be sure. That's why I didn't put her in my family tree."

"Perhaps Thomas asked his own sister to come and help Martha, perhaps because he knew he was dying...or about to leave her...or something."

"Yes. That would work too. Jemmy could have been either a Ransome or a Temporal."

"Next time you're online, search for the birth of a Jemmy Ransome or a Jemmy Temporal in the Marton parish register. Jemmy's a strange name, isn't it? I bet it's short for Jemima. Check under that name as well. I bet you won't have any trouble pinning her down."

"I'll do that, yes. But where, oh where is the grave of Thomas's father?"

"It's a mystery. But it's pretty clear that it's not here. The parish register and the churchyard agree on that."

Tom sighed and gazed around the churchyard one last time. There seemed to be nowhere else to look, and he'd found very little in the dirt that was helpful. His four times' great-grandfather was still squirming, still unsatisfied.

"Look, Tom, it's getting chilly," said Denise. "Can we be done here and go back to the coffee shop? Or do you want to look inside the church?"

"Nah," said Tom. "No point. There won't be anything for us inside. Only the highborn made it inside the warmth of the church in those days—just as long as they could afford a fancy monument. Let's call it quits. I'll take a few photos of the exterior of the church as we go."

They made their way back to the lych-gate, and as they walked through it, Tom asked, "Will you be okay sleeping with Karen tonight?"

"Sure. Provided she doesn't kick. Will *you* be all right with Harry the Bear?"

"Provided he doesn't eat me."

"You just need to survive the one night, honey."

"Don't call me honey with a bear about."

Chapter 27

Lincoln Castle
March 1804

ON THE MORNING AFTER HIS trial, Thomas Temporal was woken from a fitful sleep by the clanging of an iron key in the lock of his cell in the dungeon of Cobb Hall. Dawn had barely lifted its head. The door creaked open, and two men wearing the uniforms of prison guards entered. The first was a tall, burly man with a bushy red beard, whom Thomas knew by the name of Rufus. Thomas rather liked Rufus, and they'd developed an uneasy friendship over the past five months. The second man was shorter and slight of frame and known to Thomas only by his title, chief warder. Thomas raised himself up on one elbow. He rubbed his eyes. He sat up. Then he looked away from both his visitors and spat into the corner of his cell.

"On your feet, Temporal!" said the chief warder.

Thomas turned his head.

"Come to string me up?"

"On your feet!"

Thomas very slowly did as he was commanded, slow enough to imply that if he'd wanted to, he could have remained lying down.

Two other men then entered the room. Thomas did not know either of these men. One was well dressed in a dark suit and waistcoat and sporting a light, walnut-colored cane; the other wore a full-length apron and was bald and stocky and muscled.

"Who are these blokes?" Thomas asked Rufus, but Rufus declined to reply and remained staring straight ahead, standing stiffly to attention.

The well-dressed man, however, thought to answer the prisoner's question, "I am the armorer here at Lincoln Castle. My name is not important. This man here is Mr. Pearson, our blacksmith. We are here to measure you. Stand up straight and spread your arms out."

Thomas did no such thing, so Rufus went behind him and pushed his hands under Thomas's armpits, whispering into the prisoner's ear as he did so, "Come along now, Thomas." He lifted Thomas a little until he was straight and stretched upright. The armorer took hold of the handle of his cane and pulled at the lower end of it. Out came a wooden ruler, two feet or so in length and marked off in inches. "Notebook, if you please," he said, and the chief warder immediately pulled from his trouser pocket a small notebook and a pencil, the tip of which he licked.

The armorer walked over to Thomas and measured his height. "Five feet and ten inches," he said, and the chief warder dutifully scribbled it in his book.

"A horse, am I, Mr. Not Important?" Thomas asked. "How many hands? Good enough for Horncastle Horse Fair?"

No one answered him.

"Legs…two feet and nine inches, by my reckoning." More scribbling.

"Arms…"

Thomas did not move.

"Guard!" Rufus forced Thomas's arms out wide and held them there. "Two feet and nowt." Rufus let Thomas's arms fall back to his sides. The armorer then circled Thomas, laying his ruler up against various parts of the prisoner's anatomy as he went.

"Of the body, height…nineteen inches, breadth…eighteen inches, depth…thirteen inches. And of the head, height…nine inches, width…six inches, depth…eight inches, including the nose." The armorer turned to the blacksmith. "Anything else you require, Mr. Pearson?"

"No. That is sufficient. We'll have it finished by the end of the day."

"Very good."

The chief warder tore the page of measurements out of his notebook and handed it to the blacksmith. "Can you read this?" he asked.

The blacksmith looked at it, nodded, and tucked the piece of paper into his apron. The armorer slid his ruler back into the body of the cane. Their business seemed to be concluded.

"For what do you measure me?" Thomas asked the armorer. "A new suit?"

"Chains. For the chains, man. Did you not hear the words of Judge Monson?" The armorer shook his head at the ignorance of the prisoner and then snapped to Rufus, "Give the man some breakfast!" They all four left the room, and the iron key clanged in the lock once again, leaving Thomas alone with his thoughts.

He sat back down on what the warders laughingly called his bed: two coarse sacks stuffed with barley stubble and horsehair. And for the first time since he'd been accosted in the great room of The Plough by the elders of Saxonborough, his defiance and his contempt of his accusers dwindled away. He choked a couple of times but would not let himself cry. He held his hands over his ears and pressed them hard against his head, grinding his teeth as he did so. He wanted to say to himself that he wished he'd led his life differently, but he could not do so. For that person would not have been Thomas Temporal.

What he did wish though was that he'd joined the army rather than be a canal-banking navvy—or, better still, that he'd enlisted before ever he agreed to marry Martha. Rufus had told him back in November that King George reviewed thousands of volunteer soldiers in Hyde Park on the very day Mary was killed. Half a million people had watched the spectacle, so they said, every one of them hurling venom at Napoleon. One of those volunteer soldiers could have been him. Or he could have walked out of his parents' farmhouse at eighteen and marched proudly to Lincoln or Nottingham and signed up. He would have been given a smart uniform, a rifle. That is what a true-blue Englishman would have done. Then he would have been done with every one of the Ransomes and the Deloits and the Kirkhams who had hitherto ruled his life.

He would have made a good soldier. If he'd killed someone then, on the battlefield, he would have earned a medal instead of iron chains. A shiny gold medal. To pin on his smart uniform. He would have been respected. Unfettered. There would have been easy women at the army camps and French women too on the Continent. Perhaps Caribbean lasses, even, if he would have been posted to the West Indies. Variety and spice. He thought little of Martha anymore, and he couldn't let himself think of Mary, and he'd almost forgotten that he had a son.

The next morning Thomas awoke to the sounds of loud voices, the stamping of feet, the neighing of horses. Sometimes there was laughter, sometimes hooting and jeering. A faint morning light slanted in through the arrow slits. One of the warders brought him a plate of buttered barley bread topped with two slices of beef and a fried egg. It was the best meal he'd had in Lincoln Castle or anywhere else in the last three or four years. There was also a mug of cider. Thomas knew exactly what it signified, but he ate and drank nonetheless. Fifteen minutes later, the warder returned and removed the plate and mug. No words were exchanged.

Rufus entered his cell soon after that, followed by a man in clerical garb. Thomas recognized him. He was the curate of Saxonborough. He held a Bible in his hands and seemed diffident. Thomas rose to his feet in anger. Rufus stepped aside and stood to attention against the cell wall, all the while keeping a close watch on the prisoner and remaining alert in case he should need to rush over and restrain him.

"You!" said Thomas, pointing at the curate. "You! You are the reason I'm in here! You married me to Mary Kirkham under force. It was a knobstick wedding, nowt less. You had no right to do that!" Rufus stiffened. Thomas waggled his index finger in front of the curate's face, barely a couple of inches from his nose end. "You call yourself a man of God? Don't you know it was the marriage that twisted my head around and made me hit her? It's all *your* fault, root and branch. And now you come to my cell and confront me again? To survey the damage you have inflicted? What say you?"

"Mr. Temporal, calm yourself, please. I can explain. A group of parish officers has come from Saxonborough for the…er…the occasion. They asked for a representative of St. Swithin's to accompany them, and the vicar declined. So the task devolved to me. I had no choice. It is not my desire to be here, I can assure you. I am here purely as Christ's minion, to do his bidding. I am here to offer you the sacrament. It is a courtesy offered to everyone in shoes such as yours."

"Well, I don't want it—not from any man of the cloth and least of all from you. If God exists—and I doubt that he does—he will treat me as he will. There's nothing a sprat like you can do that will help me. Be gone!"

The curate argued against it, but Thomas was adamant and waved him out of his cell.

After the cleric had departed, Rufus reluctantly stepped forward. "Very well, then. Come along, Thomas. I'm afraid it's time. I'm sorry." Thomas gave him a despairing look, but just as on the day he'd been apprehended in The Plough, he could see no alternative but to comply with the order and walk out of the cell that had been his home for five months. He didn't give it a backward glance. He climbed the wooden ladder with Rufus close behind him.

As he ascended, Thomas was surprised by the glow of the morning overspreading him, the delicacy of which he'd been deprived of for so long, having had to make do with the narrow strips of faded gray light coming into the dungeon through the barred arrow slits that served as windows in the tower. He had never before in his life been aware of the light around him—in the morning or the evening or at any time of day. He had never noticed its intrinsic beauty. He suddenly wondered if there might have been other beauteous things in the world around him that he'd been totally unaware of. The air itself possibly. Children's voices. Starry skies. Unobserved his whole life. It occurred to him that perhaps it was only when you were deprived of something for long enough that you could truly appreciate the return of it. But now he would never know of these subtle delights…all lost, all gone.

A group of men was waiting in the small circular vestibule of Cobb Hall: the governor of Lincoln Castle, the chief warder of the prison, the court recorder from his trial at Lincoln assizes, and the undersheriff and coroner of the city of Lincoln. There were also three men from Saxonborough: Godfrey Fry, the overseer of the poor; Constable Perkin, who had apprehended Thomas the previous October; and, standing tall in the rear once again, Mary's father, James Kirkham. Mr. Kirkham seemed to Thomas much like a personification of the devil, there to supervise his obliteration from the world. Only the horns were missing and the cloven hooves. Was he even real? Thomas wondered. Could the others see him brooding back there? Perhaps it was a figment of his imagination. No, it was Kirkham, all right, just one of the many fingers in his pie. And yet in spite of all this and in spite of the horrific occasion, on the whole, Thomas felt rather proud that he could attract the attention of such a distinguished body of men.

As Thomas approached, the body of men turned as one and walked outside onto the small stone courtyard that overlooked the castle grounds. Thomas followed, and Rufus brought up the rear. As he stepped through the doorway, Thomas was struck once again by the delicate grace of the light. It had rained during the night, and now a light mist clung to the ground; but the mist was thin enough and low enough that the air above it appeared brighter and bluer than usual, and the thought crossed Thomas's mind that a good Christian would see it as heavenly.

But fast on the heels of that thought came a shock. Thomas could not believe the tapestry that was spread out before his eyes. The castle grounds were filled with people…hundreds of people. And every face was turned and raised toward the door of Cobb Hall. Toward him. As he emerged onto the courtyard, a roar arose from the assembled mouths, a frightful agglomeration of laughter, jeers, hoots, and curses. Thomas, stunned, surveyed the scene in all directions. On the grass in front of the observatory tower were stalls serving food and drink and cheap trinkets. There was a row of carts by the main gate and a row of horses tethered opposite them. A fiddler was playing a tune in front of the castle wall, and a young child was dancing. He thought it grotesque. And there was a scaffold erected on the low stone wall directly in front of him, its noose swaying in the morning breeze.

Rufus pushed Thomas gently in the small of the back and followed him down the steps from the courtyard onto the castle grounds, followed by the chief warder, the city coroner, and the court recorder. In front of the wall and under the gallows was a cart. At the front of the cart was a horse with a groom standing beside it and holding tight to its bridle. At the rear of the cart was a short ladder. Rufus helped Thomas step up onto the bed of the cart. It was then that Thomas noticed the figure of the executioner standing at the front of the cart and staring at him. The three officials climbed onto the cart as well. A hush came over the crowd. The fiddler stopped playing.

The executioner stepped forward. He took hold of Thomas's arms and placed him directly under the noose. With lengths of cord, he pinioned Thomas's arms by his side and tied his legs together at the knees. He pulled Thomas's shirt away from his neck. Finally, the executioner's lad sitting astride the stone wall let the noose descend so that the executioner could place it around Thomas's neck. He adjusted the eyelet under the angle of the jaw. The lad eyeballed Thomas's height and then carefully pulled a little on the rope that was hung over the gallows' bar until it was comfortably tight and then tied it securely around a hook set deep into the stone.

The court recorder stepped forward, and the crowd hushed completely. He addressed the prisoner, "Thomas Temporal, in accordance with the laws of Great Britain, the deliberate and humane consideration of your case by a jury of honorable men, and the ruling of Judge Monson at the Lent assizes of the year eighteen hundred and four in the city of Lincoln for the Midland Circuit, you have been sentenced to death for the murder of one Mary Kirkham in the village of Saxonborough on the twenty-sixth day of October last. Before the sentence is carried out, as is customary, I now ask you if you wish to say anything to express your contrition and make peace with Almighty God?"

Thomas kept his eyes fixed on the high castle wall opposite and shook his head.

"Then may the Lord God have mercy on your soul."

A voice shouted out from the crowd, "God bless you, Thomas!" Thomas recognized the voice of Jeb Sparks, his friend and roommate. Someone booed in reply.

"Very well," said the court recorder. "Mr. Executioner?"

The executioner stepped forward, produced a white hood from his pocket, and placed it over Thomas's head down to the jawline, leaving the neck uncovered. He adjusted the eyelet of the noose again. The three officials standing on the bed of the cart each took one step backward and placed a hand on the side of the cart to steady themselves. The chief warder looked around him and nodded to the executioner, who turned and nodded down to the groom. And it was all over with a click of the groom's tongue. The horse moved forward, and Thomas was left swinging in the air from the gallows rope. The crowd applauded.

There was no *long drop* in those days and no breaking of the neck. Thomas struggled and twitched and spluttered for two minutes before dying by strangulation. When he had not moved for a further minute, the executioner asked the groom to back the cart up under the gallows again. He then signaled to his lad, who untied the rope and let Thomas's body fall gently onto the floor of the cart. The city coroner stepped forward and examined the body. He pronounced Thomas Temporal dead. Huzzahs came from the front row of observers who heard his declaration. Several hats were thrown into the air. The executioner removed the hood and the noose. The hood he left beside the body. The noose was drawn back up into the air by his boy. He laid out the body in decent fashion, rearranging the splayed limbs. He covered the body with sackcloth. Then he and the officials climbed down and walked away.

Slowly the crowd turned its attention away from the cart and began to chatter in small groups about the spectacle they'd just witnessed. To one or two hesitant cheers, the castle blacksmith and his assistant appeared, walking across the grass carrying the iron shackles they had forged the previous day. They tossed them into the cart, where they glinted in the rising sun. The blacksmith paid his respects to the chief warder, and he and his assistant turned and walked back the way they'd come. Constable Perkin came over, shook hands with Rufus, and said in his official voice, "I'll take over from here." He climbed up into the cart, while Rufus walked away.

The Saxonborough notables chatted for a minute or two and then moved off to their own carriage parked by the castle gate. The undersheriff of Lincoln shook hands with the governor and the other castle dignitaries and left with the coroner and the court recorder. They'd done their job; the execution had been conducted in accordance with city law and custom. The governor returned to his lodgings in the Lucy Tower and had breakfast with his wife. The lesser prison officials dispersed to their various work places around the grounds. The executed prisoner was forgotten. The scaffold remained standing, now useless and ignored but still professing its power to all who caught sight of it. The groom mounted his horse and turned the cart around. The castle gates opened, and the procession of carriages and carts left the grounds, pursued by the straggling crowd of onlookers. The fiddler began to play, and the child danced.

Chapter 28

Saxonborough
March 1804

First to arrive at Saxonborough was the carriage with Godfrey Fry and James Kirkham in it, clattering down the village street a little before ten o'clock. The street was already thronged with villagers, chittering excitedly among themselves. Fry and Kirkham forced their way through the crowd and marched straight into The Plough.

"Two strong ones, if you please, Mr. Norris," said James Kirkham. "Large ones."

"Certainly, sir."

As he poured, Mrs. Hodgson and Nancy Barnes came out of the kitchen.

"Did he say owt?" Nancy asked with a wicked glint in her eye.

Kirkham shook his head.

"Nary a word," said Fry. "Nary a word. He just stood standing there with that contemptuous glare on his face."

"That *evil* glare," Kirkham clarified.

"Even with the noose tight against his neck."

"Any tears?" asked Mrs. Hodgson.

"Not a one. Stiff and straight the whole time."

"How long did he suffer?"

"A few minutes," Kirkham answered casually. "I've seen plenty take longer than that."

"And the body?"

"The cart is on its way. It should be here shortly. Where is the blacksmith?"

"He's already up Fallow Lane with the farmhands and the carpenter," said Humphrey Norris. "They've been erecting the post since daybreak. A good thick piece of wood, I've heard tell. Fifteen feet long. Not an inch less. And nigh on a foot in width. Best oak."

"Good. Excellent. It will be seen from afar and for an eternity."

Fry and Kirkham downed their drinks and set their tumblers on the counter. As they did so, cries arose from the street outside, announcing the arrival of the cart with Thomas's body on it. The two men went and looked out the window. The cart came to a halt behind their carriage, and the villagers crowded around it, hoping to catch a glimpse of Thomas's corpse and the chains that lay beside it. Constable Perkin stood up on the cart, holding his arms outstretched, and cried, "Keep your distance, ladies and gentlemen. This is not the slab at the butcher's shop. Stay back, I say. And no children!" The groom dismounted and shielded his horse from the press of the crowd. People were hurrying out of their homes and running down the street so as not to miss anything. Another Saxonborough constable appeared and helped Perkin hold the crowd at bay. Fry and Kirkham strode out of The Plough, looking perturbed.

"Best get on!" Fry shouted to Constable Perkin. "It's too much of chaos here."

"Where is the gibbet to be found, sir?"

"On the moor, down Fallow Lane. You won't easily miss it."

So the two constables settled themselves on the cart, the groom remounted his horse, and the procession continued on down the street. A few village boys ran in front of the cart, hallooing, while many ran alongside it and the older villagers walked behind. Humphrey Norris came out of the tavern to join Fry and Kirkham, and the three of them set off in the waiting carriage. As they moved off, they observed a trickle of unfamiliar carts and carriages and riders on horseback entering the village from the opposite direction after following Thomas's body all the way from Lincoln. Fry raised his eyebrows at the sight of them and muttered, "An occasion for all the county, it seems."

By the time the morbid procession neared the gibbet post on Fallow Lane, the mist had overflowed its atmospheric banks and become a fine drizzle. Farmhands were still shoveling rocks and stones into the deep hole that contained the post, firming up the foundation with soil and leveling the ground around it. Three gypsy caravans were parked off to the side, and a table had been set up in front of one of them with bottles of beer and mugs of hot tea. Several villagers were already availing themselves of refreshment. Over the next hour, onlookers arrived from far and near to watch the spectacle and celebrate justice being seen to be done—more than a hundred people, it was later reported in the *Stamford Mercury*. There was even a cartload of curiosity seekers from Marton, birthplace of the executed man.

The blacksmith and his assistant removed the body from the cart and carefully laid it down in a clearing beside the gibbet. The two constables took up positions in front of them with their backs to the corpse, staring down the onlookers and periodically warning them to "keep your distance!" The blacksmith had only once before in his life had to encage a body, and he did not relish having to do it again. His assistant carried over the chains that had been forged in Lincoln Castle, and they separated them and sorted them and set to work.

First, they encased the torso and arms in the largest and sturdiest of the cages, which consisted of six flat iron bars, two inches in width, hammered into ovals. While they were doing that, the blacksmith's daughter shaved the head of the corpse. The two men then placed leather stirrups under each foot and encased each leg in thinner and narrower iron bars, which they attached to the bottom of the cage around the torso. Crossbars were affixed at the ankles, the knees, the thighs, the buttocks, the chest, and the shoulders, and connected to the vertical members. The crowd murmured all the while and paid great attention to the work underway. When the body was firmly enclosed, the blacksmith's daughter reached for a pot and brush and smeared pitch over the hands, the face, and the head—this to allay deterioration through the action of weather. The members of the congregation turned to their nearest companion to ask why this was being done. None could say.

The blacksmith's daughter then produced the hood that had been draped over Thomas's head during the execution and made to place it over the head of the corpse, but James Kirkham intervened. He stepped forward and shouted, "No cap! Let the county forever see the face of the demon! No cap, I say!" Several male voices shouted their agreement, and so she complied. She was later to sell the death cap for two guineas to the squire of Doddington Hall for his collection of macabre relics.

Finally, the blacksmith placed the small round iron cage over the head of the corpse and fastened it tight to the top of the torso cage. He tested that the ring on the very top of the cage that enclosed the head was also firm and tight. His job was done. He stepped back with a sour taste in his mouth and swore to himself that this was the last time he would undertake such barbarous work. He turned away as three farmhands manhandled the caged corpse into position and hauled it up to its designated height to the cheers of the onlookers. The drizzle waned imperceptibly.

The rest of the day called for celebration. The gypsies sold drink to the bystanders and told their fortunes in one of the caravans for a penny farthing. A fiddler played throughout the morning. Some of the teenage girls occasionally formed up and danced a roundelay on the street. After lunch, a ballad singer from Gainsborough showed up and sang local favorites while his wife passed the hat. An old gypsy craftsman sold horseshoes, knife handles, and knitting needles from the back of his caravan. Time drifted by. The younger men and women chatted about how they'd never seen such a thing before and hoped never to see it again. The old folk, on the other hand, compared this gibbeting to ones they had seen in the past, seemingly in competition to see who among them could cast their memory back the furthest or recount the most horrific tale. Children were confined to the grass on other side of the road, playing endless games of tag.

In the early afternoon Constable Perkin noticed that Thomas's old roommates, Jeb Sparks and Danny Murphy, were studying the gibbet carefully, their eyes moving up and down the post, seeming to gauge its height and weight. "Don't even think about it," he said, pointing to them. "Don't think about taking down the body or burning it up. We will all know it was you, and you'll be taking Thomas's place in the dungeon at Cobb Hall in short order. Now clear off!" They turned and sauntered away. By midafternoon, the Saxonborough villagers and the folks from Lincoln and the surrounding villages had tired of the festivities and begun to disperse to their homes. James Kirkham, seeming to want to remain for as long as the gibbet would remain, was finally pulled away from it by Fry and Norris and taken home. By dusk, only the gypsy caravans remained. As the light faded, the wind got up fiercely and banged the gibbet irons against the post, scaring the Romany children half to death.

The gypsies were to remain camped by the gibbet for several weeks—they were safe there, for no villager dared to approach the accursed site after dark. The gypsies shaved slivers off the wooden post and sold them later in the towns as souvenirs. Then one sunny morning in late April, they, too, were gone, wandering off to pastures new. And Thomas's corpse was finally left alone, his dead eyes staring over the bleak Saxonborough moor, just as his living eyes had stared at the castle wall as he'd dropped from the bed of the cart. They did not stare for long though once the crows discovered them. Nevertheless—to the wonderment of all—the gibbet post stood for forty-five years, testament to the skill of the carpenter who'd made it and the diligence of the farmhands who'd erected it. It was not until a storm in the year 1849 that a great wind blew the post down. Amazingly, most parts of the iron cage were still intact—though heavily rusted through—and they were rapidly scavenged up by eager villagers. Some parts were sold, some were repurposed, some were kept as souvenirs. There were no traces of Thomas Temporal, however. Not tooth or bone.

Martha cast her husband behind her on the day that news reached Fallow Fields of his infidelity and his bigamy and his arrest for murder. She would never again speak of him or what he'd done. Though she was told he'd been transported to Lincoln Castle after the coroner's inquest at Saxonborough, she refused to go and visit him. Jemmy, on the other hand, was not so harsh and unbending. Thomas was her brother, after all. She felt an obligation to remain concerned about his welfare, no matter his crimes. So a few days before Christmas, she journeyed to Lincoln and spent an hour with

Thomas in his cell, watched over the whole time by Rufus. The conversation was stilted. Thomas would say little about what had led to his imprisonment and less about where it might all end. For the most part, they talked about their parents and happenings back at Marton. Jemmy left the castle none the wiser and never saw him again.

Jemmy and Martha survived the winter. Somehow. Without the ten shillings a week from Thomas. They cared for young Tom and cooked and cleaned, relying on intermittent poor relief from the parish and random donations of food from their neighbors: a dish of barley meal here, a few eggs there. Jemmy picked up occasional jobs close to home whenever she could, but it was always a struggle. On the third day of March, Farmer Deloit called on them with a basket of scones and informed them that the date of Thomas's trial had been set. Did they want to attend? He offered to take them to Lincoln in his carriage if they did. Martha said they did not. Farmer Deloit said he understood. He turned to leave but then stopped at the front door and turned back, looking decidedly uncomfortable.

"If the worst comes to the worst," he said, "you may stay on here with the boy for as long as you wish. I will find jobs for you on the farm and pay you something. And you have the parish relief. This until you…until you can find other lives to live…better lives than the ones you have now."

"Thank you very much," said Martha.

Farmer Deloit gave the merest hint of a smile and left.

A week later, one of their neighbors called and drew Jemmy out of the house into the roadway and explained to her the verdict and the sentence that had been imposed and already carried out. Jemmy was not surprised but wept nonetheless. The neighbor apologized for having to bring such awful news. Jemmy thanked her and went back inside.

Martha looked at her.

"It's all over," Jemmy said.

Martha nodded.

"From now on, whenever you walk to Saxonborough, take the long way across the fields. Do not go near Fallow Lane."

Martha nodded again.

Chapter 29

Hoyland
March 1593

A CARRIAGE PULLED UP IN FRONT of Hoyland Church. A man and a woman got out. The man hitched the carriage to the gatepost, and the horses promptly began to munch on the lush grass growing at the foot of the low stone wall that encircled the church grounds. The two visitors opened the gate and crunched up the path to the church door. The air was brisk, and the sky was a very pale blue with just a hint of high cirrus. They entered the church and looked around. It was cold and damp and deserted.

"Over this way," said the woman, leading the man toward the vestry by the sleeve of his jacket. She knocked on the door, and they walked in just as the vicar rose from behind his desk. The woman pushed the man in the small of his back to step forward, and he approached the vicar tentatively, leaning in for a handshake.

"Rimes," said the man, introducing himself. "Robert Rimes, your worship."

"I'm the vicar," came the response. "Nothing more. Benedict Massey. At your service. What can I do for you? You wish to arrange a marriage perhaps?" He glanced over at the woman, now discreetly hiding in Robert's shadow.

"Oh no, sir. We're already married. This is Alice, my wife… Mrs. Rimes." She took a small step forward but kept her hands rigid by her side and said nothing.

"What, then?"

"Well, sir, you won't remember me, but I've been here a number of times before. Five or six years ago, it must be. I'm a coachman, see. I conveyed Mr. Edward Kelley here and Mr. Dee. You know both of them, I think. And then later Mrs. Crossly. I know this church well." He cast his eyes to one side and then down. "From the outside anyway. I always waited in the coach until their business was concluded. Once or twice I partook of a draft of ale in the Red Lion."

"So? Yes?"

"And my wife has been here twice before. She attended the funeral of her mother, Joan, and then of Mr. Crossly, didn't you, Alice?" She nodded. "Alice was companion to Mrs. Crossly on that sad day. Comforted her throughout. Alice was housekeeper for the Crosslys at Ketteringham Lodge, see. For many years. Until… until…" He didn't know how to finish the sentence.

"Until Mrs. Crossly left Lincolnshire," Alice chimed in.

"Ah yes," said the vicar, looking uncomfortable. "Left Lincolnshire."

"Alice and I kept company many times in the kitchen at Ketteringham Lodge—while my master, Mr. Kelley, dallied with Mrs. Crossly. Well, not dallied in *that* sense. Conversed, I mean. I don't know what their relationship was or what transpired between them; but Alice and I, well, we fell for each other." He blushed. "We've been married nigh on four years now," said Robert proudly. "We both work for the Willoughbys at Wollaton Hall. Mr. Kelley arranged it for us after Ketteringham Lodge was sold. Wollaton Hall is near Nottingham. Sir Francis Willoughby attended Mr. Crossly's funeral. You might remember him. Very fortunate we are to have both found employment in that grand house." Alice nodded vigorously. "We have a baby as well. Baptized and everything." The vicar did not say a word during this monologue, and Robert paused as he approached his announcement of the awkward reason for their visit.

"Sir," he began, straightening the necktie he had donned for the first time for this special occasion. "You see, sir, before Mrs. Crossly… er…left Lincolnshire…she wrote a letter to Alice. She put it in the drawer of the dressing table in her bedroom with strict instructions that Alice was not to open it unless she—Mrs. Crossly, that is—failed to return from her planned trip, which she did. Fail to return, that is." His necktie felt unusually tight as he swallowed.

"I drove Mrs. Crossly on that very trip, sir. In Mr. Kelley's carriage. First here to Hoyland—as you may recall—then to Lincoln, and finally on to Saxonborough. There we stopped at the Oughtred's farm for a short while and then went on to The Plough. Sometime during that night—as best as Jane Oughtred, Mr. Stringfellow, and myself were able to surmise—Mrs. Crossly left the tavern. She either walked off into the darkness or someone came and picked her up. Unbeknownst to all. Nobody knows from that day to this where she went. Never to be seen again."

"Thank you for explaining that. I never did know the particulars of that day," said the Reverend Massey, "but I am well aware of the upshot. For Mr. Williamson, one of Mrs. Crossly's lawyers, came to see me two weeks later and started the legal process that resulted in the sale of Ketteringham Lodge and the steady flow of sovereigns into my church's coffers. Most desperately needed they were and most gratefully received. Yes. That much I know."

"Yes, of course. And all of that we later learned as well. But Alice found out soon enough that her employment at Ketteringham Lodge was to end."

"I didn't read my mistress's letter until ten days had passed without her return," Alice interjected. "She only asked me to wait three days, but I waited ten."

"Commendable," said the vicar, short of anything more relevant to contribute.

"Mrs. Crossly was very good to our Alice," Robert continued. "She left funds invested for her in the safe care of her lawyers. Alice gets a monthly allowance and a pension waiting for her in her old age. Very generous. But we both still needed to work. That was when we went to Wollaton Hall. Mr. Kelley gave our references to Sir Francis. Everyone has been most solicitous to the both of us."

"Such a lovely woman," said Alice, "Mrs. Crossly. I miss her every day. I worked at the Lodge for nigh on seventeen years, and my poor mother, Joan, was the cook for even longer. I cry at night sometimes just thinking of what might have happened to Mrs. Crossly. I would give up the allowance and the pension tomorrow just to be back at Ketteringham Lodge with her." She looked up at her husband. "Provided Robert was there by my side, of course."

"Of course." Everything was so far beside the point, and the vicar was anxious to discover the purpose of their visit. "So why have you come to see me today? Are you desirous of my help in some way?"

Robert summoned up one final ounce of courage. "Well, sir, Mrs. Crossly's letter to Alice had one concluding sentence that forced our hand, didn't it, Alice? That's why we're here today. You tell him."

Robert stepped aside, and Alice stepped forward and took up the story. "I haven't been able to let it rest. It's been preying on my mind these last five years. I suppose I should just let it pass, but I feel indebted to Mrs. Crossly every day of my life. She asked one final thing of me in the letter—once she'd described what provisions she was going to make for my welfare after she was...gone. She said that she had asked you, Mr. Massey, sir, to take care of some matter regarding the tomb of her husband, Master Richard. She didn't say what exactly the matter was concerning, but she asked me if I would kindly visit this church at some future time to ensure that the promise had been fulfilled. That's why my husband and I are here today. Do you recall the promise of which I speak?"

The vicar coughed nervously. "I do, Mrs. Rimes, I do. And I regret to have to inform you that I have not yet fulfilled the vow I made to your mistress. You must understand that there are many varied things that fill the hours of a parish vicar each and every day. And this particular one concerned something significant and rather difficult to accomplish. Nevertheless, I promise you here and now that I will attend to it within the month. Again, my apologies for the long delay."

"Thank you, sir. It is much appreciated."

"If you wish, the two of you may return in one month from now for confirmation that the promise has at last been fulfilled."

Robert spoke again, "Much obliged, sir, but I don't think any such confirmation will be necessary. We trust the word of our Lord's servant." He looked down, embarrassed at having uttered such fine words, him being a lowly coachman, and then looked back up and mouthed his prepared postscript, "And, sir…before we take our leave, sir…my wife wonders if she could see Mr. Crossly's tomb. She has often thought about it over the years. She knew Mr. Crossly very well, naturally, but at the funeral she was not able to approach the tomb to see where he lay. Those of higher birth blocked her way. She would like to say a prayer for him. She has long wished to bid him a heartfelt farewell. Would you be so kind as to show his tomb to us on our way out?"

"Why, certainly."

They walked through into the back of the church, and the vicar pointed out the stone sarcophagus resting in the niche alongside the altar. Alice Rimes went up to it and read the part of the inscription that faced outward. Her hand went to her mouth at once. She turned to the vicar. "It says here…*Ille…obiit*, sir! The same words are on my mother's gravestone. They mean *She…died.* Is my lady dead?"

"Oh no, Mrs. Rimes, she is not dead. Well…I mean…I don't know if she is dead or not. Nobody knows. Those words were inscribed at the time Mr. Crossly died. Six years ago. Do you see that there is a space after those two words? It is waiting upon Mrs. Crossly's death. In that tragic eventuality, it was intended that she would be interred herein and the inscription completed by the addition of the date of her death by our stonemason. That is all. This wording does not mean that your mistress has already passed." He paused and wondered how much more he could confide in the couple. "Actually, the bargain I sealed with your mistress concerns this very tomb and this very inscription and her interment within. However, I may not reveal the exact terms of the bargain because Mrs. Crossly swore me to eternal secrecy. But never fear, within the month all will be settled in this matter."

Somewhat, but only somewhat, relieved, Alice knelt in front of the tomb, placed a hand upon it, and offered up her prayer to Richard Crossly. Then she rose and accompanied her husband out of the church. Reverend Massey followed the pair. On the churchyard path, the vicar halted and waved goodbye to them. As the carriage pulled away, he looked about him and noticed the sexton,

Ezra Palethorpe, digging a grave in the corner of the churchyard. He walked over to him.

"Ezra!"

The sexton turned and appraised him but said nothing.

"Tell me, Ezra, do we have any imminent plans for burials in a pauper's grave?"

"Imminent?"

"Soon to come."

"Oh. No, sir. Nothing, sir."

"Any rumors, then, about impending deaths in the village?"

Ezra thought for a moment and then slowly shook his head. "None come to mind."

"A lonely widow on her deathbed in one of the poorhouse cottages perhaps?" the vicar suggested.

"Well, they do say that the widow Jackson is failing fast. Her as once ran the fish shop."

"Does she have relatives in the village?"

"I don't believe so, sir. She's an abandoned soul, poor thing. Remember that she came here from Boston to live with her son after her husband died? But then her son joined the army and was killed in France, so they say. She was left all alone, and the poor-law officers had to step in."

The vicar nodded. "Do you know her?"

"In passing, sir. She takes a drink in the Red Lion on occasion. And I used to buy cockles from her once upon a time."

"Would you say she is a respectable woman? Morally speaking. Above reproach?"

"Well, I don't know about that, sir. Old Moses goes and visits her cottage regular-like. Has done for some years. And he always winks at us in the Red Lion when she walks through the tavern door. We all know what that means. And you know how people talk. Some say she takes coins *off* the communion plate when it's passed around in church of a Sunday morning rather than putting any coins *on* it. That might or mightn't be true, I couldn't say. Gossip mostly. I think I would have to say she was *at the level* of reproach but not *above* it." He snickered softly.

"Well, it matters little, I suppose. At this point. Please keep your ear to the ground and let me know when she passes. She may find exaltation far beyond a pauper's grave."

"Right you are, sir."

A fortnight later, four people stood around a body that was wrapped in a clean white shroud and lying on the floor of the chancel of Hoyland Church: the vicar, the sexton, the sexton's boy, and the stonemason. They each looked down upon it, each perplexed as to their course of action. The vicar scratched his cheek. "The widow Jackson?" he asked.

"The same," Ezra said. "Yesterday morning. Seen lying next the fireplace by a neighbor. Through the window. Coroner said no inquest needed. *Visitation by God* would suffice."

Reverend Massey nodded. "Well, she's going in the Crossly tomb."

The three others stared at him in undisguised astonishment.

"In the sarcophagus?" asked the stonemason, eyes wide and staring.

"In the sarcophagus. That is what Mrs. Crossly wanted. I made a bargain with her some years ago. She left Lincolnshire and will not return. She did not want her husband to lie alone for all eternity, bound in stone. I can almost understand that. She wanted a respectable widow to lie alongside him. And I agreed to it."

"That don't seem right," said Ezra, pursing his lips. "Not right by my book."

"Look," said the vicar. "Your wages are being paid by Mrs. Crossly, Ezra. And have been for five years or more. Her bequest to this church was inestimable. The least we can do is fulfill her final request."

"Still don't seem right," Ezra reiterated. "Smells of sorcery."

"Don't be ridiculous."

"Ridiculous? No, it ain't, sir. No, it ain't." Ezra was agitated. "I saw what old Ironfist—Master Crossly, if you will—got up to with those sorcerers from London way back when. I looked in through that there church window up there and saw the lights flickering and the shades of spirits wandering among the wizards. In this very chancel. Saw it with my own eyes, I did. And now you want me to put a strange woman in his tomb? That ain't right nohow. Mayhap the widow Jackson was a witch herself and needs must lie alongside him to rekindle the hocus pocus."

"Silence, Ezra! I'll have no more of that kind of talk!"

"Why do we not just wait for Mrs. Crossly to pass?" the stonemason asked. "She were an upright lady if ever there were one."

"Mrs. Crossly is gone from the county. She will never return."

"Where has she gone?" Ezra asked, but the vicar had no answer.

For a moment Ezra stood in silence, shaking his head.

"This is what Mrs. Crossly wants," the vicar emphasized. "If you respect her, you must respect her wishes. Now get on with the job!"

Still shaking his head, Ezra walked over to the niche. He said, "We'll need to lift off the lid, lads. It's heavy as sin. It'll take three men and six sets of muscles."

"And all this is to remain secret, gentlemen," the vicar stressed. "It was Mrs. Crossly's expressed desire. Secret. You may not tell anyone who is being laid to rest here today. Or where. Is that clearly understood? No gossip in the Red Lion. Not a word."

The three men nodded. They surveyed the tomb and gauged the weight of the thick stone lid. Ezra took the lead, and they raised the lid and set it gently on the floor of the church. A smell of embalming materials and herbs was released. Surprisingly pleasant, they all thought. The vicar stepped backward so as not to see the contents. The sexton and his boy unwrapped the corpse, lifted it off the floor, and laid it alongside the remains of Richard Crossly. On impulse, Ezra took the hand of the widow Jackson and placed it around the decomposed hand and partly skeletal fingers of Richard Crossly—the hand that was not encased in the iron glove. "Here you are, Ironfist. A partner for the ride," he said to Richard's body; then leaning close to Richard's withered face, he whispered, "If you haven't already gone below." They replaced the lid.

The stonemason then moved forward, chisel and hammer in his hands, and knelt down.

"What date shall I carve?" He looked up at the vicar.

"Yesterday's, I suppose. At least that part will then be true."

"Tell it me the Roman way."

It took some time for the vicar to get it straight in his head and to convey it to the stonemason in preparation for the handiwork. In the end, he had to go back to the vestry and scratch it in large letters onto a piece of parchment, which he handed to the stonemason. The stonemason could not read, but he was an expert copier. Ezra and his boy quickly got bored and walked outside, their part of the day's work over. The vicar, too, felt that his participation was no longer required and returned to the vestry.

The stonemason was left alone in front of the niche to complete the inscription. After the words *"Ille obiit,"* he chiseled, *"Nono Aprilis MDXCIII."* He blew the stone dust off it and went home.

Chapter 30

Saxonborough
April 2019

On the Sunday morning, when all talk of time and ghosts and graveyards had abated and things had largely returned to normal, three of the four of them dug into their full English breakfasts in the coffee shop. Denise declined such a big meal as she was on a diet; she ate a grapefruit and a slice of toast. Karen, on the other hand, had been deprived of modern breakfasts for so long that she simply could not resist.

"What's not to like?" she asked with true Joey Tribbiani enthusiasm. "Sausage…good! Fried eggs…good! Baked beans…? Goooood! I was thinking," Karen said between mouthfuls, "if we have time, I'd like to make a couple of side trips this morning on our way down to London. I'd like to see what's become of the home I lived in for fifty years, Ketteringham Lodge. Then I'd like to take a quick trip over to Hoyland Church. Would you be okay with that, Harry? After all that happened to you there?"

"I guess so," Harry replied with no great enthusiasm. "Ketteringham Lodge is no problem. And I guess I could take one more trip to Hoyland Church without letting my mind dwell on the past—if you really have to go there."

"I do. Neither of them are far out of our way. An hour or two at most. Then we can swing across and pick up the A-1 somewhere near Grantham. I'd really like to see what Ketteringham Lodge looks like today. I'm only familiar with its Tudor forebear. And there's one or two things I need to clear up at the church. Shouldn't take more than ten minutes. Assuming the vicar's there."

"He should be," said Tom. "It's Sunday. There'll be a morning service."

"Oh, I didn't think of that. We may have to wait till it's over. Late morning, say."

"Sure," Harry replied. "We can do all of that. Tom and Denise might like to see these places they've heard us talk about so much."

"Yes," said Tom. "Very much so."

"One other thing before we go, Karen," Harry said. "Have you thought any more about what you intend to do? I'm really worried about you. What are you going to do while you're over here? How will you support yourself? And how will you go about returning to the States?"

"I don't have any answers at the moment. One good thing is that I brought all my coins and jewelry with me. I sold one of the better pieces, a gold bracelet, in Lincoln on Wednesday. That kept me going in London, and I still have cash left over from the sale. Plus, I reckon that the remaining items are worth a lot—tens of thousands at least, I'm sure of it. So my immediate financial concerns are taken care of. After that…I don't know. My dream is very modest, simply to get myself back to Reinbeck and live out my days there in peace and quiet. I guess I'll go home to my parents and see if they can accept me…a daughter repurposed as a mother perhaps. God knows what they'll think—or even if they'll believe my story. Or I could just get a place by myself nearby. I'm still thinking about that. And I'm not sure how I'm going to support myself in my old age…or if I get sick. Like Denise said, a lot of things to consider.

"And at the moment I really have no idea *how* to get home. All the strategies I can come up with seem problematic. Right now, the only thing I can think to do is to throw myself on the mercy of the INS at the embassy in London. Tell them I lost my passport and all other forms of ID. Tell them I've been living with this goofy British scientist guy, Brian Kenning, who then deserted me and took my stuff. That much they can verify. Presuming they can access a photograph of me from my passport records, I could tell them that Brian and I performed some sort of aging experiment together…and see what I've become! Doubtful they would buy that though. But I'm hoping I can convince them that I really am who I claim to be, that I grew up in Iowa, lived in Joliet, went to CIU, *et cetera, et cetera.* Hopefully, they would have pity on me and give me a one-time special dispensation to go back home. They might be amenable to that."

"Yes, they might," said Harry. "Such things must have happened before—similar ones anyway. Muggings and accidents. You're clearly not a terrorist or a threat of any kind. The only sticking point is that you appear to be way older than in any photo or the contents of any form of documentation. Your date of birth, for example, will seem impossible. They're bound to think you might be an imposter. I wonder if I should stay on with you in London to help you navigate your way back to the States. What do you think? I'm the reason you got into this mess in the first place."

"It's a thought. It would make me feel more confident. Let's think about it some more."

They finished breakfast, gathered up their belongings, and checked out.

Within an hour their car pulled up at the entrance to Ketteringham Lodge. The path into the property was just how Karen remembered it except that the fancy iron gate was gone, and a sign by the roadside said *Ketteringham Lodge, Residential Care Home.* Underneath the name were a phone number and a web address and the slogan *"Our home is your home."* Harry had no compunction in turning up the path and driving through the grounds to the front of the imposing three-story building. They came to a halt on the gravel by the front door, and all got out. Tom and Denise looked around in wonderment.

"You used to *live* here?" asked Tom.

"It's like Downton Abbey," Denise added.

"I lived on this property," Karen replied, "but not in this building. These grounds were the long-time home of the Crossly family, but this building is much more recent than the crumbling old mansion we lived in. This looks Victorian." She gazed full circle around her. "Oh no! My alder trees have gone," she said sadly. "And that pond is new. Everything's changed." She bent down and picked up some of the gravel stones, sifting them through her fingers. "These are the only things that are the same. I probably stepped on these very pebbles four hundred years ago."

The other three stared at her, lost for words.

"Let's go," Karen said abruptly, and they all got back in the car and drove off.

Hoyland Church, on the other hand, was little changed from earlier times. Karen had entered the Tudor world through the ancient Augustinian monastery known as Hoyland Abbey, but she had witnessed—and financially supported—the construction of its replacement Anglican church, the same church that now stood in front of her. The surrounding vegetation was a little different, and there were way more gravestones, but basically it was the same. After Tom and Denise had studied its exterior and compared it to the church at Saxonborough, the four of them went in through the main door. Morning service had concluded, and only the vicar was in the building, polishing the communion rail. The four of them walked over to him. He looked up.

"Can I help you?"

"You might remember me," Harry began. "I'm one of the American scientists that got involved in all the brouhaha last summer."

"Oh yes, you do look familiar."

"We've returned to take a quick look around. I hope it's not inconvenient."

The vicar bristled. "Please leave at once! You're not welcome here." He waved them toward the door. "Do you have any idea what your shenanigans cost this church? And I don't mean financially. Our reputation in the community…in the Church of England…was shattered. We're lucky to have a congregation at all. You have no idea!"

"I don't, I know," Harry continued, "and we're sorry beyond words. But it was all unintentional. And we suffered too, sir…me and this woman here. Suffered in ways *you* could never imagine."

"That matters little. The whole business is closed. Please leave."

"Sir," said Karen, stepping forward, "is the crypt off-limits?"

"Absolutely, it is!" said the vicar, on the verge of shouting. "Absolutely! Two people died down there. It's locked on the orders of the county police. Anyone desirous of access must apply to them seventy-two hours in advance and have a very, very good reason to go down there. Then, if permitted, they must be accompanied by me and a police officer. There's not a chance in Hades that you would be permitted to go down there."

"Okay, okay. I understand," said Karen. "Honestly, I do. Instead of going down there then, perhaps I could just ask you a couple of questions about the Crossly tomb?"

"That tomb was utterly violated!" the vicar continued, ignoring Karen's request. "The marble top had been knocked to the ground and smashed to pieces. It was four hundred years old! We had to bring in the stonemason from Sleaford to make a replacement. Just awful."

"You saw inside the tomb though, correct? There were still the two bodies in it?"

"Of course there were. Richard and Catherine Crossly. The remains were undisturbed."

"And the remains of the man…one hand was missing? Replaced by a metal hand?"

"Yes, yes. He was known as Ironfist, I believe. Both bodies were undisturbed, as I said."

"Good. I'm glad no damage was done to the remains."

"But the whole crypt was damp. Wet, in fact. We had to put fans down there and run them for a week to dry everything out. How the water got in there is still a mystery. The Lincoln city engineer could not explain it."

"But you tidied up the Crossly tomb and laid a new marble slab on top of it?"

"Yes, of course. And then locked the crypt up. It won't be opened again in my lifetime, if I have anything to say about it. When we say 'Rest in peace,' we mean it!"

"Very good. Thank you, sir," said Karen calmly. "That's all I needed to know. We won't bother you any further. I'm sorry for the inconvenience."

"You have no idea how much trouble it caused us," said the vicar, slowly calming down. "My religious training never prepared me for anything like it."

"No, of course not. We won't bother you further."

Karen turned and walked away, signaling the others to follow her. As they headed down the path to the car, Karen summed things up for Harry, "So Brian is still resting down there, and the Tudor vicar did what he said he would do and provided the body of a poor old pauper woman to take my place beside him. I'm good. What exactly happened down there in the crypt last August will have to remain locked up too, but I'm sure Brian's brother was behind it, wherever he is today."

"Nobody knows where John is," said Harry. "I made a few inquiries at the time but to no avail. He could be anywhere."

Chapter 31

London and Fallow Fields
January 1806

On January 9, 1806, the most lavish funeral ever seen in England took place at St. Paul's Cathedral. The procession that escorted the coffin from the Admiralty consisted of thirty-two admirals, more than one hundred captains, and ten thousand soldiers. After a four-hour service, the body was lowered through the floor of the nave and interred within the crypt in a sarcophagus originally carved for Cardinal Wolsey. The pomp and pageantry were spectacular in the extreme and thrilled the city's populace—which was surprising for the burial of the son of a Norfolk parson. But the inscription on the coffin revealed that its occupant was none other than *The Most Noble Lord Horatio Nelson, Viscount and Baron Nelson, of the Nile and of Burnham Thorpe in the County of Norfolk, Baron Nelson of the Nile and of Hilborough in the said County, Knight of the Most Honourable Order of the Bath, Vice Admiral of the White Squadron of the Fleet, Commander in Chief of His Majesty's Ships and Vessels in the Mediterranean, Duke of Bronté in the Kingdom of Sicily, Knight Grand Cross of the Sicilian Order of St. Ferdinand and of Merit, Member of the Ottoman Order of the Crescent, Knight Grand Commander of the Order of St. Joachim.*

On that same day Martha and Jemmy bundled themselves up in the heaviest coats they possessed and went to the bottom of the garden and dug a hole in the ground. They laid the body in the hole and covered it. Two days later, Jemmy went to the stonemason's workshop next to the parish church and asked if she could have a cast-off piece of gravestone. He obliged. She brought it back on a cart and scratched three letters on it with the point of a kitchen knife: T...O...M. She went down to the bottom of the garden and stuck it in the ground at the head of the grave.

Chapter 32

London
April 2019

As soon as they arrived back at their hotel in London, Tom and Denise started packing for their flight home the next morning. Harry told them they would be on their own this time—he would not leave without Karen. The four of them came together in a communal hug and promised to reconvene Stateside at the earliest opportunity. Harry then canceled his own flight and huddled with Karen to talk strategy. In the end, Karen could think of no alternative but to march up to the Immigration and Naturalization Service, explain her situation, and pray they would look kindly on her. Harry offered to accompany her to the embassy and vouch for her, but then the two of them thought better of it in light of the troubles Harry himself had had with the INS during the course of the previous summer when he'd overstayed his visa. Karen would go alone.

She made an appointment for Wednesday morning on the grounds that she'd lost her passport and all other forms of identification and needed to get back home as quickly as possible. It took three trips to the American Embassy. At the first meeting she told her tale. She'd been in a relationship with a British citizen named Brian Kenning. They'd both gone off the grid, so to speak. He was a scientist, and they'd been doing some experiments that had aged her. She could not explain it any better. They'd recently split up, and she'd been unable to recover her documentation from his place. The INS people were skeptical and asked her to return the following day after they'd done some checking.

She dutifully returned the next day and was interrogated some more. Then they made their admission to her. Yes, they'd been able to confirm who Brian Kenning was and that he was currently missing. Yes, they knew that she'd left Chicago on June 6, 2018, arrived in London the following day, and been missing since then. And yes, everything she'd said about her studies at Central Illinois University, her apartment in Joliet, and her parents' home in Reinbeck, Iowa, had checked out. They'd even contacted the Joliet Police Department and had one of their staff compare notes with the detective in charge of her missing persons case, John Dietrichson. Only one thing was amiss: every piece of documentation said she was nineteen years old, but she looked sixty if a day. She was asked to return for a third meeting on Friday, bringing a passport photo and a completed application form. This she did. She handed them over and waited for half an hour until she was ushered into an office and asked to sit.

The INS officer to whom her case had been assigned took a seat across the desk from her and looked her up and down, clearly exasperated. On the desk in front of him were a limited-validity emergency passport and a letter on State Department stationery. He had a pen in his hand. He nodded thoughtfully for a minute and then looked her in the eye. He spoke quickly and forcefully.

"What's the nickname of the University of Iowa football team?"

"The Hawkeyes. But I'm a fan of Iowa State. The Cyclones."

"Who's the governor of Iowa?"

"Er…Kim Reynolds?"

"What's the zip code of Reinbeck?"

"50669."

"What county is it in?"

"Grundy."

The officer continued to stare at her, then shook his head and signed the letter.

"We're giving you a one-time travel dispensation to enable you to return to the US. This is an emergency passport." He handed it over to her. "And this is a letter of authorization to permit you to travel—in case the officer on duty studies your passport photo and casts doubt on your age." He handed that over also. "Present both of these documents to the authorities at Heathrow Airport and you'll be allowed to board the plane. Once you get back home, you'll need to contact the State Department, Social Security, and other agencies and start the process of reestablishing your identity and applying for all the necessary documentation you're currently missing."

Karen nodded. "I understand."

"Your case is unprecedented," the officer said with a sly smile. "We've been up and down the chain of command here three times, trying to decide what to do with you. But two things are clear to me. One, you really *are* Karen Butler despite the incongruities in your appearance, and as such, you are a US citizen and entitled to return home. Two, you are definitely not a terrorist, and you are definitely not a threat in any shape or form. So at the end of the day, I feel confident in making this decision. Don't let me down. Good luck to you."

"Thank you so much," said Karen. "I can't tell you how happy I am. I've been through such a lot this past year, and always in the back of my mind was an uneasiness about how I was ever going to get back home. I spent night after night worrying about it. I even thought about going to Nicaragua or somewhere and then hiking up though Mexico and creeping across the border."

"Ha! Well, you did the right thing, Miss Butler. You should write a book about your experiences when you get back home. I would buy it."

They stood up and shook hands. Karen did her best to leave the room in a dignified fashion and walk ladylike out of the building despite her inclination to leap into the air and run headlong out into the street. If she'd still been nineteen, she might have done just that, but at sixty-nine, it wasn't really on the cards. Harry was waiting for her by the entrance and immediately knew she'd been successful. He laughed and hugged her while she cried into his shoulder.

"It's okay, Harry. All is well," Karen said, finally smiling through her tears. "I have papers!" She waved them in the air. "Go back to the hotel and reschedule your flight for Monday. Buy me a ticket too, please. I've got one more thing to do before I go home."

"What's that?"

"Make my fortune."

Karen had done her homework. She'd identified a prominent company of numismatists in the ritziest part of London, Mayfair. She left Harry in front of the American Embassy, skipped over Vauxhall Bridge, danced a jig around the grounds of Buckingham Palace, and landed on the company's doorstep just after lunchtime. She paused to compose herself. Taking a deep breath, she adopted a sophisticated air and smiled at the uniformed doorman as she entered. She strolled over to the counter, where a smartly dressed middle-aged man in a dark-blue suit and a bow tie greeted her.

"Good afternoon, madam. How may we help you?"

"I have some old coins that I would like valued."

"Certainly, madam."

"And if I approve of your valuation and your service, I would like you to put them up for auction on my behalf."

"We can do that. Most assuredly. If they meet our standards. Do you have the coins in your possession at the moment?"

"I do," said Karen, trying to sound both classy and opulent. She then added in little more than a whisper, "But I believe they are quite valuable, and I notice that there are other customers in your shop at present. I would not wish for these strangers to catch sight of my coins—for security reasons, you understand. Do you have a private room where I could show them to you?"

"Certainly. Please follow me. My name is Gordon Howard by the way," the man said as they walked. "And you are?"

"My name is Karen Butler. I have come over from America expressly for this purpose."

He led her into a small backroom, in the center of which was a wooden table with a baize top and elegant armchairs on either side of it. They took up their positions. The man, with a supercilious grin on his face, held out his left palm, fingers pointing downward, to indicate that she should display her wares on the tabletop. Karen pulled out her ancient purse, untied the strings, opened it up, and spilled twenty coins or thereabouts out onto the green baize. The man's jaw literally dropped. He looked up into Karen's face, eyes wide, and then back down at the coins. He put on a pair of gloves and gently spread the coins apart. He said nothing for almost a minute as he peered down at each one. Then again, he looked up at Karen.

"Are you serious?" he asked.

"I am," Karen replied.

"And these are all genuine?"

"They are. You may test them later."

"But I have never seen coins of this period in such immaculate condition. I'm stunned."

"Yes. They're bright and shiny, are they not?"

"Where did you get them? I cannot believe my eyes."

"I'll tell you later how I acquired them. I need you first to value them."

"Yes, of course." He swallowed hard. "Of course. Hmm. It will take a little while to come up with a preliminary evaluation. I will need the help of one of my colleagues. I myself am an expert on Celtic and Roman coinage, but our office manager knows the House of Tudor well. It may take half an hour or so."

"Not a problem."

"You are aware, I suppose, that these are very rare Elizabethan gold coins?"

"I am."

"We almost never see the like of them."

"Take your time. My afternoon is free."

"Allow me to fetch my colleague, then. And may I get you something to drink while you wait? Tea perhaps? Or coffee?"

"A cup of coffee would be nice."

"My pleasure."

The man hurried out of the room. He returned shortly thereafter carrying a cup of coffee and a plate of assorted cookies. In his wake was a bald older man clutching two battered catalogs that looked almost as old as the coins themselves. Mr. Howard indicated that Karen should sit in a leather armchair in a corner of the room, and he placed the refreshments on a tiny table by its side. "Please make yourself comfortable," he said. Karen sat down and sipped the coffee. Almost at once she dozed off, both exhausted by her walk and relieved by the events of the day thus far. The two experts went over to the table and pored over the coins. They fumbled through the catalogs and whispered to each other with astonished looks. Time passed.

Karen was woken by Mr. Howard tapping gently on her wrist. She jerked upright giving her apologies. She was urged to return to the table and sit down. The two men took up positions across from her. The bald man seated himself, while the other stood at his side. The bald man opened his mouth and eventually spoke.

"These coins…," he began and then paused and shook his head. "We have not seen such exquisite specimens in many a day. I might almost say *never*. All of them are from the Elizabethan period." He moved them around carefully with a gloved hand. "I will describe them individually to begin with and give you a very approximate estimate of their value. And by *value*, I mean our estimate of the price they might realize at auction. And this assumes they are genuine, which they do appear to be. I understand you would not be averse to us obtaining a professional certification of their authenticity?"

"Not at all."

"Very well. Then let me start with these eight gold sovereigns."

He set them out in a row in the center of the table and pushed the others off to one side.

"These eight coins are what is known as Sixth Issue gold sovereigns. Some of them appear to be *fine*, meaning that the gold content is greater than 0.99, while the rest of them are probably *crown*, with a gold content between 0.91 and 0.92. That can be determined at a later time. There are just three different kinds of mintmarks on the eight of them: the letter A, the escallop, and the crescent. I apologize for these technicalities, madam. These mintmarks date them to the early to mid-1580s."

"Yes," said Karen, "that sounds about right."

Both men instantly looked up at her. They'd assumed that she was completely ignorant about the types of coins in her possession, but perhaps she knew more than she'd let on. She would have to be taken seriously.

"And their value?" Karen pressed the bald-headed man.

"Their quality is, frankly, beyond belief. They make the *very fine* category hang its head in shame. They are *extremely fine* in my judgment—a quality we never see in Elizabethan coinage. *Never*. In fact, catalogs do not show the *extremely fine* category for Elizabethan coins. That category does not make an appearance until the milled coinage of Charles II in 1662. You see, prior to 1662, the process of making coins was by hammering. Such coins are known in the trade as *hammered*. They do not withstand the ravages of time as well as the milled ones."

"And their value?" Karen asked yet again.

"I'm going to say…roughly £35,000 each at auction."

Karen nodded her approval, though her heart leaped.

"Then there are three slightly older gold sovereigns." He slid them over to join the eight others. "They all appear to be from the Fourth Issue, dating to the late 1570s. They are all what we call *fine* sovereigns, with a gold content of about 0.994. This one is the best of the three." He pushed it forward so that Karen could see it more closely. "Notice that this coin is distinguished from the others by having no chains on the portcullis in the engraving. See? It is rarer. It is slightly worn, however, but still of *very fine* quality and worth about £40,000."

Karen looked up at him and smiled. The smile was returned.

"And then these other two are lesser sovereigns of the same time frame—*with* chains on the portcullis—also slightly worn but still *fine* to *very fine*. Worth perhaps £20,000 each. And the smaller coins here are what we call gold angels, ten-shilling coins."

"I know," said Karen, and again the men looked at her in disbelief.

"They are all from the early 1580s and worth about £4,000 each. There are ten of them."

"That's wonderful," said Karen. "Thank you so much."

"Wait. I have not quite finished," said the old man, this time breaking into an even broader smile, impudent even. "This one…" He pulled the last coin from the array and pushed it under Karen's nose. It was similar to the sovereigns but slightly smaller. "This is the crown jewel of your collection. It is a very rare gold ryal, equivalent to about fifteen shillings at the time, also from the 1580s. Do you see the figure of Queen Elizabeth with a ship in the background?" He pushed it even closer to her so that she could bend forward and view the engraved image. "It is superb! Absolutely superb! I have only ever seen one or two of them in my lifetime and none of this outstanding quality. This coin alone would make £75,000 at the very least. The very least!"

Karen coughed and then spluttered a little. "Truly?"

"I would bet my pension on it. No less than £75,000."

"So what is the total value?"

The bald man looked up at his partner, who began punching numbers into his iPhone. He looked at the screen and whispered, "Four hundred and seventy-five thousand." The bald man cleared his throat. "Our preliminary estimate of the total value of the coins laid out here is £475,000. In view of the extremely high quality and the desirability of Elizabethan coins, at a well-advertised auction, you can round that up to half a million. I believe that is what the collection would make. Subject to our own expenses, of course, and the cost of NGC certification. And all being subject to guarantees of good provenance, you understand."

"I do."

"Good. So…shall we?"

"Yes," said Karen. "I would like you to sell them for me at auction." The two men simply beamed at this news. "You will have guessed that I am American. I'd thought about selling them in New York, but then I decided they would probably make a better price over here, where people would be more familiar with them and more interested in acquiring them. I will be returning to the States on Monday. I would like to leave the coins with you. I assume you have a secure place to store them. Please have them certified as genuine at your own convenience and then set up the auction. I'm sure you will advertise it widely and permit overseas bidding. I will not demean myself by appearing to tell you your business. I will leave you my personal details with instructions as to how to contact me. And at a later date I will provide bank details for the proceeds of the sale to be transferred to me."

"Certainly, madam, certainly. It will be our great pleasure. We are most honored by the trust you place in us. Mr. Howard will take it from here." He nodded toward his companion, who simpered. "We will draw up an agreement immediately to be signed by both parties. And you can rest assured that your coins will be in good hands until the time of the auction."

"*Secure* hands," Mr. Howard emphasized.

"My name is Jonathan Tompkins by the way," the bald man said before he left the room. "I am the office manager and something of an expert on hammered coins like these. And I have to say that this is one of the two or three most dazzling collections I have seen in my forty years in the trade. I thank you, Miss Butler, for honoring us with your patronage."

Karen nodded and remained seated.

"Let me quickly start the paperwork," Mr. Howard said. "I shall return in a moment."

He scurried out of the room, leaving Karen to stare at the coins arrayed in front of her. Yes, they were beautiful. Yes, they were shiny. And yes, they'd been of value in her time at Ketteringham Lodge. The eight gold sovereigns alone would have paid her maidservant's wages for a couple of years…bought four horses for a new carriage…or paid for a couple of pairs of courtier's satin breeches. But half a million pounds? Never in her wildest dreams could she have imagined they would be worth so much today. Thank God she'd thought to stuff them in her purse before she left! Her financial future was secure.

Mr. Howard returned with a velvet bag and placed the coins carefully into it.

"There!" he said, pulling on the drawstrings and tying them. "They will be placed into proper scratch-proof coin capsules by our staff later this afternoon. Then they will be locked in our safe for the weekend. Now before you go, Miss Butler, would you be so kind as to briefly tell me how these coins came into your possession? You said you would do that. I'm on tenterhooks." He chuckled. "It will also help toward establishing provenance, you understand, which is a requirement of our company. How long have they been in your possession, might I ask?"

Karen had completed this homework assignment too.

"It's a long story, Mr. Howard, so I'll just give you a synopsis. The bottom line is that the coins have been in the possession of our family since the day they were minted. I know that's hard to believe, but it's the truth. My brother has done a lot of research on them since they came into our possession—which, by the way, was out of a safe deposit box pursuant to a bequest from our grandfather. Nobody knew of their existence until he died and his will was read. Because of this, nobody knows precisely how he obtained them. But my brother has built our family tree and developed a highly probable explanation. Most of what I'm about to tell you will mean little or nothing to you, but bear with me.

"We believe that the coins were originally owned by a woman who was one of the earliest settlers in the Virginia colony of North America. And by that I mean the Jamestown colony, not the doomed Roanoke colony. She was a lady with the adorable name of Temperance Flowerdew. She was born in Norfolk here in England. She arrived at Jamestown in August 1609 aboard a vessel called the *Falcon*. This, you will appreciate, is consistent with the dates of the coins. We believe she carried the coins on her person during the Atlantic crossing.

"Temperance survived the first terrible winter that was known as the *Starving Time*. Depredations by Indian tribes only made matters worse. They say that only sixty of the original five hundred colonists survived that winter. Can you believe it? Temperance, fortunately, was one of them. But they were reinforced and resupplied in the nick of time and managed to survive.

"Temperance Flowerdew married into the Yeardley family in 1618. Her husband served three years as the governor of Virginia and was later knighted by King James back in England. She became Lady Yeardley. And when her husband died, she also became one of the wealthiest women in Virginia. Her estate was passed down to her children—the English coins included, we presume. The family tree that my brother constructed suggests that we're descended from their second child, Argoll Yeardley. I don't remember any more than that, but I very much doubt you have any interest, in any case."

"No, it's most…," said Mr. Howard, straightening his bow tie.

"We think that the coins were preserved by these early ancestors—either for a rainy day or because there was no market for such coinage in Virginia at that time. Or perhaps they kept them purely out of sentimental value—a keepsake from the homeland, as it were—and stored them away fastidiously. The purse in which they were kept has already been dated to the sixteenth century by an American expert in fabrics." She showed the purse to Mr. Howard. "Somehow this purse and its contents made their way down the ages from Argoll Yeardley to our grandfather."

"That must be a unique set of circumstances, truly. New coins brought to America from England and never added to or traded away or disturbed in any way."

"That's what we think," said Karen, completing the elaborate lie. "Unique."

A woman entered the room carrying two sheets of paper, which she laid on the table in front of Mr. Howard. He quicky glanced them over and then turned them around and pushed them in front of Karen. She noticed that they were both already signed and dated by Jonathan Tompkins, and there was a line underneath for her to sign. She read the agreement closely and thought about it for a second or two. Everything seemed to be in order, but what did she know? She signed and dated both copies. She turned one copy back around and set it in front of Mr. Howard; the other copy she folded and slipped into her bag. In words that seemed to be popular in England at the time, *all done and dusted.*

They stood up and shook hands. Mr. Howard escorted Karen out of the building in a gentlemanly fashion. Under the canopy above the doorway, she pulled her ancient purse out of her bag and examined the jewelry remaining in it: two gold rings, a gold bracelet, and a necklace—her other bracelet having already been sold in Lincoln. *Well,* she thought, *these I can keep.* She put the rings on her fingers, the bracelet on her wrist, and the necklace around her neck. She kissed her decrepit Tudor purse goodbye, tossed it into a garbage can, and sauntered away down Grosvenor Street.

As she walked, the feel of the necklace against her skin brought to mind her suitor Edward Kelley, who'd given it to her in the upstairs hallway of The Plough so very many years ago. She began to think that she might have been too hard on him. She wondered what he'd felt about her disappearance. Had he managed to forget about her? Had his life found renewal somehow? She wondered what his fate had been. Did one of the crowned heads of Europe reward him sumptuously?

Chapter 33

Hněvín Castle, Most, Bohemia
November 1597

Edward Kelley stared for a long time through the small window of his cell at the top of the tall tower of Hněvín Castle. Twice he'd tried to escape through that window, and twice he'd fallen onto the battlements below. As a result, he now had one wooden leg and one leg so rotten and swathed in bandages that it throbbed continuously and knifed him whenever he tried to walk. He was sitting in a chair with his one remaining foot resting on a stool. On a tiny round table by his right side was a small plate of bread and sausage that he could not eat; on a similar table by his left side was a goblet of poison placed there by a guard under the instructions of his wife for the day when the pain became unbearable, which would arrive soon enough. Through the small window he could see tiny trees and clouds and a hilltop and the color blue, none of which he would ever again enjoy. All pleasure had been lost through his own foolishness. He scratched his wooden leg and massaged his infected leg and leaned back in his chair.

He should've stayed with Dee in Poland. Or in Třeboň. He was convinced he had completed his first transmutation in Třeboň, and all had been proceeding well enough there. But he'd been greedy. Emperor Rudolf had offered him even greater riches if he would come to the court in Prague and replicate his successful experiment there. He and Dee had parted ways then, Dee returning to England. That was eight years ago, and they had not seen each other since. Opulence had indeed welcomed Kelley to Prague. Under the patronage of Lord William of Rosenberg, he'd been granted estates and wealth. His family had joined him. They had prospered. And just as he'd once bragged to Catherine, the emperor knighted him Sir Edward Kelley of Imany and New Lüben. But he had been a greedy, stupid fool. For it did not last. When he'd been unable to deliver the gold he'd promised, the emperor soured on him. He should have foreseen that. Twice he'd been imprisoned, twice he'd attempted to escape, and twice he'd fallen and broken his legs. So now he found himself lodged permanently in the small cell at the top of the round tower of Hněvín Castle. Reveal the secret. Make gold. Or remain there.

He dozed. He awoke.

The Beast with the Head of a Boar was sitting in the corner again. In the shadows. The accusations began afresh.

"You are not Edward Kelley. Your name is Talbot!"

"Well, when I—"

"You were pilloried in Leicester for forgery!"

"I know, but—"

"Your ears were cropped!"

"I wear a cap to—"

"You have cheated John Dee for many years!"

"Not cheated, we—"

"You have cheated the nobility of Europe!"

"They asked me—"

"You have cheated Queen Elizabeth herself!"

"I only showed—"

"You have cheated on your wife!"

"No, I did not do—"

"You have disowned your stepchildren!"

"That is not true, I—"

"You have never transmuted any metal to gold!"

"I have indications that—"

"You have never communicated with angels!"

"The shew stone always—"

"You invented the Enochian language yourself!"

"No, I merely—"

"You were never in love with Catherine Crossly!"

"I was! I was! I—"

"You only wanted her property and escape from your family!"

"Do not say that. I—"

"You did not love Catherine Crossly, I say."

"Sir, that is—"

"The only transmutation you have ever achieved was a transmutation of yourself from a scheming young rascal to a double-dealing man of wealth!" The Beast with the Head of a Boar leaned forward out of the shadows to reveal itself in all its hideousness. "Is that not true, Master Talbot?"

"Yes, I suppose—"

"Is not every word of it true?"

"Yes."

The Beast with the Head of a Boar leaned back into the shadows.

"It is time for you to drink from the poisoned goblet, is it not?"

"Perhaps."

"Is IT NOT?!"

"Yes. Yes, it is."

"Good. Then do so."

And he did.

Chapter 34

Fallow Fields
July 1809

There were nine tongues within one head,
The tenth went out to seek for bread,
To feed the living within the dead.

THE WORDS SWAM IN THE boy's head, words he had stolen from the edge of schoolyard whisper. They stuck him with barbs, then rearranged themselves and fled from meaning. *Nine tongues? The living within the dead?* His schoolmates seemed to understand these words and even to derive amusement from them, but to him they were just echoes of something terrible beyond his grasp. Trembling slightly, the boy picked up a twig and began to skin it. A wisp of smoke trailed up into the sky from a dying bonfire in the corner of the garden. He was alone among the wild weeds, banished there by his mother the moment Aunt Jemmy had begun to talk of important things. Now their voices caught his ear and drew him to the kitchen door. Great secrets were being kept from him, he knew.

"The poor creature," Martha sobbed. "Oh, poor Tommy!"

"Allay, allay," cooed Aunt Jemmy. "Don't take on so. This burden will not press us forever. It will be lifted soon."

"Lifted from you. And lifted from me perhaps. But from the boy?" Martha's voice rose in a mixture of fear and exasperation. "Oh, Thomas, that you should do such a thing and leave your son to pay tithe on it!"

"God rest his soul."

When they spoke ill of his father—as many seemed to do—the boy looked down at the ground, ashamed but not knowing why. Anger seethed in his belly. Thomas Temporal, the father; Tommy Temporal, the son. *Tom Tit! Tit! Tom Tit!* Fingers pointing across the playground. Girls giggling in corridors.

Lonely and alone, he turned back into the summer's heat and the perfumes of gardenia and geranium. He paused by the door to the woodshed, where hung a jar part-filled with orange marmalade for the purpose of catching wasps. The poor creatures, lured through holes in the lid, could find no exit and whimpered in the sugary mire, pressing the faces of older inmates down into sweet death. Mesmerized, the boy studied the carnage. A hornet, larger than any of the wasps, hovered above the jar—it, too, summoned by the scent. It turned toward the boy, ballooned into a monster with his father's face, stuck out nine tongues, and flew up into the sky.

Shouting came from inside the cottage.

"It'll be a mercy if you'll let me do it," said Aunt Jemmy.

"No, no! Not poor Tommy, please!"

"Poor Tommy he is *now*—if you could only see it—and poor Tommy he will *remain* if the scouring of it not be done soon. Can you not see that?"

"He's but a bantling," Martha pleaded. "He ain't got the constitution for it."

The boy inhaled the smell of strife and snapped the twig in his hands. He returned to the buzzing marmalade, where he was the omniscient one.

Suddenly his aunt burst from the kitchen and hurried toward him.

"Come away from that jar, Tommy, and walk with me."

The boy's blank face, country-round and ember-cheeked, looked up at her and searched for some token of reassurance but found only marbled determination. She grabbed his hand and dragged him away from the shambles of his parentage and the security of the great and empty garden. They walked away from the cottage, down the road that led to Saxonborough, past the five-sail mill.

"Do you know Fallow Lane?"

"Aye, Aunt Jemmy, but I mayn't go there."

"And who says so?"

"Mama."

"Well, today, Fallow Lane is where you and I go."

The boy jerked on his aunt's hand and dug his heels into the dirt.

"I won't!"

"It's over Martha's naysay, true enough, but I'll act surety on it. Is there aught else?"

"There be a monster down Fallow Lane."

"A monster?"

"A boggart. It lives in the dyke and eats children. So many has it eaten, they say, that it grows fat and bold. I fear it will take a hankering for me. I'm much afeared of it."

"Aye, Tommy, your schoolfellows be part right. There truly is some monstrous thing down Fallow Lane. But it is rather the not seeing of it that will eat you whole and alive." She looked down at him and smiled a bitter smile. "Though you be young and innocent and more precious to us than a coachload of King George's gold, today you shall see this thing."

"No, Aunt Jemmy, please."

The two of them halted in the dust of a lost English lane on the blasted side of Whitsun in the year eighteen hundred and nine. Emotion simmered in the young woman's voice. She shook the lad by the shoulders. "Tommy, this thing must be done, and you mayn't swerve me from it. You need to know what happened to your father. Martha cannot do it, so the duty falls to me. God, give me the strength, for you must be told!"

The boy's lower lip unfolded in a pout. He exhaled audibly. Then just as quickly, the lip receded. A white cloud seemed to drift down out of the bright blue sky and settle over the boy and soothe him. He looked up into his aunt's eyes. She seemed more afraid than he was and sorely in need of his compliance. He was greatly fond of her also. He sighed.

"I will walk with you," he said softly, raising his small hand into hers, "if I must."

"There's my brave boy. And hearken well to me as we walk, for I will tell you as much of the story as I know. Though how to summon the voice to speak it I scarce can fathom. It is the story of why your father is no longer with us, and it is as bitter a tale as ever was told. So where to start now? Walk on, Tommy, walk on. And please look to the fields as I speak the words, or I may falter. My brother—your father—was never much of a thinker, nor even a man of God. He was always and ever a laboring sort. No different from a thousand other men hereabouts. No ideas above his station, if you know what I mean. And with a bit of a temper when he believed himself thwarted. These are just *extenuating circumstances*, as the judge called them, so I'm told. Even I cannot bring myself to use the word *excuses*.

"Now Martha—and God forgive me for the telling of it this way—can be a hard woman. Not greatly mindful of the menfolk and their needs. Inattentive to them in the loving ways, you might say. Not that I'm passing judgment, mind, just offering my observance of the same. Mary Kirkham was out of the opposite mold. Soft as a lamb and ever concerned for our Thomas."

"Who's Mary Kirkham?"

"She came from a well-to-do farming family on the other side of Saxonborough. They grow a lot of the wheat for the miller to grind back at the mill we just passed—to make the bread that sits on our kitchen table. Mary betimes worked at the inn called The Plough in Saxonborough. Served food and drink and suchlike. I walked with her a few times but never knew her well. A pretty face and a sweet disposition. Everyone said so."

"I don't know her." *Bread. The tenth went out to seek for bread. From the miller?*

"Nor any reason you should. Lord, I forget it's been nigh on six years since all this happened, and you sheltered from the gossip all that time—until you started school at least. Forgive me. Well, anyway, your father took one step too many into Mary's good graces, and like a wasp in the marmalade, he was trapped. Ah, Tommy, it's a great pity the laws of the land don't call to mind human nature once in a while. Is not our garden the fuller still with wasps when the deathtrap be open?" The boy thought for a moment and supposed that it was.

"It's a powerful yearning comes over the menfolk when they smell such sweetness as Mary Kirkham."

They reached a broad field of grain and halted, like a small army called to the front line, surveying the lay of the land between them and the enemy. Aunt Jemmy smiled down at him, ran her fingers through his hair, and gave him a nod. "Buck up, young flower. In ten years you'll thank me for this, though perhaps not before." The boy nodded back at her, and they struck out between a pair of wagon ruts that carved a path at the edge of the sprouting barley. The sun bore down and made them sweat, but they pressed on.

"Poor Mary Kirkham came with child, Tommy, and the news fair broke the back of our Thomas. Scared he was of Martha's anger and scared too that the village would turn against him and cast him out. On top of that, Mary's father and the overseers forced him to marry her. But mostly it was Thomas's temper that drove him to do what he did. Since ever he was younger than you are now, he couldn't abide being forced to do anything he didn't want to." She paused and squinted up into the sun's glare, then continued matter-of-factly. "He killed Mary Kirkham the night they were wed. In a bedroom at The Plough. Beat her to death in a fury at the cruel circumstance that had befallen him. The patrol caught him at once and carried him off. Your mother never saw him again. I only saw him the once…that Christmas…in the prison." She stared across the fields into the far distance. "It seems like such a long time ago."

She shook her head and bit her bottom lip. A slow breeze ruffled the grain stalks.

"There was never any doubting the culprit. So a man that needed succor more than the rope was hanged at Lincoln Castle. Five years ago last March."

"My father?"

"Your father."

"A very bad man?"

"I don't know. So it is said by many."

They walked on in silence. A solitary wooden post came into view, hard by the crossroads at the edge of Saxonborough Moor. Iron staves of strange fashioning were perched atop it. The boy stared, puzzled. It seemed less frightful than a thing that leaped out of dykes and ate boys.

"This is Fallow Lane," Jemmy said.

"Is that the monster?"

"It is the gibbet, Tommy."

"The what?"

And poor Jemmy Temporal, but twenty-three years of age herself and as pretty and delicate as a porcelain cup, broke down and hugged him tight to her breasts, weeping onto his hair. "Oh, Tommy, Tommy, that you should have to see such a thing! Yon cage holds the remains of your father as a warning to such others as may be tempted to murder. That is the monster they have all affrighted you of. Five years it has stood there to torment us."

The boy turned from her bosom and stared at the gibbet and felt nothing.

"And wouldn't you know the richness of it," his aunt continued. "This spring a blue tit built a nest in the hollow of raw bones that was once my poor brother's jaw. Therein it has raised a cheerful brood. Nine chicks, so John James of the village has counted." She sniffed and wiped her eyes with the sleeve of her dress. "There's a rhyme about it being passed around the village. Perhaps you have heard it? In the schoolyard?"

"No, Aunt Jemmy," said the boy, taking hold of her hand and pulling her back toward home. "Come away now."

Jemmy stared at the gibbet and what little remained of her brother and then responded to the tug of the boy's hand and turned away.

"I don't want to be called Tommy anymore," he said as they walked home. "I want to be called Thomas."

Chapter 35

Fallow Fields
February 1810

MARTHA HAD MADE UP HER mind. She'd talked it over with Jemmy and made up her mind. Life had become intolerable. She still worked in the fields for Mr. Deloit in the spring and autumn, and Jemmy kept house and did sewing for all in Fallow Fields, but they could not make ends meet. As dire as that was though, it was but the smallest part of it. Their neighbors and the villagers of Saxonborough could barely tolerate their presence. The shadow of the gibbet had spread over the entire community and could not be lifted. Though none could explicate the wrong that Martha and Jemmy had done, their existence was a stain by association. Passersby on the street turned their heads aside and hurried away; fellow members of the congregation at St. Swithin's looked up to God whenever the two of them entered the church. Shopkeepers grudgingly handed over small portions of cheese and bacon wrapped in greaseproof paper with a few coins as change but never uttered greeting or farewell. Whispers were ever in the air, if never quite heard. And though Martha and Jemmy had expected otherwise, six years had done nothing but polish the memories of the village folk and give them a vindictive sheen, even as the shadow of the gibbet darkened and spread. And now the monster was rearing up over the shoulder of young Thomas.

So Martha had made up her mind. And this morning she would take the final step to remedy the situation once and for all. She told Jemmy to watch the boy—she would be back in the afternoon. She wrapped herself up in her warmest clothes, stuffed an apple into the pocket of her dress, and was out the door. She took the long way from Fallow Fields into Saxonborough, still following Jemmy's advice so that she did not have to see the abomination that she could not bear to see and never had seen and never would see. For she was the last person on earth who needed to be taught a lesson by it—a lesson of the kind that Judge Monson had espoused; she was well schooled. When she reached the village, she headed straight for The Plough, pushed open the front door, and saw Ethel Hodgson behind the counter. She walked up to her and asked one simple question: "Where does James Kirkham live?"

"Beg pardon?"

"James Kirkham. You once told our Jemmy that you'd been to see him. I needs must talk to him, but I don't know where he lives."

"Ah yes, well, his farm is out on the Torksey road. About a half mile from here. You'll know it when you come to a bridge over the Broadholme river. They call it a river, but it's no more'n a little stream really. The Kirkham farm is on the other side of the bridge. On the left side of the road. Willow trees overlooking the stream, fancy elms in front."

"Thank you."

"You're welcome…Mrs. Temporal. Good day to you."

Martha left the inn and checked that the letter she was carrying was still securely in her pocket. Then she walked to the end of the main street of the village and turned north up the road to Torksey. Half an hour later, she arrived outside the Kirkhams' farm. It was much nicer than Deloit's. Larger and newer, with two big sheds behind the farmhouse. All freshly painted white. No chickens or pigs roaming here—at least not anywhere to be seen. Suddenly she was a little daunted. Never before had she visited such a distinguished home. Nonetheless, it had to be done. She hitched up her skirt and marched to the front door. A maid answered the chime of the doorbell.

"I'm here to see Mr. James Kirkham," she said as boldly as she could manage.

"May I ask who's visiting?"

"Please just ask him if he would be kind enough to come and see a concerned woman."

"One moment," said the maid and shut the door on Martha.

Time passed, presumably while the maid explained the mystery of the woman on the doorstep. Then the door opened, and Mr. Kirkham appeared.

"Yes?" he said, clearly not recognizing the visitor.

"You don't know me, sir. I'm Mrs. Temporal. Thomas's wife as was." Mr. Kirkham froze and made to close the door on her, but Martha was quick to continue, "Please listen to me. I have a proposition to put to you. A way to end this suffering once and for all. Please give me a moment of your time to explain. That's all I ask. Just a moment. It will be to your advantage."

Mr. Kirkham was nonplussed, but good breeding forced him to open the door and admit her. He led her into the kitchen and sat her down. "You'd better explain yourself," he said. Martha needed no second bidding. She came straight to the point.

"Mr. Deloit wants us out of his cottage at Fallow Fields. He says he loses money every day we remain there. He says he's put up with the present situation long enough on account of pity for me and Jemima and the boy. But it must end, he says. He needs a family living there that has a strong laboring father and, ideally, an older son or two who can wield a scythe. It's only business, he says. Nothing personal."

"I'm sorry to hear that," said Mr. Kirkham.

"It's no great trouble for us, though, because we want out of the place just as much as he wants us out. We've tolerated the whispers and the glares from the villagers for long enough. We thought it would fade away in time, but it hasn't, more's the pity. Got worse if anything. And now the lad has started school and he's facing bullying of the same ilk as the hostility to me and Jemima. It's become intolerable for all three of us."

Mr. Kirkham nodded. "I can see that. What do you intend?"

Martha took a deep breath. "We're done. With Saxonborough. With Lincolnshire. With England. Done. We want to emigrate and make a new start." She paused and took an even deeper breath. "We want to emigrate to America. Me and Jemmy can perhaps find husbands there—we certainly can't find none hereabouts, and the boy will be able to off-load all the baggage that he now must carry around on his back every day. He can begin a new life. We all can. In a place where the name *Temporal* means nothing to no one."

Mr. Kirkham was surprised but not critical.

"So why do you come to me?"

Martha pulled the letter out of her dress and thrust it into Mr. Kirkham's hand. "This is a letter from Farmer Deloit. It's addressed to you. It's a sort of agreement. To prove the sincerity of his offer. He signed it at the bottom, see? He says that he will pay Jemima's passage to Philadelphia. He says he will be able to recoup the cost in a year once a working family moves into his cottage. He has a distant relative in Philadelphia, a Miss Josephine Deloit, who owns a café there. He has already written to her. She will let us stay with her and find us work until we get properly settled. She will stand surety on us when we arrive. Likewise, my father has agreed to pay my passage, though I have no letter of proof from him. It only remains to find money to pay the boy's fare. Mr. Deloit says here at the bottom of the page that he promises to pay Jemima's fare, if you, Mr. Kirkham, will pay Thomas's. Then we will be set, and we can put this whole business behind us."

"Me? You expect me to pay? On what grounds?"

"So the slate might be wiped clean, sir," Martha said, surprised that he would need an answer to that question. "So that Saxonborough will have naught remaining of the terrible circumstance that descended upon it—save for the gibbet, I suppose. You will be rid of it all as well. In church, eyes will cease to pass from me, the wife of Temporal the murderer, to you, the father of poor Mary the murdered. Only then, finally, I reckon, will it end. Only when we're gone. So you will benefit almost as much as Mr. Deloit."

"And how much must I pay to wipe clean this slate on which I wrote nary a word?"

"Five pounds."

"Five? In truth?"

"With Mr. Deloit's help, we have arranged for steerage berths for the three of us on a cargo brig out of Liverpool. The fares for me and Jemima are ten pounds each. The boy's fare is five. In addition,

Jemima and I have five pounds already saved to get us to Liverpool and to stay one or two nights there and to support us for a few days once we reach Philadelphia. With a little left over for the unexpected. In sum, Mr. Kirkham, we have promissories of twenty-five of the thirty pounds we think we will need. We humbly ask you for the last five pounds. Then we will be gone from your vicinity and your daily life, if never from your memory. And you will have paid for a new life for the boy, which ought to mean something to you. Looking around at the expensive furnishings in this house, it seems to me to be a small price to pay."

"When would you leave?"

"The first crossings are in April, I'm told."

James Kirkham said nothing more. He sat quietly in his kitchen, weighing the words he'd just heard. Then he turned, left the room, and eventually returned to face Martha. He counted out five gold sovereigns into Martha's hand.

"If fortune deigns otherwise and you do not emigrate as you have just now described, then you can walk back here and return my gold."

"Yes, Mr. Kirkham, I will. We all three thank you for your generosity. Most sincerely." Her eyes began to water. "I didn't know what else to do."

"Yes. So be it. But one final question, Mrs. Temporal, before you go. Do you not have *two* children in your cottage?"

"No."

Chapter 36

London to America
April 2019

Karen's one-time passport and her INS letter passed muster with every official at Heathrow Airport, so she boarded the plane and settled into her window seat for the flight to Chicago. Harry had an aisle seat further back. The plane took off without the announcement of a delay while security escorted a passenger off the flight, which Karen was halfway expecting. Slowly her eyes closed, and she dreamed her way across the Atlantic, periodically catching glimpses of cotton-ball clouds nestled among various shades of sky blue above and aquamarine below. She didn't eat. She didn't drink. She barely moved. She landed. She had originally intended to get a connecting flight from Chicago to Cedar Rapids and then rent a car for the short drive to Reinbeck, but it had dawned on her at Heathrow that she had no driver's license and only sketchy documentation. She would not be able to rent a car on that basis.

"Not a problem," said Harry. "I'll drive you from O'Hare. We'll go to my place for tonight, and then I'll drive you from Plainfield to Reinbeck tomorrow. Or wherever and whenever you want. Not a problem."

So that's what they did. And for the rest of that week, while Harry was at work, Karen did nothing but sleep and walk Harry's dogs around the fields in back of Wheeler Road. She didn't read any of her books that were stacked on Harry's couch, and she forgot about the rest of her possessions that were off in some storage locker somewhere. She didn't watch television. She had no iPhone. She had no documentation. No purse, no billfold, no dollars. Though modern life had been the thing she'd missed the most, she did not, for the time being, avail herself of one single aspect of it. It was sufficient for her to know that it was all available once again, all around her, at her fingertips, whenever she should be ready for it. But she was not yet ready for it.

As she walked and threw sticks for the dogs, she pondered three things: the exquisite mystery of time itself; what she should do with the years remaining to her, however few; and whether or not she should make contact with her parents. The last one took up the least amount of time but was the most important; she certainly wanted to see *them*, but she was desperately afraid that the sight of *her* would be disastrous for both her mother and her father. She could not make up her mind what was the best course of action.

Also, as she walked, she realized for the first time in her life that she was entirely free of encumbrances. She was content to breathe modern American air, to walk on hardy American soil, to enjoy the natural world of animals and sky and fields. She had achieved the goal she'd set for herself at Ketteringham Lodge two weeks or four hundred and thirty-one years ago, whichever way you wanted to look at it.

Already though, unbeknownst to Karen, the powerful undercurrents of societal awareness had begun to swirl; they, too, were a feature of that modern world Karen had longed for. Two days after her arrival, a computer screen flashed in an office at the Joliet Police Department. Detective John Dietrichson looked up. It was a new message. A message from the FBI. He clicked on it and read it. A name in the FBI national missing persons file had cross-matched with a name in INS files of an arrival into the country from overseas.

Dietrichson set down his coffee mug. It was folly to delay action on FBI messages. He opened his file drawer and flicked through the many folders jammed within. He eventually pulled out the one with the words *Karen Butler* stamped in red on the tab and labeled *Inactive* on the front. He held it in both hands and tapped it on the desk while trying to remember what he could about her case. He remembered her apartment in Joliet. He could still picture the paranormal books on her coffee table, the sour milk in the refrigerator. He vaguely remembered the talks he'd had with Karen's colleagues at CIU, though he could no longer remember any of their names. How long ago was it? Nine months? Ten?

Of course, he could very well remember all the hoopla concerning the deaths of Frank Koslowski and Dan Patzner. That had been big news for months. In fact, it was just about the biggest case that had come before their department in years. But that wasn't his turf. Their cases had been assigned to other detectives. Homicide. His only role in it all was to locate the whereabouts of Karen Butler, the vanished student.

He opened the folder.

On the inside front cover was a list of phone numbers.

He began with the first one on the list, her cell phone. It was dead. No surprise there. He next called the company that managed her apartment. They said they'd reclaimed it in the fall, and all her stuff had been removed by some friend. No forwarding address. He called her office phone number at CIU. A grad student answered. He said he'd taken over Karen's office at Christmas time and knew nothing about her. The next number on the list was Karen's emergency phone number, that of her parents in Iowa. He called them.

The rotary phone in the parlor of the Butler residence rang. Karen's mother answered it.

"Mrs. Butler?"

"Yes."

"My name is John Dietrichson, Mrs. Butler. Detective Dietrichson. I'm with the Joliet Police Department. You may remember that I talked with you and your husband when you came over last July. After Karen went missing? Yes?"

"What?" Mrs. Butler said, her voice quivering. "What's happened?"

"Just to confirm first, you are the mother of Karen Butler, is that correct?"

"Yes."

"Very good. Well, we received word this morning that Karen arrived at O'Hare on the twenty-second on a flight from London to Chicago. That was Monday. Were you aware of this?"

Mrs. Butler let the receiver slip from her ear and pressed it against her chest. "Larry! Come here! Now!" Her husband hurried in from the kitchen, asking what the matter was. Mrs. Butler thrust the receiver into his hands and said, "You take it!" After a repeat of the introductions, the conversation continued.

"As I was telling your wife, we received word here at Joliet PD that Karen returned to Chicago on Monday."

"Really? I can't believe it. It's been…months. We thought she might…might be…"

"So you didn't know?"

"No. We've had no word from her since she left last summer. Nothing."

"Well, she's been listed with the FBI as a missing person ever since then. And the FBI and the INS cross-check their lists by computer every day. Karen's name popped up on Monday. The FBI called us this morning. Apparently, she has returned to the US."

Karen's father placed his palm over the mouthpiece.

"It's true!" he whispered to his wife with a mixture of excitement and apprehension. "The detective says she's come back." He returned to the call.

"I just checked," Dietrichson continued, "and she no longer has her apartment in Joliet. The leasing company took it back after she'd been gone for some months and quit paying rent. And you say she has not shown up at your house?"

"No, she hasn't. And she hasn't called us either. Why hasn't she called us? Surely, she would have called us as soon as she landed? Are you sure it's our Karen?"

"The INS certainly thinks so."

"Could someone have stolen her passport and be impersonating her?"

"Unlikely."

"Then where is she?"

"We want to know that too. Because she's still on the missing persons list, we need to find her, confirm her identity, and then we can take her off the list and close the file—at least the file we have on her here at Joliet. Perhaps you'd like to ask around any family and friends whom she might have contacted. Could you do that?"

Karen's father was not pleased with the detective's last remark. "If she hasn't contacted us, then she won't have contacted them!"

"Probably not, no. But still..."

Karen's mother whispered to her husband, "Is she in any trouble?"

"Is she in any trouble?" he asked Dietrichson. "What with the two deaths and all."

"No, no. I just need to confirm that she's returned. So you don't know where she is?"

"No. I already told you. You're the police. You find her!"

"Well, we will be looking obviously. You're our first port of call."

"What about her college friends? What about that bearded freakster? Have you asked any of them? Were any of them on the flight with her? Do your job!"

"Yes, Mr. Butler. As I just said, we intend to do all of those things. Starting today. Please call me if Karen shows up. She's not in any trouble. We just want to close our file on her." He read a phone number to Mr. Butler, but he did not write it down.

"All right, then."

"All right. Thank you for your time, sir. We'll be in touch."

Mr. Butler hung up the phone. His wife came over, looking anxiously into his face, and clutched his arm.

"They say she's returned," he said, staring off into space. "She's alive."

The next name on Dietrichson's list was Connie Cammaretta, Karen's workmate, who'd first advised them of Karen's disappearance. He called her. She could not help. She'd heard nothing from Karen since her disappearance. And although she pressed him, the detective would not reveal what new information he had about her.

Finally, Dietrichson called Harry Groh's cell phone. He first apologized for calling him. He said he'd tried to find Karen by calling her parents, but they'd had no contact with her. He was simply the next in line. Harry was reluctant to say much because he knew that Karen was enjoying her isolation and privacy for the time being, but when pressed and threatened with a follow-up investigation, he admitted that, yes, Karen Butler had indeed returned and was temporarily staying with him in Plainfield.

"I need to see her for confirmation," Dietrichson said.

"Do you really?" Harry replied. "She's been through a lot. She's enjoying a quiet time for a while. Can't you just take my word for it?"

"No. I need to see her. Operational procedure."

"Is this something to do with the CIU deaths in England?"

"No, it's not."

If the deaths of Koslowski and Patzner had occurred in Illinois, there would have been a much bigger inquiry than the one that did take place. Probably their files would still be open—perhaps their FBI files still were; but for deaths overseas, there was little more that the Joliet PD could do. The files had been closed at the end of the calendar year, and no one was in any hurry to reopen them. There were other fish for Homicide to fry. Karen had been cleared at the inquiry by Harry Groh's testimony—at least for the death of Koslowski and, by extension, for the death of Patzner. Perhaps that last decision had been hurried, but there'd been no subsequent complaint registered and work had moved on.

Dietrichson mulled over the importance of Karen's return in comparison with all the other cases piled on his desk. "Perhaps a phone call will suffice," said Dietrichson. "Do you have her number?"

"She doesn't have a phone anymore. It was lost in the UK."

"Well, can you have her call me, then?"

"I guess. All right. I'll have her call you."

"Tomorrow if you would. Then I'll close the file."

"Okay."

"Thanks a lot."

Harry returned home that evening and talked to Karen as soon as he walked through the front door.

"Joliet PD wants to talk to you," he said.

"What? How did they find out about me?"

"From the INS passenger list. The detective on the case is a nice-enough guy. Name of Dietrichson. Connie talked with him when you first went missing, and I talked with him later after I came back from England at the time of the inquiry. He called me this afternoon as soon as he got word you'd returned. He said he wanted to meet with you in person for confirmation, but in the end, he said a phone call would suffice. You just need to phone him and tell him you've returned from England, and that should be good enough. You can use my phone tomorrow morning."

"Okay. I guess I can do that."

"Have you thought any more about going to see your parents?"

"I can't decide what to do, Harry. I've been thinking so hard about it. On the one hand, I think perhaps they've already come to terms with the…let's say…the absence of their young daughter. Perhaps they've reached a certain level of acceptance. They're living with it. And perhaps that's better for them than the sudden appearance on their doorstep of an ancient, wizened, zombie daughter. How horrendous would that be? It could totally freak them out. What do you think? I just can't make up my mind. I'm leaning toward letting them simply get on with their lives. I'm thinking it's better that I not tell them I've returned."

"They already know," said Harry.

They already knew. The decision had been made for her. If they already knew she'd returned, then she couldn't not go see them. Willingly, Harry took the following day off. Early in the morning, Karen called the Joliet PD and resolved her situation with Detective Dietrichson. Immediately afterward, Harry drove her over to Reinbeck. What happened on the doorstep Harry never knew. Karen and her parents talked for twenty minutes. It didn't go as well as Karen had hoped but not as badly as she'd feared. After an inquisition concerning her childhood and her family that was much worse than the one the INS officer had inflicted on her in London, her parents conceded that perhaps she could be their daughter. They opened the door to admit her. Karen turned to Harry and gave him a thumbs-up and a wave and disappeared inside. Harry drove home. The next morning, Karen walked into town and bought a cell phone. She was in America at last.

Chapter 37

Philadelphia
May 1810

The day had finally come. Six weeks of rocking and rolling and all the associated distress were nearing an end. Finally. The pools of vomit and urine—garnished with other bodily fluids and an overabundance of salt—which they'd tried so hard to avoid as they stepped gingerly across the floor in midocean, had at last ceased to slosh about and begun to congeal by the time they arrived in the calmer waters of the Delaware Bay. The *Gleaner* headed for the narrow entrance to the Delaware River and slowly came to a halt. The passengers forced themselves to swallow their misery and summon up a little excitement. Everyone expected to be told to gather their belongings and be prepared to leave the ship, but it was not that easy.

The master, Elisha King, climbed down the ladder to the steerage deck, followed by two uniformed officers. The *Gleaner* was a small cargo ship, only 370 tons, supplementing its income from transporting goods—seventy-two cases, casks, and hampers of merchandise on this trip—by filling half its hold and a couple of spare cabins with passengers. On this trip there was just one cabin passenger, a handsome lawyer named Edward Gullorny, and perhaps thirty-five steerage passengers, nearly half of them children. Martha and Jemmy joined the other adults in a semicircle in front of the master.

"Ladies and gentlemen," Elisha King began, "welcome to America! Your long journey is almost over. We are anchored temporarily in the outer reaches of the Port of Philadelphia. Behind me are two officers of the port authority. Inspector O'Rourke is here to explain the immigration procedure you will have to go through upon landing. But before that, Dr. Matthew Potts must examine all of you—including the children—for contagious diseases. Cholera, plague, smallpox, scarlet fever, typhoid fever, yellow fever…they have all been brought into this country by immigrants in recent years. Yellow fever, in particular, has been a scourge in Philadelphia. The year 1793 was a killer. But do not be alarmed, ladies and gentlemen. Those diseases were mostly carried by the poor and the destitute from tropical countries and from the larger cities of the developing world. You are all respectable, fare-paying passengers from England, so it's highly unlikely that you carry any such diseases. Nevertheless, American law requires that Dr. Potts examine each of you before you can be allowed entry into our country. So gather up your children and form a line against that wall. When Dr. Potts signals you, please step forward to be examined."

"Yellow fever? What's that?" Martha whispered to Jemmy. "I've never heard of it."

"I don't know. It sounds awful."

"Where's Mr. Gullorny?"

"Probably already been given a quick going-over in his private cabin. Just a lick and a promise, I'll bet. Him being so posh."

"*You* wouldn't say no to a lick and a promise in his private cabin," Martha said with a giggle, and Jemmy giggled too for the first time in six weeks. Then, overhearing the immigration officer chatting with Elisha King, Martha asked her sister-in-law, "And what is impressment?"

"I don't know."

"Well, the master just told that inspector there hadn't been any during the voyage."

"That's a good thing, I suppose."

They shuffled forward, Martha holding young Thomas in front of her by the shoulders and pushing him forward when appropriate. Eyes were examined for trachoma. Ears, nose, and throat for symptomatic onset of disease. Breathing for a possible heart condition. A few simple questions and a search for the kind of bewildered gaze that might signify mental problems. Scalp infection. Lameness. Pregnancy. No more than one minute per person. Every passenger on the *Gleaner* was passed fit for entry. The immigration officer told them only one thing: that they would have to complete a declaration form upon landing, and it was important that they answer each question truthfully. Or they could be deported. And that was that. The two officials went back up the ladder and departed from the side of the ship in a cutter. Elisha King thanked the passengers for their compliance with regulations and went back up the ladder himself.

"We'll be landing in about one hour," he added over his shoulder.

Elisha King returned to the captain's cabin and completed the ship's manifest that would be required by immigration authorities. He double-checked the listing of passengers and noted below it that the same number of passengers that had departed from Liverpool had arrived in Philadelphia. One small boy, Peter Proudfoot, had succumbed to acute diarrhea and been buried at sea; one baby girl had been born midocean and given the name Ruth because one of the passengers, a minister, informed her parents that the biblical Ruth had been a gleaner. Ruth was lovely, and her smile sustained some of the more anxious passengers through the final weeks of the voyage. Elisha King signed the manifest with a flourish.

Land they did. The *Gleaner* went a little further up the Delaware River and inched its way alongside a small pier. Ropes were thrown and the ship tied up tight. The passengers disembarked, thanking Master King for affording them safe passage across the ocean as he stood at the end of the gangplank to wish each one of them success in their new homeland. They waited while the crew unloaded their baggage, together with the commercial merchandise. Then they made their way through immigration, which turned out to be not nearly as demanding as they'd been led to expect. The form consisted of one page only: name, age, place of origin, sponsor in America, address in America. Jemmy had to complete their three forms because Martha was illiterate. Landing cards were pinned to their lapels. Next came a currency exchange. Martha emptied all that remained of the English coins in her purse onto the desk, and the cashier counted them out at a little over three pounds. He placed them in his cashbox. He then reached for a second box and counted out twelve dollars onto the desk. All three of them watched the process intently.

"We'd been told we would get five dollars for every pound," said Martha, looking up at him.

"You would have done a couple of years ago, ma'am," the cashier responded. "But not anymore. The rate's gone down to four since the war in Europe flared up again."

"What war?"

"You didn't know you were at war with France?"

"Oh, that. My husband mentioned it years ago. We never saw no sign of any war in Lincolnshire—except for one or two missing young men. I didn't know we were still waging it."

"'Fraid so. Twelve dollars. Next!"

Martha gathered up the unfamiliar coins, and she and Jemmy stared at them. Gold and silver and some kind of base metal. Eagles everywhere, though they didn't know what an eagle was. They showed the shiniest of them to Thomas, and then Martha slid them carefully into her purse. The family behind them in line shoved them, and they moved on.

Finally, there was a ticket office. Many of their fellow passengers lined up to purchase stagecoach or steamboat tickets for cities up and down the east coast, while a few brave souls were headed inland. Martha and Jemmy did not need any tickets. "How do we get to the center of the city?" Martha asked a police officer. He pointed to a line of horse-drawn cabs waiting beyond the exit gate. Martha nodded, and she led Jemmy and Thomas through the gate. Stepping through that gate seemed to them like their first steps on American soil, for there, on that soil, they were free, at last, to do whatever they desired. They went up to the first cab in line. "The Pine-Apple Café," Martha enunciated in a loud and clear voice. "It's on Juniper Street."

"I know it," the cab driver replied. "Twenty cents." He got down and helped them load their bags into the cab. One bag each was all they had. When they were seated, he clicked his horses away from the line and onto the roadway and off up High Street toward the city center. The adventure had begun.

Thomas Temporal was asleep when he heard the words "Fine morning!" coming from somewhere outside the room. He was drifting back to sleep when he heard, more clearly this time, the words

"Past six o'clock and a fine morning!" He opened his eyes. He didn't know where he was. The light through the window didn't have that pale, misty texture that was usually associated with Lincolnshire fields in the springtime. He looked around him. He was lying on a dirty mattress on the floor of an unknown room, covered with a sheet that had once been white. He saw that on the other side of the room was a proper bed with two figures lying on it. Mother and Jemmy. He sat up. Aunt Jemmy heard him rouse up and turned toward him.

"Where are we?" he asked her.

"We're in America," she whispered.

"Oh."

"Past six o'clock and a fine morning!" Fainter now.

"Who is that?"

"The watchman, I think."

"Do they not know the time in America?"

"They do. He's just being helpful."

"Oh."

"Sleep a little more, Thomas."

He lay back down, but he didn't sleep. He was not in Fallow Fields anymore. He would never see his school friends again. The cottage was gone. The garden was gone. The jar of marmalade and the wasps were gone. He was in America at last.

Chapter 38

Kankakee
April 2019

Tom and Denise both went back to work the day after their return to the States, but Tom had a hard time concentrating on investment portfolios. The past kept intruding on the present. Lines of gravestones overlaid lists of company stocks, and the rows and columns of his spreadsheets were outlined by the fretwork of a rood screen. During the evenings of that first week, he double-checked the digitized parish registers of Lincolnshire, focusing this time on the late eighteenth-century baptismal, marriage, and burial records that he had previously found so hard to decipher. He searched for *Ransome* and *Temporal* family members in Marton Parish, as Denise had suggested.

With the utmost concentration and care, he was able to confirm the baptisms of Thomas Temporal in 1779, Martha Ransome in 1779, and Jemima Temporal in 1786. So if nothing else, he'd determined which side of the family Jemmy came from, and he now knew the precise ages of Martha and Jemmy when they emigrated to America, thirty-one and twenty-four respectively. And the more he thought about it, the more he became convinced that this Thomas Temporal was the father of his letter-writing ancestor. Had to be. However, Tom didn't find the searches satisfying. Computer images had become boring. He longed to run his fingertips over old paper in dusty ledgers or tap his knuckles against oak and stone. Tapping a mouse just wasn't the same.

On the Saturday morning of that first week back, he pulled the old trunk out of their hall closet and went through it again. He unfolded all the ragged clothes and examined each item carefully—front, back, and inside—but they held no secrets. He studied every piece of paper but found nothing prior to 1920. He pulled out the tartan bag and looked inside at the broken chair leg. He drew it out and turned it over in his hands. The feel of the heavy dark wood was gratifying but unhelpful. As he was putting it back in the bag, however, he noticed a horizontal slit in the top of the interior lining. It seemed to be a crude sort of pocket. He reached inside. It ran all the way to the bottom of the bag. He delved deeper. Near the bottom of the pocket the tips of his fingers touched a piece of paper. His pulse quickened. Very, very carefully he lifted it out and placed it on the floor. He checked all around the pocket, but there was nothing else in it.

Tom sat cross-legged on the floor of the hallway, not moving, just musing on what he might have discovered. Denise was in their bedroom. She'd switched on music, and a mournful song was spreading through their apartment. Tom lifted his head.

"What's that song?" he shouted to her. She came to the door.

"You don't know it? It's an old Scottish ballad. *Flowers of the Forest*. It commemorates the defeat of the Scottish army at some battle or other centuries ago—I forget which one. It's so lovely."

"It is."

"The women and children are grieving for the loss of all their young men. It's a lament. This is the version by a woman called Isla St. Clair."

"It's so beautiful. Play it again."

She did so.

Tom looked down at the tartan bag. *This bag, too, might have come from Scotland a long, long time ago*, he thought. *Just like the song. Forgotten soon after it came into existence, but still functional today. Still of value. We skip from car to desk to supermarket and back again and never think of the past. Never think of where everything came from, all those things we hold dear. Many of those people and places and events of the past were far more meaningful than the mundane crap we prize today. They need to be drawn out of the shadows and thrust in front of our faces. If we could fully imagine and truly appreciate the fear in the hearts of those young Highland men standing in line with claymores in their hands, the grief in the hearts of their mothers and wives and sisters afterward... well, would we be so overjoyed to win a scratch-off?*

Tom set the tartan bag aside and picked the piece of paper off the floor. It was an extremely old envelope—older even than the letter written by his ancestor. Squashed flat, thinned *in extremis,* and much faded. A light sepia in color. He saw at once that this envelope had gone through the mail. It was addressed to *Mrs. Jemima Bovey, 12 Juniper Street, Philadelphia, Pennsylvania State, North America.* Aunt Jemmy! It had to be! Bovey must have been her married name. Yes... Bovey, the sea captain!

He called Denise to come see and walked it over to the dining room table. He handed it to her, and she stared at it and handed it back.

"It was in a pocket inside that tartan bag!" Tom exclaimed. "I never noticed it when we looked at the bag up in the attic. An old letter! Very old!" He took off his glasses and examined the envelope. There was a circular postmark in the upper right corner. "The postmark says 'Lincoln AP 23 1835.' It came from England."

"Sent from Lincoln on April 23, 1835, I guess that means. Wow!" said Denise, also starting to get excited. She walked around to his side, and they studied it together.

"See here," Tom said, pointing. "There's a square red handstamp next to the postmark that says *Paid*, with the rest faded away. Looks like it's a date. And there's a handwritten scrawl underneath it that says... what is this? It looks like *20c.*"

"No stamps."

"No stamps."

"I'd better do a little research for you on how transatlantic mail worked back then."

"Hmm."

Tom laid the envelope on the table.

"I'm scared to look inside," he said after a pause. "It's so fragile."

"That didn't stop you opening your ancestor's letter."

"But this one is even more fragile. It looks like it would fall apart at a touch."

"Is it sealed?"

"It seems to have been sliced open at the top. All the way across. But the front and back covers are stuck together."

"How about I get some tweezers?" Denise suggested.

"Good idea."

She went into their bedroom and returned with a pair.

"Here. Give it a try."

Tom lifted the envelope off the table and probed at the slit. He was able to insert the tip of a tweezer into one corner and very carefully slide it across the top until it was fully opened. He gently blew into the opening, and slowly the front and back covers of the envelope parted. He looked inside.

"It looks like a letter," he said. "What now?"

"Just put the tweezers in and see if you can grab it and pull it out."

Tom tried but had no success.

"It's stuck," he said. "Whatever's inside is stuck to the envelope."

"Try to work it free at the edges, but don't pull on it."

"I'll try. I don't want to rip anything."

Eventually, after a great deal of wiggling and jiggling, the tweezers emerged clutching a folded letter. As Tom moved to lay it down on the table, a piece of gray newsprint fell from between the folds and floated down onto the surface of the table.

"There's stuff tucked inside the letter," Tom said nervously. At once, another piece of paper dropped out, and Tom quickly set the letter down on the table.

"Get me a clean sheet of paper, please," he asked Denise, and she returned from the desk and laid a blank white sheet on the table in front of him. He very carefully picked the two pieces off the table with the tweezers and laid them on the white sheet. Then he took hold of a corner of the letter and gave it a quick shake. Five or six additional scraps fell out, some of them an inch square or larger. All of them extraordinarily delicate.

"They look like bits of old newspaper," said Denise, and Tom agreed.

When all the contents had been assembled on the white sheet, Tom was finally able to unfold the letter.

"It's definitely a letter," he said. "It's a bit faded…and the edges are frayed…but I can read it." So he did, out loud.

Harold Temporal
Stow Park Road, Marton
Twenty-first of April 1835

My dearest Jemmy,

I hope you and Benjamin are well and Ben and Evelyn also. I am sorry not to have written to you before, but you know I am not much with the pen, and your mother has always done it in the past. It is now twenty-five years since you left England.

I am sorry to have to tell you that Mother passed away last week, the eighteenth. She was seventy-six years of age and had been very weak and bad of her breathing since Martinmas. She will be greatly missed, but try not to distress yourself. It was God's will. I am a poor creature myself these days, with legs all but worn out from the ploughing, but thank the Lord I am still on this earth. He has already bestowed seventy-nine years on me, which is enough. A girl from the village comes to help me.

I don't know what else to say. The past thirty years of my life have been much overshadowed by the crimes of your brother. When we emptied Mother's purse yesterday, these newspaper cuttings fell out. I don't know why she kept them. But I thought you should see them as I believe you know little about the fate of our Thomas. I know that his Martha shielded the two of you from the worst of it at Fallow Fields. Throw them on the fire if you prefer.

I don't expect to see you again in this life, but I remain, as always, your loving father.

Harold

Tom set the letter down on the table. He was trembling slightly, and his eyes were moist. Denise didn't look at him and didn't know what to say. She thought it might be better for him to be alone with his thoughts for a while, so she volunteered to go to her computer in their bedroom and look up the process of early transatlantic mail service. Tom nodded but was clearly far away in another land and another time. When she returned half an hour later, she saw a jigsaw puzzle of shredded pieces of old newsprint laid out on the sheet of white paper. Tom was earnestly scribbling notes on a pad beside it.

"Don't breathe, they go everywhere," he told her without looking up. "I've finally got all the pieces organized. I think they're all there. And they're all the right side up. They're extracts from old newspapers. There are two distinctly different sets. I could tell that at once by the slightly different shades of gray of the paper. See?" He pointed from one set to the other and back again. "I suppose I'll have to glue them down eventually, but not till I've got them both transcribed. That's what I've been working on." His eyes rose to meet hers.

"They're about Thomas's father," he said simply, "and it doesn't look good."

"I'm not surprised," replied Denise, "judging by the wording of the letter. Read them to me. Go on."

> A shocking murder was perpetrated on Wednesday last in the parish of Saxonborough near Lincoln, on the person of a young woman, whose body was found in a bedroom of the local inn, with the head dreadfully fractured. A man named Thomas Temporal, a navvy on the dykes, was compelled to marry a woman on the same Wednesday, whose name was Mary Kirkham; she was pregnant, and is supposed to be the poor creature found murdered. An inquest was held on the body on Friday, when the jury returned a verdict of willful murder against the above man, and he was on Saturday committed to Lincoln Castle. A broken chair leg was found in the bedroom; and, it is supposed, was used as the instrument of destruction.

Thomas Temporal was executed at Lincoln, on Friday last, for the murder of Mary Kirkham at Saxonborough in the county of Lincoln in October of last year. He acknowledged his guilt to the clergyman who attended, and to the keeper of the prison. At ten in the forenoon, his body was taken from the castle, and hung in chains on Saxonborough Moor. He was born, according to reports, at Marton, near Gainsborough, in the county of Lincoln. Great numbers of people went in order to see the body hanged to the gibbet-post. He was measured for the irons on the day before his execution. At that time all his fortitude appeared to forsake him, for the first time, and when taken to the gallows, he did not so much as hold up his head.

Tom read out the two newspaper articles in a dull monotone. When he'd finished, he gave Denise a brief contextual summary. "They both come from a periodical called the *London Courier*. The dates were scribbled on the back. The first one is from October 31, 1803. The second is from March 12, 1804. So they're about six months apart. The first one reports the crime committed by Thomas's father. The second one describes his execution. I guess this means it took six months to try, convict, and execute him."

"Holy shit," said Denise. "I can't believe it made the national press."

"Thomas wasn't kidding when he said in his letter that he thought his father was a bad man. What a massive understatement."

"And the chair leg in the tartan bag—"

"Was the murder weapon, presumably, yes. Preserved somehow down the years. For some ungodly reason. My guess is that Jemmy brought it over from England in the bag and then added the letter from her father at a later date. They were stuff she thought should be kept but stuff she never wanted to look at again. And somehow the bag got passed on down to our branch of the family—perhaps given to Thomas directly or one of his children."

"Yes, that would make sense. Oh, Tom, I'm sorry that your ancestor's origins are so dark." She walked over and put her hand on his shoulder. "Everything seemed so exciting and fascinating when we first found his letter."

Tom nodded and said, "Who would kill a pregnant woman like that? It's too horrible to contemplate."

"Do you think it was his baby she was carrying?"

"I don't know. The articles don't make that clear. The first article says he was *compelled* to marry her. So either it was his baby and he didn't want it, or it was someone else's baby and he *most certainly* didn't want it. It could be that she'd been unfaithful to him. That would at least provide a motive."

"Either way…"

"Right. And what in God's name is a *gibbet post*?!"

"I've no idea. More computer work needed. And speaking of computer work—though it's small potatoes now—I did solve the mystery of the envelope. Postage stamps didn't come into existence until 1840. That was when the famous Penny Black was issued in England. And also, generally speaking, at that time it was the recipient of a letter who paid for it, not the sender."

"Really?"

"Yes. Jemmy would have paid twenty cents to receive the letter, probably at a Philadelphia post office, and the envelope was then hand-stamped *Paid*."

"I guess junk mail put a stop to that practice."

"Ha! So how does all this new information stack up against the baptism, marriage, and burial records you've located so far?" Denise asked.

"Well, let's start with that first newspaper article. It was dated 31 October 1803, but it doesn't say what day of the week that was. Can you look it up?"

"How do you do that?"

"There are historical calendars on the internet."

Denise searched her iPhone.

"Found it. 1803…Britain…October…31… It was a Monday."

"A Monday. That means *Wednesday last*, like it says, would have been the…twenty-sixth."

"Correct."

Tom searched through his computer notes.

"The twenty-sixth. Okay, that jibes perfectly with the marriage record I found for Thomas Temporal and Mary Kirkham at Saxonborough. They were legally married in the local church on that day, just like the article says."

"He was *compelled* to marry," Denise emphasized.

"Right, right. Compelled. Because her father found out she was pregnant no doubt."

"I wonder how far along she was."

"No way to tell from this extract."

"But Thomas was already married to Martha and had a son. Why didn't he tell the vicar? The church would never have agreed to marry a man who was already married to someone else—no matter what the girl's father wanted. Seems like it would have been easy for Thomas to avoid marrying Mary Kirkham if he didn't want to. *Sorry, fellas, gotta get home to the wife and kid.* Simple." Denise frowned and rubbed her forehead. "Perhaps he thought it was easier to keep quiet than to create trouble. Perhaps Martha and their son lived sufficiently far away that he thought nobody would ever find out that he was already married…that he could keep it a secret. Maybe he truly wanted to marry Mary. What do you think?"

Tom didn't reply. He was still searching his computer notes and the register entries he had found previously. "So this means that the Saxonborough marriage entry is correct. But that was also the day that Mary Kirkham was murdered—"

"Strictly speaking, she was Mary *Temporal* when she died."

"True." Tom's eyes suddenly lit up. "Oh, that might explain why I didn't find Mary's burial at Saxonborough in the days following the twenty-sixth. I only searched under the name *Temporal*, but she might have been buried as Mary *Kirkham*! Would you want your daughter to have the surname of the man who'd just killed her?"

"I would not. No way!"

Tom quickly went to his family history website and searched Lincolnshire burial records. And there he found it. He read out the entry from Saxonborough Parish, "'October 28. Mary Kirkham, alias Temporal, aged twenty, found murdered in a tavern bedroom. The coroner's jury returned a verdict of willful murder against her husband, Thomas Temporal.' Seems like nobody thought of her as a Temporal."

Denise jumped up excitedly from her chair.

"Wait, wait! That little cracked gravestone in Saxonborough churchyard! Remember? The one you couldn't read very well. What was the date on it?"

Tom scrolled to his transcription of it and recounted, "Mary Kirkham, something the twenty-sixth, 1803. Followed by that little poem starting 'In Bloom of Life.'"

"Something equals October! Get it? That wasn't the grave of James Kirkham's wife—Mary's mother—like we thought. That was the grave of Mary Kirkham herself. That was her little tombstone. Hastily put together perhaps, under the circumstances. And once again, she has her maiden name. You can bet that old James Kirkham would have forbidden the name of Temporal to be carved on the tombstone of his poor daughter."

"Or ever mentioned in his house again. Yes! It all makes sense. And the wording on the tombstone is much more appropriate for a young girl like Mary Kirkham, who was indeed *in bloom of life* and was indeed *snatched away*, just like the inscription said."

Denise nodded and thought of the implications of such a murder occurring in a family in a tightly knit village community. "You can hardly blame Martha and Jemmy for emigrating."

"No."

They both sat quietly at the table, taking in the new revelation about the horrible crime that Tom's ancestor had been guilty of, sipping on coffee, fiddling with table mats. Then Tom tilted his head to one side.

"So…that second newspaper entry…it's dated March 12, 1804. What day of the week was that?"

"Monday again," said Denise after a quick search. "The *London Courier* must have come out every Monday."

"This means that Thomas was executed on…March 9. He was executed at Lincoln, but his body was taken to Saxonborough. So why didn't I find his burial in Saxonborough Parish records for something like March 10 or 11? Let me look again." He went once again to his family history website. "There's nothing," he said. "I looked all through March and all around Lincolnshire."

While he'd been doing that, Denise had been studying her iPhone.

"That's because he wasn't buried," she said, looking up at him.

"What?" said a startled Tom.

"I just looked up the word *gibbet*," she said. "Here's the definition, 'A gallows with a projecting arm at the top from which the bodies of criminals were formerly hung in chains and left suspended after execution.'"

"You're kidding me."

"No. There's even a picture of one here. Look. It's a kind of metal cage."

"They did that sort of thing? I can't believe it. It's not that long ago. And Britain was…was…the pinnacle of civilization back then. I can't believe it. How long was the body left hanging there?"

"Indefinitely, it says here. To warn the local people against committing murder or something equally heinous themselves. In time the corpse would have decomposed naturally…or been preyed upon by animals and birds…or I guess the post could have been blown down. It says that sometimes friends of the gibbeted man would come at night and burn down the post and the body with it. But one thing's for sure: there was definitely no church burial. Nothing that would appear in parish registers."

"That's sick."

Tom drifted off, and Denise discreetly left the room once again.

We all look into the future, don't we? Tom thought. *Every one of us. We construct these vague and varied scenarios of the way the world might look on down the road, not to mention the way we ourselves might look. And then we try to visualize how the two would mesh together. Which futures best suit us? Which futures could harm us the most, hold us back? Subconsciously, we weigh the probabilities of every alternative that comes to mind. And then we make decisions: which subjects to study in college, where to live, whom to marry.*

But we also look into the past. Just like I've been doing these last few months. Those images are more distinct, but there are way more of them. When it comes to the past, it's not so much which one is preferred, as a driver of future action, but what is the meaning of each one. What is the significance of each one. Which ones should we draw lessons from, which ones can be set aside. Then, too, we make decisions. But the glow of each nugget of the past is tainted by our own biases. Things emphasized out of pride, things tucked away out of shame. Past events are modified before they are assessed. We all do it.

And after that, at symbolic moments in time—the death of a loved one, the loss of a job, the outbreak of war—we stand on our two feet in the present and weigh the future and the past. On one pan of the scale is the breath of the Almighty, on the other the fog of memory. Not a blueprint for accuracy by any means. Nevertheless, we stare at the needle shading the scale, breathe deeply, and take a step forward.

But, Tom suddenly realized, *as soon as our foot touches the ground, the earth shudders. The sky blinks and twitches. The future is now different; the past has mutated. Some of our hopes for the future have dimmed. Some have brightened. The contours of the world to come have buckled and bent. Not only that, some of the things we did in the past we now regret more, or less, and things that were once distinct in the past but had been hidden away now step out from behind a screen and confront us. Those young men on the Highland battlefield, the* Flowers of the Forest, *they stepped out from behind the fir trees with claymores in their hands. They had weighed their futures. They had recalled their childhoods, their mothers, their sisters milking the cows. But their reading of the needle against the scale had been sorely wrong. They were cold in the clay within a week. Had Mary Kirkham misread the needle? She was in the churchyard loam within two days of her wedding.*

The Scottish lament flowed through the apartment, and Tom was overcome with sadness.

And my past is changed too from this day and forever. My five times' great-grandfather just stepped out from behind the trunk of my family tree holding a broken chair leg. Blood on his hands. How now do I put one foot forward? I am descended from a murderer.

Chapter 39

Philadelphia
1810–1821

For Martha and Jemmy, America was a never-ending Tilt-A-Whirl at the same time exciting and scary and unsettling to the stomach—not that much different from their ocean crossing. Everything they encountered was unfamiliar to them. The grocery store was a nightmare. Coins were indecipherable, and many times storeowners would laugh at what they were offered by way of payment. When they did buy the correct food item, Miss Deloit had to tell them what it was for and how the dish was made and how long to leave it on the fire. They had to learn what an icebox was and how to use it to lengthen the lifetimes of the café's delicacies.

It was not just the national differences that made life hard for Martha and Jemmy; it was also the switch from a rural to an urban environment. And in some ways, this was harder to adjust to. No reassuring sunsets and sunrises painted the horizon. Green vistas had vanished and been replaced by ugly gray walls and rooftops. Gone were the adorable badgers, foxes, and hedgehogs that had sniffed their way across the grass at Fallow Fields; in their places were noisome skunks, aggressive and befingered raccoons, and a horrible round ball with a rattail that the locals called a possum—all of them intent on sampling the varieties of garbage stacked behind the café. Just awful. And they were warned that outside the city there were even more dangerous *critters*; did that mean *creatures*? Jemmy thought so, but Martha wasn't sure. Those predators had names like cougars and coyotes and bobcats, and they seemed to prefer children to garbage. Further south there were alligators, snakes...Enough said. They stayed in their small city block, oppressed merely by heat and humidity and biting insects.

The only thing they had in common with the other residents of Juniper Street was that they'd come from someplace else. But that was a theoretical consolation only, as all of them had their own words for food and coins and animals—not to mention unfamiliar accents for describing them in English. Even among the immigrants from England, they met few people who'd heard of Lincolnshire and no one who'd ever been there. However, they did learn a few things about Dublin and Kingston and Milan, for all that was worth. It took them months...years...to feel comfortable in their new surroundings. Jemmy, as pretty as she was, was immediately taken on by Miss Deloit as a waitress in the café, doubling sales by all accounts. Poor Martha took on whatever work she could find, mostly as a washerwoman for neighboring homes and businesses.

For young Thomas it was easier. He had less to forget and a greater capacity to assimilate. He quickly took to school, where every boy was different and doing their best to fit in. Nobody called him *Tom Tit*. Nobody pointed at him and denigrated his father. *Temporal* was the equal of *O'Rourke* and *Bianchi*. He grew like a weed on the streets of Philadelphia. Before long he was using words and expressions that Martha and Jemmy did not understand. They soon looked to him to explain the coinage and teach them the bestiary.

While Jemmy was amused by the strange distinctions between the two sides of the Atlantic, Martha shrank from them. Her pale round face became blotchy from the hot sun and the daily lavage of steam from her washtub. Lines spread across her forehead and down her cheeks from the apprehension she could never rid herself of. It had been her idea to emigrate, and she was the one paying the price. If it hadn't been for Jemmy and Thomas, she would have thrown herself off the Pennypack Creek Bridge. She would never marry again, she knew that now. She could not talk to these foreign men—even the ones who tried their best to coax her. She had no alternative but to struggle and toil, her face in other folks' dirty underwear each and every day.

If all this was not enough, things got worse just two years after their arrival in Philadelphia when President James Madison saw fit to declare war on Britain for a variety of nebulous grievances. Being English suddenly became a blemish. In her café, Miss Deloit quickly turned French. On the street nobody cared where Thomas came from. But Martha was frightened; she stayed indoors for a long time thereafter and would venture out only to pick up or deliver laundry. Jemmy had to do all the shopping, trying her best to disguise her accent and avoid the use of words and phrases that would betray her roots. If caught out—if the grocer's assistant asked her, "Are you English?"—she would laugh and say, "Of course not, I'm Irish," or Norwegian or South African or some other nationality that would be unfamiliar to them and elicit a blank stare. And as she walked home, she kept her head down when approaching the lines of American soldiers and sailors headed to or from the port district, off to fight her countrymen or just returning from one of the skirmishes. Nevertheless, Martha, Jemmy, and Thomas survived the three years of conflict unscathed and emerged from them a little more American and a little less jittery.

There was one thing, however, that enraptured all three of them from the day they stepped off the boat: the fruit. For folks brought up on two varieties of green apples and sour berries plucked from hedgerows, the fruit in Philadelphia was out of this world. The native fruits alone were far more delicious than anything they had eaten back home: strawberries, the first fruit of the spring; black and red cherries; melons, both water and musk, brought down from New Jersey; blueberries; peaches...The list went on and on. The taste buds marveled.

But it was the imported tropical fruits that thrilled them the most: the pineapples, mangoes, oranges, limes, and lemons. Exotic in the extreme. The Pine-Apple Café specialized in tropical fruit concoctions of all kinds. Ice cream, sorbets, sherbet, compote, jams and jellies, punch—they all made their way onto the shelves and tables of the café; and it was terribly hard for the three of them to keep their fingers from sampling each one. Martha was even invited by Miss Deloit to make some of her special orange marmalade, an art she'd acquired on the few and unpredictable occasions when Seville oranges had managed to find their way to Fallow Fields. It proved surprisingly popular among the café's customers.

The tropical fruits were delivered weekly to the café by the captain of a small cutter that plied its trade between Kingston and Philadelphia, and one day the captain came up behind Jemmy as she was shelving jars of apricot preserves, slipped his arm around her waist, and kissed her tenderly on the neck. He joked that he was sweet on her. Ha! They were married the following year. This was in 1814 when Jemmy was twenty-eight. On the day of her marriage, she announced that from that moment on she was to be called Jemima Bovey. Jemima Bovey was a lady of elegance; Jemmy Bovey was a whore. The change was accepted by everyone but Martha and Thomas.

There were three bedrooms above the café. Miss Deloit had the best and biggest one to herself naturally. Jemima and Captain Benjamin Bovey installed themselves in the second best, while Martha and Thomas shared the third with a curtain draped across the middle of the room. It was understood to be just a temporary arrangement, but it lasted six years. Martha continued to work as a washerwoman, and Thomas left school early and became apprenticed as a carpenter. Jemima very soon had a baby boy and then a baby girl, who both slept in the second bedroom with her and her husband—when he was not away at sea. The accommodation upstairs was tight, but none of them could see an alternative, not even Miss Deloit, who could easily have asked them all to leave but was uncertain whether living alone at her age would be more comfortable than having distractions all around her.

Then one hot Sunday evening in early August of 1820, the household was gathered around the kitchen table in back of the café eating a dinner of pepper pot and rusk cakes. Jemima had made the pepper pot from tripe and ox feet and chilies to give them a good sweat—and subsequently a cool evening—on the heels of a stifling day. It worked well. Captain Bovey mopped his brow and rubbed the back of his neck with a handkerchief. But Martha began to sweat more than the others—profusely in fact—and came close to passing out at the table. They helped her to a chair, where she lay on her side shivering and moaning.

"It's not the pepper pot," said Jemima, laying a palm across her forehead. "She has a fever."

"A high fever," Miss Deloit confirmed, repeating Jemima's test.

"Let's get her to bed."

The following morning, Thomas ran into the Boveys' bedroom early, without knocking, and said, "Aunt Jemmy, come quick. Mother's worse."

The three of them hurried across the hallway and straight to Martha's bedside. Her eyes were red and inflamed, and the skin of her face had a strange yellow hue to it. She struggled to sit up and muttered, "I feel funny. I don't know." Right after saying that, she leaned over the side of the bed and vomited a dark-brown liquid onto the floor. All three of them took a quick step backward. Thomas felt like he was about to throw up himself.

Benjamin's brow furrowed, and he said, "It's the yellow jack."

Jemima looked up at him in terror. "What? Thomas, go and wave down a cab!" Thomas turned and stared at his aunt, his face pale as alabaster. "A cab!" she shouted. "Quickly now!"

Within the hour they were in a small annex of the city hospital by the Schuylkill, which had opened just the previous week as a temporary isolation facility for those stricken by the new wave of yellow fever. Martha was bled and purged and told to rest. Jemima stayed with her throughout the afternoon, holding her hand. At four o'clock, Martha roused up a little and pulled Jemima toward her. A strange, stilted conversation ensued.

"This is the end for me," said Martha.

"Don't talk like that," Jemima replied. "You're in the hospital now. The doctors will take care of you."

"There's nothing they can do. I've heard stories of the yellow fever."

"Nonsense. They're treating you well here."

"I don't mind to end it, Jemmy. Honestly, I don't. While coming here was a good thing for you and the boy, I've seen only the rough end of it. In my head I still live in Fallow Fields and weep."

"Oh, Martha," said Jemima, saddened to hear what she'd suspected for a long time. She tightened her grip on Martha's hand, shook it, and said, "Don't say things like that. Pull yourself together. We can get past this."

"Do you remember when the master of the *Gleaner* talked to us in the harbor ten years ago? He said the words *yellow fever* and neither of us knew what it was?"

"I remember."

"You said to me that it sounded awful."

"I remember."

"Well, now I know just how awful it is."

Jemima didn't know what to say to that and waited for Martha to start up again.

"Jemmy, you must never tell Thomas anything. Do you promise me?'

"What? Don't you think he deserves to know?"

"I don't. You showed him the gibbet against my wishes—"

"And I think it helped him. In the long run."

"I don't think it did, Jemmy. I don't think it did."

"Well, he was only a boy then. He's a man now. It will not unbalance him now."

"Do not tell him!" Martha growled, pulling Jemima even closer to her. "I'm on my deathbed. You must promise me."

"All right, all right."

"The gibbet was one thing. That was his father. But this is a bigger thing. You must never tell him different. You surely can see how important it is to me." She stared fixedly into Jemima's eyes as she said those ten words. "Thomas is happy to live with the world as it is. Fallow Fields must remain locked and barred—as tight as the cottage door was on that day we left for Liverpool. Do you recall? Do you promise me?"

"Very well, Martha. I promise. Now rest some more. Sleep if you can."

"Thank you, Jemmy. And thank you for everything you've done for me. I can never repay…" Martha closed her eyes and sighed, and by the evening, she was dead, one of eighty-three souls who perished in that final visitation of the yellow fever that had plagued Philadelphia for more than thirty years. She was forty-one. Afterward, they rarely spoke of how Martha had come to contract the disease. When they did do so, they attributed it to contact with one of the poorer households for whom she washed clothes, though in the back of each mind was the likelihood that she'd been bitten by a mosquito brought home by Captain Bovey from Jamaica in one of his crates of pineapple or secreted in his clothing.

Thomas took the death very hard. The curtain in the third bedroom was taken down so that, so it seemed, he could be tormented by the sight of his mother's empty bed every night and morning. He'd come all that way across the Atlantic for a better life, only to have his mother snatched away from him at such an early age. It wasn't fair. It wasn't right. It unsettled him greatly. No matter how tenderly he was cared for by Aunt Jemmy and how respectfully Captain Bovey treated him, the fruits of Philadelphia had soured. He finished his apprenticeship and went to work for a contractor building homes in the Northern Liberties. He was good at his work, but he didn't much care for it. It was too repetitive. He began to itch for something different, something removed from the hot and filthy city air. He longed for a place where he could breathe deep and have a view of mountains or fields to look at every morning. A stream to wash his face in. A home with a bedroom that had no curtain and no memories.

ONE YEAR AFTER MARTHA'S DEATH, in early September of 1821, Thomas and his workmate, Batch Coleman, were sitting under a tree at a construction site eating lunch and drinking bottled beer. Batch spoke up, "Do you remember my cousin Albert?"

"Him as came to your birthday party last year?"

"The same. Well, I got a letter from him yesterday."

"Yeah?"

"Yeah. From Fort Dearborn."

Thomas shook his head.

"It's in the Illinois. On one of the big lakes. Remember it was burned down by the Potawatomi a few years ago?"

Thomas shook his head again.

"Well, it was. But it's been rebuilt since, and there are a lot of log cabins surrounding it. Albert stayed at the fort for two weeks. He says in his letter he's off now to a place called Galena to mine lead."

"I wouldn't want to do that. Sounds dangerous."

"Albert says there's a lot of money in it."

"Enough to pay for your funeral perhaps. Is that what you want to go and do?"

"No, no. Not that."

"Hmm. So what else did he say?"

"Okay, so he said he met the man who runs the township surrounding the fort. His name is—" Batch fumbled in his pocket for the letter, pulled it out, and unfolded it. "Alexander Wolcott. A physician and the Indian agent for the area. Albert says he's real important. Albert says they're desperate for construction workers, especially carpenters. They have plans to grow the township into something big."

"So?"

"So didn't you say you wanted to go out west? Now that your mother has passed. Didn't you say you were tired of Philly and the heat and all? That you wanted to breathe fresh air again? You talk about it all the time."

"Yeah. I know. Ten years in this city is enough for me. And now the ties are broken."

"Albert says that the country out there is magnificent. Shall we go? Make a new start? What do you say? Albert says he gave my name to this Mr. Wolcott. Recommended me to him, like. So there's already an open door."

"But isn't it still dangerous out there? I don't need to get scalped this year."

"No, I don't think it is anymore. Albert says not. He says there was a treaty five years ago with the Potawatomi and the other local Indian tribes. We gave them a thousand dollars' worth of merchandise, and they gave us the land around Fort Dearborn. They're still allowed to hunt and fish in the wilder parts of the territory. But no more scalping. He says the Indians are actually quite friendly now, helpful even. What do you say? I tell you, I'm bursting to go."

"How in hell's name would we get there?"

"Albert says you head for a town called Wheeling. It's just outside Pittsburg and about halfway between Philly and this Fort Dearborn. He says it's pretty easy to get to Wheeling. Not comfortable by any means and rough and rocky in places, but well-traveled. You go out of Philly on the Lancaster turnpike and take the Pennsylvania road through Bedford and Greensburg to Pittsburg. Then southwest a little ways to Wheeling. And then ask." He laughed uproariously. "Wheeling is kind of a fork in the road apparently. It's the place where you cross the Ohio."

"How do you know all this stuff?"

"Albert told me some of it, and I talked to a buddy of mine who works in the mayor's office. Anyway, from Wheeling you can either take a steamboat down the Ohio to a place called Louisville and continue on a bit further to pick up the Mississippi to St. Louis. I'm sure you've heard of St. Louis. Or you can cut across from Wheeling to Fort Dearborn, direct-like. That's what Albert did. He says that way's rougher and more devious, but at least it's flat. Not like what we'll face crossing the Alleghenies."

"Do we take a coach?"

"I think so. Many families take their own Conestogas, but single guys like us don't need to haul chests and children. We can take a stagecoach, I think."

"And how long would it take?"

"That I'm not sure. Albert said it took him three weeks to get to Pittsburg. That's with crossing the Allegheny Mountains. After that he didn't say. Perhaps it would take…let's say…five weeks in all to reach Fort Dearborn. Does that sound about right?"

"And the cost?"

"Twenty dollars? Thirty? Albert didn't say."

"I've got that much saved already. I can save more by next year."

"We could go once the weather's good and the snow's cleared off the mountain passes. May or June next year?"

"I'm not sure, Batch. Do you think we should? Seriously?"

"There's opportunity out there, Thomas. Boundless work and good money. A huge lake to sail on. Hills and forests. Plus, we have a contact in this Wolcott feller when we get there. I don't see how we could fail. I'm going to say…yes!" He punched Thomas on the shoulder.

"Let me think about it. I need to talk to Aunt Jemmy first. Fort Dearborn sounds like such a tiny little place, a flea at the wrong end of a telescope."

"Albert says there are already fifty or a hundred people living around it with more coming every day—all needing homes, cabins, stores. He says they plan to incorporate it in a few years. They're going to call it by its old French and Indian name, which was…" He fumbled through the letter to the last page.

"What?"

"Chicagou."

Chapter 40

Chicago and Kankakee
1854–1858

Thomas Temporal and Batch Coleman remained in touch over the years even as they both married, built families, and hopscotched around the city. They'd lived in Chicago for thirty years and mostly forgotten all they'd ever known about Philadelphia. Once a year, a few days before Christmas, they'd get together at the old Green Tree Tavern at Lake and Canal to catch up. They'd frequented the place for at least twenty years. This particular year, 1854, right after they'd ordered their drinks and begun to reminisce, a stranger walked up to the bar and ordered a single corn whiskey. He took a gulp, swiped his hand across his mouth, and asked the barkeeper, "Is this Wolf Point?"

"Well, that's what they sometimes call it," the barkeeper replied, "or used to call it. It's really just a fork in the Chicago River. Why do you ask?"

"I'm thinking of building a store somewhere near here."

"It's a good location, sir. Of course, you'd probably do better on the east side of the river, closer to the center of the city, but…still…there's lots of action here on the west side too. Growth potential. Plenty of small boats dock hereabouts. And there's the ferry."

"That's what I was told. And they say it's expanding every day. But…Wolf Point…it set me to thinking…wolves. Are there any around here?"

"Wolves? No, not so much these days."

Batch Coleman, who'd overheard the drift of the stranger's question, could not resist opening his mouth. "Scarcely a wolf to be seen nowadays, sir," he said. "Pardon my butting in. But when this place was built—back in the thirties—there were plenty of wolves living in the woods to the west of here, and they visited regular." He turned his head toward Thomas and asked, "Do you recall George Allen?"

Thomas nodded vigorously and chimed in at once. "Wolves used to come here every evening back in them days," Thomas said. "The landlord kept pigs in the stable yard, and one summer there was a wolf would come every night and steal a piglet. Just the one. For his supper. The same thieving critter every night. So the landlord paid his buddy George Allen to take his gun and sit up in a corner of the stable yard all night. So he did. Perched on a bar stool. Still and silent."

"When the wolf came for his supper that night," Batch continued, "George shot him clean through the belly. One shot."

"*However*," said Thomas, pausing for effect, "the bullet struck a watering can and glanced upward through the weatherboarding and into one of the upstairs bedrooms. Bounced off the headboard and into the jaw of a sleeping guest!"

"Clean into his jaw!" said Batch, laughing. "Not deep, mind. Just a quarter of an inch."

"Not deep, no. Just a gash. But the man came thundering downstairs with a towel pressed to his mouth and the bullet in his other hand. Slammed it on the counter where the landlord was dozing. Demanded all kinds of compensation. But the only thing Mr. Cox would do for him was to promise to cook him bacon for his morning breakfast."

Batch and Thomas laughed loudly, and the stranger chuckled along.

"As if it were from the saved piglet," Batch explained. "Bacon!"

"I understand."

"Yep, there were plenty of wolves around here in them days," the barkeeper affirmed. "It was before my time, but I've heard you could sit on the front stoop and shoot them of an evening. There used to be a painted sign of a wolf hanging above the tavern door. Gone now though."

"And one other time," said Thomas, "just up West Water Street, as it was called then, a horse had died by the roadside, under the trees, and a pack of wolves descended and began to devour the carcass. Such a howling as you never heard this side of Gehenna. Old Mrs. Cox came out the side door of this here tavern and saw them. Screamed the once and fainted on the spot. They would've waltzed over and gnawed on her too, but Mr. Cox heard the commotion and dragged her back indoors, feet first. What a palaver! It took five men with guns to disperse the pack. The men dragged what was left of the horse carcass into the barn and buried it the next day."

"To prevent the varmints reassembling," Batch explained.

"How many wolves were there?" asked the stranger.

"I didn't see them myself," said Thomas, "but Mr. Cox reckoned twenty at least. Fighting each other to get the best parts."

"Liver and kidneys and such," Batch said in a knowing kind of voice.

"Good God."

"But don't worry," said Batch. "You'll be safe these days. There's more storefronts now than there was then. More people about. The wolves have turned back west." They resumed drinking. "It's still called Wolf Point though," Batch said to conclude that particular topic.

"You built much of this tavern, did you not, Batch?" said Thomas.

"That I did," he replied. "For Mr. Kinzie. I did all the weatherboarding and plasterwork on this here first floor." He looked up and around the room, proud of his handiwork. "Got well paid for it too. Mr. Kinzie was a fine and generous gentleman. I wish there were more like him. That would've been in '32 or thereabouts."

"Chicago was full of land speculators in those days," the barkeeper added. "There were public sales and auctions every month. No place to bed them at night. In the early days of the Green Tree, so I've heard, they often had three in a bed: the outside two lying as normal and the middle one arsy-varsy with his feet up at the headboard. Madness, it was. Somebody made a lot of green out of it. More than I've ever made."

"Not only that, I can remember when there were mattresses all over the floor of this here bar. For the casual buyers and sellers and workmen," said Batch. "I saw them most nights."

The stranger nodded and finished his drink. He expressed his gratitude to all around him, asserting that they had reassured him to the point of a positive decision. He scurried off to survey the bare land around the point, particularly up West Water Street. Next year the man built his store at the end of Lake Street on the west side of the river. This proved wise in retrospect, for everything on the east side was burnt to a crisp seventeen years later in the Great Chicago Fire, which, though it jumped across the river from south to north, close by Market and Franklin, was never quite able to leap across it from east to west at Wolf Point. Thus, the Green Tree Tavern survived too.

When the stranger had left, Batch and Thomas turned inward again.

"So what are you up to these days?" Batch asked Thomas.

"I've been working these past months on the Central Union Depot," said Thomas. "Down where the river meets the lake, you know. It's hard work, but the pay's very good. Things might change though, I'm thinking. Last week I had a chat with Boyington, a young man from out east who's been doing the drawings for the depot. He told me he'd landed a new assignment downstate. He was designing the county courthouse at a place called Kankakee."

"Never heard of it."

"Me neither. It's fifty miles or so south of here, he says. Five days by wagon, three hours on the railroad. Apparently, it's going to be the next big city to burst forth in the Illinois. The Illinois Central completed the tracks between here and there a year or so ago, and now immigrants are hurrying down there by the bushel load to build up the place. French Canadians mostly, they say…but Belgians and Scandinavians too…Germans and Irish working on the railroad…all kinds. Boyington thought it would be a good place for me to move to. Developing fast. More carpentry than you could imagine. He said he would talk to the management and see if they'd make me a supervisor on the courthouse project and give me a pay raise. He seems to like me—well, my work at least—and the pride I take in it."

"Wow. That's going back to frontier days. Like when we first came to Chicago, remember? Fur traders…Indians…trappers. Remember how we had to cut down the trees ourselves to make logs for our cabins that first year?"

"We sure did. And it's funny you should mention that. Boyington said the square on which they're going to build the courthouse used to be a Potawatomi council ground! Can you believe that? Remember how we were afraid we might be attacked by the Potawatomi out here?"

"You thought you would be scalped!" said Batch.

"I did! How times have changed. It seems like this big group of investors—they call themselves the Associates Land Company or something like that—financed the railroad depot down there in Kankakee. So when it came to a discussion of which town should be the county seat, they pushed for Kankakee. Naturally, they would, wouldn't they? Originally the county seat was going to be in a different town nearby. Boyington called it *Moments* or something like that. But last year the company doubled down and promised land and cash for the building of a county courthouse. So Kankakee won the day."

"Money talks."

"Loudly in these small towns. Louder 'n a foghorn."

"So they're about to begin work on a fancy building to house the county government. Cunningham won the contract, and I've just been offered a job with them, thanks to Boyington. Not as supervisor, mind, but with a hefty raise. I'm thinking I'm going to go. Try something new. You wanna come too?"

"Nah. We're all set on Ashland. Kids in school and all."

"Sure, sure."

"Have you seen the plans for the courthouse? What kind of a building is it gonna be?"

"Boyington showed me his plain drawings. Three stories, brick and limestone. A dome on top, as I recall. I might get to work on the jail on the first floor. That would be a lark. Never done that kind of thing before. No idea how you secure the iron bars so they can't be torn out. One huge courtroom on the top floor. They'll probably have me working on the interior walls and floors—stuff I can do with my eyes closed."

"You sure you want to move? Drag the kids down there?"

"I think so, Batch. Since Fiona passed, I've lost the taste for my house and neighborhood. Her memory is just everywhere. Seeps out the walls like French perfume. No escape from it. I haven't mentioned moving to the kids yet though."

"How old are they now?"

"George is eleven, Martha eight, and Henry…he must be about four, I guess. Yes, that's right, it's been four years since I lost Fiona."

"Are there schools down there?"

"I don't know. Maybe a one-room schoolhouse I could get George into. The young'uns don't need schooling yet."

They drank in silence for another minute or two.

"Do you remember my cousin Albert?" said Batch.

"Him as went off to mine lead in Galena?"

"Good memory! Well, he finally quit that kind of work last year. He's in Chicago now. He's got a place on Philo Carpenter's old piece. I saw him in August."

"Yeah? What's he doing now?"

"He's a landscape gardener. Still digging, but soil now, not rock. Easier on his bad back."

"He must be over fifty by now. I can't believe he lasted so long at that lead mining."

"He'd have liked to have stayed longer at it, truth be told, but the work changed. It used to be all outcrop work—you know, hacking into the side of a hill. He could do that well enough. But then they found out there were tons more lead ore below the waterline. Bosses set their minds on deep mining. Line their pockets a tad thicker. They asked for a hundred men to go down a hundred-foot shaft at the Jamestown Diggings. They said pumps would keep the water out."

"Jesus."

"Well, Albert said the fuck with that. He handed his pickax to the manager and headed for Chicago."

"You sure can't blame him. A hundred-foot shaft down underground? It's an accident waiting to happen. It could flood anytime and drown him. And who knows how much lead dust was already fixed in his lungs after all those years."

Batch nodded. "He does cough a lot. Good job they were mostly mining in the open air all those years, or he'd be dead by now."

More thoughtful drinking time.

"So you're going downstate, then," Batch said. Less of a question than a sad reflection.

"I've pretty well made up my mind. Probably sign on next week."

"I might not see you again."

"I'll make a point of coming to Chicago every Christmas," said Thomas. "Don't worry."

They clinked glasses and quickly changed the subject.

The Sunday after his catch-up with Batch, Thomas sat around the breakfast table with his three children. He was nervous. It was a big decision for himself, and he'd realized overnight that it was a big thing for the kids as well. He set his coffee mug down and drew a deep breath.

"Kids," he said, "we're moving."

All three children sat motionless, their eyes glancing from one sibling to the other. Suddenly, Martha's face wrinkled up, and she gave out a single, gentle sob. At the sound of it, Henry let out a loud cry and began bawling. George remained motionless.

"Kids, kids, don't worry! Everything's going to be just fine. The new place will be better than this one, I promise."

"Where are we going?" asked George, ever the thoughtful one.

"We're going a ways downstate. Not very far. I got a new job—a better job—in a place called Kankakee. I'm going to be helping them build the new courthouse down there. It's an opportunity not to be missed."

"But what about us? What about our friends?"

"It'll be better down there, believe me. Plenty of fresh air." That didn't sound like much of an allure even to Thomas. "You can learn to fish and hunt. Sail. Ride a horse. You'll find plenty of new friends."

"But I don't want to do those things. Will there be a school?"

"I'm not sure, Georgie. I don't know yet. But you'll get used to it, I know you will. No different than when I came from England to Philly. And then from Philly to Chicago. It takes a little time, but you'll call it home soon enough. Quit crying, Henry…Martha. We wouldn't be going if I didn't think you'd like it. Okay?"

"When will we leave?"

"In a week or two. It's not decided yet."

The children calmed down eventually, and Thomas took them to church and then for ice cream. By the evening they'd adjusted somewhat to the idea and begun to ask him questions about what they would encounter in this strange new place they could not pronounce. Thomas made up answers as he himself had no idea what the place would be like. As he tucked Martha and Henry up in their shared bed that night, he whispered to the pair of them, "I promise you one thing. You'll each have your own bed in Kankakee. I'm going to make them myself. I'm resolved. One bed each." They seemed to like that idea. "And we'll go down there on the railroad!" Henry squealed with delight and laughed. Thomas pulled an imaginary cord above his head, simulated a train whistle, and cried, "All aboard the Illinois Central! Next stop, Kankakee." Martha laughed too this time. Thomas tucked them in, kissed them, and said, "Sleep tight, kids, tight as two bugs in a rug." They turned outward and closed their eyes and were soon asleep. Thomas wished he felt as confident as the confidence he'd instilled in them. He went across the room and bid George a goodnight also.

George offered the same back to his father and said firmly, "I'll make sure we're all right down there, Father."

Thomas teared up and had to turn away.

They had a great time on the railroad train, but their four smiles faded when they alighted at the tiny clapboard station house in the middle of nowhere. With its white picket fence, it looked no different than the tiny farmhouses they'd passed on their three-hour trip through the flat countryside. Even Thomas was taken aback by the primitive structures around him. Cunningham's people had arranged temporary accommodation for them, so they went there and made the best of it. It would be two years before Thomas was able to find a decent, affordable plot of land and build them a good-sized home with the help of his colleagues and fill it with well-made wooden furniture he built himself: four beds upstairs, the minimum requirement, a promise he could not break.

What made a city? Where and when Thomas was a child and was still called Tommy, it required a cathedral. He could very vaguely recall seeing the main tower of Lincoln Cathedral far away on the eastern horizon. Reputedly, it was the tallest manmade structure on earth for 238 years until the central spire was blown down in a storm in 1548, the year that John Dee celebrated his manhood and Thomas Digges was a bawling two-year-old. It was the cathedral that made Lincoln a city. That was the rule. In the American Midwest, however, such rules did not exist. All that was required to become a city, seemingly, was for the inhabitants of a town to decide they were worthy of being one. In the case of Kankakee, this had happened the year before Thomas and his children arrived. A petition was sent to the governor, and he said, "Okey dokey," and Kankakee City was born. And why not? It had a couple of thousand inhabitants, a hardware store, a drugstore, a bank, a blacksmith and a gunsmith, and no less than three newspapers. Who needed a cathedral? Who cared if there were a million acres of marshland just to the east, crawling with beavers, Indians, and outlaws? It was a city if it thought itself one.

Thomas worked hard on the courthouse from the outset, being given responsibility for all the interior work. He hired one of the boss's nieces, Willa Cunningham, to come and keep house for them three days a week. Mornings she washed and cleaned and sewed and prepared food. Afternoons she taught Martha and Henry to read and write and gave them very basic instruction in American history and world geography. At the same time, she supervised George as he bent over a desk that his father had built for him and educated himself. He read whatever books he could find—he could never find enough—and filled a journal with notes and thoughts. Often he would ask questions of Willa, but more often than not, he would end up answering them himself. From two o'clock to three o'clock, winter months excepted, she took the three children outside and let them hurtle around the streets and gardens playing made-up games. It worked out well. They began to like Kankakee. They began to forget Chicago.

One day, when Thomas came home from work, George met him at the front door and took his coat and hung it up for him. That was unusual. He waited while his father removed his boots and sat down in his armchair. Then he brought him his pipe and tobacco and matches. When his father seemed relaxed and comfortable, George sat down on a stool in front of him and said what was on his mind.

"Jake came 'round to play today."

"Hmm," Thomas replied, puffing on his pipe till it took.

"He said he went to see his grandpa at their farm in Momence at the weekend. His grandpa said that Jake could go and work there over the summer, and he would pay him. A dollar a day. To do easy stuff like weeding and hoeing. So it set me to thinking. Where's my grandpa at?"

"You remember Grandpa McCann. We used to go to his house in Garfield Park."

"Not on mother's side. On your side."

Thomas took the pipe out of his mouth and stared into the corner of the room. "Grandpa Temporal is dead, I'm afraid. He died back in England before we came over here."

"Oh. I didn't know that. What was he like?"

"I don't know, Georgie. I don't remember him at all. He died soon after I was born."

"What kind of work did he do?"

"I don't know."

"And my grandma?"

"Grandma Temporal died in Philadelphia. Right before I came out to Chicago. She was a lovely lady. You would've liked her. Her name was Martha, same as your sister. I'm sorry, Georgie, but you have no grandparents to visit or go work for. And now that your mother's passed, I'm afraid you've just got me and Martha and Henry. The four of us will have to take care of each other. If it's summer work you're interested in, I'll pay you a dollar a day to help me with the woodworking. Learning the trade might stand you in good stead in the future."

George bowed his head. "I'll work with you in the summertime, but I don't think that's what I want to do my whole life. With respect. I've been reading a lot these days. About how the country is run. How the state is run. That's what I'm interested in mostly."

Thomas sucked on his pipe and said, "You'll make me proud, Georgie, I have no doubt."

On September 25, 1858, Thomas Temporal stood on the steps of the Kankakee County Courthouse listening to Senator Stephen A. Douglas address the crowd. Thomas was proud beyond words to have received a printed invitation card for the event, even though George had had to explain to him some of the more esoteric words on it and even though it didn't actually have his name on it. And he didn't mind in the least that he was positioned off to one side on the back row of an assembly of city dignitaries—one of just five Cunningham workers permitted an exalted position on this great occasion. The five had built it, the five deserved recognition. And though Thomas was unable to spot them, he knew that his children were standing with Willa somewhere in the throng of two thousand folks spread out in front of him. He wore a black suit bought special and a dark-blue tie that George had had to tie for him. He wore neither one again until the day he was buried in them.

George was now fifteen and took a great interest in Senator Douglas's words. Martha was twelve, and Henry was eight, and the two of them crouched down and whispered jokes to each other and made rude comments about the skirts and trousers and legs of the adults in front of them. George turned to Willa and asked, "Is Nebraska a state?"

Willa was taken aback. "What? A state? No, I don't think so. I think it's the name of the land to the west of us. Across the Mississippi River. I think. Why?"

"Mr. Douglas just said he thinks that the people who live there should be able to decide for themselves whether they can own slaves or not. Did I hear him right?"

Willa gave him a wan smile and slowly shook her head.

"That's what he said. I can't believe it. He thinks one man can own another man? Buy him…sell him…like in a store? There's a young black man from Bourbonnais who we see from time to time down by the river. He's no different from me. Two arms, two legs. A head on his shoulders. How can he be owned?"

"I don't know. It's just what some people think."

George listened intently. Senator Douglas's words were clear and forthright. He did not invest in figures of speech. One thing was never similar to another thing; no flowery comparisons were tossed to the crowd. George liked how he spoke, but he didn't like the words he used. However, many around him cheered him on and jeered when the views of his opponent were described. George was surprised and pressed Willa on the matter.

"He said that Mr. Lincoln wants to make Illinois a colony for free black men, but I don't think that's right from what I've read. Mr. Lincoln just thinks that black men are entitled to the same rights as white men. Wherever they may choose to live. Like it says in the Constitution. Willa?"

Willa smiled at him again and put her arm around his shoulder. She leaned in to him and whispered, "I don't know about such things, Georgie. Perhaps the time has come for you to be *my* teacher."

George smiled back at her. "Did you know that Father came from a place called Lincoln? In England. Across the sea. Do you think Mr. Lincoln is named after that place? Wouldn't that be something?"

"It would. Perhaps he is."

"When I'm old enough to vote, I will vote for Mr. Lincoln. And if there is ever a fight with these slave-owning people, as some think there will be one day, I will fight for *his* side. *By* his side."

Chapter 41

Kankakee
June 2019

"I GOT A MESSAGE!" TOM SHOUTED in a lazy voice that seemed to struggle to escape from his vocal cords. The humid air tamped down and flattened his words. There was no reply. He was sprawled in a lawn chair on the patio with his laptop on his knees. Laden with Gulf moisture, the summer air had already worked its way up the Mississippi and collapsed, exhausted, over central Illinois. There it had encountered layers of high-altitude smoke from a wildfire somewhere out beyond Kansas. God had whisked the hot, wet air and the fine, dry smoke into a creamy broth of haze that stretched far beyond the row of spruce trees marking the property line. And seemingly knowing themselves to be behind in the calendar, mayflies hovered over the pond beyond the trees and periodically ventured onto Tom's patio, stopping and starting like miniature drones over a desperate battlefield. Dragonflies darted among them, guiding them to their targets. The mayflies eyed Tom, shivered, and sped off. In the distance, someone was playing eighties pop hits: "Just another manic Monday. I wish it was Sunday…"

"It *is* Sunday," Tom muttered with a degree of annoyance but tapping his toes nonetheless. "My fun day. Thank you, Bangles." He was getting drowsy. He turned toward the back door of the apartment and repeated, louder, "I said I got a message!"

Still no response. After staring at his computer screen a little longer, scared to click on the icon, he set his laptop down on the picnic table and went to the back door. He slid it open and shouted through the screen door, "Denise, I got a message!"

"What?"

"On my family history site. Someone posted a message."

"Well, open it! I'm busy."

He walked back to his chair and picked up his laptop. He clicked on the message.

> *Hello, TTemp1. My name is Maxine Reed. I am thirty-four years old, and I live in King's Lynn, Norfolk, England. I was looking through my DNA matches just now and saw that we are fourth to sixth cousins with 48 cM shared DNA, whatever that means. I looked at the tree you uploaded and saw that our ancestors come from the same area to the northwest of Lincoln. I have not uploaded my tree yet, but I've done a lot of work on it and have more than a thousand ancestors identified! If you're interested, we could see how we are related. Maxine.*

Tom immediately typed a reply and sent it.

> *Hello, Maxine. My name is Tom Temporal. Thank you for contacting me. You have done far more work than I have on your tree! Mine's just a sapling! I'm afraid I only know the two names* Temporal *and* Ransome. *Both families came from Marton, a village near Gainsborough that you might have heard of. See if either of those names are in your tree. I live in America, by the way. Best Regards, Tom.*

He closed his laptop. A different song was now cajoling him. "♪ *Hush, hush, keep it down now, voices carry…* ♪" Another of his favorites. Just hope it doesn't go on 'til Tuesday. He checked to see if the afternoon's baseball games had started yet, closed his laptop, and went back inside. Denise was making salad.

"So you got a message at last," she said. "I told you you would."

"Some woman in England. Maxine Reed. We're matched as distant cousins. She looked at that little tree I posted, and she says her family came from the same part of Lincolnshire. She wants to follow up on it."

"What did you tell her?"

"I said we didn't know much about my origins, only the names Temporal and Ransome and that they came from Marton. I told her to check for them in her tree. Sounds like she's done way more research than I have."

"See how she responds. Some of these family history wonks have been digging for years and years. Obsessed. She might come up with something helpful. Do you want salad for lunch?"

"Sounds good." He exhaled loudly and slumped down in a kitchen chair. "Man, it's really hot out there." He grabbed a paper towel and wiped the back of his neck. "Wouldn't it be great if she's already mapped out the Temporal family? My job would be over, and Thomas could rest in peace. That would be awesome."

Tom didn't hear back for three days, and then one evening, when he and Denise were sitting on their couch watching TV and he was fiddling with his computer, he saw that he had another message. He clicked on it. It was a response from Maxine.

> *Hello, Tom. Sorry for the delay. It was nice to hear from you. I'm afraid I don't have either of those names in my tree, but never mind. If we share DNA, then there must be some connection somewhere. A branch of my family lived in Lincolnshire until about 1805 after which they moved to Norfolk. My Lincolnshire family comes from the following towns and villages: Lincoln itself, Scampton, Nettleham, Saxonborough, Broadholme, and Torksey. Some of the family names associated with these places are: Hildred, Mitchell, Atkinson, Kirkham, Webster, Holland...and loads more! Let me know if you recognize any of these names and places. I'm a schoolteacher. What do you do? Maxine.*

Tom jerked upright on the couch.

"What the fuck!"

Denise turned to look at him but said nothing.

"That can't be right!" he exclaimed. "What the fuck!"

"What can't?"

"Maxine just sent me some place names and family names to see if I recognized any of them. Saxonborough, yes, of course… but there's also…Kirkham." He turned to look at her. "That's not possible."

"Kirkham? It must be a mistake. She must have gotten the relationships wrong in her tree. No Temporals or Ransomes, you said?"

"No. She just sent a list of possible names, one of which is Kirkham. I don't recognize any of the others."

"But how is that possible? If your connection is truly through a Kirkham, then your relationship to Maxine must date back much earlier than Thomas. Into the eighteenth century or even earlier. How else could you be related to a Kirkham?"

"But it would be a huge coincidence for the name Kirkham to pop up twice," said Tom. "Two trees connected in two places: an early relationship and then Thomas and Mary later. What are the odds?"

"I suppose it's possible that the two families knew each other from way back."

"But they lived in different villages. Marton and Saxonborough are too far apart. No, it can't be that."

Denise pondered the conundrum for a moment.

"Well, I suppose it's possible that Thomas and Mary Kirkham had a child *before* she died. The pregnancy at the time she was murdered could have been her second. *Their* second. Do you think? Is that possible?"

Thomas was shaking his head. "That doesn't seem likely either, does it? Such a child would've had to have been born in…hmm… in about the middle of 1802 at the latest. But the baby Tom that we know about was born in mid-1801. There doesn't seem to be enough time. And surely Thomas was still with Martha at that time."

"Unless he was having it off with Mary Kirkham on the side."

"That's possible, I guess."

"But there was all that palaver about Thomas being forced to marry Mary. If her parents were so incensed, then that anger would've manifested itself the first time around, not in the fall of 1803. They would've forced Thomas to marry their daughter the first time she got pregnant. If they already had a child, then her getting pregnant a second time would be no big deal."

"No. And then, of course, she died, so there was no possibility of another child born *after* 1803…"

"No. So let's think about the alternatives—*a*, it's unlikely to have been an earlier Kirkham relationship, and *b*, it's unlikely to have been an earlier or later child with Mary. Seems like it must be *c*, the one she was carrying when she died. But that's not possible either."

Denise switched off the TV and turned to face Tom. "What if the newspapers got it wrong," she said. "What if she *had been* pregnant, and that was the gossip the newspapers heard when they investigated. So that was what they reported. She had *been* pregnant, but her baby had been delivered before she was murdered. Then Thomas's mother would be Mary and not Martha. Then you've established the DNA connection."

"But Thomas said in his letter that Martha was his mother. And why would Martha take on the upbringing of the bastard child of her husband and his mistress? People don't do that. They certainly didn't do it in the old days. No, there must be some other explanation, an option *d*."

"Well, neither Martha nor Jemmy married a Kirkham, and then they were all off to America, ending the possibility of any connection past 1810. So to my mind, either Mary was Thomas's mother or there's another connection further back in time."

"Or it's all a big coincidence and my connection to Maxine is not through a Kirkham but through one of the other names she mentioned. Further back in time. A name of which we are unaware."

"Or Maxine simply fucked up."

Thomas squeezed his eyes tight shut and scratched the back of his neck.

"Let me see if I can get some more info from her to narrow things down. I'll send her a brief message—no frills or thrills—merely suggesting that we might have a Kirkham connection and asking for further details about that family. I really don't want to start crunching all those other family names into my computer just to look for new connections. That could take months...years...with no guarantee of success."

"Right. Best to start with the elephant in the room."

Tom thought for a few minutes, then typed a response.

> *Hello, Maxine. Thanks for sending me that information. I'm thinking that our connection might be through the Kirkham family of Saxonborough in about 1800 or so if that is consistent with what's in your tree. Could you further enlighten me about this Kirkham family? Then perhaps I can pinpoint the connection. I work in a bank in the city of Kankakee, which is an hour's drive south of Chicago. Best regards, Tom.*

Although it was past midnight in the UK when Tom sent his message, Maxine must have been awake and working on her family history because a reply came within twenty minutes. Denise leaned over, and the two of them read it together.

> *Hello, Tom. Well, I can definitely confirm that the Kirkham family* did *come from Saxonborough (and from Torksey, which is close by). So...bingo! I have traced them as far back as Elijah Kirkham at the beginning of the eighteenth century. He was born at Torksey in 1706. After him the next three eldest sons in line were all born and lived at Saxonborough: William born in 1731, James born in 1760, and Joseph born in 1781. Joseph moved to Norfolk and had two children there: Mary born in 1808 and Matthew born in 1810. Matthew continued*

> *the Kirkham line here in King's Lynn, but I haven't done any more recent Kirkhams because I am descended from Joseph's daughter, Mary, who married a Robinson in 1830. Hope this makes sense! Can you see where you fit in? Maxine.*

"See here!" Tom said, pointing at the screen with growing excitement. "Here's James Kirkham! That's Mary's father, the man whose gravestone we found in the Saxonborough churchyard. And unless I'm very much mistaken, the birth year Maxine gives is exactly the year we calculated from his gravestone, 1760."

"You'd remember that better than me," Denise replied, also pointing at the screen. "And look here, he had a son, Joseph, born in 1781. Mary's brother. A couple of years older than her. This is the first we've heard of him."

"I wonder if Maxine has discovered Mary. I wonder if she's on Maxine's tree."

"She says that Joseph moved to Norfolk and had family there. That would make sense."

"After his sister was murdered. He left to escape the scandal in Saxonborough, yes."

"And see, this Joseph had a daughter whom he named Mary. I bet she was named in memory of his poor dead sister. That would make sense as well."

"And if Joseph was the only son of James, then that would explain why we didn't find any more recent Kirkham graves in the churchyard. The Kirkham name died out in Saxonborough."

"You could probably learn more about this Joseph Kirkham online if you care to look." Denise paused and looked Tom in the face. "So how will you respond to Maxine's message?"

"I don't know yet," Tom said, setting his laptop aside and getting up. "Do you want a drink?"

"I'll share a beer with you," Denise replied, so Tom went to the kitchen and came back with two half-filled glasses.

"I think perhaps we've got all the pertinent information from Maxine for now. If I want to fill in the Kirkham branches, I can do that myself. I just have to be sure, first and foremost, that I am really and truly related to them through Mary. How the fuck do I do that?"

"Well, the way it's looking right now, your Thomas was the son of Mary Kirkham, conceived somewhere in that tiny window between when his father left Martha and his son and when Mary died. A window that's no more than a couple of years wide. I don't know how you're going to prove it one way or the other."

"I don't see how either. But I really don't want to have to trawl through early eighteenth-century parish registers looking for an earlier Temporal-Kirkham marriage or something like that. It'll ruin my eyesight."

"The problem is that the saga is drifting away from official records," said Denise. "Toward things that happened in the dark. Behind closed doors. Things that probably few people even knew about at the time. Nobody wrote that stuff down. Nobody went and got it sanctioned in church."

Tom nodded. He returned to his laptop and quickly typed a terse message back to Maxine.

> *Hello, Maxine. Thanks for sending that Kirkham line. I think I might be descended from James Kirkham through a daughter of his named Mary. She would've been Joseph's sister. I don't have anything more to say at the moment about them. Let me think about it some more and do some more background work. I'll get back to you. Again, thanks much for your help. Tom.*

Tom did think about it some more, and he did do some more background work, but he didn't get anywhere with either one. He couldn't see how to make further progress. He was frustrated, but other things came up as the weather heated up. Work at the office got busy, and genealogy drifted out of his mind. A short email from Maxine three days later kind of brought the matter to a conclusion for the time being.

> *Tom, I didn't know Joseph had a sister. I'll have to look her up. Glad I was able to help. Perhaps we can exchange trees at some point. Maxine.*

As soon as he read the message, an idea leaped into his head.

"I need to talk to Karen Butler," he told Denise.

"Why?"

"I've a feeling Karen knows more about what went on in the bedroom of The Plough back in 1803 than she told us in Saxonborough. She said she distinctly remembered passing through the *t⟨sub b⟩* state on her way back to the present. Yes? Do you remember that she said she saw some *really freaky stuff*? Those were the exact words she used—I remember them clearly. Well, perhaps there's more. Perhaps there are clues lodged in her memory that will help us put this Kirkham mystery to rest. I need to talk to her."

"Okay. Do you know how to find her?"

"Harry Groh will know. He'll have her phone number, and he knows how to get to her place in Iowa—presuming that's where she's settled. I'll give Harry a call and then go talk to her."

"I'm sure she'd appreciate a friendly face."

Chapter 42

Philadelphia
September 1870

HENRY AND MARTHA TEMPORAL ENTERED the Pine-Apple Café with the trepidation of two naive young Midwesterners adrift among throngs of bustling people with citified East Coast ways—ways that were nothing at all like they encountered in laidback Kankakee but something similar to what they could recall from growing up in Chicago. It was early in the morning though, and the café had no customers yet. They walked over to the counter together, but Martha deviated before reaching it and plopped herself down in a chair, tossing her valise onto a nearby chair in the process. She quickly removed her headscarf and undid the top button of her dress. Her hands flopped down on the table. She looked utterly exhausted.

"What can I get you, sir…madam?" said the man behind the counter. "We got a consignment of limes in from Mexico just this Monday. Our lime sherbets are going fast. Would you like a sample?" Henry shook his head, but Martha raised her hand. "Certainly, madam. One lime sherbet bite coming up." He turned and prepared a small paper cup for the lady. Henry took it off the counter and handed it to his sister.

"Actually, we're here searching for someone," said Henry. "We've come all the way from Illinois on the railroad. Stepped off the train just half an hour ago."

The man turned to look at him. "From Illinois? Truly? Why, that must be a wearisome journey."

"Three days in all. Stopping in towns we never heard of. Forever changing trains. My sister here can barely stay awake."

"Just to find someone? Who is it you are looking for?"

"A woman by the name of Jemmy."

The man shook his head.

"Jemmy Temporal."

"Temporal? Why, that was my mother's name! Before she married my father. It's an old English name, I believe." He paused for a moment until the connection dawned on him, and then exclaimed, "Oh, *Jemmy*! That *is* my mother. But she goes by the name of Jemima. I've not heard her called Jemmy for…well, it must be fifty years or more. So it must be my mother you're seeking. Can that be right?"

"Excuse my mistake," said Henry. "You see, me and my sister here…we are Temporals too. I am Henry Temporal, and she is Martha Temporal. We believe that we are kinfolk to your mother."

"Really? Kinfolk, you say? How remarkable. Well, I am Ben Bovey." He offered his hand across the counter and vigorously shook Henry's hand as soon as it was offered. "How are you related?"

"Well, your mother was the sister of my grandfather, I believe. I don't know what kind of relative that makes her to us. Great-aunt perhaps?"

"And you came all the way from the Illinois to find us? How remarkable!"

"Well, you see, our father passed earlier this year. And after his death, we discovered that he'd written a letter just before he died. We found it in the drawer of his desk. The letter was addressed to his children and those who would come after them. In the letter, he mentioned that he was brought up by his mother and his Aunt Jemmy in Philadelphia above a place called the Pine-Apple Café. Right, sister?"

"Right," said Martha, and she took the letter out of her purse and waved it in the air. She unfolded it and read an extract from the first page, "'My aunt's name was Jemmy. She worked as a waitress in the Pine-Apple Café owned by Miss Deloit, a relative of the farmer whose land we had lived on back in England. We all lived above the café on Juniper Street for ten years.' It was these words that brought us here today."

The man tilted his head a little and closed his eyes. Then he opened his eyes very wide, snapped his fingers, and pointed to Henry. "You mean Thomas!" he exclaimed.

"That's right!" said Henry.

"Thomas! Yes! I remember Thomas. He and his mother lived here with us, just like you said. He was always nice to me. When I was four or five, he would play stickball with me in the street. He must have been fifteen or sixteen then. He was always encouraging me and praising me. A lovely young man! He went out west when I was...what...maybe seven years old? We never heard from him again. It must be fifty years ago, if a day. That's incredible! And you are two of his children." He beamed from Henry to Martha and back again. "Well, I never."

"We are, indeed," said Henry. "Yes, we are. Henry and Martha. And we had a brother, George, who was killed in the Civil War. Thomas had three children in Illinois."

"After all these years."

"And you must be...," Henry began but then faded away.

Martha, who'd been rereading her father's letter while the two men talked, suddenly asked, "Was your father a sea captain?"

"He was! He was! Captain Benjamin Bovey!"

"The letter says that Jemmy married a sea captain. But father had forgotten his name."

"He was a Benjamin, and so am I!"

Ben Bovey walked out from behind the counter and went over to the table where Martha was sitting. He sat down in a chair beside her and Henry joined them.

"May I see the letter?" Ben asked. "Certainly," Martha replied and handed it over to him. He read and began to quote from it. "Look what it says here, 'Aunt Jemmy took up with a sea captain. I don't recall his name. They were married a few years after we arrived and had two children.' That's me! I am one of those two children. I'm Ben! And the other one is my sister, Evelyn. She lives in New York City now. They are us!" He seemed utterly amazed to find himself mentioned, as a child, in a letter from far away brought to him by strangers.

He continued reading and quoting, "'My mother died of the yellow fever in about 1820.' Yes, I remember that! It was in the summertime. Thomas rushed into our bedroom early one morning. Woke all four of us up at once. My father and mother jumped out of bed and ran into the other bedroom. Evelyn and I, we just sat up in bed looking at each other. We were very young. We didn't know what was happening. So we went back to sleep. We never saw Thomas's mother again. I didn't know she had the yellow fever. Nobody ever said. It was a scourge in Philly in those days. Thomas left us not long after his mother passed. Went to seek his fortune out west, they said. My mother cried and cried the day he left."

"And do you see the reference to a Miss Deloit?" asked Martha.

"Yes, yes! She owned the café in those days. I'm talking before 1820 or so. Perhaps 1830. More than forty years ago now anyway. I remember her as this old spinster lady who had her own room here. A very fancy room it was too. Lace and leather and knickknacks of all description on the shelves and mantle. Framed pictures around the walls. Evelyn and I were not allowed to go in her room, but occasionally we would push open the door and gaze at the forbidden delights. Very prim and proper was Miss Deloit."

"What happened to her?"

"Well, she had to give up running the place. She just got too old for it. My mother and father decided to buy her out. Miss Deloit offered them a deal they couldn't refuse. That would be in…perhaps 1830. I don't rightly remember. She continued to live on in her own room and ate her meals downstairs with us. Quite content she was. She died a few years later—the year before my father perished."

"Perished? Oh dear, I'm so sorry to hear that," said Martha.

"Lost at sea. He was bringing a cargo up from Kingston as he'd done many times before. Many, many times. But this particular time a terrible storm blew up off Rokers Point in the Bahamas. Unexpected. The ship was lost. No wreckage was ever found."

"That's terrible," said Martha. "Not having the chance to say goodbye."

"Yes, it was terrible hard. For Evelyn and for my mother especially."

"And what happened to Jemmy…Jemima, forgive me?" Henry asked.

"Happened?"

"Hmm."

"Why, nothing happened. My mother is upstairs resting as we speak."

"She has not passed, then?"

"No, no! She's still with us, thank the Lord. A sprightly eighty-four. The Temporal blood is rich, sir! It bodes well for you two!"

Henry and Martha looked at each other with smiles on their faces. "Father's aunt is still alive!" Henry said to Martha.

"We did not expect it," Martha responded.

"We thought she must have… We did not expect it."

"The only problem is that she is almost completely blind now," Ben said with some sadness. "It has gotten worse these last couple of years. But I'll take you up to see her. She will be thrilled to bits. Just let me close up the shop."

Ben walked to the front door, flipped the sign on it, and rejoined them.

"Follow me, Temporals!" he ordered, and upstairs they went.

A slight, delicate woman with a straight back and light-gray hair was sitting in a dining chair by the window, her face turned toward the morning sunlight streaming through it from the street. Behind her, on the lavender-colored wallpaper, President Lincoln stared down Queen Victoria in paired lithographs, symbolizing either dual or divided loyalties of the members of the household. Who could say? Perhaps they themselves did not truly know how they felt about such things. Jemima smiled as they entered the room.

"Benjamin?" she said in a confident though shaky voice.

"Mother, we have guests."

"Guests?"

"I think you will know who they are. Please compose yourself and be prepared for a surprise."

Jemima tilted her head to one side and opened her sightless eyes wide in anticipation.

"They are two of the children of your nephew Thomas."

Jemima said nothing for a moment. Her son's unexpected words took time to register. Then she burst into tears. It took Ben several minutes to calm her and dry her eyes.

"Thomas? Thomas has come to see me?"

"Not Thomas, Mother, two of his children. Henry and—"

"Martha," said Martha.

"Tommy has children now?"

"My father had three children," Henry explained loudly, leaning in toward her as if she were deaf as well as blind, "but sadly our brother, George, was lost in the Civil War. There are just the two of us now. We have come from Illinois to see you."

"And how is my Tommy? I have not seen him these many years. So very many years."

"I regret to have to tell you," said Henry, "that he passed away earlier this year. In the month of April. He had not been well for some years before that."

"Tommy has died? I cannot believe it. My poor little Tommy." Tears came into her eyes again, and she fumbled in the sleeve of her dress for a lace handkerchief. "By rights, he should not have died before me."

"He was in his late sixties...perhaps seventy even. He once told us that he did not know when he was born, so none of us ever knew his true age, but he lived to a ripe old one! Ha! Happy, hale, and hearty for the most part."

"Seventy? It's not possible. He was a young man when last I saw him. How time does fly." She dabbed her eyes. "We heard nothing from him after he left us and went out west. Not a single letter. Where did he settle?"

"In Chicago at first. He married there, and all of us children were born there. Then not long after Mother died, we moved downstate to Kankakee when that city was in its infancy. Our father was an accomplished carpenter his whole life. He helped to build the county courthouse there. And many, many homes for the early settlers."

"Yes. I remember when he apprenticed over on Sassafras. On his first day there he didn't know a nail from the head of a hammer, poor boy. But he was a good listener and a good learner. Martha and I always said he would prosper."

"And you, Mrs. Bovey. To be frank, we did not expect to see you today. We surmised that you must have passed during the long time that Father had been gone. But you have blossomed!"

"Blossomed? No," said Jemima. "The blossom fell many years ago. And then autumn took the leaves. Winter is upon me."

"But you look so spry."

"That is an illusion," said Jemima, drifting quickly away from her visitors and any message they might have brought her, deciding to explain her frailties first. "Inside this skin it is a different story. Every part of my body has a complaint. Each morning the parts discuss among themselves which one will step up today. The teeth say they are in a good mood, ask the hips. The hips say we are recovered from last week's ailment, and it is the turn of the small of the back. They soon reach their decision—at just about the time I rise of a morning. I suppose some people hate the parts of their body that rebel and aggravate them. I don't. I ask them to gather round, and I say to them, 'We are all in this together. Each of you must do your best to help the others.' And they do try. The eyes, in particular, are pitied by every part of me. The eyes weep and regret that they can no longer help the fingers to sew, help the feet to find direction. But the other parts do not resent their impotence. They sympathize and help them out as best they can. Thus, like a wagon on the Oregon Trail, we continue our journey, leaving nothing behind, making the best of each day. The lame dogs snuggle with us at night."

"You are a lesson to us all," said Martha.

"And what of your mother, the wife of our Tommy?" Jemima asked with a kind of delicate eagerness.

"Her name was Fiona. She was of Scotch heritage. I do not know when her family came to this country. She and Father were married in Chicago in 1840." Henry's head drooped. "Tragically, she died giving birth to me, the youngest. In 1850. The doctors worked hard to save her, but to no avail. Father was distressed beyond belief. He blamed himself for making her deliver at such an advanced age."

"What age was she?"

"Mother was forty-two."

"Not so very old. Many women have children at such an age. Older."

"I think Father was just distraught that he'd lost her."

"Yes, that would be it. And your ages, then?"

"I am Henry. I am twenty years old. Martha is twenty-four. Our elder brother George was twenty-two when he was killed in Alabama."

Jemima did not reply. Her shoulders slouched a little, and her hands clutched each other in her lap. Ben noticed this and said, "Let me get you some tea, Mother. You look a touch pale."

She raised her head toward the sound of his voice and said, "Tea, yes, that would be nice. For all of us."

Ben left the room, and the three of them sat in silence, slightly uncomfortable after the thrill of the introductions, wondering in which direction to head next. Neither Henry nor Martha seemed eager to bring up the subject of their father's letter lest it prove distressful to Jemima.

"We brought Tommy over from England on the boat," Jemima offered up to the silence. "Such a good boy. Six weeks at sea and him sick most of the time. But he never complained. Then or thereafter."

"Can I ask…why do you refer to him as *Tommy*?" said Martha. "He never used that name around us. Not once in his entire life."

"*Tommy*? Oh, that's what we called him back in England when he was just a little boy. To distinguish him from…" Her lips closed.

"Distinguish him? From whom?"

"It is of no matter. From his father perhaps. Our cottage was filled with that name in those days."

"He was always *Thomas* in Illinois."

"Yes, yes. He would be. He actually insisted that he be called by that name before ever we left Liverpool. I remember well the day he instructed me. I think he wanted to use the same name as his father—when he learned that his father was dead. It was the day I showed him his father's resting place."

"His grave?"

"Not exactly." Jemima turned away, then quickly turned back and said, "But you have not told me why you are here! How did you even know of my existence and where to find me?"

"That is rather a long story, I'm afraid," said Henry. "Why don't we wait until your son brings you some tea to revive yourself."

They didn't have to wait long. Ben entered the room with a tray. He took a cup and saucer off it and placed them on the table beside Jemima's chair. "Here you are, Mother," he said and guided her fingers to the handle of the cup. "Careful now!"

Jemima picked up the cup and took a few sips, then used her other hand to find the saucer and place the cup down on it. "Nothing is easy anymore," she said. "Once upon a time, it was the eyes who told the fingers what to do. But these days it is the fingers that help the eyes. Teamwork. No matter. Please proceed."

Henry and Martha helped themselves to tea first.

"Father died in April," Henry began. "But it was not until June that we could face the task of sorting through his papers. We thought there might be unpaid bills and suchlike." Martha nodded. "But everything was in order fortunately. We did find one unexpected thing though, a letter. It was addressed to us, his children, and to succeeding generations, I guess. We had no idea that he'd written this letter. Just two months before his death. It came as a great surprise."

"And what did the letter say?"

"Well, first of all, Father spoke very highly of his mother, Martha—"

"After whom I am named," Martha interjected.

"And of his Aunt Jemmy. You."

"That's what he always called me," said Jemima fondly, "even when he was grown and was asked not to." She smiled at a memory in the corner of the room.

Henry waited a moment, glanced at his sister for approval, and then pressed on.

"He described what he could remember of his childhood, which was actually very little, and how he came to America. He mentioned the Pine-Apple Café in Philadelphia. On Juniper Street. Which guided us here today."

Jemima held out her hand. "Can I hold the letter?" Martha passed it to her, and she gently caressed the front and back covers, staring up at the ceiling the whole time. Then she unfolded it and riffled through the six pages. "I can see him writing it," she said. "He is seated at a desk. Looking down at his fingers holding the pen. Thinking of us all. Our Tommy." She held out the letter, and Martha took it back.

Henry and Martha hesitated, again not sure how to proceed. Henry nodded to Martha, who swallowed hard and said, "Mrs. Bovey, we have come to see you primarily because of some of the things Father said at the end of his letter. He said that he felt… insecure, shall we say—had done his whole life—about his roots. He said he knew very little about his father and was worried that he was a bad man. He knew nothing about his birth, his family, his early childhood. Back in England, you understand. He even had some kind of intimation that his birth was miraculous…magical even. He said that he didn't have the right words to describe this feeling, and we don't understand what he meant by the words that he did use.

"He said that nothing had been told him directly when he was growing up in England—at least nothing that he could remember. It was only overheard gossip, schoolyard whispers and taunts, mutterings at late-night family gatherings. And nothing at all was ever mentioned after your arrival in Philadelphia. He said it made him anxious, not to know the answers to his questions. His dying wish, if you like, was for someone who came after him to discover the answers. Tell his descendants. Dig the dirt and plant him firmly in the family tree, so to speak. That is what has driven us here today."

"Of course," said Henry, picking up the conversation as his sister's voice trailed away, "we did not know if you were still alive. We knew that Father's mother, Martha, our grandmother, had died before ever he left Philadelphia. He said so in the letter. But we thought there was a chance that we could find someone here who could shed light on things. If only candlelight."

"And we have been most fortunate to find you, dear Mrs. Bovey," said Martha, reaching out to hold Jemima's left hand. Jemima picked up her teacup with her right hand and took more sips from it before placing it back on the saucer, perhaps to give her a little time to process her thoughts. "Can you assist us? Can you tell us anything about Father's early years? Can you help him to rest easy?" Martha tried to be both forceful and considerate at the same time. "Of course, we do not wish to distress you in any way. If these topics are too painful to recall, please say so, and we will not press you."

"It can come as no surprise to you," Jemima responded, "that I know almost everything you ask about. There are only one or two aspects of the life of Tommy's father, my brother, that are forever closed off to me. As regards Tommy himself, all is an open book. But…" She turned to look in the direction of their voices and smiled in a melancholy way. "But regretfully, my mouth must remain closed. I can tell you nothing. Though it is not for the pain of telling it."

"Why? Surely, with Father now in his grave…"

"That does not matter. I made a promise years ago that I would say nothing more to our Tommy about such things, and to my mind you have inherited that obligation. I'm sorry. What I know must be buried with me in my grave."

"But it is something Father wanted most sincerely."

Jemima's eyes moistened again. "Once before, when Tommy was but a young boy, I tried to tell him a truth. Show him a truth. Martha said at the time that it was a mistake, and she might have been right for all I know. It certainly sowed confusion in his mind. Martha said it would. And now perhaps I make a second mistake by not telling more to you. Is it fair that a woman who loved each one of them so much should have to take an action that hurts one of them either way? Whether I say or do not say. Why would God inflict that on me? Why?"

It was not a question to be answered, so Henry and Martha just waited for Jemima to continue. It seemed to them that she'd wandered far away and could not easily be led back. They let her go where she wanted.

"It might have been better, in the very beginning, if I'd never accepted my brother's urgings to leave Marton and help out his wife in Fallow Fields while he went off laboring and carousing with never a care for either one of us. Then I would not be here now. I would not have suffered all this pain. I could have married Billy Allsop from Gate Burton and lived a settled life on his farm. He wanted me badly. He doted on me. And he was a true gentleman. I would still be in Lincolnshire today with Lincolnshire children and Lincolnshire grandchildren all around me. But I decided to agree to our Thomas's plea and see what a harvest I reaped!"

"Mother, Mother," said Ben, coming to her side and putting his arm around her shoulders. "Do not take on so."

"Oh, Ben! I mean no disrespect to your father or to you and Evelyn. Do not think that. You mean the world to me. But these people who have come here today…Tommy's children, forgive me… have pushed me back across the ocean. They ask me to recall his days in England, and I cannot do that without recalling my own!"

"They intend no hurt."

"I know. I know it. I'm sorry for my outburst. Please forgive me."

Henry and Martha murmured their appreciation of her words. They looked at each other and at Ben Bovey. Was it time for them to leave? They were at a loss.

"I'm sorry, but a promise is a promise," Jemima continued, seeming to near the end of her monologue. "I can tell you nothing more. Here is what I suggest you do. I am an old woman, mind, so my judgment might be even less sound now than it was the day I led Tommy out of our garden and across the fields so many years ago. At the end of the day, you must do whatever you think is best. But what I suggest is that you take that letter and fold it back up and seal it with wax and leave it in a safe place. One day, someone will find it, someone who may be able to fulfill Tommy's wishes—your son, your grandson, who knows. But it cannot be done today. Not by me."

"Very well, Mrs. Bovey. We will do as you say."

"And alongside the letter you must place something else."

"What is that?"

"The bag that you will find in the bottom of my wardrobe. Benjamin?"

"Yes, Mother." Her son went and opened the wardrobe and poked around in the bottom of it. "This tartan one?"

"Yes, the tartan bag. I brought it over from England on the boat with some of my brother's old work clothes and a few of Tommy's baby clothes. Just as souvenirs. And one or two other mementos. Do not open the bag though, children, I beg you. Simply store it with the letter for safekeeping. They all belong together. They are memories of a time long gone. They may be of value to future generations, but I am done with them."

"Yes, Mrs. Bovey," said Martha, "Thank you."

Martha turned to her brother and said, "We can store them in that old trunk for now."

Chapter 43

Fallow Fields
May 1804

The woman waited under a tree until Martha Temporal had closed the cottage door behind her and set off across the fields to Saxonborough. When Martha was far enough away, the woman hurried to the door and knocked on it loudly. She was carrying a bundle in her arms. She knocked again. A keening east wind swept across the flat countryside and seemed to rebound off the whitewashed plasterwork into her face. She shivered as she waited—or trembled; sometimes it's hard to tell the difference. Eventually the door opened.

"Yes?"

"Beg pardon, miss. Are you Jemmy Temporal, sister of the late Thomas Temporal, God rest his soul?"

"I am. Who are you?"

"I'm Ethel Hodgson, housekeeper at The Plough in Saxonborough. I don't think we've ever met, but one of our maidservants, Nancy Barnes, knows you and told me where you live."

"Nancy? Yes, I know Nancy. We've been out walking betimes. What do you want?"

"And was that Martha Temporal, Thomas's wife, who just left for the village? Widow, I should say, I suppose. Beg pardon."

"It was. My sister-in-law. What is it that you want?"

Before Ethel Hodgson could reply, a sharp cry came from the bundle she was holding in her arms. Ethel looked down at it and then offered it up to Jemmy in outstretched arms.

"This is Thomas's son," she said.

"What? No," Jemmy replied. "Thomas's son is sleeping in his cradle in the front room. This is not his son. You are mistaken."

"But it is," Ethel continued. "There is much that needs to be explained. May I come in?"

Jemmy leaned forward beyond the door frame and glanced up and down the deserted, windswept lane, looking for nobody in particular, gossipmongers.

"I suppose you'd better."

Mrs. Hodgson came inside, and Jemmy closed the front door behind her rather reluctantly. She didn't offer Mrs. Hodgson a seat or take the bundle from her. It seemed like either would indicate some kind of acceptance of the story to come. So Ethel just stood there, burdened, in the tiny entrance hall of the cottage and said what she'd come to say.

"You know Thomas's story, of course—what happened to him over these past few months. I didn't see you at the trial though. Nor Mrs. Temporal."

"We did not attend the trial. Martha couldn't face it."

"No. I quite understand. But I believe someone must have told you by now of all that was revealed concerning that dreadful day last October. Well, Miss Temporal, it was me who found Mary Kirkham's body. Me. I heard the commotion in the bedroom and hurried up the stairs. Thomas darted past me and ran out the tavern door." She could hardly find the fortitude to continue, but she forced herself, staring all the while down at the floor. "I couldn't believe what I saw in that bedroom. I can scarcely speak of it even now. Mary was lying on the bed covered in blood. Her nightdress…no, enough of that. I went to help her but didn't rightly know what was best to be done. And that's when I saw it."

"Saw what?"

"The baby's head."

"The baby's head?" Jemmy asked. She pointed to the bundle. "This baby?"

"Mary was dying, but she was also giving birth. I wouldn't have thought it possible if I hadn't seen it with my own eyes. What was I supposed to do? I didn't rightly know. I ran to the window to shout for help, then quickly returned and delivered the baby. I'd done the same thing many times before, so it wasn't a big problem for me, though I could barely see what I was doing through my tears. I cut the cord and tied it with a ribbon from Mary's hair. Then I carried the baby to one of the empty rooms until I was ready to leave for the day. Washed it some. It was a boy."

Jemmy was speechless. At first she thought this must be some kind of trick being played on her to unload some unwanted, inconvenient bastard child, but if this truly was Ethel Hodgson, then that seemed unlikely. She began to think it must be true. "Mary Kirkham delivered this baby on the night our Thomas killed her?"

"Yes. And somehow I've managed to keep him alive since then. He's a sturdy little mite. I've fed him and cared for him in my cottage all by myself. I didn't know what else to do. He's about six months old now. He's lovely. See!" Ethel gently uncovered the face of the baby and presented it to Jemmy's eyes. "This is your nephew," she said. "It's nothing short of a miracle."

Jemmy stared at the baby in wonderment but could not speak or touch him.

"What was I supposed to do?" Ethel continued, seemingly in hopes that honest elaboration would wash away her own uneasiness about what she'd done. "I couldn't let him just die there, could I? That wouldn't have been the Christian thing to do at all, would it? I felt I had to save him. I showed the baby to Mary after I'd delivered him, and I swear to God she smiled at him just seconds before she passed. It was like she'd forced herself to stay alive until that moment. Honest to God. I've not told anyone about this. I didn't tell Mr. Norris or the servants. I didn't say nothing in court. But now that he's alive and well, I've come to realize that I can't keep him. I don't have the time, and he's not my responsibility. So what am I supposed to do? I went to see Mary's father yesterday, James Kirkham up on the Torksey road, but he wouldn't have nowt to do with him. *'Categorically not,'* Mr. Kirkham said. Some bastard offspring of their murdered daughter? *'No, ma'am. Not in this house. Not ever. Please leave at once.'* I couldn't believe it. His grandson 'n' all!

"So I came here. You needs must take your nephew and bring him up. He's the son of your brother and Mary Kirkham. I can't think of anyone else who'd take him. The parish might, but they would be the ruin of him. None of this is Mary's fault, mind. She was the sweetest thing. We all thought so. She was just captivated by your brother. After all, he was a ladies' man. All the kitchen agreed on that. God's gift to women, Nancy said. And for a while he loved Mary back. Probably. But that all changed when she came with child. He was already married to Martha, see, and had just wanted a fling—though none of us knew any of this at the time. There were other girls waiting on his charms. He had his pick, you might say." She raised her head then and looked into Jemmy's eyes. "But I didn't come here to speak ill of your brother, Miss Temporal. It's not my place to do that."

"I know our Thomas right well, Mrs. Hodgson. I know what kind of a man he was. I also knew Mary Kirkham a little. She would sometimes walk out with Nancy and me and the other village girls. I did think highly of her."

"I'm at my wits' end. You must take him."

She pushed the swaddled baby up against Jemmy's chest.

"But I live with Martha now," said Jemmy. "Our poor Thomas's wife, now widow, as you say. She will not take to the boy, considering his parentage. You can't expect her to. And she has her own son to care for."

"Then *you* must be mother for him, Miss Temporal. Martha can love her own son, and you can love this one. You can share the upkeep of the two babbies together."

Jemmy shook her head slowly. She looked out the small window beside the front door and stared at the fields and the sky. Her future seemed to be ever drifting off track in directions she'd never planned and for reasons not to her liking. But she was never one to shirk her duty. She pursed her lips and turned back to appraise the visitors.

"Let me see him," she said hesitantly, opening her arms.

Ethel handed the child over and watched as Jemmy brushed the blanket away from his cheeks and chest and smiled at him. The baby smiled back and brandished his two tiny fists. "He is lovely, right enough." Jemmy clenched her jaw and grimaced. "I can't think what's best to do at the moment. Leave him with me, then. For now. I'll see how we take to each other. And I'll see how Martha takes to him. I'll come by The Plough in a couple of weeks and let you know our decision. I'll let you know if we think we can keep him."

"God bless you," said Ethel. "I didn't know where else to turn. Perhaps I did the wrong thing to save the child in the first place—it might have been better to let him die with his mother, and then they would be together in paradise now. Or perhaps I should have told the whole truth in court and let the parish decide. Or even just left the babby on the doorstep of his grandfather Kirkham. I cannot resolve these things in my mind, even though I have wrestled with them for nigh on a six-month. Bless you, Jemmy Temporal." Ethel started to tear up with relief.

"I will come and see you in two weeks," Jemmy said. "I promise. But be warned, there's a chance that I will bring the baby with me to give back to you."

"I understand. Truly, I do."

She smiled down at him. "But one way or another, this mite must survive."

It didn't take two weeks. Just five days later, Jemmy entered the front door of The Plough and asked to see Mrs. Hodgson. Ethel emerged from the kitchen and greeted Jemmy with a friendly smile. "Miss Temporal! How are you today?" She paused. "I see you are empty-handed."

Jemmy looked around to see if there was anyone within earshot and then spoke up in a shy whisper, "We've decided to keep the baby. Martha and me. We've taken a shine to him these past few days. He's been as good as gold and happy as a sandboy. We're going to give him the same name as his father, so we'll have two young Toms in the household." She giggled. "That's going to cause confusion down the road, I suppose. But it seemed the right thing to do as both babies are the sons of our Thomas and equally loved. The child has no paperwork, I know, but we'll worry about that later as well. We'll get him baptized when we can find the time. So there'll be two women and two children in that cottage up Fallow Fields. I don't know how we'll get through it, but we're going to give it our best. It can't be worse than this last winter was for us. Anyway, Martha and I are agreed on it. We'll take the lad."

"Many thanks again," said Ethel Hodgson. "I think it's the best of many bad solutions to a vexing problem." She looked away, thinking back to that frightful evening. "But I have to say, somehow I do feel like he's a gift from the Almighty. There was something about the look in Mary's eyes as I held him up for her to see. Like some higher power was looking at him through her eyes and was relieved to see that he'd survived the birth. Perhaps the Almighty has some special plan in store for him. If that be true, Miss Temporal, you'll get your reward in heaven. Our Lord will see to that."

"Perhaps, but it's a right heavy burden to have to carry till then, knowing, too, that we'll never all be reunited with our Thomas up there in the firmament. And that Thomas will never see neither one of his sons there. He's gone to a different place, I fear."

Together they bowed their heads respectfully at the thought. Jemmy turned to leave, but as she did so, Mrs. Hodgson reached under the counter and called her back.

"If you're keeping the baby, then you'd better take this as well."

She handed a wooden stick over the counter.

"What is it?"

"It's the chair leg that Thomas wielded to kill Mary. The constable left it in a corner of the bedroom. It lay there a good two weeks. None of the servant girls dare touch it for fear it be cursed. Mr. Norris wants it out of here sharpish. You take it. Such a thing will turn Martha's head and your own head, but it may be meaningful to the child in the future. Who knows, perhaps one day he can take out his anger by hurling it at the gibbet post."

Chapter 44

Reinbeck, Iowa
June 2019

AND SO IT CAME TO pass that Tom Temporal and Karen Butler sat side by side in wooden rocking chairs on the back porch of the Butler residence in Reinbeck. The morning passed in a slow dream, alternating between periods of drizzle and feeble sunshine. The branches of every tree hung motionless, dripping. Tom and Karen stared straight ahead as they conversed, and the flatness and uniformity of the landscape induced monotony into their speech and a perceptible hiatus between statement and response, question and answer. Despite, or perhaps because of, the blandness of their surroundings and the absence of distractions, their minds synchronized the moment their rocking motions did, and their age difference melted away.

"How's life treating you?" Tom began.

"Let's just say I'm content," Karen replied.

"And your parents? Have they fully accepted you?"

"My mother, yes. My father is still of two minds. I think he finally accepts that I'm me, but he can't yet get his head around the aging process. He doesn't believe my explanation. He can't think of any other explanation. So there's still a puzzle in his head over my changed appearance."

"You can understand that."

"I can. And I'll keep working on him. Perhaps over time he'll find a way to come to terms with it. But for now…well…he treats me no worse than he did before I left." She chuckled. "Plus, there's now an added touch of respect for the elderly lady in the house."

"Well, that's something, I guess."

"The three of us get along pretty well. I'm happy about that. I help my mom out with housework, cooking, stuff like that. One good thing that's happened is that I made a whole bunch of money selling my Tudor coins in London. The company I was dealing with held the auction last week. They said it was their second biggest sale ever. I'm due to receive $384,000 net of everything. They'd said I might get half a million—pounds at that. But I'm not about to sniff at three hundred and eighty thousand dollars."

"Jesus! Fantastic!"

"All I need now is a bank account to deposit it in." She chuckled again. "Must get on that. Anyway, that amount of money should be sufficient to see me out. Which reminds me…I need to get a new driver's license too. Don't know if I can easily navigate that process. We'll see."

"And what do you do with the rest of your time? When you're not shucking corn."

"I sit in this chair a lot. I look at the fields, and I remember and reflect. I've signed up to teach a class at the local community college in the fall, *Early Colonization of North America*. I'm excited about that. So I've been preparing lectures. I'll probably tell them more about Sir Walter Raleigh than they care to know! He hit on me twice! I also haven't given up on the idea that I mentioned once before of writing a journal article on my paranormal experiences—a kind of sequel to Brian's paper in the *Journal of Paranormal Phenomena*."

"Will you give it that title you joked about…something to do with time being spiral?"

"*The Spirality of Mirrored Temporal States*. Yes, probably. I can't get that title out of my head. But I haven't done much work on it yet. Just a few scribbled notes about stuff I'm liable to forget otherwise." She paused a moment. "I read a lot. I'm reading about the philosophers' views of time…and of existence. Anything that will help me to understand how and why I went through the ordeal I did. And to reach a level of reconciliation."

"Well, you're the expert now. Perhaps it's incumbent on you to put the philosophers straight. Knock their heads together."

"Yep. Think about it, Tom. I've been nineteen in 1537. I've been sixty-nine in 2019. For a brief moment, I was sixty-nine in 1803. Nobody knows more about time than I do!"

Tom nodded and then raised the topic that had been the primary motivation for his visit. "Speaking of 1803, I'd like to talk a little bit about your transition back to the present—and particularly about your passage through the base year. If that's okay with you."

"Go ahead."

"When you described it to us back in Saxonborough, you mentioned seeing some *really freaky stuff* as you passed through the *t⟨sub b⟩* state. Those were your exact words. They've stuck with me ever since."

"Uh-huh."

"A man with a stick…a bloodied young woman. That part I don't remember as clearly."

"Yes, well, that was the essence of it. And the woman was floating a foot above the bed. Maybe eighteen inches. It all passed extremely quickly."

"So do you know what was happening? Have you thought any more about it?"

"I have no clue what it was I was looking at. A murder perhaps? It was such a brief glimpse. Why do you ask?"

"Because Denise and I think we know what you saw. We found a letter in a bag that had been sitting in our attic for ages. Inside the letter were two newspaper clippings. They described the murder. The man brandishing the stick was my five times' great-grandfather Thomas Temporal. And the bloodied woman was a local girl called Mary Kirkham. Thomas had been forced to marry Mary earlier in the day, and then he killed her that same evening. Probably out of pure rage."

"Shit."

"I know. So it did have something to do with my family."

"I'm glad you found that out," said Karen, "but I'm sorry the end result was so gruesome."

"But I need to press you on the matter. You're the only person who has any first-hand information about the murder, however minimal. Let me start by asking you this. How long were you in the *t⟨sub b⟩* state, do you think?"

"No more than ten seconds."

"Ten seconds. Okay. Can you describe exactly what happened during those ten seconds?"

"Well, I was deep in my zeta trance, aiming for the present time frame. You know all about that. I suddenly became aware that the light in the room had changed slightly. It had gotten a little brighter. In just a second or two. Don't ask me how I knew this. My senses are very acute when I'm in zeta. So I wondered if I'd arrived in the present. I forced my eyes open a tad, and almost immediately I saw the very faint outline of the man with a stick raised above his head. It sure didn't give me the impression of being 2019. Also, the light was flickering like candlelight, suggesting a time before electricity. These were tiny clues, but I couldn't be certain where I was. So I opened my eyes a little further.

"The images then became a bit more distinct. And that was when I noticed the young woman behind him. Pressed up against the wall. Suspended above the bed. For about three or four seconds, I stared at the scene. Then I knew for sure that this was *not* 2019. Instinctively I knew it must be the base year and that what I was seeing was the event that had triggered the temporal tsunami. The appearance of the woman looked very much like the appearance of Abbot Gervase that Brian and I had seen in the Hoyland base year. And there were all the same associated phenomena—the shimmer of an electrical discharge along the frame of the iron bedstead, little sparks and flashes of light around the woman, the swirling air…a high-pitched buzzing sound all around the room. I knew at once where I was. And I also knew the danger, that my contact would be broken, and I would be washed up on this alien shore, never to reach my goal. So I quickly closed my eyes and returned to the sensory deprivation tank—as I like to refer to it—and headed onward… onward to the present. And I succeeded. Here I am."

"And that all happened in about ten seconds?"

"Yes. No more."

"Let me ask you about the woman, then. Did she appear to be…pregnant?"

"As a matter of fact, she did. How could you possibly know that?"

"It was in the newspaper reports. Why didn't you mention it before? In Saxonborough?"

"I don't know. It seemed a bit…unsettling. I thought you might all be grossed out by the thought of a pregnant woman being killed. So I kept it to myself."

"And you're sure about this?"

"Ninety percent. Why?"

"Because the child she was carrying could be important. I'll explain in a minute."

"Okay. Moving on."

"What you say confuses me though. The newspapers at the time said she was pregnant when she was killed…but I don't see how she could have been. From what Denise and I have been piecing together, that baby has to have survived. Somehow."

"Well," said Karen, pausing even longer than usual, "it might have."

"What do you mean?"

"Well, normally you might expect that a woman in her situation would have her hands positioned under her bump, in the typical support-and-protect posture—perhaps with one hand raised to try to ward off the blows from her assailant. But when I saw her, she had both hands *on top of* the bump. Neither hand was raised to protect herself. And her legs were spread wide apart. There was blood on her legs. I got the impression that she was not so much holding the baby inside her and protecting it, as…as trying to…in some way…push the baby out. She was straining in a downward direction. It's not easy to describe."

"Push the baby out? Seriously?"

"That's the impression I got. The woman was extremely distressed and very badly injured, but protecting herself did not seem to be nearly as important to her as delivering her child. I don't know.

She must have known that if she died, then her baby would die too, but that perhaps there was a chance to save it this way. But the images faded, and I closed my eyes. I saw nothing more."

"So perhaps the baby survived."

"I'm only saying it's a possibility. I saw nothing more."

"I don't suppose you could see the baby's head?"

"No."

"If the baby did survive, that would explain everything."

"How do you mean?"

Tom smiled but continued to stare straight ahead. "It's a long story, but the overview of it is that I learned a little while ago that I have Kirkham blood in my veins. The same blood as the murdered woman. The only way that could happen, Denise and I figured out, is if my ancestor Thomas was somehow born of the relationship between his father and Mary. It didn't seem possible that they could've had a child before this one, but if the child did not die in The Plough that night, then that child could be Thomas, and his mother would then be Mary Kirkham, not Martha, and the DNA match would be confirmed."

"You're saying that this Mary Kirkham safely delivered the child she was carrying even as she was being murdered? Is that even possible?"

"That's what I'm saying. I would think that anything could be possible in that ecstatic state. What happened to Abbot Gervase and Mary Kirkham was identical in that respect. I think you might have provided the solution to our mystery, Karen."

"Hey, I did nothing but float through time."

"And it does seem that Thomas's birth was miraculous, as he intuited. Lord knows how."

Neither of them spoke for a while as they reenacted Karen's story and gauged its veracity. Then Tom returned to Karen's experience and asked her what she'd learned from it all.

"What have I learned? Hmm. What *have* I learned? Well, for one thing, I've learned that there's much about the interconnectedness of the past, the present, and the future that mankind has yet to discover. The more I think about it, the more I realize that Brian and

I, together, have grasped the essence of it, yet only scratched the surface." She looked up to the heavens as if searching for the significance of it all and then looked back down at the horizon and continued, "We have discovered—by experiment, mind you—that this interconnectedness is not just the musings of philosophers, not just mental constructs for Kant and Hegel to argue over. It's a real property of the natural world…the physical world. And it's intimately connected with human existence.

"What Brian and I have discovered is that we…all of us…have the potentiality for existence at any moment during the entire lifetime of the universe. Brian might have called it a nonzero probability, I'm not sure. The present is not unique for us. It's not merely a question of *now* and a lifetime that is contained…constrained…within a period of a hundred years or so following our birth. Not at all. It is incorrect to say that we have a zero probability of existence outside this hundred-year window. It's not forbidden in any kind of quantum mechanical sense.

"It's my belief that the wise men of old had stumbled upon this possibility, but what none of them realized is that there is a necessary spatial component to the interconnectedness. What we have is not a temporal continuity but a time-space continuity—if Einstein would permit such an expression. I hesitate to use the word *continuum* because Brian always stressed the existence of discrete temporal states. That part is a bit beyond me. But anyway, the spatial aspect is something I conceived after thinking about the similarity of Saxonborough and Hoyland and realizing that what we'd experienced at Hoyland was not a one-time, one-place phenomenon. The past, the present, and the future, as they relate to the human experience, are interconnected in different ways in different spatial locations. In theory, to my mind anyway, any set of time-space pairwise coordinates ought to be theoretically accessible. But I'm not completely sure about this. There could be some locations where there is no interconnectedness, and the probability of human existence at any time period other than the present one is precisely zero. But most everywhere else it is not. It only takes human intervention to uncover and exploit these pathways—an appropriate base year, a zeta field, and the knowledge and will to take advantage of them."

"You thought of all this by yourself?"

"Not by myself entirely. Brian and I talked about it a lot in those long, TV-less Tudor evenings. But the spatial aspect is mine alone, I think. You see, Brian never knew about the time warp at Saxonborough. He never knew there were gateways elsewhere."

"So that's the essence of your discovery."

"It is. And do you know what it implies? Think about it. It means that it ought to be possible to transition into the future. Essentially that's what I just did, didn't I? I went forward in time from 1588 to 2019. Imagine a set of spatial coordinates…a place…where a time warp will be created in the future…by someone experiencing the same kind of ecstasy as Abbot Gervase or Mary Kirkham. In other words, a *t⟨sub b⟩* state out beyond 2019. Like 2050 or 2100 or further out. Then if I could figure out where that place was, I could go there and transition to a mirror *t⟨sub -n⟩* state far out into the future. How awesome would that be!"

"You've got to be kidding me."

"Absolutely not. There's no theoretical impediment to it at all. I would never *do* it, of course, but I *could*."

"How could you ever know the correct spatial coordinates?"

"That's the difficulty. I also don't know how many such places there might be—spread across all of time when you think about it. At the moment we know of just two, Hoyland and Saxonborough; but there may be more. Perhaps many, many more. Who knows. I remember that Brian thought that other such locations might exist wherever spirits…ghosts…angels…whatever…have been reported. Lourdes, Mons, Versailles. He mentioned several when we talked about it. Perhaps it might be possible to think of similar places that could conceivably host miraculous events in the future. I'm thinking about places that are presently the subject of conflict, controversy, confrontation…places like the Temple Mount, the Potala Palace, the Yasukuni Shrine. Who knows what dramas might be enacted there in the future.

"*Or*—think about it this way—it could be that a few people have *already* glimpsed the future at sites that will *become* the locations of base states in the future. Sites that are at present unknown. These people simply did not recognize what they saw. Think about St. Neot in our very first encounter at Hoyland Church. Neot saw into the future. He saw Brian, John, and Harry peering into the niche in the wall of the church. But he had no idea that he was looking at people from 2018. He had no reference points by which to assign it to a future year. He simply rationalized it into a distorted view of his present time. He decided the figures must be Guthlac, Bartholomew, and Waltheof—people and saints from his present time, from 1057. It would be no different today. People would be on the internet, on morning talk shows, in the tabloids, describing the weird shit they'd seen, with never a clue that they'd witnessed something futuristic."

"I think you're right. Just like Neot, they would have no reference points."

"So it would just require someone like me to find one of these places and go there and jump into the future! As I said, awesome! No other word for it."

"Wow. You're something else, Karen."

Karen again looked up into the sunny, drizzly sky and then returned to the big picture.

"This interconnectedness along the great river of time actually brings me a kind of peace, Tom. In a sense, all the people that I've loved and cared about are still with me. All equivalent, no matter when in time I loved them or cared about them. My one and only Brian; his brother John and his Aunt Polly; my buddy Dan Patzner; our servants at Ketteringham Lodge, Joan and Alice and Nicholas; our great friend William Cecil from Burghley; even Edward Kelley… They're all…What's the word? Available to me. All equally accessible. Undead, if you like. Because if I wanted to, I could go and visit any one of them tomorrow. It's as if they're all waiting patiently in adjoining rooms for me to come and give them a great big hug. I like that.

"And going back to what I said before, I'm convinced that mystics have had a sense of all this since forever. It's just that the true meaning of their words has been lost in translation or has not correctly registered in our minds. The other day I came across something that's written in the Bhagavad Gita. I don't know how old it is or what the writer was thinking about at the time, but it meshes perfectly with my beliefs. I want the words carved on my gravestone,

Never was there a time when I did not
exist, nor you, nor all these kings; nor in
the future shall any of us cease to be.

Chapter 45

Kankakee
June 2019

As soon as Tom returned from Iowa, he huddled over his laptop for an hour. The next morning, he resumed the work, the kitchen table covered with his notes and sketches.

"What on earth are you doing?" Denise asked him.

"I'm redoing Thomas's family tree."

She peered at the screen and said, "Impressive."

"I've put in all his close relatives, together with all the years of their births, marriages, and deaths that I know of. Also the places where those events happened."

"Very impressive."

"It's not complete, of course. Never will be. And I've not connected it up to the present. But I feel like I've done enough. There will always be outliers and uncertainties, but I think this chart has the essential information that Thomas asked for." He tapped on the computer screen.

"It does," said Denise.

"And see…I put him in the center and highlighted him in yellow."

"I see that."

Tom leaned back in his chair, admiring his work. He was clearly proud of himself. Then he uploaded the information to his family history website, printed out a few copies, and downloaded the file onto a flash drive. He sent a brief message to Maxine Reed to tell her to check out his updated tree. Then he switched off his computer.

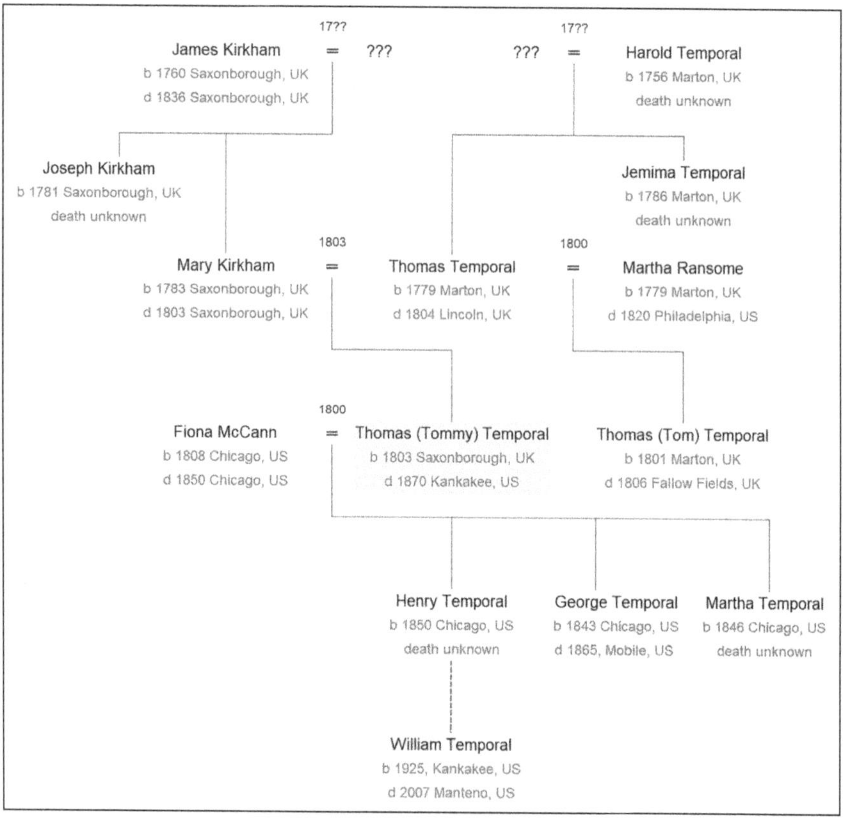

"Get ready. We leave in five minutes."

"Where are we going?"

"Just a couple of miles. You'll see."

They drove out of Kankakee on Highway 113 that ran northwest alongside the Kankakee River. Traffic was light, and the day was fine. Denise had a printed copy of Tom's new family tree on her lap, and as they drove, she studied it. "I still don't quite understand these two babies," she said. "How did you disentangle them?"

"It took me a little time, but I think I have it straight now. The first thing we know is that Martha and Thomas had a baby who was baptized Thomas Temporall, with two *l*s. Remember? I found that in the online parish registers back in February. He was baptized on April 12, 1801, in Marton. Let's call him *Tom*, as his parents did, to distinguish him from his father. The three of them moved to the hamlet of Fallow Fields soon afterward, but it didn't take long for Thomas to stray and get involved with Mary Kirkham at Saxonborough. Now from what Karen told me and from other clues, I figure that Mary gave birth to a son on the night she was murdered. That was on October 26, 1803. The newborn seems to have been taken in by Martha and Jemmy. That was a bit hard to accept at first, but then I realized that the baby was Jemmy's nephew by blood, and he had no one else in the world to care for him. I figure they accepted him into their household at Fallow Fields out of love with a dash of charity.

"They gave this second baby the name *Tommy*, just like the letter said. He was also the son of Thomas, but they threw in a name variation to distinguish him from both his father and his little half-brother. Interestingly, the name Tommy means *twin*. Did you know that? Coincidence probably. Now presuming that Tom was still alive when Tommy appeared on the scene, my guess is that for the most part, Martha looked after Tom, and Jemmy looked after Tommy. That would make sense. Tom would be about two-and-a-half years older than Tommy. I realize that the composition of the household was very unusual, perhaps unique, but I can imagine that it functioned pretty well. There was probably more than enough love to go around once father was out of the picture.

"Moving on, from my DNA results it's clear that Tommy was the one who accompanied Martha and Jemmy to America. No doubt about that. So what happened to Tom? He didn't come with them to America, and he wouldn't have been left behind. Therefore, he must have died sometime between 1801 and 1810. Right? It's a bit of a leap of faith, I know. But I read Thomas's letter again and rediscovered these words: *'The first thing I remember is the sound of weeping, a high-pitched yowling, a steady sobbing, and a quiet whimpering. Three different kinds. I don't know who they were. I was little more than a baby then.'* Remember that? Three people. Well, surely that was little Tom dying, and Martha and Jemmy weeping for him. I checked online, and the earliest age for memories is typically two and a half to three years of age. So I figure that's how old Tommy was when his half-brother died. So it was probably in 1806 that Tom passed away.

"Do you see what Martha and Jemmy did? There's no record of a church burial for Tom, and Tommy had no baptismal papers. So…a simple solution was to have Tommy assume the place of Tom. Right? They probably buried Tom in their backyard. Instantly, then, Tommy had legitimacy and documentation and could accompany them to America. My guess is that Tommy changed his name to Thomas sometime between 1806 and 1810 when the clashes of nomenclature had gone away. The key upshot of all of this is that Thomas was actually two-and-a-half years younger than we thought. And younger than he himself thought. He was only six and a half when he came to America, not nine. That explains why he had only a vague recollection of his childhood in England. He was only a little kid."

"Brilliant, Tom. Absolutely brilliant." She looked up and gazed around her to see where the car was headed. After three miles or so, Tom slowed down and made a right turn into the parking area in front of a large cemetery. Denise looked at him. "Here?"

"Both Thomas and his son, George, are buried here. I found that out from a website called *Find a Grave*. Come on."

They got out of the car and located the two headstones adjacent to each other. George's was a small stone, only about a foot tall by two feet wide. It had six horizontal lines of inscription: *George Temporal; Died; Apr. 9, 1865; Aged; 22 Yrs.; Co. D 76 Ill. Vol. Inf.*

"That last line means he was in Company D of the Seventy-Sixth Illinois Volunteer Infantry Regiment," Tom explained. "The date of his death is the date that the Union forces assaulted Fort Blakely just outside Mobile. It was essentially the last big battle of the Civil War—and it was largely ineffective, fought just hours after Lee had surrendered at Appomattox."

Tom took a photo of it and then squatted down and patted the top of it.

"George," he said, "your father told me he loved you and was very proud of you."

Thomas's memorial was larger but had no more information on it than George's: *Thomas Temporal; Died; Apr. 26, 1870; Aged; 69 Years; God rest his soul.*

"That should say 'sixty-six and a half years,' of course."

"Of course."

Tom took a photo and then knelt down beside his ancestor's grave. He reached into his pocket and pulled out a penknife. With it he dug a small hole in the dirt up against the headstone. He put the penknife back in his pocket and withdrew the flash drive he'd prepared earlier. He placed it in the hole and covered it up. He tamped it down and smoothed the disturbed soil over it. He placed the palm of his hand on the middle of the headstone.

"This is what you asked for, sir," he said. "You'll find yourself sitting under your family tree, at the center of the group, with the sun shining down upon you and all your relatives gathered around you. You can rest peacefully now."

He looked up at Denise and gave her a single nod.

She gave him a single nod back and said, "Job well done."

He stood up, and they lightly fist-bumped.

They linked arms and walked back to the car.

About the Author

David Streets was born in England but has lived in suburban Chicago for most of his life. He is an environmental scientist with advanced degrees in physics. He specializes in the study of air pollution and how to control it so that we can all breathe easier. He has helped to improve the air in many parts of the world, particularly Asia. He is a world-renowned researcher with more than three hundred publications in scientific literature. He was a named contributor to the work of the Intergovernmental Panel on Climate Change, which was awarded the Nobel Peace Prize in 2007. In his childhood, he spent many hours in gloomy churches, wondering if they were haunted and how it might be possible. This led to his first foray into the world of fiction, *The Time Quantum*, with a science-based explanation of the appearance of ghosts. In this sequel, *Temporality*, the theory is further elaborated and the characters fight the implications thereof.

Milton Keynes UK
Ingram Content Group UK Ltd.
UKHW042349130923
428564UK00022B/120/J